Meredith Angelson

NATHANIEL RICH is the author of *The Mayor's Tongue*. His essays and short fiction have appeared in *Harper's Magazine*, *The New York Review of Books*, *McSweeney's*, and *The New York Times Magazine*. Born in New York City, he now lives in New Orleans. For more information, please visit www.nathanielrich.com.

Also by Nathaniel Rich

*The Mayor's Tongue*

Additional Praise for *Odds Against Tomorrow*

Winner of the Inaugural New Orleans
Library Society Fiction Award

"Rich displays both enthusiasm for his subject and evocative linguistic flair. . . . In just a few pages, he paints a convincing and dreadful portrait of a city about to be destroyed, a city so insensate and self-involved that it fails to recognize when it's staring doom in the face."
—*The New York Times*

"As a study of catastrophe, this novel chills and convinces. Contemporary dystopian fiction cannot rely on fantasy but must engage more rigorously, as Rich does, with the natural world: J. G. Ballard's *The Drowned World* via David Attenborough."
—*Financial Times* (London)

"One of the best rewritings of the ark myth." —*The New York Observer*

"Rich is an imaginative storyteller, and his vivid vignettes are peppered with factoids that seem just true enough to be frightening. . . . He shows that living with your eyes focused on the distant horizon can blind you to what's happening right in front of you."
—*The Boston Globe*

"Captivating . . . Rich enchants with vivid characters and attention to their idiosyncrasies. . . . The accessibility of both the story and the science in this highly approachable novel makes the read all the more exciting and terrifying. Five stars."
—*Time Out* (New York)

"An exceptional work, often humorous—if darkly so."
—*Bloomberg News*

"Prescient and disturbing . . . A premonitory dissection of New York's pre- and post-Sandy state of mind." —*The Dallas Morning News*

"Highly anticipated . . . *Odds Against Tomorrow* sweeps you along on a current of high anxiety." —*Chicago Tribune*

"The novel moves fast, bathed in a hallucinatory glow, and the centerpiece depiction of post-hurricane New York gives the book a prophetic quality." —*The Cleveland Plain Dealer*

"Amusing and petrifying by turns, this is near-future fiction with an edge of the real." —*Nature*

"Recent current events have conspired to make this chilling novel even timelier. . . . Mitchell's intensely fraught journey from man of intellect to man of action is one the reader will not soon forget." —*Publishers Weekly* (starred review)

"This literary thriller is blessed with a propulsive plot, macabre humor, several richly developed characters, and serious ethical and philosophical issues, all lightly clothed in skillful writing. Highly recommended." —*Booklist*

"[Rich] addresses [his subject] with poise and the kind of gallows humor that would make Don DeLillo, Joseph Heller, and Gary Shteyngart proud." —*Full Stop*

"Rich zeroes in on our collective anxiety with a story of wild-eyed ingenuity that is both meditative and propulsive. . . . It's also nearly impossible to put down." —*Kirkus Reviews*

"If the books to come are half as good as Nathaniel Rich's novel *Odds Against Tomorrow*, there may be a silver lining to the end of the world." —*The Santa Barbara Independent*

# ODDS
# AGAINST
# TOMORROW

## NATHANIEL RICH

PICADOR ⊞ FARRAR, STRAUS AND GIROUX ⊞ NEW YORK

I want to thank Yaddo, the Rockefeller Foundation's Bellagio Center, Beatrice von Rezzori and the Santa Mad-
dalena Foundation, the Danish-American Writers Retreat at Hald Hovedgaard, and the Kenneth Shapiro
Studio in the Maine Woods for providing shelter during the storm. Readers Meredith Angelson, Sam Axelrod,
Eric Brown, Joseph Kanon, MK, David Yourdon, and Captain Caridad annihilated microbursts of prose. To
Sean McDonald, Elyse Cheney, and Emily Bell, a deluge of gratitude.

www.picadorusa.com
www.twitter.com/picadorusa • www.facebook.com/picadorusa
picadorbookroom.tumblr.com

Picador® is a U.S. registered trademark and is used by Farrar, Straus and Giroux under license from Pan Books
Limited.

For book club information, please visit www.facebook.com/picadorbookclub or e-mail marketing@picadorusa.com.

Lyrics from "All We Have Is Now," by the Flaming Lips, used by permission of the Flaming Lips.

Illustrations by Oliver Munday
Designed by Abby Kagan

The Library of Congress has cataloged the Farrar, Straus and Giroux edition as follows:

Rich, Nathaniel, 1980–
    Odds against tomorrow / Nathaniel Rich. — 1st ed.
      p.   cm.
    ISBN 978-0-374-22424-0 (hardcover)
    ISBN 978-1-4668-3675-4 (e-book)
    1. Scientists—Fiction.   I.  Title.
  PS3618.I3334 O44 2013
  813'.6—dc23
                          2012028928

Picador ISBN 978-1-250-04364-1

Picador books may be purchased for educational, business, or promotional use. For information on bulk purchases,
please contact Macmillan Corporate and Premium Sales Department at 1-800-221-7945, extension 5442, or
write specialmarkets@macmillan.com.

First published in the United States by Farrar, Straus and Giroux

First Picador Edition: April 2014

10   9   8   7   6   5   4   3   2   1

FOR MY BROTHER

# Contents

## Part One

Brugada        3
The Futurist        13


## Part Two

Every Silver Lining Has a Cloud        95
Sternman        160


## Part Three

Future Days        201
Flatlanders        294

# Part One

New York makes one think about the collapse of civilization, about Sodom and Gomorrah, the end of the world. The end wouldn't come as a surprise here. Many people already bank on it.

—SAUL BELLOW

## Brugada

---

The way other people fantasize about surprise inheritances, first-glance love, and endless white empyreal pastures, Mitchell dreamed of an erupting supervolcano that would bury North America under a foot of hot ash. He envisioned a nuclear exchange with China; a modern black plague; an asteroid tearing apart the crust of the earth, unleashing a new dark age. Such singularities didn't frighten him, he claimed; they offered freedom. They opened wormholes to a sublime realm of fantasy and chaos. Worst-case scenarios, he said, were for him games of logic. How vast a nightmare could he imagine, and to what level of precision? What was possible? What should we be afraid of?

We knew that Mitchell's "logic games" line was a bluff. Worst-case scenarios filled him with very real terror. Late in the evening he raced out of his bedroom in a panic, cheeks flushed, eyes haunted. He flipped on his desk lamp, pounded numbers into his calculator, and scrawled equations and odds ratios. It was a near-nightly ritual. The next morning we'd find him there asleep, face-down on his papers, his cheek ink stained with numbers like a prison tattoo.

None of us, to be clear, lost any sleep over Mitchell's prophecies.

We thought he was a little mad, and a little depressed, even by U. of C. standards. He may have understood numbers, but everyday life was too complex for him. We felt for him, we did—he'd had it tough from the start. His name was its own kind of worst-case scenario, a throwback to an era of midwestern Anglo-Saxon gentility. *Mitchell.* Who named their child Mitchell? Parents with high aspirations and antiquated ideals. From his mother, a stout, fair Missourian, he inherited a twangy Ozark accent, flat russet hair that lay on his head like straw at the bottom of a pigpen, and a loathing for Overland Park, his native suburb. His father, a Hungarian refugee who owned housing projects in east Kansas City, contributed an eccentric, brooding manner and a depressive sense of humor. At first we wondered how Mitchell had been admitted, but it soon became apparent that he was a mathematical zealot. During orientation he wore a series of gray T-shirts bearing the faces of "Legendary Statisticians" (this written in a pompous cursive): C. R. Rao, Leonardo Fibonacci, Andrei Nikolaevich Kolmogorov. We hadn't heard of any of them. We suspected that Mitchell had silk-screened the shirts himself. If he wasn't a mathematical genius, something else was wrong with him.

Put out of your mind, if you can, all the posters and magazine photographs and T-shirts bearing Mitchell Zukor's own face. Try to imagine the great man as a college student. You would not have recognized him then. Clean-shaven, round faced, eyes dark and hooded. He was flagrantly rust belt. He looked like a swing voter. The old-fashioned crew cut, the neck reddish with razor bumps, and his retiring, timid manner gave the impression of a perversely premature descent into middle age. Had he not been assigned to our dorm, we likely wouldn't have considered him more than a curiosity, like the chairman of the college Republicans who slept in his bow tie, or the sad, skinny girl who walked around campus cradling a ragged teddy bear.

As might be expected, he was always with the computer: in the lab during the day and at his desk in the common room at night. When friends visited, he'd participate amiably enough in the conversation for a few minutes, though before long he'd retreat to his screen, scanning the Web for articles about artificial intelligence or manned space exploration or the lives of great mathematicians. I'd glance at him uneasily from time to time. Why wasn't he trying like the rest of us? His hunched back, expanding the fabric of a Peter L. Bernstein T-shirt, projected absolute indifference. Even when he was eating midnight takeout, or watching cable news, he seemed lost in the higher questions.

⊡ ⊡ ⊡

I came to know Mitchell casually over the years, but I can't say we had any particularly meaningful interaction until shortly before graduation. I'm referring to the Puget Sound earthquake.

It's been written that Mitchell saw it coming, Seattle—that he tried to tell the world, but no one would listen to him. This, I feel confident insisting, is pure mythology. Mitchell was prepared for disaster, sure, but he had no better idea than anyone else what was going to unfold that Tuesday. I know because I was with him.

It was a chilly autumn morning in Chicago. We were in Cobb Hall for Introduction to Russian Literature, a.k.a. Sputnik for Nudniks. A fraction of the students were first-years genuinely excited to read Tolstoy, but most were fourth-years like Mitchell and me, who needed the credit to graduate. On that terrible morning, shortly after we sat down, a murmur spread through the four-hundred-seat auditorium, growing in intensity and volume. There followed a burst of laughter and then another. My first thought was that the professor, Dziga Olesha, had canceled class, but the laughter was too harsh, too peculiar, and not at all mirthful. It was surprised, uncomfortable, even slightly deranged, the stifled sound a husband might make upon interrupting his wife and her lover:

laughter as defense mechanism. In row after row, like the reverse of a wave at a baseball game, the students bent over their laps and activated their portables. I was reaching for my own when Professor Olesha entered.

He was a muscular man, low to the ground, with a bushy Leninite mustache and a supercilious varnish over his eyes. His blue oxford flapped open at the collar, exposing a repugnant coil of black hair. He pressed a button, and the large screen over the stage illuminated with an image of a municipal garden.

"The family estate of Alexander Pushkin," muttered Olesha.

A girl in the second row shook her hand in the air. "Professor?" Olesha, ignoring her, clicked his remote.

"*The Bronze Horseman*," said Olesha. The statue appeared on the screen—the powerful horse bucking from its mountainous plinth.

Several other hands went up. Portables buzzed. A shimmer of hysteria passed through the room.

"What's happening?" Mitchell whispered to me.

"Professor *Olesha*," said another student. Someone coughed. Someone choked.

It was no use. Olesha, in his clotted voice, read from the poem:

*"Rushing through the empty square*
*He hears behind him as it were*
*Thunders that rattle in a chorus*
*A gallop ponderous, sonorous*
*That shakes the pavement."*

"Olesha!"

The professor looked sharply down from the stage, a lock of hair falling over one eye.

"What is this?" The disgust was plain on his face.

"Professor? There has been a huge earthquake. In Seattle."

Olesha squinted. "Explain yourself."

"Seattle. The city is destroyed."

Olesha swept the hair out of his eye. "I see." Feedback squealed over the speakers. "I am sorry to hear this."

He called up the next slide: a portrait of the young poet, his cheeks furred with muttonchops.

"On June sixth, 1799, Alexander Sergeyevich was born."

Two dozen students rose loudly to their feet, gathering their laptops and bags, pushing their way out of the lecture hall. There was a tussle in the row ahead of us. A female student, her face heavily flushed, had become entangled with the boy sitting beside her. In her frustration she shoved him.

*"My brother lives in Seattle!"* she shrieked. She ran up the aisle sobbing.

Olesha could no longer ignore the tumult. Red with rage, he pounded the lectern twice. "For anyone who is serious about this course, I will conduct the rest of the lecture across the hall." He marched out. Nobody followed.

Five seconds later the portrait of Pushkin flickered off the giant screen. Someone was manipulating the remote control. The lights dimmed, and a live television feed came on. The reporter's voice was loud and hoarse in the speakers. We saw incoherent flashes of flame, glass, metal, sea. No one spoke. We were trying to understand what we were watching. Beside me Mitchell was shaking. He shielded his eyes like a child at a horror movie.

I hardly need to rehearse for you the emotion of that day, the confusion and terror, but certain images I will never forget. A naked child, covered in ash, walking dazed through a mountain of rubble. A helicopter, its blades spinning frantically, sinking slowly into the sound. A convertible impaled on a stoplight. A dozen bodies running madly in every direction, silhouetted against a swelling wall of flame. The news reporter, no doubt in shock himself, stopped talking.

The images cohered into a narrative and we began to make sense of it. The silence in the lecture hall was broken by three screams in rapid succession. These were followed by the muted whimper of hundreds of people weeping. Cell phones buzzed. But most of us stayed in our seats, transfixed by what we were seeing. Everything happened very slowly. The network, having lost several of its street feeds, held for several minutes on an overhead shot of the Seattle harbor taken from the vantage of a looming blimp. Great billows of smoke obscured downtown, so the extent of damage was unclear. For all we knew, there might have been, beneath the blooming clouds of ash, an abyss as deep as the center of the earth. "We want to hold our breath," said the news anchor, stuttering. "Let's not jump to any conclusions." A correspondent called from a parking lot in North Seattle. "There is a complete cessation of regular life," she said. "Everyone is standing outside, staring at the ground. Waiting. Staring at the ground." The anchor thanked her. "We want," he said, "to hold our breath."

It seems horrible now, but I remember laughing. It started in my stomach, a light, ticklish sensation like a bubble rising, rising in my chest until it burst out in a wild guffaw. Nobody noticed—there were a lot of odd, uncontrolled noises in that lecture hall. The thought that made me laugh, though it is not at all funny in retrospect, was this: I felt that I had entered Mitchell Zukor's head. Sitting in that hall as the smoke plumed on the screen, I felt as if I were eavesdropping on one of Mitchell's nightmares. I felt very close to him then.

But when I glanced at Mitchell I saw that he had turned away. Something else had claimed his attention. I followed his gaze to the other end of our row, where an auburn-haired girl had collapsed awkwardly in her seat. Her head was twisted to one side, and her arms dangled crookedly beneath her. She was alone. In the commotion no one else seemed to have noticed her.

Mitchell shot past me, racing down the row, knocking his kneecaps against the chairs as he went. I followed, glancing back and forth between the images of the atrocity and the fainted girl. The juxtaposition was unsettling. It was as if somehow the monster on the screen had reached its talons into Cobb Hall and snatched one of us.

When I caught up to Mitchell, he was frozen, hunched over the girl.

"She needs fresh air," I said.

At the sound of my voice he spun around. His eyes were large and white.

"She didn't faint," said Mitchell.

"How do you know?"

He pulled himself to one side so I could see the girl's face. I didn't recognize her.

"It's *Elsa*," said Mitchell. "It's Elsa Bruner!"

### ▫ ▫ ▫

Mitchell had first seen Elsa Bruner on a visit the previous October to the Student Health Service. Mitchell was on good terms with the people at SHS—a regular customer. They knew all his specials before he sat down. What would it be this week? A red, scaly patch of unknown provenance? Neck lump? Vague pain about the groin? The nurses welcomed him with patient smiles and made him wait until they had treated everyone with unimagined health concerns.

That particular October morning the doctor had called Elsa Bruner's name and a pallid, slender, but seemingly healthful girl stood up. She met with the doctor for ten minutes and, after signing a form at the front desk, went on her way. She was not especially attractive or even distinct—a small nose, reddish brown hair hanging loosely to her shoulders, soft eyes spaced slightly too far apart, a delicate chin—and Mitchell would have immediately forgotten her had he not seen her medical form when he checked out. (Mitchell, the doctor had cheerily informed him, was merely exhausted and overstressed; he did not have Crohn's disease.) Elsa's medical file, thickly stuffed, was still lying on the counter, and Mitchell couldn't help but notice, printed in large caps on the top of the front page, the word "BRUGADA." Other than several cardiologists in the medical school, Mitchell was undoubtedly the only person on campus who understood the meaning of this word.

"It's a heart disorder," he explained in the dining hall that night. "It can strike you dead at any time. But otherwise you're completely healthy."

"That's a thing you made up."

"A girl at U. of C. has it. A second-year. Her name is Elsa Bruner. She was at SHS this morning."

"Her heart stopped?"

"No. She was probably there for a routine EKG."

"Is she hot."

"Don't you get it? She can drop dead at any time."

We gave prudent nods. "So she's desperate."

Mitchell ignored us. "Can you imagine?" he said. One of his hands began absently to pull at his hair. "She's a walking worst-case scenario. How does she get out of bed?"

We murmured halfhearted words of concern, but it was too late. We'd lost him. He stood up, shaking his head, and walked out of the dining hall, into the cold night.

Mitchell must have thought about Elsa Bruner often, but I don't recall that he mentioned her again, and I know he never talked to her until the day of the earthquake. I also know that he never returned to the Student Health Service.

◻ ◻ ◻

The lecture hall was nearly empty when the two paramedics arrived. Elsa was sitting up in her chair, her hand on her heart. Mitchell's hand was on his heart too. He was having pains.

"How do you feel?"

She didn't appear to hear him. There was a quavering, absent curl to her lips. "It happened again."

She closed her eyes.

"Elsa?"

"I'm only resting," she said, blinking. "It's over now."

She tried to wave the paramedics away, but they ignored her and slapped a blood pressure cuff around her arm. They scanned her student ID into a black machine that resembled a credit card reader. A buzzer sounded and a red light flashed. This seemed to alarm them.

"Ms. Bruner? We need to take you to the hospital. Are you able to walk?"

She nodded and rose stiffly from her seat.

"Do I know you?" she asked Mitchell.

He shook his head and introduced himself.

"I'm sorry you're . . . sick."

"You didn't do it." She pointed to her heart. "I did. I did it all by myself."

The two paramedics, each holding one of her tiny elbows, escorted her from the hall.

On the screen a section of the Alaskan Way Viaduct, clogged with morning commuter traffic, collapsed. The giant concrete slab dropped twenty feet, shattering on the pavement below like a pane of glass. The cars bounced like dice.

◫ ◫ ◫

When we graduated in June, the panic raised by the Puget Sound earthquake had become part of us. It was slapped across our faces like a birthmark. We were dubbed Generation Seattle. Both the best and the worst suddenly seemed possible. Elsa Bruner, I learned, had dropped out and started a cooperative farm in Maine.

Mitchell, like so much of our class after Seattle, moved to New York for a financial consulting job. We fell out of touch. I never saw him again, at least not in the flesh. I wish I could say that we'd been the best of friends, but today I consider myself lucky to have known him at what, I now realize, was a crucial stage in his development.

To tell the truth, I was as shocked as everyone else when I found out what happened to Mitchell Zukor.

# The Futurist

―

# I.

The Seattle settlements, to be certain, unnerved nearly every private enterprise in America. But no company had greater cause for anxiety than Fitzsimmons Sherman, which employed more than three hundred workers in offices honeycombed across the seventy-fifth and seventy-sixth floors of the Empire State Building. The Empire State was the most disaster-prone building in America. It had to be evacuated nearly once a year—for no-fly-zone infractions, bomb threats, tropical storms, and blackouts. Fitzsimmons Sherman was the building's largest tenant, and its wealthiest. After the Supreme Court affirmed the record settlements, Fitzsimmons's chairman, the ursine, mouth-frothing Sanford "Sandy" Sherman, called an emergency board meeting. The executives and their team of lawyers assembled early one June morning at Sherman's Sagaponack estate. The windows of the conference room were fogged over with the mist that rose from the ocean. The executives hovered like seagulls over a spread of bagels, lox, and sturgeon. The expensive fish seethed a salty, humid aroma, indistinguishable from the smell of dirty dollar bills.

Once everyone was seated, Sandy Sherman, standing at the end of the massive oval table, asked a question that had haunted him for years: "If the Empire State Building fell, how much would it cost Fitzsimmons? Could we avoid paying as much as our friends in Seattle?"

Fitzsimmons's friends in Seattle had paid dearly. The loss of life, though regrettable, they could overcome. It was the loss of capital that brought the chief executives to their knees. Even before the ground stopped trembling, the families of the earthquake victims had enacted that uniquely American mourning ritual: they filed class action lawsuits. The lawsuits alleged that the corporations that held offices in downtown Seattle had needlessly endangered their employees' lives. The companies, in other words, were asked to pay for their dead.

The business leaders of Seattle were outraged. How could they have foreseen the horrors that had engulfed their city? How could they have known that the Emerald City Tower would compress like an accordion or that the black windows that sheathed the seventy-six-story Columbia Center would shatter like a mirror? Sure, they understood the general threat. A significant earthquake struck northwestern Washington every twenty years, and a megathrust earthquake—greater than 9.0 on the Richter scale—every three or four centuries. The Juan de Fuca tectonic plate, located just fifty miles off the coast, was the site of the largest earthquake ever to have struck North America, the Cascadia megathrust earthquake of January 26, 1700. But what were the odds that Seattle would be hit by another Big One anytime soon? In the first decade of the millennium Seattle had relaxed restrictions on building heights in order to encourage downtown growth. If the city's Department of Planning and Development had approved plans to build skyscrapers, how could the CEOs be expected to know better? They were in the businesses of Internet commerce and banking, after all. They knew nothing about seismology. They were masters of industry, not masters of the universe.

The juries saw images of the bonfires that engulfed the Seattle Art Museum and the white geyser of glass that shot into the clouds when the Central Library imploded. A dozen times they were forced to watch the famous video of the Space Needle falling, its tip piercing the dome of the planetarium, popping it like a blister. They learned that seismologists had given Seattle an eighty percent chance of being hit by a megathrust earthquake before 2060; that the high-rises were known to be vulnerable; that aftershocks, some of them large earthquakes in themselves, would continue for years, perhaps even a decade. They listened to 911 tapes, recorded statements by people who had watched their husbands and wives plunge into Elliott Bay, and heartbreaking testimonies from the children of the deceased. Yes, someone needed to pay for this.

And so the business leaders of Seattle, having already suffered immeasurable financial losses, were ordered to pay settlements to their employees' families. Blood would be converted into treasure.

The exchange rate was brutal. That's because the insurance industry, after the terrorist attacks at the turn of the century, had discontinued major catastrophe coverage. The corporations' insurance plans were worthless. This was a catastrophe in itself. "My God, what did we do to deserve this?" said one business leader to *The Seattle Times* shortly before his firm sent him to a weeklong sensitivity retreat on Fidalgo Island.

Sandy Sherman therefore found himself in a difficult position. Fitzsimmons's insurance plans, because of the prohibition on catastrophe coverage, would not protect them. But fleeing New York City, or even the building, was inconceivable. The firm would be perceived as craven, weak, fearful. Or worse: un-American. Shares would cannonball. No, they had to stay put.

"Fitzsimmons is on its own," bellowed Sherman. "So what now, boys?" he added, despite the fact that in the room there were seated two female executives and five female secretaries, all of whom were now busily investigating the carpet.

Sherman's underlings mimicked expressions of perplexity. They knew better than to speak up, so it is impossible to imagine how long the room might have remained silent were it not for the interjection of a junior account associate from the Department of Equity, Assets, and Derivatives who was in attendance only because he had been asked to serve as proxy for his vacationing boss.

"I don't mean to sound morbid," said this junior associate, but his voice caught. He was distracted by something outside the window. The fog had cleared, and a pleasure yacht could be seen gliding just off the coast. The lights in the cabin were out, and nobody was on deck. It seemed, in fact, that nobody was on the boat—that it had been cut loose from its mooring and was drifting toward the ocean. *Was it possible that there was nobody on the boat?*

Thick necks chafed against starched collars as the pink faces turned to regard the young man.

"Excuse me," said the junior associate, his fingers shaking under the table. "I just mean to say that, if our building collapsed, then . . ." He trailed off, his cheeks flaring with panic.

"Speak up," Sherman yelled.

"Sorry. I was saying, if the building collapsed—"

"*Yes?*"

"—if the Empire State Building was destroyed, wouldn't we all be dead?"

Nobody stirred. The junior associate was extraordinarily conscious of the fact that he was being observed, for the first time in his career, by the distinguished executive board of Fitzsimmons Sherman. He pictured in his mind an amoeba squirming under a glass slide.

"I mean," he said wildly, "there wouldn't be anyone left to pay out damages to the victims' families. So perhaps the whole question is moot."

Sherman looked down at his papers as if he had suddenly noticed a typo. The older men chuckled silently. The young associate, having never ventured higher than the seventy-fifth floor, was evidently unaware that no executives actually worked in the Empire State. They maintained offices there, of course—with chocolate leather couches unbroken by sitting and dim mahogany lamps that emitted insufficient light for reading and tufted, untrammeled carpets, soft as sea moss—but only the department managers and their staffs reported to the building.

A senior executive remarked upon the escalating price of insurance premiums and the men took that as a cue to resume their breakfast. They made loud smacking noises as they chewed, and gulped their coffee with great thirst. Sherman required coffee to be served at room temperature so that it could be imbibed quickly, like water.

The only thing resolved that day was that Mitchell Zukor, the outspoken junior associate from the Department of Equities, Assets, and Derivatives, would be given a new assignment. He would estimate the company's financial losses in the case of a catastrophe. It seemed a logical first step. The kid was said to be a mathematical wizard—a quant, in the old terminology. This would be a good test for him, a job that demanded statistical expertise and attention to detail. It would also teach him a lesson.

# 2.

"What will it cost me?" shouted Mitchell.

He was alone in his office on the seventy-fifth floor, 940 feet above the sidewalk. It was not a large office: four feet wide by six feet long. Mitchell had read that solitary cells in U.S. federal prisons had to measure at least six by nine. It was impossible to think coherently in a room so small and plain, and so insanely bright—for the fluorescent ceiling lights never turned off. Sandy Sherman had seen to that.

Mitchell had spent every night since the Sagaponack meeting—thirty-four long, debilitating nights—in this fluorescent cell. He was taking the project to heart. After two months in the Basement (as the seventy-fifth floor was known at Fitzsimmons), this was a chance to show Sherman that he was better than the Department of Equity, Assets, and Derivatives. A little luck, and he might even be promoted to the Penthouse (the seventy-sixth floor), to Risk Analysis. Risk was all that interested him; it was all he wanted to do. Really it was all he *could* do. Event trees, optimism bias, binomial distribution, base rate fallacy—these were his long-lost friends; he missed them like old stuffed animals. But there were no entry-level positions in Risk. You had to make it elsewhere first. And finally he had his opportunity. Risk, he hoped, would be his reward.

Sherman's secretaries sent Mitchell records that listed his colleagues' age, gender, salary, and aggregate profit earned for Fitzsimmons. The names had been replaced by fourteen-digit identification codes, but they were not difficult to crack. After ranking them by salary, Mitchell found himself. He was second from the bottom. Of course he was. It was his own fault. He'd had inquiries from other firms—including the colossus itself, Brumley Sansome—but Fitzsimmons had pursued Mitchell most aggressively, and he hadn't wanted to leave anything to chance. During spring break of his senior year Fitzsimmons flew him business class from Kansas City to New York, fed him venison before the interview and oysters afterward, and in a paroxysm of gratitude Mitchell had accepted the recruiter's first offer. Others, evidently, had bargained.

Mitchell's assignment, it soon became clear, was simple: he was to calculate the price of each Fitzsimmons employee's life, in dollars. As Sherman began to grow restless for results, Mitchell's calculations became increasingly gnarled and complex. He created indices of medical records, expense reports, and personal days used; graphs showing expected future earnings, incentive pricing, value added per quarter. The numbers kept coming at him, growing like vines out of his computer, wrapping around his ankles, binding him to his swivel chair. His job was not to predict longevity—though longevity was one consideration. For the purposes of this assignment, a person's value meant the value of his life to Fitzsimmons Sherman.

The work often required him to type the word "future" into his search engine—as in "future holdings" or "future cost of" or "future mass destruction"—and a peculiar advertisement began to pop up. "FIND OUT WHAT THE FUTURE WILL COST YOU," it said in austere small caps. If you clicked on it, you were taken to the website of a company called FutureWorld that offered consulting services in "future prediction." The site was a single page, linking nowhere. It listed only a phone number and e-mail address beneath the firm's logo: an elegant pencil sketch of an open window. Mitchell often found himself, especially late at night, staring at this page in a trance. If he jumped out of the open window, where would he land?

The advertisement flickered across the screen enough times that it began to feel like a taunt.

"What will it cost me?"

The sound of his own voice disturbed him—hysterical, hoarse, echoing down the hall. He paused to see whether someone would come to his door. No one did. It was unwritten office protocol at Fitzsimmons to ignore stray agonized screams.

Mitchell continued in a whisper. "I work in the tallest building in the biggest city in the richest country in the world. So what's my future? *Annihilation?*"

He closed his eyes and tried to clear his head. But it was no good. He could feel his old pursuers, the cockroaches, feasting on him. In moments like this he imagined thousands of them, tiny hairy-legged critters climbing the walls of his stomach. Their food was fear, and they ate ravenously, lip-smackingly. No, there was nothing to do but keep working. He was getting close. The numbers were beginning to tell a story.

Shortly after three in the morning Mitchell typed "future value calculator compound interest" and the FutureWorld logo popped up. Without thinking, he composed an e-mail to the address listed. "What *will* the future cost me?" he wrote. "Can I afford it? Will I pay with my life?"

On his desk he noticed a can of ginger ale he'd opened several hours earlier, and he took a sip. As soon as he put it down, his e-mail icon brightened—a new message. It came from FutureWorld:

Dear Mr. Zukor,

Thank you for contacting FutureWorld. I'm so glad you did.

FutureWorld is a private consulting firm—in a manner of speaking—based in New York. We specialize in minimizing losses that may result from unforeseen or worst-case-imaginable scenarios. We will study your company's holdings, predict all possible future outcomes, highlight the most grievous, and explain what options might be available to you. Most important, we can indemnify you against liability claims brought against you in the wake of a catastrophe.

I hope we can discuss the details of a potential partnership in person.

Since you work in the Empire State Building, you are ideally suited for our services.

> Thanks,
> Alec Charnoble
> Director and Founder
> FutureWorld

Mitchell suspected from the speed of the reply that the note was automatically generated. But what was this business about being "ideally suited" for catastrophe insurance? And how did the computer know that he was in the Empire State Building? He would call this man's bluff—this "Alec Charnoble."

Dear Mr. Charnoble,

It appears that you are awake at this late hour. If so, might you be available for a meeting? You can come to my office in the Empire State Building. Let me know if I should expect you.

> Thanks,
> Mitchell Zukor

He clicked back to his spreadsheet. In two adjacent columns he'd listed every Fitzsimmons employee number and the annuity owed to them should they be killed on the job. To calculate this figure, he had written a formula that took into account age, marital status, health rating, number of dependents, professional standing, salary level, and vacation day usage. It looked like this:

$$\bar{A}_x = v^{k+1}\,_kP_x q_{x+k} \sum_{j=0}^{m-1} \frac{P_{x+k}\,v^{-j/m}}{m\left(1 - \frac{j+1}{m}q_{x+k}\right)\left(1 - \frac{j}{m}q_{x+k}\right)}$$

Mitchell scrolled down to his own listing. He had no dependents or spouse and one of the lowest salaries on staff. So despite his young age, the value of his life to Fitzsimmons Sherman ($266,213) was significantly lower than the lives of most of his colleagues. He even came in below Lucy Fleishaker ($271,533), the assistant manager's chubby, doe-eyed secretary, owing to the fact that she was the sole caretaker of her epileptic older sister and therefore listed a dependent on her tax form. He thought of how few people depended on him—of his slumlord father and his mother, a matriarchal tornado tearing across the midwestern plains—and he started to wonder whether $266,213 was much too high.

The e-mail icon illuminated.

Dear Mr. Zukor,
I agree. There is no time to lose.

Thanks,
Alec

Mitchell reread the note, the ginger ale going flat on his tongue. The intercom rang. It was the night guard at the desk downstairs. Mr. Zukor had a visitor.

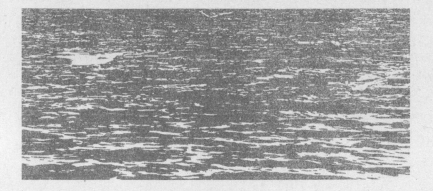

# 3.

"Mitchell," said Alec Charnoble, extending a long, bony arm. "If I may."

It was not a bright idea, he realized now, inviting a maniac to his office at four in the morning. Even his most masochistic colleagues had gone home—even the tactical research analyst across the hall, who every night wandered the corridors repeating phrases that he seemed to find soothing, such as "Gaussian processes are stochastic processes, stochastic processes are Markov processes, and Markov processes are Gaussian processes." The international market analysts—the BSE Bears, the Bolsa Bulls, the Hang Seng Sheep, the Micex Mice—they were on the clock all night, but they worked upstairs in the Penthouse. It had occurred to Mitchell, just before the elevator chimed, that he had blundered into a new type of worst-case scenario. The worst scenarios were always the ones you didn't anticipate, at least not until too late, but now it was so plainly obvious that he couldn't believe he hadn't seen it coming: the madman would be very strong, he would have tools, large, dull steel tools, and a metal glint in his eye.

But when the elevator doors parted, Mitchell was surprised to see a man who seemed nothing like a killer, at least not the kind who committed the act in cold blood. Alec Charnoble more closely resembled the type of businessman who, with the press of a button, detonates mortgages or pension funds in some suburban hamlet on the other side of the country. He was tall but thin, with a weak, hollow chest, wheaten hair, and gray oval eyes. His navy pin-striped suit and yellow tie were cleanly pressed; despite the hour he seemed as alert as a bright bronze bell.

"Alec Charnoble," said the man, his face creasing in a tight grin.

Without asking permission, Charnoble carried a chair into Mitchell's cubicle, so that the two men had to share the space. Their knees grazed.

"I never listen to preambles," said Charnoble, "so I won't bore you with one."

Mitchell shifted in his chair and his leg pressed against Charnoble's. A tepid queasiness passed over him like a blush.

"Imagine something terrible happens," said Charnoble.

"I do. Often."

"*Really.*" Charnoble frowned, impressed. "It should not be difficult for you then. Well, say this building is destroyed. So-and-so many people die—"

"So-and-so?"

Charnoble pushed back his shirtsleeves as if he were preparing to conduct some serious bit of manual labor—to dig a grave, for instance. Mitchell noticed that Charnoble wore two watches, one on each slender wrist.

"You need an example? Take Seattle. You've seen what happens. It's really not fair, is it. The victims' families take out their anger on the corporations. The company's investors, tallying their massive financial losses, are equally enraged. Why didn't you move the office out of danger? Why didn't you plan for this? The investors, like the families of the dead, also want money."

Charnoble tapped his forefinger into his palm in somber emphasis of his point.

"Money," he repeated. "Money. Money. Money—"

"Listen," said Mitchell. "I'm just about to finish a project here. Can you leave me your card?"

Charnoble pretended not to hear. "The corporation," he continued, "has only one response: *We didn't see it coming either.* Unfortunately, as we've seen in Seattle, this response doesn't hold up in court. And because they have no catastrophe coverage, they're out, at the very minimum, several hundred million dollars."

Mitchell saw that he was going to have to wait this through.

"Listen," said Charnoble. "I'm not immoral or anything like that."

"Of course not."

"It's only that disasters happen, no matter how much you prepare. Just because you build a bomb shelter doesn't mean you'll be inside when the bombs fall. And if it's not a bombing, it's a war, a tsunami, an envelope stuffed with ricin. An *earthquake*."

He appeared to be a snake, this guy. But he wasn't quite guileful enough. The real reptiles never look like reptiles—they're too skilled at camouflage. Still, it made Mitchell wonder: When he went on about his worst-case scenarios, did he sound like Charnoble? He doubted it. He didn't have the rank phoniness, the condescension, the folksy camaraderie. People like Charnoble—and Fitzsimmons was full of them, especially in Securities and Lender Finance—were interested in risk for purely financial reasons. They saw the wedges that risk offered, the way you could use risk to get between clients and their money. Mitchell's fear, on the other hand, was real, hot, viral. Just the previous night he couldn't sleep because he'd been trying to figure out why a global pandemic as severe as the influenza of 1918 hadn't recurred, and whether one was imminent. He had read about a new superbug called New Delhi metallo-beta-lactamase, or NDM-1. This Indian bug was a product of the twenty-first century, resistant to antibiotics. In the last four decades, scientists had discovered nearly no new antibiotics; an airborne mutation of NDM-1 would be unvanquishable. It would quickly contaminate every hospital in the world. There would be no cancer treatment, transplants, care of preterm babies, even tonsillectomies or appendectomies, without the risk of fatal infection. NDM-1—this was the kind of thing that Mitchell pondered. Not just NDM-1, but also its inevitable heirs: NDM-2, NDM-3, NDM-4, each mutation more aggressive than the last. The youngest child always caused the most trouble. Until the next one came along.

"As we've learned," Charnoble continued, "whenever there's a catastrophe, Corporate is vulnerable. Corporate has to clean up the mess—in a manner of speaking. This is where FutureWorld comes in."

"So FutureWorld protects the company against disaster? That's impossible."

"You're right. We don't protect. We *advise*. We predict catastrophes, calculate their costs, and help our clients avoid unnecessary risk."

Mitchell sat with this for a second. "What's in it for them? The clients, I mean. If another earthquake comes, they're doomed, no matter what advice you've given them."

"If a disaster does occur, we serve as a hired scapegoat. We indemnify you when your insurance company won't."

"We're talking great fires, twisters, solar storms."

Charnoble nodded. "Suitcase bomb, water supply poisoning, hantavirus. In court, the corporation can testify that they hired FutureWorld, a risk management specialist. They paid us eight hundred and fifty thousand dollars a year—"

*"Eight fifty?"*

"That's just the retainer. The point is that the client can say, 'If our business was not sufficiently prepared, it is the fault of Future-World, whom we hired to advise us—at the formidable rate of eight hundred and fifty thousand dollars—for this exact service.'"

Mitchell couldn't figure out why Charnoble was trying to win him over.

"So we would pay for the right to blame you."

"Exactly," said Charnoble. "So you can't be accused of negligence. This is, in legal terms, a buck-passing. A ripcord. Future-World serves as a get-out-of-jail-free card. In a manner of speaking."

"So you're offering catastrophe coverage. You're offering a service that insurance companies no longer offer."

"I'll put it like this. When, after 2001, insurance firms stopped providing catastrophe coverage, a void was created in the market. We plan to fill that void."

"But how?" asked Mitchell. "I mean, if a worst-case scenario did occur, wouldn't FutureWorld have to pick up the bill, like an insurance agency? One disaster and you'd be bankrupt."

"No," said Charnoble. His fingernails were working half-moons into his palm now. He seemed pleased with himself. "No, we wouldn't have to pick up any bill."

"Who, then, would pay?"

"Nobody," said Charnoble, and it was as if a white sheet of paper had passed over his face. His features became flat and blank. Even his voice had lost its modulation. "Nobody," he said, "pays at all."

Mitchell suspected that Charnoble had accidentally said something he wasn't supposed to say.

"You've left something out," said Mitchell. "I've added it all up, and it doesn't come out right. You protect your corporate clients. But who protects you? What protection do you have that an insurance company doesn't?"

Charnoble laughed. "You're good at mathematics."

"This is only basic algebra. But a variable is missing."

Charnoble seemed to be weighing something in his head. On one side of the scale was prudence. On the other side was his pride. A grin slowly started to work its way across his face and Mitchell could tell that pride was tipping the scale.

"How familiar are you with the concept of limited liability?" said Charnoble at last.

"I didn't go to law school."

"Let me try again. Two weeks after the Seattle settlements were announced, the governor of New York signed a routine piece of legislation called the Recommit to Civil Service and Pensions Act. It moved money between different state retirement funds, but that doesn't matter. Like any bill in this state, it contained earmarks—funding for a hospital in Syracuse, a park in Batavia, a salmon-counting project in Lake Ontario. But none of that matters either. What matters is that the state senator from the Twenty-fifth District—that's the district that includes Wall Street—inserted his own earmark. It's one sentence long. It offers what lawyers call 'a defense to liability claims.' It applies to any property owner in possession of a building with an occupancy greater than two hundred persons."

"Just about every office building in the state, in other words."

"That's the first part of the sentence. The second part says that if the property owner has made a 'reasonable, good faith effort' to protect his building against acts of God—by, for instance, spending a substantial sum on precautionary measures—he is indemnified. He can't be subject to civil suits like those we saw in Seattle."

"And that's it?"

"Similar limited liability statutes were passed after the savings and loan crisis, after nine eleven, after Bernie Madoff. It's nothing new. You just have to know the right state senator."

This man was up to tricks. But there was a solid and compact logic to what he was describing. The first rule of investment was that chaos breeds financial opportunity. And this was a chaotic time. Mitchell was beginning to see it now.

"We make recommendations to our clients about how to reduce their exposure to catastrophe," said Charnoble. "But we're merely consultants. If our recommendations are insufficient, we're not liable. And our clients, as long as they pay for our services, are not liable either."

Charnoble paused to let that sink in.

"Think of a money-laundering operation," he continued. "Dirty money goes in, clean money comes out, no one breaks a law, and everyone is cleared. And everyone is *rich*. We protect our clients against risks, and we protect them from lawsuits. The statute protects us. And the good senator from the Twenty-fifth District will not have to worry about fund-raising this year. Everyone wins. In a manner of speaking."

"So you just happen to know the right state senator?"

"Not me—I don't. But Brumley Sansome's legal counsel does."

So Charnoble was a Brumley man. That meant he was either a genius or a crank. He had impressed powerful people in his past.

"That makes sense. Only Brumley would devise something this devious."

Charnoble's grin was a fault line splitting open a freeway. "Look, these old shops—they're like spiderwebs." He gestured at the spreadsheets on Mitchell's desk. "We're the flies. Before I started FutureWorld, I was just like you—a quant. I would've been stuck there forever, pricing risk, valuing employees' lives. The same grunt work you're doing at Fitzsimmons."

Mitchell turned the spreadsheets facedown.

"After Seattle," continued Charnoble, "Brumley saw an opening. That's what they do, after all. They see windows of opportunity and they jump through them. They understood how consulting could indemnify. It's an old trick, really. McKinsey, Bain, BCG—they've been swiping clients from the old insurance Goliaths for more than a decade now. Consulting firms are more nimble, and much less regulated, than the insurance multinationals. Seattle only confirmed that we don't even have to compete with insurance firms for catastrophe money. Catastrophe is all ours. We're going to make a killing."

"In a manner of speaking."

"Exactly!" Charnoble's eyes glittered like mica. "Brumley spun FutureWorld into its own company—the way JPMorgan did back in the nineties with RiskMetrics. They needed a quant to lead it, and I was there."

Mitchell had studied RiskMetrics in Advanced Financial Engineering. The firm's statistical model was now obsolete, but it had been the pioneer in the field, the Ford Model T of the risk industry. For all his sublimated deviousness, Charnoble knew the literature. He had mastered Risk; he had studied the canon.

"Brumley doesn't want our competitors to catch on, at least not until we've cornered the market. So we have our own office, our own LLC, our own stationery."

"Where is FutureWorld's office?" asked Mitchell.

"Downstairs. Second floor. How do you think I got here so fast?"

"Oh. Right."

"It's temporary, though, this address. Brumley leased the office before I was brought in. It's not good for FutureWorld to be in the Empire State Building. Too hot."

"You think something bad is going to happen? Based on your research?"

Charnoble pursed his lips.

"Another attack?" Mitchell groped absently for his calculator. "What are your numbers?"

Charnoble laughed—a cold, sickly expulsion of air. "You'll have to hire FutureWorld in order to find out. To find out what the future"—and here he took a histrionic pause—"will cost you."

At the elevator bank Charnoble handed Mitchell a business card.

"I bet Fitzsimmons is happy with you. You must be good."

"Equity, Assets, and Derivatives isn't hard. It just eats your life."

"There's something about you," said Charnoble. "I'm not sure if you're aware of this, but, well, it's your eyes."

"Sorry. My eyes?"

"They communicate urgency. Urgency, and even fear—fear of a great danger coming on."

"That probably explains my success with women."

"It's a gift I don't have," said Charnoble. "I can't imitate it either. No matter how much I practice in the mirror."

"You practice in the mirror?"

"It's essential, in this line of work, to frighten clients. To convey a sense of implacable doom, in a manner of speaking. I'm no good at it. I come off as too cheerful or else too nervous. See, Mitchell—I know my limitations."

Charnoble's finger found his palm and twisted inside it.

"It's not difficult to scare people during hard times," he said, taking a confidential tone. "The challenge is to scare them during the hopeful times, in the lulls between catastrophic events, when FutureWorld's services start to seem like an unnecessary luxury. When I look at you I start to believe that another disaster is fast approaching."

"It's late."

"Don't take it the wrong way. All I mean to say is, you're a natural."

The elevator chimed and Charnoble slinked inside. Just before the door closed, a weird lopsided smile crawled onto one side of his face. Then he was gone.

Mitchell wondered what Charnoble meant by "the wrong way." Did business zeal make Charnoble pray for atrocity?

But half an hour later, as Mitchell sat in the backseat of the company sedan, the tinted windows muting the dawn, he wondered whether, in some hidden zone in his brain, he prayed for atrocity too. If you devoted your life to the contemplation of disaster, then wasn't an incident-free existence an empty one? Put it this way: if you planned for disaster and none ever occurred, you were a fantasist. But if a disaster you predicted did come true, then your life had meaning. You weren't just an expert. You were a prophet.

It was at moments like this that Mitchell's thoughts turned to Elsa Bruner.

# 4.

He hadn't needed to open the envelope, which was heavily creased and smudged with dirt, to know that it contained a bomb, or at least superfine toxic dust. He had been expecting something of this sort; given the current national mood, it was only a matter of time until next-generation radicals began mailing bombs to the country's largest corporations. But when Mitchell flipped over the soiled envelope—was the dirt, in fact, *human feces?*—he saw Elsa Bruner's name. This barely diminished his anxiety. His forefinger trembled as he tried to slide it under the crease. It was as if his finger were connected to a stranger's hand.

His agitation multiplied with each sentence he read. The first peculiar thing he noticed about the letter, other than the fact that it was drafted in pencil, was its intimate, almost confessional tone. It was written in the voice of a lifelong friend who was resuming a conversation begun long ago. "Hi M.," she had written.

Elsa began the letter by explaining that after her "close call" on the day of the earthquake, she had been admitted to a hospital, where she was given a heavy dose of quinidine to combat her arrhythmia. If Mitchell hadn't called the paramedics, she might have died. She apologized for her behavior that day—she hadn't been thinking clearly. Her fainting episode, she explained, had been caused by a rare genetic disorder called the Brugada syndrome, which she didn't describe beyond calling it "boring."

One might have expected the letter to end there. A thank-you note demanded no further elaboration. But elaborate she did. Elsa proceeded to update him on what had happened to her since that day. She explained that she had never returned to college and instead moved to a tiny village in Maine called Starling. Her boyfriend's father owned property there: Camp Ticonderoga, a summer camp for boys on a horseshoe-shaped lake twenty miles northwest of Augusta. The camp had gone out of business several years earlier, and its log cabins had been yielding to the encroaching wilderness. The father had struggled to find a buyer, so he agreed to let his son and Elsa, along with several friends, convert the hundred-and-fifty-acre property into a working farm. It all seemed very convenient. Did Elsa know about the property before she started dating the boyfriend? She didn't say.

They arrived in late March, when a fragile crust of frost still covered the ground and sheer flakes of blue ice floated in the lake like tiny glaciers. In April, under Elsa's direction, they tilled the baseball field and planted tomatoes, squash, and cucumbers; in the riflery range they concealed a square plot of marijuana by planting rows of sunflowers around its perimeter. They played volleyball, lit giant bonfires, and had dance parties in the old assembly hall. They paddled canoes out to the raft and jumped screaming into the frigid green water. They bunked in a farmhouse that had once served as the camp's infirmary. There was no Internet service and no cell phone reception until Augusta, which is why she had to send her letter by post.

And that was it. She signed the letter, "Goodbye, Elsa (The Fainting Girl)."

Mitchell was baffled. His first conclusion was that the letter was a request for money. Since he started at Fitzsimmons Sherman, several friends had already written to request his patronage. They never asked him outright, of course—the e-mails were always carefully oblique. They began with a couple of paragraphs of stale banter, reminiscences, and old jokes before succumbing to the inevitable: Would you like to "invest" in my noise band's debut EP? Would you like to be an "executive producer" of my documentary film about chocolate cigarettes? Would you "subscribe" to our online literary magazine? The message was always clear enough: We're struggling artists. You have money now. Can you give us some?

But Elsa hadn't mentioned money. Perhaps the boyfriend's family was providing subsidies. If anything she seemed oblivious to such concerns.

A more logical explanation was that Elsa Bruner had gone mad. The lack of oxygen to the brain while her heart had momentarily stopped was the most likely cause. It wasn't just the "Hi M." business, the inexplicable familiarity, that seemed off. Mitchell had also noticed egregious inconsistencies in her behavior that suggested impaired cognitive faculties. Elsa had realized, for instance, that were it not for her proximity to a first-class university medical center, she would have died during her Brugada episode. Yet now she had decided to move to a farm in Starling, Maine, of all places, some *twenty* miles from the nearest city. Not that Augusta's hospital was a state-of-the-art operation—did they have any physicians who had ever treated, or even heard of, Brugada syndrome? Besides, Elsa didn't have access to the Internet or telephones, so calling an ambulance would be out of the question. And if that weren't enough, she was submitting herself to a frightening cocktail of activities that seemed designed to induce cardiac arrest: strenuous exercise, narcotics, and physical shock (jumping into a freezing lake). Perhaps her letter was a thinly disguised plea for help.

Yet he wasn't certain that was right either. There was no indication of panic in her language. In fact she seemed remarkably composed, equable, cheerful—even strangely *reasonable*. Nor was there anything remotely flirtatious about the tone. She had gone on about her boyfriend, after all. The whole thing was nonsensical, and though the letter seemed to demand a response, Mitchell didn't know what to say. He removed from the bottom drawer of his desk the box of company letterhead he had inherited along with the office. Since all his correspondence was conducted electronically, he had never used it—nor, it seemed, had his predecessor, or the one before that, because the pages had acquired a faded, rust-colored border. Under the Fitzsimmons Sherman logo, instead of Mitchell's name, it read DEPARTMENT OF EQUITY, ASSETS, AND DERIVATIVES. He shuddered. How had the acronym never occurred to him before?

He stared blankly at the page. He wasn't going to lecture her about all the ways in which she was risking her life, nor suggest that she move to New York City, where she could be examined by the best doctors in the world. That would hardly be tactful. Really he just wanted to ask her how she did it. That is, how did she live each day knowing that because of an electrical glitch, at any moment her heart, for no particular reason, could stop beating? How could she babble on about planting squash and sunflowers while all along hummed the constant threat of annihilation? For all he knew, in the time it took for the letter to reach his desk, she might have had another attack.

Short of discussing any of these things, he'd be forced to write about himself. But there was little worth reporting on that subject. He couldn't, for instance, explain to her the perverse truth about the day of the Puget Sound earthquake: how, as the chaos burst onto the screen in Cobb Hall, after an initial moment of panic he had been overwhelmed by a profound, almost ethereal sense of calm. That was why he'd been able to help her. For the first time in his life he hadn't been alone with his fear. On that Tuesday morning *everyone* was Mitchell Zukor. Everyone obsessed over Richter magnitudes and fatality tolls and worst-case scenarios. He had read that Cassandra, during the sack of Troy—even as the temples incinerated and the women were dragged from their homes by their hair—had watched calmly from behind her loom. He now understood why.

It would be just as distasteful to talk about his work for Sandy Sherman, the worst-case scenarios and death statistics. But that was his whole life: the Empire State Building, his anonymously furnished apartment on East Thirty-seventh Street, and the night terrors that brought on the cockroaches and their quick hairy legs.

It then occurred to him that a single interesting thing *had* happened. Not extremely interesting—he hadn't figured out how to deflect incoming asteroids or anything like that. But it was rather mysterious, a pattern of behavior that had no rational explanation but, once initiated, seemed fated to go on indefinitely.

One afternoon during his lunch hour he had found himself, for no particular reason, turning west on Thirty-second Street at Fifth Avenue. It was only two blocks south of his office, but he had not been on that street before. Yong Su, a Korean restaurant a dozen yards from the corner, was serving a dish called bi bim bap. He'd never heard of bi bim bap—for that matter he'd never even eaten Korean food—but he ordered it. Soon a large bowl, the color of bone, was brought to his table. In it was arrayed a pinwheel of pickled vegetables—wedges of bean sprouts, spinach, cucumbers, carrots, mushrooms, and shredded radish—resting on a hassock of steamed white rice. A fried egg on top. It was one of the best things he'd ever tasted.

He returned to Yong Su two days later, then three times the following week. Soon he was there every day. He developed a cordial, well, "friendship" wasn't the word, but acquaintance with the waitress. Not that he knew her name or anything about her— he wasn't even sure, now that he thought about it, whether she spoke more than ten words of English. Yet every time he ordered his bi bim bap, she gave him a brief, knowing smile, and he smiled back.

Very quickly Yong Su became the highlight of his day and, to be honest, a not insignificant part of his life. By ten in the morning he was already thinking about his slow, deliberate walk to the restaurant; the satisfaction of placing his order, the three plosive detonations of *bi! bim! bap!*; the way the tacky surface of the black vinyl tablecloth clung to his fingertips; the bitter vinegary burst when he bit into the white radish; the waitress's watery smile. This went on for a month.

Then one day he did something he could not explain. At the entrance to Yong Su, instead of turning inside, he kept walking. It so happened that two doors down, there was another Korean restaurant, Soowon Galbi. Soowon Galbi also served bi bim bap. Mitchell told himself he was there for variation, but he wasn't sure if that was quite right. As it turned out, the Soowon Galbi bi bim bap was just as delicious as the Yong Su bi bim bap. The waitress at Soowon Galbi was older than her counterpart at Yong Su, but there was something pleasantly maternal about her, and they soon developed their own rapport. After two weeks of committed patronage, she stopped bothering with the menu and, with a wink, delivered a steaming bowl of bi bim bap as soon as he sat down. He found their routine oddly reassuring—or was it reassuringly odd? And yet the next week something must have come over him because he crossed Thirty-second Street and discovered a new restaurant: Moo Dae Po II. The bi bim bap at Moo Dae Po II was excellent. The cycle repeated itself, but now, after three weeks at Moo Dae Po II, he found himself sitting in a booth at Chosan Galbi, pretending to scour the eight-page menu as if he didn't know exactly what he would order. He figured he'd eat at Chosan Galbi for the next few weeks, get to know the waitress there— who seemed very kind, if not particularly loquacious—and see how he felt then.

Satisfied with this account of his life in New York, Mitchell signed the letter, addressed the envelope to Elsa Bruner care of Camp Ticonderoga, and dropped it in his out-box.

A week later Mitchell received an old Camp Ticonderoga postcard. The image showed two ten-year-old boys in bathing suits and life vests paddling a canoe across a green lake. A dark wood loomed in the background. The boys were smiling giddily, as if sharing some private hilarity. He turned the postcard over.

"Mitchell," Elsa had written in her neat, girlish script. "Your note upset me. You seem deeply unhappy. I wonder if Fitzsimmons is the problem."

She signed it "The Fainting Girl." Beneath she had drawn a small pencil sketch of a girl lying on the bottom of a canoe, $X$'s for her eyes and a large $O$ for her mouth.

Mitchell felt a sharp, almost overwhelming pulse of nausea.

But why? He stared at the drawing for several seconds. Then he figured it out. He realized that he couldn't tell whether the girl in the canoe was supposed to be asleep, or dead.

# 5.

The subject line read "YOUR PRESENCE." Body of the e-mail: "REQUESTED."

The e-mail was not entirely unexpected. Still, as with any communication from his boss, it upset his nerves. Sandy Sherman's e-mails, with their infantile reliance on the upper case, always seemed like threats.

Mitchell had asked for a meeting with Sherman to discuss his valuation project. Twenty-four hours after Charnoble's visit, Mitchell had finished calculating the total life worth, in dollars, of every employee on the seventy-fifth and seventy-sixth floors of the Empire State Building. The project finally behind him, he felt he'd earned a chance at Risk. Out of the Basement and into the Penthouse.

When Mitchell entered Sherman's office he noticed that the caps lock key on the computer of Sherman's secretary was held down permanently with a thin strip of duct tape. Sherman insisted on giving his two assistants the corner suite; he used the smaller adjacent room, intended for the secretaries, as his personal office on the few days every month that he came in to work. In that room there was space for only a single desk and a folding chair. Sherman invited Mitchell to sit in the chair. Sherman stood in front of the desk, so there was little separation between his crotch and Mitchell's chin. Mitchell worked in one of the largest buildings in New York City, but he was constantly finding himself sharing miniature spaces with other men.

"Strong work," said Sherman, pointing to Mitchell's reports. They were the only papers on his desk. There was also a stopped clock and several paperweights. The desk was a prop. Mitchell sympathized with the desk. But he barely glanced at it, transfixed as he was by Sherman's head. It was bald and white and as big as a drum, sprayed with red freckles that proliferated in density toward the crown. The effect was not unlike a giant nipple. Despite the fatness of his cranium, Sherman's center of gravity was low, in his haunches, so that his hips buckled and it seemed as if, at any moment, he were about to spring. Men of Sherman's stature are often compared to bulldogs, but he reminded Mitchell more of a jaguar—albeit one in captivity, fussed over and overfed. He had that animal's dangerous, false languor in his eyes, a stare that lulled its object into quiescence before, all of a sudden, it attacked. Sherman saved his fangs for those further up the food chain, but Mitchell still viewed him with the quaking insecurity of a grazing imbecilic herbivore.

"I'm grateful for your efforts regarding this delicate matter," said Sherman. He absently caressed his belly. "We appreciate it."

A sudden lightness tickled Mitchell's brain, and it occurred to him that this might be a good time to ask for his promotion. He told himself to speak. But he didn't speak.

"You're quick with numbers. It's a quality that seems to have gone extinct among today's graduates. They think that as long as you can punch numbers into a calculator, you're a mathematician. Not so. And you, Mitchell—you understand that. You show real cleverness in this department."

"Thank you." Mitchell's voice was quick with humiliating eagerness. "I think, given the opportunity, I might display talent in several different departments."

"I agree. In fact I had another department in mind. Equations and Vectors. We could use you there."

Mitchell smiled awkwardly, as if posing for a camera that wouldn't click. The guys in E and V were glorified accountants. Their job was to devise algorithms and formulas to predict complex market activities and the rate of return on various investments. Even his DEAD colleagues seemed lively compared with the forsaken souls in E and V. They were the nerds of the quant world. Which was saying something.

"Actually," said Mitchell, the words coming too quickly now, "I was hoping that you might consider me for Risk."

Sherman smiled generously, as if indicating that he would be so good as to pretend Mitchell had never raised the subject.

"Or—" Mitchell stammered, "there's another idea I was considering. I've been approached by a risk consulting firm called FutureWorld. Given my experience with the evaluation project, I thought I could serve as a liaison. You see, they've worked out a new kind of business model. It's quite ingenious—"

Sherman, wincing with confusion at this sudden barrage, silenced Mitchell with a firm nod.

"Risk requires a certain social, ah, aspect that I'm sure is beneath you," said Sherman. "We tend to give those jobs to former college athletes—you know, big men on campus. Those jobs require salesmanship. Large personalities, camaraderie, wooing. Sure, they have to handle some quantitative analysis, basic stochastics and econometrics, but nothing more advanced than that. A brain like yours is better suited to pure statistical work. You know, the mathematics that are too tricky for computers. Delta-gamma approximations, Monte Carlo simulations, Hull-White, Cox-Ingersoll-Ross, Heath-Jarrow-Morton, whatever else those boys do behind the curtain. Frankly I don't understand half that crap, but I'm told it's a hell of an exciting field."

Sherman paused, his eyebrows flexing like caterpillars. Mitchell was reminded of the cockroaches, which happened to be furiously incubating in his gut that moment.

*What's your secret, Elsa Bruner? Why aren't you afraid? What do you know that I don't?*

"This is between us," said Sherman, "and I wouldn't admit it to the frat boys. But I envy you. You quants—it's like you have your own secret society. A secret language and a secret world. And it's all up here."

Sherman pointed to his own head, which in that instant reflected the fluorescent ceiling light into Mitchell's eyes.

"Tomorrow you will be shown to your new office." He seemed to notice the gloom in Mitchell's face, because he added, "Don't worry: you won't even have to change floors."

Mitchell trudged back to his desk. His nameplate had already been removed from the door. They had placed on the filing cabinet his few personal belongings—a warm can of ginger ale, the postcard from Elsa, and a pair of framed photographs his mother had sent him the day he was hired. In the first photograph he was two years old, bouncing on her lap. Rikki looked concerned. At that age Mitchell was already behaving strangely. He had developed a habit of taking long pauses before speaking—a tic that Rikki blamed on having a nonnative English speaker for a father. It took a speech therapist to explain that Mitchell's hesitation was not caused by any mental impairment, but by an unusual compulsion to speak in complete sentences. He did not respond to a question until he formulated his answer in his head and mouthed

it to himself, making visible lip movements. There were other pe-
culiarities. At three, observing an elder cousin struggle to read
from a schoolbook, he glanced at the page and pronounced the first
paragraph flawlessly. Seeing the astonished faces around him, he
burst into tears.

The second photo was taken less than two miles away, on the
steps of the New York Stock Exchange, during the Zukors' first
family trip to the city. Mitchell had been only twelve years old—
too young for a hypersensitive child from Overland Park. He'd
wanted to visit the aquarium, but his father, old Tibor, commanded
the cab to drive straight to Wall Street and Broad. Police barricades, surging citadels of silver glass, pewter-faced men in loos-
ened ties and sweat-damp shirts—Tibor had called the financial
district a jungle, but to Mitchell it seemed more like a watch with
intricate parts, constantly ticking, ticking. Or was it a time bomb?
On a tour of the Stock Exchange, the traders' urgent sign language
and exasperated hectoring were too much. Mitchell covered his
ears and the chaos became an insane pantomime, adults playact-
ing like children. When he saw tears in Tibor's eyes, Mitchell
thought that his father must have been similarly affected. But Tibor was moved for a different reason.

"This is where America happens," said Tibor. "Where *we* happen." His passion for old American movies surfaced whenever he
found himself overpowered by emotion. "'Greed is good,'" he said.
"*Wall Street*, starring a certain Mr. Michael Douglas." Mitchell had
nodded solemnly in agreement.

Tibor felt indebted to Wall Street because he owed his pros-
perity to a quintessentially American idea. He'd learned as a young
man that it was possible to buy cheap residential property with
very little money up front, just so long as you could secure, ahead
of time, enough tenants who agreed to pay rent in cash. Even more
incredible, one could win government funding for this scam,
under the premise that each new building would create affordable

housing in poor neighborhoods. Slumlords were the foundation of any strong community, Tibor would regularly declaim, though never, to his credit, with sincerity. But now his slums were fading, and so, it seemed, were Tibor and Rikki. Every time Mitchell looked at this photograph he wondered whether his parents were about to enter their own worst-case scenario.

The Zukorminiums, as they were called by local activists, required extensive repairs. Extensive demolition would be better. They stood in Kansas City's depleted Blue Valley industrial zone, adjacent to a condemned textile factory that still hiccuped orange puffs of overheated asbestos. Tenants had complained about the conditions before, but few lingered long enough to cause trouble. Since Seattle, however, there had been petitions, demonstrations, clench-fisted aldermen making speeches. Tibor was too old to be a slumlord anymore. His tenants and their community backers wanted to hurt him. They would gleefully dismember the poor old Hungarian refugee.

Mitchell felt for Tibor, he did, especially tonight as he prepared to leave his vacated Fitzsimmons Sherman office for an empty apartment and a nice long evening of panic. Sometimes Mitchell even saw himself as a kind of slumlord. Only his slums, his own private Zukorminiums, were inside of him. A vast array of necropolitan towers, rotting and structurally unsound. And how were they doing these days, his inner slums? They were not doing well. They, too, were in disrepair. The pipes were blocked, the air-conditioning cut out, and at night the cockroaches raced up the walls.

# 6.

Microwaves were all right—as long as you stood in the next room while they operated. Put the frozen burrito in the oven, set the timer, press start. Then run.

Mitchell felt desperate sitting there on the couch, a paper plate and plastic fork on his lap, while the microwave whirred in the kitchen. It wasn't the plastic, or the couch's sour, pasty smell, so much as it was the waiting. He had waited patiently for college to end so that he could join Fitzsimmons Sherman, where he had waited patiently for a chance at Risk. Then came the valuation project—and failure. But why? Had he disappointed Sherman? He didn't think so, but it was impossible to know. In any case, that opportunity had passed, and he would have to wait once more. When he woke the next morning, his career—and, by minimal extension, his entire life—would change. He would be an E and V man. He might have to wait there for a very long time.

The microwave bleated. He nudged the burrito onto the paper

plate, which sagged from the heat. Perhaps he was being too hard on himself. Hadn't he felt the same kind of dread before starting at Fitzsimmons? When he learned that he would be working on the seventy-fifth floor of the Empire State Building, he had done some research on elevator accidents. To his horror, he immediately discovered that the most catastrophic accident in the history of building transportation technology was called the "Empire State Building incident." On July 28, 1945, Lieutenant Colonel William Franklin Smith, Jr., a twenty-seven-year-old B-25 bomber pilot, was flying through increasing fog from Bedford, Massachusetts, to Newark Airport, where he was to retrieve his commanding officer. Twenty-five miles short of Newark, Smith radioed the air traffic controller for a weather report. "From where I'm sitting," said the controller, "I can't see the top of the Empire State Building."

But Smith continued toward Manhattan. After passing the Chrysler Building, he became disoriented when a sudden burst of air pushed the airplane to one side, and he turned right instead of left. Within seconds he crashed into the seventy-ninth floor of the Empire State Building. The hoist and safety cables of two of the elevators snapped. One of these elevators, which was being operated by a woman named Betty Lou Oliver, plunged from the seventy-fifth floor—*the very floor Mitchell would be working on.* Luckily for Betty Lou, who was cowering in a fetal position on the floor of the elevator, the falling car compressed the air in the shaft, creating a landing cushion that softened the blow at the bottom. She broke her back and both legs, but survived.

Mitchell skipped the elevator. But after climbing seventy-five flights of stairs, his suit—a Hungarian tri-blend inherited from Tibor—was nearly translucent with sweat, and he had decided to run the numbers. In the United States there were 900,000 elevators, each serving an average of 20,000 people per year. That meant eighteen billion passenger trips per year. These trips resulted in twenty-seven deaths. The chance of dying in an elevator accident was therefore one in 10.44 (repeating) million—about equivalent to the odds of dying from a dog bite, according to the National Safety Council odds-of-death chart he kept in his wallet. This made him feel easier about entering the metal box every morning but he did find himself crossing the street whenever he saw a dog.

It hadn't been lost on him that FutureWorld's office was on the second floor.

After three bites he dumped burrito, plate, and plastic into the trash. Though it was barely dark outside he slipped off his loafers and lay on top of the balled-up sheets of his unmade bed, his laptop opened on his chest. He found New York State's online legislative database. He searched for "Recommit to Civil Service and Pensions Act," and a link was produced to State Finance Law § 307. Under section 52, subsection F, sub-subsection 3, he found what he was looking for:

(3) Defense to liability claims.

Legal indemnification against liability claims that should result from i) acts of God or ii) acts of war shall be assumed by any person or incorporated agency that holds legal title to a Group B building with a permitted occupancy of two hundred or more persons, provided that he/she has made a reasonable, good faith effort to protect his/her building from said circumstances through substantial investment in precautionary measures, or services thereof.

Mitchell closed his laptop and then his eyes. He was asleep within minutes, a deep, rich sleep. He hadn't slept so well in months—no cockroaches, no nightmares of flashing steel and glass, just milky oblivion.

---

The next morning Mitchell called in sick for the first time in his professional career. He removed from his wallet the business card with the line drawing of the open window, and he decided to jump out of it.

Charnoble picked up in the middle of the first ring.

"I wondered when you would call."

He offered Mitchell eleven thousand dollars to start the next morning. The check would arrive in less than an hour by messenger. (Mitchell considered asking that a copy be sent to Sandy Sherman, but then his survival instinct set in.) Charnoble didn't try to hide his relief on the phone. "We've had a number of applications but there was no one with the right mix of technical knowledge and personal despair."

As soon as Mitchell hung up the room became very dark. What had he done? Had he gone *insane*? Was this, finally, the path that had been chosen for him: madness? He'd shown a talent for it in the past, he would admit that, a flair for madness, but he never believed it was his true calling. He tried Charnoble again. But this time, as in a nightmare, the phone rang and rang. No answering machine. He looked again at the business card, made sure he had the right number, and dialed again. Still no answer. He had a picture of Charnoble hunched over the phone, his eyes wide, watching it ring, cackling uncontrollably.

But all things considered, wasn't it a greater risk to remain at Fitzsimmons? An eternity in E and V—that was a risk he couldn't take. Better to start at FutureWorld and quit if things went badly rather than return to Fitzsimmons and E and V. *F—E—V*: if you squinted, it almost spelled FOREVER.

He called his parents.

"FutureWorld? Isn't that a village in Walt Disney?" said Rikki.

"In Budapest," said Tibor, "there was a social committee called the Future World. Their job was to assassinate nationalistic journalists. Sorry—torture first, then assassinate. I promised myself never to speak of the thing they did to my friend Laszlo. You think you can trust a business with that name?"

"It is a dopey name, FutureWorld. But I'm glad you've found something that excites you."

"Poor Laszlo. He was never the same man once they were done with him. If, after such an experience, you could even call him a man."

Mitchell took a deep breath.

"I'm being paid eleven thousand dollars today and sixteen thousand dollars a month. That's before incentives and bonuses kick in. It may increase when we take on more clients."

"'Yippie-kay-yay, motherfucker,'" said Tibor.

"Tibor!" said Rikki.

"*Die Hard*, starring a certain Mr. Bruce Willis."

Mitchell hung up the phone and looked around his apartment, as if for the first time. He had never given much thought to its appearance before—after work he tended to rumble directly to his bed and tip over like a felled tree. And he rarely saw the place by daylight. Not that it admitted daylight. He had only a single, grime-coated window in the living room, which faced the ramp leading from Third Avenue onto the Queens Midtown Tunnel. By day the window cast a narrow rectangle of light onto the floor; at night the tunnel's marigold glow suffused the living room like a nuclear sunset. This was an unhappy apartment. It was not just depressing—it was itself depressed. The baleful wide-screen television glaring at the melancholy mouse-colored couch. The metal desk as heavy as a tombstone, supporting the computer's glassy slab. The unvarnished teak coffee table supporting a pile of withered science magazines and heavily fingered books (on top lay Becker's *The Denial of Death*: "The irony of man's condition is that the deepest need is to be free of the anxiety of death and annihilation; but it is life itself which awakens it, and so we shrink from being fully alive."). And in the corner of the room, the pelican mouth of the forlorn brown briefcase that Tibor had bequeathed him as a graduation present. Every object was despondent, numb, heavy with exhaustion.

Things outside weren't any better. Seattle had inspired a new wave of street preachers to evangelize midtown Manhattan. They must have been having success with their donation boxes because they were fruitful and they did increase. They competed for the busiest intersections, standing across the street from one another, raising the volume on their loudspeakers until they drowned out the honking horns. They preached apocalypse and lifted signs written in magic marker: GOD IS ANGRY WITH THE WICKED EVERY DAY. THE STARS WILL FALL FROM THE SKY. IT REPENTED THE LORD THAT HE HAD MADE MAN ON THE EARTH, IT GRIEVED HIM AT HIS HEART. But it was the crowds that surprised Mitchell. They weren't merely assembling—they were listening. This was a notable development in the world capital of cynicism.

Charnoble's check arrived within the hour. Mitchell took it straight to his bank and decided to celebrate with a lunch at Chosan Galbi. On Lexington Avenue he passed a particularly animated preacher who balanced himself precariously in the basket of a shopping cart. He was cloaked in nothing but a brown canvas tunic cinched around the waist with a dirty string. Not a bad idea—it was another hydrant-bursting, brownout-warning, macadam-melting summer day, the kind of day when people went to movies for the air-conditioning. But this urban apostle had attracted a crowd, roughly a dozen people. They removed the pods from their ears, the sunglasses from their eyes, and peered up at this man. Even Mitchell paused.

"Meat?" said the preacher. The cart was unsteady beneath his feet, skipping on the pavement with each violent swing of his arms.

"Meat and bones and water?"

"No!" shouted a young woman, sitting erect on her bicycle seat.

"Is that all we are?" It was a loud voice, a rhetorician's voice. He spoke like someone accustomed to standing at a pulpit in a mega-cathedral somewhere, lecturing a suburban congregation attired in their Sunday best. This shopping cart, his manner suggested, was only a temporary embarrassment. Sweat beaded under his eyes and dripped over his cheeks. The sides of him, visible through the tunic's gaping armholes, were also wet.

"Intricately wired meat? Meat sending signals to meat through electricity? Where is the mystery in that?"

His audience nodded. It wasn't just a performance. These people were paying witness. A feeling was building. An urban malaria, a future-affected anxiety disorder. Whatever kind of disease it was, it had become infectious.

The bi bim bap at Chosan Galbi that day tasted rancid. Mitchell couldn't finish it. Next to the register the restaurant offered a stack of free postcards. Mitchell chose one bearing an image of bi bim bap and, using the cashier's pen, addressed it to Elsa Bruner.

"By the time you get this," he wrote, "I'll be a futurist."

# 7.

After a tense exchange with one of Sandy's secretaries ("Mr. Sherman will not be pleased," she said breathlessly when he presented his letter of resignation. "Mr. Sherman will not be pleased one bit.") Mitchell took the elevator from the Fitzsimmons offices down to the lobby of the Empire State Building, then changed for an elevator that went to the second floor. He stepped into a long hallway. On the doors were stenciled the names of various law and accounting firms. Finally he reached a door without a name. Instead there was a brass panel embossed with the familiar image of an open window. Mitchell opened the door and entered a small foyer.

Charnoble was seated there, facing him, not three feet away. His bent posture and mortified grin indicated that he'd been waiting there for hours. He wore the same navy pin-striped suit and yellow tie as at their first meeting. His hair was slick and tamped down, and his briefcase balanced gingerly on his pointed knees. As the door cracked open he leaped into the air.

"Welcome!"

"Thanks. I have a box upstairs—"

"We have to leave. Now, I'm afraid. Potential client. A big one. Law firm downtown. You'll get a chance to settle in later. But first, quickly—"

Charnoble produced a camera, and before Mitchell could understand what he was doing, the flash went off.

"Brumley Sansome insists," said Charnoble. "For their file. Security purposes."

Over Charnoble's shoulder Mitchell saw, side by side, beyond the foyer, an identical pair of large rooms. They did not resemble private offices so much as banquet halls. The only wall decorations were digital clocks. There appeared to be one on each wall. At first Mitchell assumed that each clock gave the time in a different international capital, but upon scrutiny he realized that they were all precisely synchronized with one another. Were they also synchronized to the watches on both of Charnoble's wrists? It couldn't be otherwise.

The offices were minimally furnished. At the far end of each— some thirty or forty feet from the entrance—stood a small desk approximately the size of a chopping board. It was large enough to accommodate a micro laptop and a box of tissues. Tall rectangular windows looked onto Sixth Avenue.

"Imposing, no?" said Charnoble. "Big spaces with small furniture create a mood of dread. Perfect for client meetings."

Downstairs, a long black car was idling at the curb. Charnoble didn't give any directions. The driver knew where to go, and he drove aggressively. He assaulted the busy midday traffic, and the traffic yielded to the expensive car. The traffic supplicated. Mitchell wiped the sweat off his forehead with his suit sleeve and tried to ignore the roaches that nibbled away at his stomach lining.

"It's best that I do the talking," said Charnoble. "It's a trial meeting, in a manner of speaking. I've prepared a script." He clutched a folder in his hand. The pages inside were thick with blue ink: diagrams, statistics, color-coded graphs. When Mitchell squinted to make out the text, Charnoble turned the folder over on his lap. Mitchell decided the best thing to do was close his eyes and banish any thought of Fitzsimmons Sherman.

The car glided to a rest in front of a black tower, the headquarters of a major international law firm called Nybuster, Nybuster, and Greene. Charnoble explained that Nybuster represented several small sovereign nations, as well as corporations in more than forty countries. The firm's representative was a very young man wearing a mohair three-piece, no doubt bespoke, and a checkered tie the color of a faded dollar bill. A fatuous smirk was slapped across his face like a price tag. He had trim golden-brown hair, a manicured five o'clock shadow (though it was ten in the morning—did he shave in the middle of the night, was that what you were supposed to do?), a robotic chin, and bright, malicious eyes. The eyes had the cocky look of inherited fortune and disinherited ambition. Mitchell was not surprised to learn that the fellow's name was Nybuster: Ned Nybuster. The three of them sat at a conference table covered by white glass. A tray of cheese, cut fruit, soy wafers, and deli sandwiches had been laid out alongside miniature water bottles, each of which contained no more than a mouthful of liquid. The young Caesar grabbed an entire bunch of grapes, lifted it above his head, and pulled off the lowest-hanging orb with his lips.

"So-o-o-o," said Charnoble, with a thin smile. He was already in full ingratiation mode.

"How does this work?" Nybuster had an effortlessly loud voice, a well-fed voice. "You guys are like economic soothsayers?"

"In a certain sense—"

"I once went to a fortune-teller. She said the path to success would be long and difficult." He frowned playfully.

"We are future-based consultants," said Charnoble, trying again. He removed a digital recorder from his suitcase and pressed the record button. "We help you to build a risk-aware culture. We create scenarios to prepare your company for whatever the future might hold."

"I'm thinking the future holds money. Lots of it. Kind of like the past and the present."

Charnoble explained that he would record each session to comply with federal insurance briefing regulations. The recordings, along with reports that FutureWorld would issue after each meeting, would indemnify the firm should it ever be tried for castastrophe negligence in a court of law.

"What kind of catastrophe? New York doesn't have earthquakes."

"Perhaps not," said Charnoble, and Mitchell had to bite his cheek to restrain himself from correcting his new boss. "Plenty of catastrophes are possible, however."

Nybuster flung a pin-striped leg on the seat of a swivel chair. "So what are we talking about here? Is it total bullshit or just credible bullshit? Entertaining bullshit, actually—that would be ideal."

"Right." Charnoble took a deep breath. He had a pained expression that Mitchell had not seen on his face before. Was it anxiety? Could this be Charnoble's first consulting session too? "Scenario one," said Charnoble. "China declares war."

"The yellow claw," said Nybuster, winking at Mitchell. He leaned back in his chair as if expecting to be fanned by palm fronds.

Charnoble began by listing the number of ways in which the American markets were dependent on Chinese monetary policy. Then he reviewed Nybuster, Nybuster, and Greene's specific Chinese accounts, explaining how each would be affected by an outbreak of war. Charnoble's script wasn't bad, but the delivery was tedious. He might have been reading his tax statements. Mitchell's eyes watered. His hair was still damp and frizzled, his skin dry. He had shaved poorly and had barely seen the sun in weeks, except through tinted glare-resistant office windows. His eyes didn't open all the way. And after a single restful night, the cockroaches had returned. But they weren't alone. They had brought with them a new friend: a kindly bald Spanish gentleman named Pedro Brugada.

Pedro and his brother Josep, Spaniards who practiced in Belgium, were the first Westerners to identify a condition they first described as *tristeza del corazón*, "heart sadness." In 1987 they observed a three-year-old Polish boy, Lech, who experienced fainting spells with a terrifying frequency. The boy's sister had already died from the same mysterious disorder. The Brugadas found additional examples of this condition and, in 1992, the Brugada syndrome entered the diagnostic lexicon. But Easterners had known about it for centuries. In Japan it was called *Pokkuri* ("unexpected death at night"), and in the Phillipines it was known as *bangungut* ("scream followed by sudden death"). In the northeast of Thailand, where it struck young men disproportionately, it was known as *lai tai*, or "death during sleep." *Lai tai* was believed to be caused by the ghosts of dead women who kidnapped young men to serve as their husbands in the underworld. The Thai men of this region, in a desperate effort to trick the succubi—or at least to turn them off—went to bed every night dressed in drag.

In his second letter to Elsa, Mitchell had asked whether she was certain that she had this condition. The first indication, she wrote, came when her father dropped dead on a public bus when she was seven years old. His last checkup had revealed an unusual ditch in his electrocardiogram reading, but he was a healthy, fit man and no one suspected heart problems. Elsa had several fainting spells in high school, however, and her doctor noticed the same peculiarity in her EKG. After excluding everything else, a cardiologist tested for Brugada. It wasn't an easy test. To test a patient for Brugada, you have to kill her.

At the hospital they inserted a catheter into her groin, feeding the tube through the femoral vein into the heart. A pacemaker was attached to the end of the catheter. It sent an electronic signal, forcing the heart to skip a beat. The heart of a patient with Brugada syndrome cannot handle this stress. If the heart stops beating, it means Brugada is present. Elsa's heart stopped. Less than two seconds later they defibrillated her.

"What was it like to be dead?"

"It was the most excruciating sensation I've ever experienced," she wrote. "Defibrillation contracts every muscle, so your body leaps from the operating table. The constriction is so painful that it momentarily jars you from sedation and you awake, with a shock, in the middle of the air."

The memory of this image made Mitchell's fingers shake, beating erratic rhythms into Nybuster's conference table like a frustrated drummer. He squeezed the rim of his chair.

But Nybuster hadn't noticed. His face was a portrait of abject boredom, a child forced to sit with a tutor while his friends play at recess. He had finished the grapes and was now using the branches to pick the fruit out of his teeth. In the last ten minutes, as Charnoble had gone on about the state of China's ballistic technology, Nybuster hadn't once glanced in their direction. Finally he swung around in his seat, put his feet back on the ground, and turned to Charnoble.

"Would you please arrive at your point?" he said. "I don't understand how any of this is useful to Nybuster, Nybuster, and Greene. We're comfortable with our client base, our risk exposure. Our firm has been in this business for more than four decades. Our formula has not let us down yet."

Charnoble glanced between Nybuster and Mitchell, his finger twisting in his palm. For all his reptilian maneuvering, his conniving ratiocination, he was obviously not adept at selling fear. The problem was that he didn't truly *believe* it. Charnoble was right. He needed someone like Mitchell.

Nybuster stood.

"Sorry, chums. I'm going to have to ask you to tell the rest of your report to the tape recorder. I have business." He started for the door. Charnoble's widening eyes and whitish blond hair made him look like a scared little boy. Mitchell rose from his chair.

"Mr. Nybuster."

Nybuster turned. He appeared surprised to learn that Mitchell could speak. In fact he appeared surprised to see that a third person was present in the room.

"I'd like to tell you what's going happen in about ten years, once Beijing attacks. Before the first missile lands in Times Square, Nybuster, Nybuster, and Greene will be ruined. And I don't just mean the firm. I mean your private wealth, your legacy, your next of kin."

Nybuster squinted uncertainly.

"Come again?"

"It's going to be ugly," said Mitchell. In his mind he saw a body levitating above an operating table in a paroxysm of infinite agony. He allowed his fear to radiate out of his eyes. He would use the fear.

"Go on." Nybuster seemed, for the first time all meeting, to be listening. He scooted back to his seat. "I want to hear the ugly."

"OK," said Mitchell. "Right. Well, for instance, China blockades Taiwan." Mitchell hesitated, glancing at Charnoble. Charnoble was nodding eagerly, grateful.

"China has threatened it before," Mitchell continued. "It's just a matter of time before it happens. The Taiwan Relations Act mandates that any act of aggression against Taiwan be considered a threat to the security of the United States and will trigger the use of military force."

Nybuster nodded, taking this in.

"The U.S. sends missile carriers to the Taiwan Strait. China bombs Taipei. The U.S. bombs Beijing. China starts firing intercontinental ballistic missiles at San Francisco, Los Angeles, and Seattle. Jin-class submarines surface off the Atlantic coast, launching warheads at Boston, Miami, Washington, D.C., and New York."

"Mm."

"Nybuster, Nybuster, and Greene's employees will all have fled the city for the heartland, or Canada, or Mexico. Or they'll have died. Either way, it's irrelevant. The country as we know it will be gone. Where the major cities once stood, there will now be only radioactive wasteland. The economy as we know it will cease to exist, and every equity—except some of those listed on the Hong Kong and Shanghai exchanges—will plunge close to zero. The dollar will be inflated beyond all possible utility, and those unlucky enough to survive the initial blast will be forced to employ a highly volatile bartering system, with water and food the most expensive commodities."

"Good God," said Nybuster. "But you're not exactly telling me anything new, are you? Or particularly useful. Listen, I'm out of time."

"But there's a more likely scenario," said Mitchell. He felt something powerful moving through him now, a dark energy. "China blockades Taiwan; the U.S. sends missile carriers to the Taiwan Strait. China threatens to bomb Taipei—but they *don't* act. They're not stupid. Sure, they've threatened a first-strike nuclear attack at the first sign of U.S. aggression, but they don't want to bring on the apocalypse. Taiwan isn't worth the loss of every major Chinese city, the massive destabilization of the yuan, the collapse of the economy."

"Right, but—"

"Imagine, instead, a low-grade attack. Chinese sleeper agents are activated in every major U.S. city. Cyberattacks strain the electrical grid, checkerboarding it. Kidnappings, corruption, political murders begin to occur. Slowly at first, then more frequently.

Why? No one knows. Policemen are assassinated by the dozen. Prominent journalists begin to vanish. The managing partner of your own firm is going out for his early-morning swim at his home on Long Island when a band of Chinese agents stun him with a taser and throw him into the back of an armored truck. Your managing partner wakes up in a dungeon, four levels below Canal Street, his wrists cinched to his ankles, an apple in his mouth."

"Are you aware," said Nybuster, in an uncharacteristically quiet voice, "are you aware that the managing partner of Nybuster is my father?"

"Certainly he didn't mean to suggest," said Charnoble, "in a manner of speaking—"

"That will be fine," said Nybuster. "Zukor, you have my attention. Please, continue. By all means—continue. What happens to my father in the dungeon? Begin with the part about the apple."

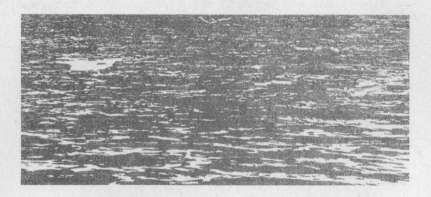

# 8.

The pitiful little cardboard box containing Mitchell's possessions from Fitzsimmons Sherman awaited him at the FutureWorld office, accompanied by a brown envelope imprinted with the familiar sketch of the canoe and the girl with *X*'s for eyes—the latest missive from the Maine hinterland. Elsa had enclosed an article from a scholarly journal, *Current Biology*, titled "The Fearless Wonder." The subject of this study was a forty-four-year-old Iowa woman, Sarah Axon, who possessed a deformed amygdala—the almond-size mass of nuclei in the brain that controls the processing and recognition of fear. If the Brugada syndrome was a human worst-case scenario, Sarah Axon's condition approached a human best-case scenario. When her amygdala was damaged by a childhood fever, she lost the ability to experience fear. But other than that she was unchanged. The study described how she handled snakes and tarantulas with glee, frolicked through haunted houses, and returned at night to a park where, just days earlier, a man had threatened to kill her. The aggressor, a "drugged-out" derelict, had stuck a knife to her throat, yelling, "I'm going to cut you, bitch!" To which Sarah Axon placidly responded, "If you're going to kill me, you're going to have to go through my God's angels first." The man with the knife ran away screaming.

When asked why she would reach into the mouth of a snake that she knew to be poisonous, and caress, with unusual tenderness, its flicking tongue, Sarah explained that she had been overcome with "curiosity." The word recurred frequently in the article. Sarah was curious to know what a haunted house monster's face felt like, so she poked it (causing the person wearing the costume to recoil in fear). When she was asked what went through her head when she watched horror movies, she replied, "I experience an overwhelming feeling of curiosity."

Fine—good story. But why would Elsa send it to him? She was like an alien who beamed into his office once or twice a week with bulletins from a planet in some distant solar system where the laws of gravity didn't exist. Down was up, dark was light, and no one was afraid of anything. Elsa and Sarah Axon and the rest of their kind lived suspended in a permanent condition of hopeful, childlike, brainless bliss. Did they come from some highly evolved future, or were they refugees from a distant, primordial past? Logic would say the former: evolution ruled against the fearless. The dodo, the most trusting and friendly animal that mankind had ever encountered, was first identified in 1581. The bird was extinct less than a century later.

On the final page Elsa had scrawled a comment in the white space at the end of the article. "I wonder if there's a correlation between fear and curiosity," she wrote. "More fear = less curiosity about the actual world?"

Mitchell puzzled over this. Was Elsa chiding him? He doubted it—she was too generous, too uncalculating—but the question unnerved him. It was a question, after all, that Mitchell often put to himself. By focusing on the worst-case scenarios, did he cut himself off from the smaller, but more immediate problems? The personal crises, the mundane dramas and trials that had everything to do with daily life but nothing to do with the larger-scale crises? Was his whole fascination with worst-case scenarios in some way frivolous? A lark?

A glance at his odds-of-death chart (death by earthquake, 1 in 153,597; death by air accident, 1 in 5,862; death by accidental poisoning, 1 in 139) was enough to call back the cold reality of the numbers. Worst-case scenarios did come to pass, after all, and if FutureWorld didn't worry about them, who would? He was on the vanguard of a new industry—nightmare analysis—and he was proud of it too. He was a fear professional now, and he was being paid lucratively for the specialized skills he brought to the job.

But there was more to it than that. Unlike Charnoble, he was not a cynic. Wouldn't these consultations perform a valuable service for his clients, apart from indemnification? He would force them to look out the windows of their skyscrapers and see what was going on. Inside the glass towers it was the twenty-first century—fiber optics, silent supercomputers, temperature control to the tenth of a degree Fahrenheit. But just outside, where the thermostat was wildly out of control, it was still the Dark Ages: pantomiming prophets, barefoot beggars, plague and pestilence.

"I know more about the actual world than most people," he wrote to Elsa on FutureWorld stationery, his pen chiseling deep indentations into the page. It was impressive stationery—a significant improvement on Fitzsimmons Sherman's thin-grade, laser-printed stock. The paper was a cotton and hardwood blend, with deckle edges, the open window logo embossed in magenta dye at the head and, in the center of the page, a faint "FW" watermark, visible only when you held it up to natural light. It said FW, but it communicated Brumley Sansome.

"It's curiosity that's my problem," Mitchell continued. "I wish I didn't want to know the first thing about plate tectonics or nuclear war, but I do. So I learn more. And the more I learn, the more I find there is to fear."

In the following weeks, as July collapsed into August, letters began to arrive nearly every day. Neither of them waited for responses before sending a new one. So several dialogues were conducted simultaneously. But the conversation, in a certain sense, remained the same. They both had information that the other craved.

Mitchell asked questions about Ticonderoga in the hope that Elsa would explain why she had decided to risk her life for the privilege of living on an isolated farm like an Okie homesteader. But she didn't disclose her secret. Instead she sent news of solar tubes, bidirectional net meters, and metal flashings; lists of crops and the seasons in which they would be planted; and long-range plans—they were replacing the tennis courts with gardens, repairing the pump in the artesian well, insulating the administrative buildings for use during the winter months. It soon became clear that it wasn't only a change of scenery she was after, or a desire to get closer to nature. No, Elsa had higher ambitions. She said she wanted to develop an entirely new way of living. "Rationality has made a mess of this world. Rationality isn't helpful or useful, and it's certainly not exciting. We want to trust our impulses more." But what were those impulses? What were they telling her to do? Were they like the voices telling Marshall Applewhite that in order to ascend to the alien spaceship trailing the Hale-Bopp comet, he and his followers had to swallow applesauce spiked with phenobarbital?

In his own letters Mitchell made a point of listing the virtues of metropolitan life, primarily the attractions of total convenience: the way the city handled essential services such as food and waste with optimal efficiency, leaving you with more time to do, well, whatever was important to you. He tried to introduce her to some basic econometric principles—Markov systems in particular—that might help her make decisions more logically, but he encountered resistence. It didn't matter; his point was simple: they had urban farms in Brooklyn and rooftop gardens all over Manhattan, if that's what she wanted. He didn't mention that the most idyllic moments of his childhood were spent floating, carefree, in a canoe across Little Elkhart Lake, where for three summers he attended a wilderness camp for boys. (At the age of eleven he left that for the Young Scholars mathematics camp at the University of Chicago.) Nor did he mention New York's doctors, the hospitals, the world-class cardiologists—but he figured he didn't have to. Wasn't it clear what they were talking about?

This theme kept recurring, an undertow that threatened to tug them out to deeper waters. Elsa asked, for instance, why Mitchell kept plastic sandwich bags filled with cash hidden in his freezer.

"In case ATMs stop working. Say there's a massive blackout.

Or a bomb. Or an electromagnetic pulse radiation. Awfulness can happen at any time. That's what's so awful."

These were the words they used, but what they were really after went unspoken. Mitchell wanted to know how she defeated, or ignored, the fear of a death that would likely come for her soon. And Elsa seemed eager to prove her case to him, to persuade him that she had figured out how best to survive a chaotic universe. But why? Why should she care what Mitchell—a financial consultant who plotted disaster and figured out how to profit from it—thought about her little utopian agricultural experiment?

He was thinking about this in his gigantic empty office on the second floor of the Empire State Building. The newest letter from Elsa Bruner lay on his desk beside a report from the World Health Organization titled "Dengue and Hemorrhagic Fever: An Emerging Public Health Threat in the United States," a file containing new telemetric readings of unusual growth activity in the Yellowstone caldera, and an article from *Nature* titled "Recent Contributions of Glaciers and Ice Caps to Sea Level Rise." It was astonishing how much bad news was generated every day. You had only to pay attention—subscribe to the right newsletters and academic journals—and you could see the information accrete, like matter spiraling around a black hole.

The newest letter from Elsa had little to it—she complained about the unusually pungent and penetrating heat that had smothered the Northeast all summer. The depth of the Housatonic River in Connecticut was at a thirty-year low, and there had been a pageant of spontaneous fires through central New Jersey, spreading from house to house, jumping over distances as long as a basketball court. The same signs, she wrote, were evident at Ticonderoga. The well was drying up; the fields were turning to dust; the evergreens were brown. But what struck Mitchell about Elsa's note was a throwaway line right at the end, set off from the rest. She had written:

"Is it odd that we read each other's thoughts but never hear each other's voices?"

This had stuck with him, stuck in the folds of his brain like gum to the sole of a shoe. There was something here. He didn't think she was proposing that they speak on the phone. That would be difficult, since she had no phone line or Internet connection at Ticonderoga and she drove into Augusta no more than once a week. But the intimacy of that line (*we read each other's thoughts*) forced him again to wonder why she was writing him so enthusiastically. Was she merely lonesome? Bored? That didn't seem right. She had endless work to do in the fields. And she had plenty of company— not just her boyfriend but the friends who bunked at the farm for weeks at a time, usually after their rock bands broke up.

But who, besides Mitchell, was willing to suggest to her, however timidly, that she was putting her life in danger? Not her comrades on the farm. The boyfriend, as far as Mitchell could tell, was doting and subservient, committed to her plans. Elsa's father was dead, and her mother, a retired social worker on disability, was absent, a burnout in Boulder. Nobody would question her but Mitchell.

So maybe Elsa, deep down, didn't *want* to hear his voice. The distance sanitized the conversation, gave it an academic quality—a correspondence course in self-denial. The strangely antiquated act of exchanging letters allowed them a phony sense of detachment. It would be considerably more difficult to have to respond to a live person, ready with spontaneous retorts. When you looked at it this way, her letter-writing mania began to make more sense. She wasn't trying to persuade Mitchell Zukor that she was doing the right thing with her life. She was trying to persuade *herself*. She had asked whether excessive fear could insulate you from the actual world. Perhaps Mitchell's letters were as much of the actual world as she could tolerate.

Almost immediately after the encounter with Nybuster, Charnoble ceded control of client meetings to Mitchell. It was clear the kid had a special talent for conceiving cataclysmic scenarios.

"You're like an exorcist in reverse," Charnoble told him over the office intercom. Since their desks were at the far ends of their respective offices, Charnoble had to walk thirty-five feet to his door, step into the adjacent room, and then advance another thirty-five feet to Mitchell's desk in order to have a face-to-face conversation. It became office policy to use the intercom instead, though Mitchell still jumped every time the reedy crackle of Charnoble's voice disrupted the woolly silence of his vast empty chamber.

Mitchell pressed the intercom button.

"What do you mean, 'an exorcist in reverse'?"

"Instead of warding off demons," said Charnoble, "you summon them." There was a pause, but since the static continued to emanate from the machine, Mitchell knew Charnoble was preparing another thought. "I think the word is 'necromancer.'"

Mitchell pressed the intercom. "We really need to move to a different office," he said.

"You don't like the intercom system?"

"I don't like being in the Empire State Building. It is not safe, and it is not good for business."

"I agree, but Brumley won't approve anything until our client list is larger."

Mitchell pressed the intercom button, then removed his finger. He'd had enough of the intercom. It was making him feel as if he were delusional, hearing voices. He pushed himself away from his small desk, walked across the ivory carpet, and entered the foyer. Charnoble's office door was closed. Mitchell knocked tentatively, but he was impatient to continue the conversation, and knowing that Charnoble was merely sitting at his desk across the room, he opened the door.

The room was empty.

# 9.

Mitchell began to spend most of his time at the library. He requested books on the engineering of New York skyscrapers, bridges, and highways. He found information that he could draft directly into his fear reports. He learned, for instance, that three-quarters of all city water lines had exceeded their design life, many by a century. The suspender bars that held up the Brooklyn Bridge had been snapping with alarming regularity since 2010. If the four ventilation fans on either end of the Holland Tunnel were to break down, drivers would die of carbon monoxide poisoning before reaching New Jersey. More violent crimes were committed in the Thirty-fourth Street BDFM subway station than in any other in New York. On the RFK Bridge there had for many years stood a sign that read IN EVENT OF AIR ATTACK, DRIVE OFF BRIDGE.

He examined so many topographical and geological maps of the city that the librarian informed him, in a hushed voice, that he had been added to an FBI watch list. He printed out stacks of reports prepared by international aid groups and government agencies. He started to think of them exclusively as acronyms: FEMA, USCG, NOAA, NYSOEM, DHS, ARC, DOT, DIA. He devised an acronym to remember all the acronyms: FUNNY DADDI. Yes, just like Tibor and his rib-tickling tales of the Hungarian pogroms.

Mitchell became gluttonous for information. The disaster research he'd done in college now seemed amateur, pathetically incomplete. He'd never had access to such resources before—an endless supply of industry and government reports, internal corporate records, and the use of proprietary software that Charnoble had imported from Brumley Sansome's Risk department. But his greatest resource was time. For ten hours every day he was free to devour the raw data of disaster. The more he consumed, the more his appetite grew. The thousands of facts he ingested daily kept out Brugada, his parents, and the emptiness of his spooky, squalid orange-lit apartment. The facts were thrilling. Manhattan's highest natural elevation was Bennett Park, an outcropping of schist in Washington Heights, 268 feet above sea level. Its lowest point was the Battery Park City Esplanade, seven feet above the Hudson River. A fault line ran across 125th Street and any day could trigger a magnitude 6 earthquake. Mitchell memorized the Richter scale and its equivalencies. An earthquake measuring 4.0 was equivalent to the detonation of a small atomic bomb; a 7.1 was as destructive as the largest thermonuclear weapon ever tested. About twenty 7.0s occurred annually, and one 8.0. The only thing in this world that could compare with the propulsive energy of an 8 or 9 earthquake was a previous 8 or 9 earthquake. In the great Panamanian quake of 1882, an 8.1, the force of the tremor broke some coastal homes in two. A young married couple, who slept on adjacent single mattresses, awoke to find themselves separated by a widening bay, their house split clean in half—she on the mainland, he on a tiny islet drifting away from her, into the sea.

Hurricanes were measured by the Saffir-Simpson scale, winds

less than 118 mph by the Beaufort scale. Tornadoes were charted by the Fujita scale, named after Professor Tetsuya Fujita of Kitakyushu, Japan, a man known in press reports as "Mr. Tornado." Through his work on tornado classification, Mr. Tornado discovered a peculiar meteorological phenomenon that he named a "microburst." A microburst was a strong, localized air current that caused wind to change direction and speed rapidly. Mr. Tornado determined that this freakish phenomenon was responsible for most unsolved airline crashes. Mitchell had never heard of microbursts before and was terrified by the thought of them. The microburst, he decided, was Brugada's meteorological equivalent: a small vector of chaos that could destroy life, unexpectedly, at any moment. For a long time he paused over the microbursts.

FEMA advised American citizens to keep in their homes, at all times, an emergency supply kit. This kit was to contain a wrench or pliers to disable utilities, a whistle, and a NOAA weather radio with tone alert. Books, games, and puzzles were also recommended. Disasters were like crime scenes: after the initial violence there was a lot of waiting around. If you kept yourself entertained, there was less opportunity for panic.

The new information crystallized in his brain. Wasn't this the work he was born to do? His juvenile obsessions had prepared him well. He sometimes wondered whether he could remember details about emergencies more vividly than anecdotes from college or childhood. As he worked his mind opened up and he plowed himself into it. Brain ate heart. That's not to say he was turning cold or emotionless—just the opposite. The bad news brought a rush of excitement; it fortified, too. It reached an intimate part of him. It didn't merely feed his fears, it also fed his fascinations. The information had a way of seeping into his higher thoughts. After a while he began to feel that he *was* the information.

He went further afield, into doomsday prophecy and eschatology. It was tremendous fun. He read Nostradamus, Malthus, Al-

vin Toffler. He read Prophets and he read Revelation. Seven-headed
dragons, locusts with man-faces wearing crowns of gold, a sea of
glass mingled with fire—Mitchell loved Revelation. The Chris-
tians were excellent worst-case scenarists, even better than the
Jews. They were terrified in Technicolor: green dragons, swirling
orange fires of hell, scarlet demons.

During consultations his clients nervously swiveled in their
ergonomic leather-padded office chairs as he guided them through
scenes from Hell. It felt good to spread the darkness around. Misery liked company, but Misery loved a party festooned with rotting
flowers, gaudy balloons inflated with cyanide gas, human piñatas.

Before long Mitchell had established a repertoire. With a new
client he began by discussing Sino-American military conflict,
and for the next several meetings he rounded out the war quartet
with hour-long sessions on Iran/Israel, India/Pakistan, and the
Koreas, war-gaming the rapid ascension to regional, then total
nuclear war. Five thousand nukes were on active, hair-trigger
alert all over the world, many aimed at financial centers. Even a
"small," regional nuclear war, such as Iran and Israel exchanging
bombs, would kick up enough ash and particulate residue to dim
the sun and cause global crop failure. A billion people would
starve to death. Buried beneath the Ural Mountains, in the heart
of Russia's nuclear command and control system, there existed a
doomsday device code-named PERIMETR. Though it was built
during the Soviet era, it remained operational. Should Russian
leadership be overthrown, a computer would automatically send
launch orders throughout the country to nuclear missiles that
would fire to all corners of the world. Half of mankind would be
vaporized.

He then turned to public health scares: the mass production of
tainted meats; the poisoning of the water supply; a gas explosion
in the sewers; an airborne toxin that escapes from a chemical factory on a windless day and floats into a major city; an explosion at

a nuclear power plant, such as Indian Point, just thirty-five miles from New York. Indian Point sat on the intersection of two active seismic zones—a fact that was not known when the plant was built in 1962. Then there was the possibility of a pandemic. It would originate in Asia, perhaps Thailand. A little girl who tends the chickens on her family farm wakes up with a fever and a headache. The next day she can barely move; by evening she has developed a painful cough, vomits blood. The desperate parents roll her in a wheelbarrow to the nearest hospital, where X-rays show a shadowy white mass, about the size of a penny, in one of her lungs. The girl dies, horribly, two days later, but not before she has sprayed billions of viral particles into the air around her. Hospital workers carry the disease home to their families and transmit it to fellow commuters on the public buses. A few days after that a woman boards an airplane at Suvarnabhumi Airport headed for San Francisco. She has a headache and a mild sore throat. Within two weeks, sixty million people are dead.

Mitchell segued gracefully into a special feature on terrorism: attack by post; bombing by shoe, suitcase, or truck; air attack; attack by radioactive agent; suicide bombings on Fifth Avenue and Wall Street. A cyberattack releases the account numbers, passwords, and holdings of the clients of a major international bank. A cyberattack reveals corruption in the Supreme Court. A cyberattack launches bombs (see War, above).

Then earthquakes, floods, wildfires, and tsunamis. He learned that scientists had detected fault lines in a five-mile-wide volcano situated on La Palma, one of the westward Canary Islands. When an eruption causes the crater, and its half-trillion tons of rock, to break apart and slide into the ocean—and this is a geological inevitability, only a matter of time—it will trigger the largest tsunami in recorded history. The great wave will travel across the ocean faster than an airplane. It will take eight hours to reach the

Atlantic Seaboard, by which time the crest will be half a mile above sea level—more than twice the height of the Empire State Building. And then that wave will crash.

There were also the threats of a solar storm that would reset the planet's magnetic field, a deep freeze, hailstorm, hurricane, tornado, asteroid, volcano.

"There is no volcano in New York City," said Nybuster.

"That's what you'd like to believe," replied Mitchell. "You would like to believe that very much."

A few sessions—a reprieve, really—on minimal, localized assaults: employee sabotages company's finances; employee leaks industry secrets to competition; employee blows his brains out at his desk; employee goes on office-wide shooting rampage. A gun is fired in the United Nations. Sarin gas is released into the subway system. An aqueduct that supplies drinking water to the city is poisoned. The complications he explored were extravagantly detailed, tendinous, delicious.

Finally, large-scale fiscal fiasco: the dollar collapses; a major foreign currency fluctuates violently; the real estate market slides eighty percent; the World Bank files for bankruptcy; commodities soar, leading to food riots and political instability. And peak oil millenarianism: electric grid crash; the collapse of industrial agriculture, travel, and international trade; a return to premodern agrarian life; mass starvation; the wilding of the suburbs.

So Elsa, tell me, how's that for the "actual world"?

The research came easily enough, but Mitchell struggled to prepare scripts for his presentations. Before each meeting, misshapen blocks of facts drifted through his mind with jagged edges that never properly aligned. He glanced at his notebook and found nothing but disarranged sentences and abandoned phrases, with no logical progression between them. It was only when he began to speak, his clients struggling to determine the veracity of what he was saying, that he could truly visualize the horrors he was paid to predict. His eyes would float faraway and water slightly, and a Cassandra prophecy would unfold in full paragraphs. Occasionally he thought of the street preachers on the busy midtown corners spouting revelation fantasy—and felt momentarily sick. But he forced himself to remember that with him it wasn't phony spiritualism. It wasn't an act. It was more like a feat of transference.

He was visiting the place he often went at night, after the cockroaches stopped scurrying up the walls of his stomach and he shuddered into a restless semiconsciousness. It was a nightmare city, a phobopolis. It came to him in a blur of flashing metal and glass. The chaotic anxiety of his bullet-train dreams would abate, like the players of an orchestra finishing their tuning exercises just before the theater lights dim, and he'd find himself in a silent, glass-windowed apartment. He was high off the ground, so high that he couldn't see the bases of the other skyscrapers. The sky was a rich, bright blue and the enormous steel edifices soared both as high and as low as he could see. He suspected that the towers never stopped, but extended infinitely in either direction. They were slender, the towers, and they swayed lightly. In the windows of the other skyscrapers stood people, peering out, just like him.

He found it calming, during consultation meetings, to imagine that his clients were the skyscraper dwellers from his dreams, staring forlornly from their glass windows, emasculated by anxiety. Seeing them there, imprisoned in their identical white rooms and looking back at him with straining eyes, Mitchell regained his nerve and began to speak about what would happen when disaster struck.

It also helped when they sweated. Whenever Mitchell held client meetings in his office, Charnoble turned the thermostat five degrees higher—just warm enough for beads of perspiration to appear beneath collars and in armpits, but not enough to make it plainly uncomfortable. After all, it was always at least twenty degrees warmer outside. It had been a savage, unusually arid summer, and the heat was getting into the brain. It had begun to appear on the release forms filled out by prospective FutureWorld clients. When asked for the most immediate challenges to the health of their business, two different representatives—from a perfume company and a firm that manufactured artificial sweeteners—had cited "catastrophic drought." It had been a slow summer for news, and the tabloids trumpeted stories that normally wouldn't have received front-page headlines. The city had been spared blackouts, but during a particularly strong heat wave in July, when the temperature hit 106, cars broke down in the streets and city workers watered the George Washington Bridge with fire hoses to prevent it from locking when its plates expanded. The Delaware and Catskill reservoir systems were in danger of emptying, and boil-water advisories were issued on the worst days. Plant watering was discouraged; bottled water was hoarded. The streets became strangely quiet. The Department of Health and Public Hygiene issued statements advising New Yorkers to "Slow Down" and "Think Cool Thoughts." At John Day High School a fifteen-year-old football player, after being denied a water break by his coach, sat down Indian-style on the fifty-yard line and expired. The coach was charged with manslaughter. (Mitchell suspected Brugada.) In Ridgewood, the corpses of Harold and Caroline Crowder, who had been married more than sixty years, were found in an elevator that had become stuck between the first and second floor of their home. The excessive heat in the steel box had melted their kidneys.

The coverage of the heat wave and the drought, however exaggerated, seemed to contribute to the anxiety that had settled like a poisonous cloud over the country after Seattle. This worked to FutureWorld's advantage. Nothing better prepared the mind for future fears than present anxieties. And so the ads were being clicked more frequently, and clients like Nybuster were discussing

FutureWorld confidentially at midtown lunches, in Ivy League clubhouses, in Southampton swimming pools. More New Yorkers were beginning to wonder what the future might cost them.

On August 16, FutureWorld signed its fiftieth client. Charnoble mentioned that Brumley would be happy to consider a new office.

Mitchell's mother—decent, homespun Rikki in Overland Park—fretted about him. She began to call more frequently.

"I'm just not sure it's so healthy."

"The scenarios, they're a type of logic game. A puzzle."

"These things you're reading so much about—are you afraid of them actually happening?"

Mitchell bit his lip.

"No."

Rikki snorted. She always could tell when he was full of it.

"You know your father still has nightmares about the revolution. I worry you've somehow inherited his fears."

"Everyone has fears. It's just a matter of controlling them. You must have fears yourself."

"Of course I do. Senility. The Zukorminiums—what a job they're doing on poor Tibor. And concern for my son's well-being. That most of all."

"So how do you overcome them?"

"I try to put them out of mind. Avoid a roving imagination and idle reveries."

"I have a different strategy," said Mitchell. He leaned back in his chair, his free hand gravitating to his head. The hair was getting thinner, it seemed. When he grabbed a fistful and pulled, several strands came away. Was this normal? The orphaned hairs collected on his desk. "I imagine a scenario in the greatest detail possible. That way I can figure out how unlikely it is to come true. Fearing the worst usually cures the worst."

"You're in New York now. You don't have to deal with all the little indignities of small-town life. Or slumlord life. Everything is just so little here."

"Sometimes I feel like a slumlord. Only the slums are inside me."

"What?"

"Um, just that I feel—"

"Stop with the nonsense. Listen, you have a good job. You are your own man. You don't have to be afraid of vast global tragedies that will not harm you. These scenarios are abstractions. Put yourself in the world. Be a person of action. Go outside. Take a walk in the park. I'm worried you're burying yourself under books and charts."

"A bomb on the crosstown bus would harm me," said Mitchell passionately. "It would harm me a lot."

He closed his eyes and saw bright sky, metallic dazzle. He was exhausted. An excess of fear did that to him. It exhausted his clients too. Nybuster lasted just over a month of meetings before losing his patience. By the end of August he had begun pacing around the room, nodding absently during Mitchell's presentations.

"Be honest with me, Zukor. Nanobot invasions? Really?"

A look of concern flashed over Charnoble's face, but by now he knew better than to interrupt.

"All right," said Mitchell. "I will get into the heavy shit."

"That's what I wanted to hear," said Nybuster. "Extreme terrorism? The bosses want to know more about that."

Mitchell paused. He needed to try a new tactic with Nybuster. He remembered the street preacher on Lexington Avenue. There was something to that man's act. The feverishness of it, the hot-blooded fantasy, the grand emotions. If a man attired in a brown canvas tunic cinched with string could make a living at it, then why couldn't Mitchell? What did he have to lose? He counted silently to ten, then inhaled deeply.

"The End of Days."

"And that would be?" said Nybuster, smirking.

"One day your employees start complaining about insomnia. Many of them call in sick. Those who do show up wear gloves in the office and never remove them. Why? you ask. They don't respond."

"Mm."

"Show me your hands, you say. They refuse to show you. You physically force your secretary to remove her gloves. The gloves are filled with blood."

"What?"

Charnoble was getting a look that Mitchell hadn't seen since their first meeting together—a white sheet of paper passing over his face.

"You run her hands under the faucet," Mitchell continued. "When the blood drains away, you can see the identical cuts on both her palms. The cuts are in the shape of a cross. You see what I mean."

"Actually? I don't."

"She has received the stigmata." He watched Nybuster closely for his reaction. It seemed to be taking. He thought of his father walking door-to-door in east Kansas City, selling the poor bastards on the merits of life in the Zukorminiums. So this is what it was to *sell*. Tibor hocked Zukorminiums; Mitchell hocked fear.

Charnoble busily screwed his fingernails into the palm of his hand. It appeared that he was trying to give himself a stigmata.

"The stigmata?"

"The stigmata. You see, your secretary is one of the chosen ones."

"Chosen? For what?"

"You wake up the next morning to the sound of a trumpet call. The sun is turning black, like a rotten lemon. At the northern end of Broadway, seven horses appear in the middle of the avenue. They are as white as ivory. Astride the beasts are horsemen cloaked up to their eyes in dark canvas garments. The horses begin to march downtown.

"The East River has turned into blood. The Harlem into blood. The Hudson—also blood. Blood spurts out of the tap. There is a red ring around the shower drain. Blood comes out of there too."

Nybuster was baffled. Baffled, but transfixed. Mitchell could tell what Nybuster was thinking: *Where is this maniac going? What's next?* And that was the crucial question. As long as Nybuster wanted to know what happened next, the consultations would continue, and so would the referrals, the money, the information. The whole exhilarating cycle of doom.

"The blood is thick and dark, almost black," said Mitchell. "It clots the pipes. Plants and crops start to wither. People raid supermarkets for bottled water. When that runs out, they start drinking the blood."

Nybuster stared in wonder. Charnoble was pressing one hand over his mouth.

"The blood is nothing like normal human blood. It tastes awful."

"Zukor? Are you all right? Alec, is he all right?"

"This taste," said Mitchell, "this is the taste of the future."

# 10.

The floor tiles in the bathroom were Florenza porcelain. The bathroom tiles were Verdana porcelain. The countertops in the kitchen were Caledonia quartz and Caesarstone quartz, and those beside the washer and dryer were Lacava polished marble. Mitchell didn't know what any of this meant, but he figured that every proper noun could accurately be translated as "expensive." The ceilings were nearly twice his height, and the floors were paneled with a white hardwood oak so pale that he periodically glanced behind him to see whether the soles of his shoes were leaving a trail, like a mud snail. But it was the living room—what just several months earlier, fresh from campus, he would have called a common room—that contained the apartment's most astonishing feature: the windows. Only "windows" seemed too pedestrian. These were giant, luxurious, undulating sheets of glass, like fun house mirrors, only transparent. His broker, Pam Davenport, described them as "free-form," which he could see was another way of saying "curved." They spanned from the floor to the ceiling and were impossibly clean. You felt as if you were about to jump out of an airplane.

"Splendid, no?" said Pam Davenport, grinning like she had annealed the glass herself. "Didn't I tell you?"

Charnoble had recommended the broker ("top-class all the way," he had said, blinking). When Mitchell called her, he explained that he wanted something nice. After all, he owed it to himself. His commissions at FutureWorld were increasing considerably, and he'd been there only two months. He wanted to make a broad gesture. He had tried to make one a week earlier, when he sent his parents a check for five thousand dollars.

"What is this?" said Tibor. Mitchell could tell from the way his parents raised their voices that they were standing hunched over the phone.

"This is dopey," said Rikki.

"I have more than I can use."

"It's wonderful you're making this money, but you should hold on to it. You're too young to be parting with your salary."

"Here's the thing," said Tibor. "You never know when you might need this. You never know anything."

"I just thought you guys might need it."

*"We don't need your money!"* shouted Tibor.

"Maybe," said Rikki in her most gentle tone, "you could figure out a better use for it. Like finding a new apartment."

She was right. When he first saw his current apartment, it had struck him as oddly familiar. He had found comfort in the lack of natural light, the stucco walls smudged with grease, and the pathetic meagerness of the kitchenette, its stained Formica and tin sink. When he e-mailed photographs to his mother, she was able to explain why this was.

"You moved into a Zukorminium?" she wrote.

This was not the only fact that had recently become clear to him. He had spent months, for instance, trying to distill from Elsa's letters some kind of general philosophy of fear avoidance that he could appropriate. Her achievement was incredible to him. She had to know the numbers: a person who has suffered a Brugada episode has a ninety percent chance of having another one. The chance that she would die from a Brugada episode was eminently reasonable. It was eminently imminent.

Early one morning, in an effort to exterminate a particularly virulent posse of cockroaches, Mitchell had done the dreadful calculation. It could be reduced to a single number: 1 in 53, or 1.89 percent. These were the odds that a Brugada patient who had already had multiple syncopes would have a fatal attack in the coming year. That was exponentially more likely than the odds of dying from drug or alcohol abuse (1 in 10,837) or an accidental injury (1 in 2,454). There was no mathematical analysis that could make that 1 in 53 less frightening. When you broadened the time frame, the numbers only became uglier. The odds of a fatal syncope in two years: 3.7 percent; in five: 8.7 percent; by the time she turned thirty: 13.2 percent. But Elsa, like curious Sarah Axon in Iowa, seemed oblivious to fear. To some extent, her trick seemed to lie in a delicate combination of denial and distraction. She did this mainly by focusing on pragmatic matters, on hard labor. But all her talk of sowing, plowing, and installing photovoltaic cells seemed to be the manifestation of a larger philosophical strategy. If he could only isolate this strategy, he might be able to use it himself. This was what he was trying to get at in his letters. It wasn't easy; he couldn't just ask her *How do you overcome your fear of imminent death? Can you teach me?* The difficulty wasn't that these questions would be embarrassing or cross some line of decency. They *would*, of course, but he held back for a different reason: he was afraid that Elsa might reveal herself to be less carefree than she appeared. That she might say something truly horrifying like *What do you mean? I'm terrified! I'm paralyzed with panic. I can barely get out of bed. I keep my hand on my heart at all times in the crazy hope that I'll be able to feel it beating funny and act before it's too late.* So instead Mitchell had to get at the answer through swipes and squints and intuition. His mission was made more challenging by the fact that Elsa rarely took a serious tone and flitted around from subject to subject. It was like trying to steal the trick of camouflage from a butterfly.

"Spalike," said Pam Davenport, who had led him into the bathroom. "The bathtub is Kohler."

Mitchell nodded. "Colder than what?"

He caught his image in the fog-proof mirror above the sink. He had the subtracted look of an automaton or mannequin. Very well—it was to be expected. Something *had* been subtracted. FutureWorld was working. Not merely as a business but as a treatment. It was better than any mood drug he'd ever taken—and he had tried them all, but none for very long, out of fear that they might mangle his synapses. FutureWorld was more focusing than Adderall, more calming than Ativan, more elating than Klonopin. It was a better soporific than Sonata. The only negative side effects were fatigue and nausea. And those he had already.

His research alerted him to countless new worst-case scenarios, but the time and resources afforded him by the job allowed him to undermine each scenario with rigorous precision. He could exactly determine, for instance, the likelihood that New York's water supply would evaporate in the next year (impossible), or that an earthquake would dissever Manhattan at 125th Street (exceedingly unlikely). An astronomer at NASA's Near-Earth Object Program Office at the Jet Propulsion Laboratory in Pasadena explained patiently to him that the odds of an asteroid crashing into the earth and unleashing a new dark age was on the order of ten to the minus eighth power per year, and one in a million in the next century. This number was further mitigated by the odds that human civilization would figure out a way to block an asteroid by the time one arrived. The asteroid scenario was not going to happen. But if a giant rock did come close to hitting Earth, Mitchell knew exactly which aerospace and defense companies would profit.

So it was a dream job—it quelled his nightmares. One by one the fears were dissipating. Even figuring out Elsa's golden secret was beginning to seem less important to him. He was starting to suspect that she had no secret. She may have convinced herself that she started the farm for altruistic, utopian reasons, but the truth of the matter, he now believed, was that Ticonderoga had been designed as a fortress. She had locked herself away from cardiologists and hospital beds, from a life lived in perpetual uncertainty. At Ticonderoga she could control every aspect of her existence— the food, the energy, the people. At least that's how she tried to play it off. In fact she had only created the illusion of control. The whole thing was so clear, so logical, he was amazed she hadn't seen her own behavior for what it was. She was either in denial or terror stricken. Either way, she was trapped.

Mitchell, on the other hand—Mitchell was free! Thanks to FutureWorld, thanks to Alec Charnoble, the old strictures were coming undone. Take, for instance, this situation with the drought. Elsa had written again to tell him how bad it was up on the farm. The tomatoes were exploding on the vine, the corn tasted burned. Her entire utopian fantasy was on the verge of shriveling up. There was a note of despair in her letters—which, by the way, had been coming less frequently. In fact, it had been something like three or four days since he'd heard from her. It made sense, this reluctance to write. It was becoming clear that it was simply unrealistic for a bunch of college kids without any agricultural expertise, or even experience, to start a farm. Unrealistic? "Insane" was a better word.

Nor was Mitchell concerned about the drought. In the past he would have turned, frantically, to his research, calculating the odds that the water scarcity might bring about a disruption in the food supply, a hoarding of goods, rapid inflation. It's true that the water table numbers weren't promising, but that was hardly remarkable. Nearly three billion people on the planet lived in water-stressed regions, places of continual drought. He did the research as always, but now he used the numbers as a salesman would—to recruit new clients, to catalyze their fears. It had become a game to him. FutureWorld had transformed him from a neurotic paranoid into something much stronger, more powerful: a businessman. To prove this to himself, he had called Pam Davenport and asked to see her finest apartments.

"The market in the financial district has shown some signs of loosening up," she had said on the phone. "Especially the high-rises. The images from Seattle rattled some nerves, I'm afraid. But we can direct our energies further uptown, if you'd prefer—"

"No," said Mitchell, an edge in his voice. "The financial district is perfect."

*This is where America happens. Where we happen.*

"Very good. If the high-rises don't bother you, we can begin with Eight Spruce Street."

He let her describe the building, but he knew the details already. At seventy-six stories, Eight Spruce Street was the tallest residential tower in New York. In high winds it could lean fourteen feet in any direction. At Fitzsimmons Sherman he would stare at it from his window on the seventy-fifth floor and wonder why in the hell any human being would consent to living 867 feet off the ground in the middle of one of the world's most dangerous airspaces.

After Pam Davenport had finished showing him the concealed "self-closing" bedroom drawers, which slid tight with a plaintive whisper, she led Mitchell to the windows. He had been waiting for this. So, it seemed, had she. With a quick, joyful intake of breath, she walked up close to the glass and then, to Mitchell's alarm, leaned her forehead on it.

"A view like this," she said, her mouth releasing an oval of fog onto the glass, "makes you feel like queen of the city."

Maybe. You certainly could see a lot of it. There was the Brooklyn Bridge, its ramps spooled like a pile of gray snakes. The water from this height was a thin navy border between the ashy flanks of Manhattan and Brooklyn, and the downtown skyscrapers, the ziggurats and belfries and minarets built in tribute to American industry, seemed plain and quaintly chunky, like the building blocks preschoolers played with, or Legos. It all made his legs feel very stiff. He thought of the skycity of his dreams and wondered whether some part of his brain—his amygdala, perhaps—had modeled those slender, infinite towers after Eight Spruce Street.

"Check this out," said Pam Davenport, beckoning him forward. "You can see all—the way—down."

He blinked, and the city began to canter diagonally across his vision. He tried to back away but his legs were too stiff.

"Mr. Zukor? Is everything all right?"

The window plunged at him. It socked him in the nose. He bounced off the glass and slid clumsily to the floor. Pam Davenport shrieked. All he could think of was the boy at John Day who sat down Indian-style on the fifty-yard line and died. When he opened his eyes there was a streak of blood across the glass, parallel to the Brooklyn skyline.

He heard his broker's heels tapping on the hardwood, and then she was beside him with a wad of damp paper towels. She pressed it to Mitchell's nose. The cold, pinkish water seeped down his lip and dropped onto his tie.

"Oh dear," she said, and ran back for more paper.

He felt a sucking sensation in his right nostril. He snorted and a clot of blood exploded in the tissue.

"Oh my God," said Pam, returning. "Is it broken?"

Mitchell explored the bridge of his nose with his free hand. He couldn't remember whether the bumps and crevices he felt were the same old bumps and crevices, or whether his collision with the window had broken new ground and altered his entire facial topography.

"I guess it was the heat."

"The quality of the air-conditioning units is simply unacceptable for a new building." She looked more closely at him. "Do you have any medical condition I should know about?"

It really had been some time since Elsa had written. Five days? Six? This was unusual. Had he offended her? His last letter had been his most direct to date. He had explained that at Future-World he had learned that facing his fears head-on was the best way to defuse them. The window, at least, seemed to disagree.

The water seeped beneath his collar and onto his chest. When he realized that Pam Davenport had been mopping his face for several minutes with disintegrating paper towels and speaking in a hushed but increasingly hysterical voice, he forced himself to stand, using the wall as support.

"Listen, Pam," he said, "maybe this isn't such a hot idea after all."

On the street, stumbling back to the subway, his hand pressing a paper towel to his nostril, he passed an old firehouse mobbed with schoolchildren. A fireman was blasting them with a fire hose. The ecstatic children screamed as they galloped through the jet. The water pooled around the gutter, which had been dammed by a weir of plastic bags. Three dogs, their owners trailing, cantered over to the puddle and began to slurp. The owners did not interfere but watched their dogs with expressions of profound longing.

## II.

In the FutureWorld foyer Charnoble was waiting for him, consulting the watches on either wrist.

"We have our man from Edison Telecom in ten minutes."

Mitchell walked past him, into his office.

"He wants to go over brain tumor epidemic scenarios again. Are you still fresh on the tumor scenarios?"

"In a decade, four percent of his workforce will develop gliomas," said Mitchell impatiently, crossing the vast carpeted expanse. "Three percent acoustic neuromas, two percent salivary gland tumors, one percent meningioma, another five percent benign tumors. Financial damages can be extrapolated accordingly. OK?"

Mitchell removed from his desk drawer Elsa's most recent letter. He read it over, looking for clues to her silence. There was her usual canoe sketch, the same neat schoolgirl's handwriting. You'd think that if something were wrong you'd be able to see it in the handwriting, but penmanship that graceful indicated reason, orderliness, calm. Could it be some kind of subterfuge? He didn't think Elsa was capable of subterfuge.

It was not a particularly long letter. She spent most of it re-counting problems she'd had keeping the artesian well clean—because of the drought it had drained and was beginning to develop mold. She joked about one of her more avid comrades on the farm who had argued in defense of the mold, which after all was a colony of living organisms. "According to him, fifty-pound sacks of powdered milk are better than cartons of organic milk but not as good as milk squeezed out of our neighbor's goats. Shopping for overalls in Augusta is better than shopping for overalls online, but weaving our own overalls out of hemp is better still. Nudity is best. Toothpaste without fluoride or parabens or propylene glycol is essential, but baking soda and peppermint oil does the trick fine, and a mush made out of crushed pine needles and dirt is ideal." Elsa seemed in good spirits. There was nothing to indicate that she wanted to cut off contact with Mitchell.

"Any mail today, Alec?" he called out.

"Just the normal things."

Mitchell ran back across the long ivory carpet to the small waiting room where the day's envelopes and packages lay stacked on a coffee table. He hoped there wasn't a letter from Elsa in the pile and he was afraid that there was not a letter in the pile and he was afraid that he was afraid.

"I'm still going to need you in the meeting," said Alec. "He's paying to see you, after all. They all pay to see you."

"Start without me."

Mitchell flipped through the envelopes. There was the usual assortment of doomsday paraphernalia, the daily harbingers of things to come: the September issue of the *Food Safety Magazine*; a carton of ciprofloxacin; a report he had ordered from the Federation of American Scientists titled "Updated International Nuclear

Warhead Database"; and the annual statement of the Reinsurance Industry Consortium, the association of gargantuan corporations that insured insurance companies. But no sign of Elsa's canoe. The old familiar fears started growing inside him like a tropical forest.

Charnoble glanced between Mitchell and one of the clocks on the wall. "Is there something wrong?" he said. "You don't look good."

Mitchell went back into his office, running across the carpet this time, and typed some words into his computer. When the phone number came up, he called it.

"ER. Augusta General."

"Do you have a patient in your hospital named Elsa Bruner?"

There was a pause. In the background a man was screaming, the type of noise a dog would make while getting run over by a bus.

"Hold on."

Charnoble paced into Mitchell's office and pointed to one of his watches. Mitchell held up one finger.

The woman came back on the line after a few seconds. Or minutes. Time was beginning to get strange.

"Here's the number."

"The number?" said Mitchell.

"You got a pen?"

The woman gave him a telephone number with a Maine area code.

"What is that?"

"That's the number they left."

The screaming got worse. Mitchell had to raise his voice to make himself heard.

"The number that *who* left?"

"Hold on," said the operator. The line was pulsing. "I have to take this."

Mitchell hung up and dialed the number. After four rings a man picked up.

"Ticonderoga."

Mitchell didn't understand.

"Hello?" said the man. "Who's that calling?"

"I didn't think—I thought Ticonderoga didn't have a phone number."

"What? Why'd you call then?"

Mitchell shook his head. Nothing made sense.

"Hey," said the man, in a sudden rage. "Is this some kind of joke?"

"Listen," said Mitchell. "Is Elsa there? Elsa Bruner?"

There was a delay. When the man spoke again his voice was quieter, defensive.

"Who is this?"

"Mitchell. Zukor. I'm a friend of Elsa's."

"Huh. Then I guess you haven't heard."

Mitchell closed his eyes.

"No," he said. "I haven't."

# Part Two

*Soon all sorts of strange things will come. No longer will things be as before.* —WASCO TRIBE PROPHECY

## Every Silver Lining Has a Cloud

## I.

"Your coffin's here."

"Wrong number!" Mitchell hung up—or tried to. His hand was trembling just enough that the receiver jarred against the plastic teeth on the telephone's base. He used both hands to steady it into the groove.

The phone rang again.

"Sucker?"

". . . This is Mitchell Zukor."

"Two twenty-three East Thirty-seventh Street calling. You got a coffin here."

"I'm not expecting a coffin."

"Who is, right?" The doorman chuckled to himself. "There's some guys got a large wood box and they want me to sign."

Now Mitchell understood.

The day of the purchase, when he awoke—from a dream of swaying, infinitely tall glass towers and a sky as bright as a nuclear flash—he felt that some gear in his brain had broken. The engine still revved, but the apparatus was beginning to grate and stutter, and despite the fact that there were not yet any outward signs of malfunction, he knew that after a few more revolutions the parts would grind themselves into dust.

Like an android Mitchell had gone through that morning, sorting his disaster folders into alphabetical order (anthrax, botulism, Crimean-Congo hemorrhagic fever . . . ), scheduling meetings, dialing voice mail. It was only after he deleted his messages that he realized he hadn't been listening at all, didn't even know who had called or what they wanted. All he could think about was how Ticonderoga *did*, after all, have a phone line. Which meant that Elsa, the fainting girl, had lied to him. Of *course* Ticonderoga had a telephone. Probably a satellite connection too. Laptops and portables, no doubt. So why, then, this mad determination to write letters? Did Elsa think that if they had spoken by phone, Mitchell would have been more insistent? That he might persuade her of the absurdity of her decision to live on a half-assed farm in the middle of nowhere with a flock of third-generation hippies who washed their bodies in the lake and brushed their teeth with a paste of crushed pine needles? It would seem that his original hunch had been confirmed: Elsa wanted to read his thoughts, but she didn't want to hear his voice.

Still, it shouldn't have mattered. The poor girl had been asking for help—begging—in the only way she knew how, but he had been too dumb, or weak, to do anything. Deep down, did some part of him *want* her to suffer? Would that have proved his point? Then again, what else could he have done? Rented a car one Saturday morning, driven to Maine, and kidnapped her, checking her in, against her will, to Mount Sinai or NewYork-Presbyterian? There were laws against that. A more puzzling question: How had he allowed himself to be lured into her fantasy? And why had the news of her attack, so predictable and logical, disturbed him? Terrible things did happen. Wishful thinking was negligent, dangerous, and, in the case of Elsa Bruner, might even prove homicidal. But if Elsa were guilty of denial, Mitchell at least was an accomplice. And that was the old, familiar problem. Analysis without action.

He had fled the FutureWorld office that day at noon, driven by an outrageous hunger. Cheeseburgers—he wanted cheeseburgers with a desperation that made his eyes water. At least he assumed it was his desire for cheeseburgers that was making his eyes water. But his hunger was extinguished almost immediately by the sight of a rat. It was not just any rat. As a New Yorker of nearly three months' standing he was well acquainted with the local vermin. They were citizens too, after all: the pigeons queuing at the street corner, waiting for the light to change; the rats loitering on subway platforms; the bedbugs snuggling in the mattresses, preparing for dinner. But lately New York's second-class citizens had been behaving strangely. This rat on Thirty-third Street, for instance, was attacking a garbage bag with an epileptic fervor. Having perforated the black plastic with its fangs, it tried to tear an opening by whiplashing its head with sudden jerks. It looked terrified, as if it weren't trying to remove food from the bag, but seeking shelter inside it. New York rats had a reputation for haughtiness—they knew they were going to outlast you, it was just a matter of time, so could you please stop getting in their way?—but recently their confidence seemed shaken. Was it simply the heat? The unfair, merciless, dominant heat? Or did they know that something was coming? The animals were always the first to know. It was that way with the warming world—the polar bear experimenting with anorexia, the marmot cutting short its hibernation, the American grizzly emigrating to Canada. And now the native New Yorkers were behaving erratically as well. The rats were traumatized; the pigeons neurotic, their dirty beaks nodding incessantly, like meth addicts; the roaches were downright hysterical, running suicides across the sidewalk. And maybe Mitchell was imagining it, but he could swear that every single infant in every single stroller was shrieking. Could they sense it too, the newborns? Could they sense this tremendous thing, whatever it was, that was coming for them all?

Where had his thoughts taken him? Ahead was the navy ribbon of the Hudson River, evaporating in vaporish wisps into New Jersey. Behind him a sky bridge that supported trees and dangling vines. Beside him a wide glass window inscribed with vinyl block letters, each letter a different shade of neon:

PSYCHO!
WHERE DO YOU GO WHEN YOU SLEEP?

The canoe rested on a podium in the middle of the gallery floor. The hull was painted in a kind of camouflage, only the colors, instead of being greens and browns, were a nightmarish swirl of orange and cerulean and bloodred.

As soon as Mitchell stepped into the refrigerated art gallery he was approached by a delicate young man with pointed elbows, a too-clever smile, and glasses with translucent rims. The man closed the distance rapidly; he held a damp Dixie cup of ice water in his outstretched hand. Mitchell took the water gratefully, winced when the ice touched his gums. Before Mitchell could understand exactly where he was or what was happening, the attendent launched into a prepared speech. The current exhibition, he explained, featured the work of a group of young artists from the eastern Canadian provinces. These artists aimed to combine sixties psychedelic art with the folkloric art of First Nations tribes. The New Psychedelia School, they called themselves. "Rationality has made a mess of this world," read the artist's statement, posted on the wall. "We want to trust our impulses more." Mitchell knew he had heard it somewhere before. The attendent indicated a series of portraits in which the subjects' skin was peeled away to reveal bright patterns

of stripes and polka dots. There was also a set of naked manne-
quins that were extraordinarily lifelike below their necks, with
hair and pores, though they had the faces of animals—bears and
giraffes and swans. But Mitchell didn't care about any of this. He
just wanted to look at the piece titled *Psycho Canoe*.

The canoe, explained the attendant, was made by a young
Nova Scotian woman named Sylvan who collected objects from
her natural environment and painted them in unexpected ways,
using organic laminates and gold leaf and nontoxic enamel in an
effort to capture the eternal unity of—

"Is it a real canoe?" Mitchell asked. "Functional, I mean."

"Sure. Even comes with two wood paddles. One of my favorite
things is the fine detail she gave to the gunwales. If you'll come
closer."

"How much?"

The kid nodded politely and made a show of going over to his
desk and consulting a price guide. He returned with an ironic
smile. A smile of ironic regret.

"For this work we have set a price of twenty-nine thousand
dollars."

Mitchell laughed, and the attendant, assuming that Mitchell
was astonished by the price, joined in. Mitchell supposed that he
was, in a way, laughing at the price—but not because it was high.
He could buy the *Psycho Canoe* with just the cash stacked in his
kitchen freezer. He had $38,140 at last count, eleven green-gray
bars, like dull chips of limestone, each individually sealed in plastic Baggies. When he reached $20,000 he had removed the ice
trays to make more room. At $30,000 he had thrown out the rest
of the frozen burritos.

The gallery attendant's conspiratorial smirk was beginning to
irritate him. Did the fact that Mitchell's shirt was soaked through
with sweat, or that his hair was uncombed and his eyes crazy—did
the attendant find that amusing? Did he think that Mitchell

couldn't buy an expensive piece of art on a whim? This kid who, no doubt, was himself a struggling artist. See the tattoo, some kind of green flower, creeping above the margin of his shirt collar by barely an inch—but what calculation had gone into that inch! And those worn brown loafers, certainly his only good pair, purchased by his parents so that he could look respectable at his first job, at a Chelsea gallery with slate floors and theater lighting. Would he have given the same smirk to Alec Charnoble, or Ned Nybuster? Mitchell was finished being underestimated. Sandy Sherman had underestimated him, as did so many of his new FutureWorld clients—they paid their fees happily and sat through the consultation meetings in order to satisfy the requirements of the liability claims law, but they were slow to believe the horrors that Mitchell forecast. And Elsa, for that matter, hadn't listened to him either. And now she lay in a coma at Augusta General. Mitchell reached for his wallet.

"Do you deliver?" he said.

The attendant flinched. It was barely perceptible—a slight recoil, the boy hunching an inch or two as if in response to a light blow to the stomach—but it gave Mitchell immense satisfaction. He felt that he had proved something. But what, exactly? And to whom?

◻ ◻ ◻

The purchase of the Psycho Canoe was not the only evidence that the new Mitchell acted in ways that would have baffled the old Mitchell. In the weeks since Elsa's attack, something had ruptured. It was as terrifying as it was liberating. His old life had peeled away like a label, and his old habits had lost their appeal. The catastrophe literature that arrived in his office every day began to pile up, unread. He shunned the library. He even lost his desire to calculate disaster odds. Elsa was right. By concentrating on the large-scale disasters he had missed the one unfolding right in front of him: Elsa herself.

His brain didn't shut down entirely, however. He was thinking, all right, it was just that the *thinking* part of him was increasingly removed from the *doing* part. During consultations with his clients he perceived Mitchell Zukor from a great distance, observing his actions unfold as if from miles away, peering out an oval airplane window or watching himself on a movie screen from the back row of the theater—a form of disengagement he had read about in firsthand descriptions of warfare. He watched himself take risks that weeks ago would have been inconceivable. He rarely looked before crossing the street, relying on sound and peripheral vision. He drank water directly from the tap. He held his cell phone next to his brain, neglecting to use his headset. He even let it rest in his front pocket, next to his testicles. What did he have to lose? Or, for that matter, to gain?

He'd read in a biography of Kurt Gödel that the great mathematician, after finishing work on his incompleteness theorems, suffered a breakdown and became incomplete himself. Sad old Kurt refused to leave the house, stopped washing, even abstained from eating. His weight dropped to sixty-five pounds and ultimately he died of starvation. But before he succumbed he developed one final application of his theory. He argued that the incompleteness theorems—which said that certain universal truths cannot be proved by rational thought—were themselves proof of the existence of God. Gödel's suffering must have been tremendous, but in those final years his genius reached a new plateau. By withdrawing himself from Earth, he was able to perceive other planets, other universes, other realities. After his death they found in his rolltop desk a page of butcher paper on which he had scrawled his final thoughts. He had written, "There exist other worlds peopled by rational beings of a different and higher kind."

"What do you want me to do with this coffin?" yelled the

doorman into Mitchell's ear. "I tried using the passkey to your apartment, but it seemed there was some other lock on the door."

There were, in fact, four other locks on the door, including a biometric panel that clicked open only when Mitchell touched his right forefinger to a sensor he had screwed into the jamb.

"I'll be there soon," said Mitchell, whispering so that Charnoble didn't rush in. "Just sign for it, please."

"And leave it in the lobby? I can't. It's a fire hazard!"

Very well, Mitchell thought as he hung up, but this fact in itself was hardly notable; the city was full of fire hazards. It was September now, and the drought had become increasingly dire. Back in July, Elsa had described particles of soil and dust floating through the Maine air, and the same thing was now happening in New York. The garbage was airborne. Plastic bags, newspapers, leaves that had cracked and fallen from the dehydrated trees—autumn had been prematurely induced. In the parks the parched soil solidified in crumbling beds of craquelure. The bodegas sold air-filtering masks imported from Japan. There were designer masks and low-end masks, louvered models and formfitting models, omega-pleated models for women with smaller faces, models with nose pads, nonstick models, and models that came equipped with damp filters containing SoothOn, a mentholated vapor laced with benzocaine that created the "sensation of throat-soothing steam" every time you exhaled. The local news anchors debated which models were the safest and most fashionable.

Most New Yorkers carried on with their usual activities, pantomiming quotidian normalcy, as if nothing were wrong. But a quiet lethargy had jammed the city's clockwork. Pedestrians zombified at the curbs, cyclists walked their bikes through the traffic, cabs inched, trains stalled. Subway platform fainting spells became so common that EMS workers set up triage posts at the Grand Central, Borough Hall, and Times Square hubs. And the sky—everybody was talking about the sky. It was brassy, smoldering. But even though the days were sunny and bright, the haze, which rose from the pavement in velvety curtains, reduced visibility to less than a square block. Garbage burst into flame spontaneously, but the fire department had been ordered to let these small fires burn themselves out. There was no water to spare. They had to save the water for the expensive fires, the ones that threatened full city blocks and office towers and glassy high-rises. In neighborhoods in upper Manhattan and the outer boroughs, the city had cut off the fire hydrants, complaining that too many kids were popping off the fireplugs, turning them into fountains. There was not enough water left in the reservoir for such frivolity, said the fire commissioner. Civil rights groups had filed suit.

Mitchell pushed through the revolving door in the lobby of the Empire State Building and broke into a sprint. The heat stopped him flat after half a block and he burst into a coughing fit, hacking out thick gobs marbled with black dust. He wondered what was in the dust. That morning the Air Quality Index had crested to 240, which put it safely in the Very Unhealthy zone (defined by the EPA as "everyone may experience more serious health effects due to airborne toxic particulate matter"). The whole Northeast was blanched, wilting. If only a big storm came along, said the meteorologists. Better yet, a *series* of big storms. If only.

By Third Avenue Mitchell was dripping on the sidewalk, big globular drops. The ovals of sweat that had spread concentrically outward from his armpits and neck had reconnoitered on the front of his shirt. Or was his stomach sweating too? Yessir. The stomach and the groin and the back had all jumped into the pool. The only part of his body that was not slick with moisture was the inside of his mouth. He had entered a new hell, and he was burning up. But it felt good, these flames, felt right. After the tepid limbo of the last three weeks, he welcomed the demotion to a lower circle. He welcomed the flames.

As promised the long wooden crate lay across the lobby, at a gratuitous angle—it could have been nudged in such a way that it didn't block the entrance, but the doorman was proving a point. Mitchell held up one finger as he slipped past the doorman, who was muttering vile things in a Slavic language, and raced up the stairs. He removed ten twenties from the freezer—his face gasping in the cold air—and returned to the lobby. The first three twenties made the doorman stop cursing. The next five made him help Mitchell carry the Psycho Canoe up the stairwell. Two more twenties—and the reassurance that the box did not contain a coffin or a body—convinced him to help Mitchell break apart the crate. The doorman brought up a hammer and a bar. It took ten minutes. The planks of wood lay in a pile in the center of Mitchell's living room like a pyre.

"Do you want me to take the wood away?" asked the doorman, eyeing the freezer.

Mitchell declined. He wanted to be alone with his canoe.

It occupied most of the living room. In order to clear enough space, Mitchell had to fold the plastic dining table, move it into the closet, and shove the couch into the corner. As the sky darkened, turning from pearl to mouse to soot, he ate dinner in the canoe, pensively dipping cold leftover spring rolls into cold, gelatinous duck sauce. He removed his shoes and pants. He fell asleep there with the television on, his head under the bow seat. It was a cosy berth, there in the hull of the Psycho Canoe. For the first time in two weeks—since he'd heard about Elsa—he slept like a corpse.

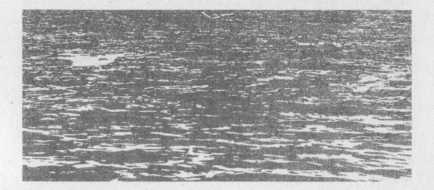

# 2.

Charnoble stepped into Mitchell's office, scissors in one hand and a long red ribbon, trailing to the ground, in the other. When Mitchell turned to face him, Charnoble sliced the ribbon in half.

"We're moving on up!"

The ribbon slithered to the rug. Mitchell waited patiently.

"I've been thinking about it, and I agree with you. We need a new office. Being in the Empire State Building undermines our authority."

"Our safety, really. It undermines our physical safety. That's the issue."

"Don't worry, I've found a place. We're going to get out of this death trap."

"That's good news," said Mitchell. He looked around his office, taking stock as if for the last time: the bare walls, the four clocks (one per wall), the low ceilings, and the expansive ivory carpet, its dense piles no doubt flourishing with bacteria (staph and E. coli assuredly, with even odds on salmonella). In the middle of the carpet lay a cardboard box, delivered that morning, that contained a pair of Day-Glo-orange PFDs, personal flotation devices. He figured they could serve as cushions for his canoe-couch.

"I've decided to let you go free," Charnoble added, smiling with every tooth in his head.

*"Free?"* Mitchell's intestines clenched. Would he have to beg Sandy Sherman for his old job? Maybe he could sell the canoe back to the gallery—that would buy him a couple of months.

"You don't need me on your consultations anymore. You'll be flying solo."

Mitchell exhaled. "Are you saying that you won't accompany me to the terror meetings?"

"I trust you, Mitchell."

"It won't be a problem."

Nor would it make much of a difference—Charnoble, after all, had been increasingly absent in the meetings. But Mitchell asked for a raise nonetheless. Charnoble granted it before the words left Mitchell's mouth. He seemed surprised that Mitchell hadn't asked for more.

It was difficult to tell exactly when it started, but there was no denying it now: FutureWorld had entered a boom period. Even before the raise, Mitchell's commission-based salary had inflated spectacularly. And from the moment the Psycho Canoe had arrived at his apartment, the old Mitchell gradually began to return. His obsession with issues of cause and effect, interconnectedness, fate, and doom had never been stronger, so his mind was particularly well prepared for apocalyptic visions. Elsa's blind optimism had deluded him, but her influence was beginning to wane. As the shock of her attack receded, he began again to see the world for the thermodynamic time bomb that it was. He resumed his old habits, stalking the library and monitoring daily disaster news from around the globe. It soon became clear to him that, during his brief vacation, conditions had only gotten worse. He could feel it intuitively: disaster was real, and it was coming fast, like an asteroid plummeting from the sky. Perhaps it *was* an asteroid plummeting from the sky. Something giant and obliterating was rapidly encroaching. What did it matter whether it were a bomb or an earthquake or a drought?

His Cassandra tales grew more persuasive, more specific. Perhaps too specific. During consultations he wrote calculations on a whiteboard, teaching them to his clients like a satanic high school algebra teacher. His favorite was the one developed by a Stanford statistician that predicted the odds of a nuclear war in the next year:

$$\lambda_{CMTC} = \lambda_{IE}\, P_1\, P_2\, P_3$$

$\lambda_{IE}$ was the annualized probability of an event that could lead to a nuclear showdown (or Cuban-missile-type crisis). $P_1$ was the probability that such an event actually results in a showdown. $P_2$ was the probability that the crisis leads to the launch of a nuclear weapon. And $P_3$ was the probability that the initial nuclear bomb results in a global nuclear war. Multiply the factors together, and the answer came out as one in ten. Every single year, in other words, there was a ten percent chance that the species would extinguish itself.

He had no great advice to offer his clients about this fact. He just wanted them to understand the likelihood that they would be incinerated shortly.

"You won't be able to say no one warned you," he said.

He could see the increasing discomfort, even alarm, on their faces. It was evident in the tight set of their jaws, their crimson eyes, their yellowish skin, the fingernail marks in their palms. He realized that the more strongly he believed his prophecies, the more strongly they did. It helped that anxiety was in the air. No longer was it free-floating. It had coalesced, settling into something heavier, tangible—a sludge of anxiety. You had to wade through it on the way to work; it sucked you down from underfoot, like quicksand.

In this light, the young, low-level financial associates who met with him suddenly seemed pitiful. They didn't realize what they'd gotten themselves into. Like him, they had come from distant cities and towns to New York, hoping to make their fortune. Out of their element, without anyone to advise them, they bunked in dormitories dressed up as apartments in overpriced midtown highrises and spent excessively on sushi, online dating, tailors, executive haircuts. But they were blind to their fate. They didn't realize they were being fed like virginal sacrifices into the maw of history, of twenty-first-century global capitalism, of vast, complex systems that were wildly beyond their control. He wanted to help them. In his consultations he would explain to these young financial associates why, despite the suitsandties-Christmasbonuses-gymmembership-nightclubbottleservice-steakhousesplurges, they still woke up in the middle of the night with violent images in their brains and screams building in their chests. Mitchell's scenarios reassured them that they had good reason to be afraid.

The drought helped. The weathermen, their credibility shot, were taking a beating. Out of desperation—or panic—they began to predict rain. They pointed to tropical storms in the Caribbean: imposing Irma, ominous Ophelia, promising Philippe—but all veered out to sea before making the Atlantic Seaboard. They pointed to a chain of hurricanes developing off the coast of Mauritania, another promising development. The Eurasian snow cover was higher than the previous year, broody cumulonimbus clouds were gathering just two hundred miles off Florida, and the sea surface temperatures in the tropics were at ten-year lows. Hopeful signs all, but still there was no rain. Faith in the meteorological industry fell to all-time lows—not that it had far to fall. Even the local anchors were getting into the act, using their meteorologists for easy punch lines. One of New York's most beloved weathermen, Channel 4's "Big" Henry D., normally a frothsome, jovial personality, was reduced to euphemistic expressions of melancholy and long, half-coherent lamentations. "When the heavens are shut up and there is no rain because your people have sinned," said Henry D. one night, the anchorwoman gaping gobsmacked across the news desk, "then what can we do? O Lord, what can we do?"

It made sense to Mitchell. Frightened people didn't want bromides, expressions of hope, happy predictions. They craved dread, worst-case scenarios, end times. What would the future cost them? They wanted to hear that the price would be exorbitant.

This was excellent news for FutureWorld. FutureWorld would provide. FutureWorld would take their money. Oh God yes, we would.

⊡ ⊡ ⊡

The new office consisted of eight linked rooms on the fourth floor of a tower at Columbus Circle. This glass monolith seemed only marginally safer than the Empire State Building, though Mitchell had at least dissuaded Charnoble from choosing an office on the twenty-seventh floor. It had dawned on him that Charnoble's priority wasn't safety, but the appearance, at least to an untrained eye, of safety.

"Uptown," Charnoble kept saying. "Always wanted to make it uptown."

"What do you mean?"

"Downtown is for the wealthy," he said, clarifying. "But uptown? Central Park South? That's for the *rich*."

Charnoble began to hum "Uptown Girl" through his fat, grotesque jackal grin. It occurred to Mitchell that Charnoble's mouth had been put there by mistake—it was much too wide for his face.

With business growing, FutureWorld had to expand. Charnoble's first hire was Mary Tewilliger, a woman in her late sixties and a secretary of the old mold. She had worked in Brumley Sansome's Risk department since the twentieth century. She won Mitchell over with her wrinkled forehead, proud chin, sagging elbows, and the agitated, bushy gesticulations of hair on either side of her face. Because she insisted upon being addressed as Ms. Tewilliger, behind her back Charnoble referred to her simply as Tewilliger. Or Old Tewilliger.

A week later Charnoble introduced Mitchell to a second hire. Jane Eppler was just out of Wharton Business, with a philosophy degree from Princeton. She had won an award for her senior essay on Antisthenes, the original Cynic. Jane was attractive in the pert, suburban, midwestern tradition, and she spoke with a sensual underbite. She seemed self-conscious about her pedigree, so she tried to baffle expectations by using coarse language. Yet some vestigial attachment to her Catholic upbringing seemed to prevent her from using actual obscenities. The first time they met, she told Mitchell that the elderly male professors at Wharton were "predatory, palsied panty sniffers." Winnetka, where she grew up with her three sisters, was a "geektown" where "gap-toothing" a star athlete or a teacher was the only way to get noticed (Mitchell didn't ask whether Jane had been "noticed"). She added, over the course of conversation, that Antisthenes was a "stone-cold Matterhorn," that the Stoics were "slophouse peen-munchers." This talk was exhausting, but it was also clearly an act, and an essentially defensive one at that. She used conversation to win concessions and deflect her own insecurities. And Mitchell couldn't help but be charmed by the unguarded, intimate way she glanced at him whenever he taught her things about the job. She wore tastefully small, expensive gems in her ears and cleanly pressed navy suits; her brown hair bobbed gently on her shoulders when she exited a room. Charnoble had hired her to be a second Cassandra.

"I'd like to learn from you," said Jane as Mitchell helped carry a box of her textbooks into her office—*Statistics for Business and Economics*, *Elementary Probability Theory*, *Wall Street Words*. "Alec says you're a genius."

"Really," said Mitchell. "He said that?"

"Well, not exactly. He said you were a 'terrorist—in the new sense of the word.' He called you a 'natural born terrorist.'"

"Mm. That sounds more like him."

Yes, she would be good at the job, just not for the same reasons that he was good at it. Unlike him, Jane had no apparent fear of catastrophe. She didn't believe for a minute anything she was asked to prophesy.

At Charnoble's request, Mitchell sat in on Jane's first sessions, but it was already clear that she'd developed her own routine.

"Can we drop the technical mumbo jumbo?" That was the kind of thing she said to clients. "I'm going to level with you," she said. "The numbers don't lie." This was boilerplate stuff, fed to her by Charnoble, and all an act—Jane was a quant at heart. As if to dispel any doubt, she tacked to her office wall on her first day of work a series of Poisson distribution charts she had drafted on loose-leaf graph paper. The charts predicted the number of nuclear accidents each year, the number of goals scored by the Chicago Blackhawks per game, the spread of bird flu from point of outbreak, Manhattan traffic accidents, congressional sex scandals. Every day at lunch she added new data points, the charts on her wall solidifying into a rolling mountain range of bell curves.

"Keeps me in the world," said Jane, apologetically, when she caught Mitchell staring at them. "I know—dorky."

"No, it's *not*," said Mitchell, and they were both momentarily alarmed by the emotion in his voice.

But Jane avoided discussing Poisson distribution models in her consultation meetings and, for that matter, the jump-diffusion model, the constant elasticity of variance model, and the generalized autoregressive conditional heteroskedasticity model. She saved those for their work sessions. In her consultations she kept it easy, personal. The saleswoman's flirtatiousness came naturally; the hucksterism appealed to her mischievous nature. She didn't come across like Mitchell, an Old World avenger with a ten o'clock shadow. Jane was a sister figure or even a girlfriend—someone her predominantly male clients could confide in. They wanted, it seemed, to protect her.

Inevitably it turned out that Jane and the client shared some mutual acquaintance or personal interest. This was possible because she conducted extensive background searches before the first meeting, investigating her clients' social lives just as assiduously as Mitchell researched the science behind his scenarios. She ran identity checks, posed as a potential employer to request information from college registrars, and scoured social networking sites.

She was a good student, but a better actress. In meetings she pulled her chair close to the client's, moving to the same side of the table if possible, and made constant physical contact: she patted a knee, caressed a shoulder. From the first handshake she was in command. When she finally turned to Mitchell's dark prophecies—for she loved his scenarios, called them "hilarious"—the effect was deadly. It gave Mitchell a special thrill to hear her interpretations of his scripts. In her delivery, his grave warnings were transformed into come-ons:

"Fear is the oldest, most effective security system we have. So don't *fear* fear—*embrace* it."

"I'm not here to talk to you about fear of the future. I want to tell you about the future of fear."

"The world began without man, and it will end without him. Until then, there's FutureWorld."

Her clients were pinned like lepidoptera specimens. They were in love. They wanted *more*.

As FutureWorld grew, so did the firm's advertising budget. Their logo—the pencil sketch of the open window, curtains blowing out—began to appear on subway platforms. Mitchell and Jane were on the way to lunch when the crosstown bus passed by, the FutureWorld logo pasted across its side. Next to the logo was a new slogan purchased by Charnoble from an advertising firm for twenty-five thousand dollars: "In a deceitful world, FutureWorld is a beacon of truth."

"*Truth*," said Mitchell, shaking his head. "It ought to be 'At the end of the tunnel—more tunnel.'"

"In the darkness of the storm," intoned Jane, "a ray . . . of darkness."

Mitchell spoke less frequently with his parents. On the phone with his mother he felt like a fraud.

"Are you living well?" she asked him one night.

"Living?" he asked, confused. For a second he actually couldn't understand what she meant.

"As in life? That thing we do when we're not sleeping?"

"Oh sure. *That* thing."

"Mitchell?"

He composed himself so that he could respond with the proper degree of enthusiasm.

"I'm living great, Mom. Don't worry about me. How's Dad?"

The thing is, he *was* living well in New York, at least if you went by his dinner receipts and pay stubs. He was a big business success. He made thirty-two thousand dollars in August. All signs seemed to indicate September would be even better. But the personal cost was extravagant. His heart was bankrupt. He was in emotional foreclosure. He felt more isolated than ever before. Once he even took the company car downtown to Chosan Galbi, but the waitress didn't recognize him.

"FutureWorld," said Mitchell. "Bad things come to those who wait."

"FutureWorld," said Jane. "Despair springs eternal."

At night he wrote letters to Elsa. He sat in the Psycho Canoe and read them over to himself before sending them—sometimes printing them out as many as a dozen times, marking them up with his pencil, trying to find the exact right words. But he never could. As he read them disembodied phrases jumped out like images in the magic eye books he obsessed over as a kid:

*. . . I should have realized . . .*
*. . . in the future . . .*
*. . . New York hospital . . .*
*. . . false complacency . . .*
*. . . I'm sorry . . . I apologize . . . I'm sorry . . .*

She didn't respond, of course. She couldn't. When he called the hospital—just about every afternoon—they reassured him that her condition was stable. As if that were a good thing.

There was in his head a grim compatibility between this absence of communication with Elsa and the absence of rain in New York. He began to develop, with Jane's help, a drought scenario for FutureWorld. They studied the Rainfall Anomaly Index, the Palmer Drought Index, the Normalized Difference Vegetation Index. Jane drafted a Poisson chart to help determine the drought's likely duration, which only confirmed the obvious—rain was long overdue. And Mitchell built narratives that drew from historical anecdote. He'd been researching the Dust Bowl. The dry soil rising like steam from the earth, the houses entombed by dirt, the black clouds filling the sky like coal smoke, the birds choking, disoriented, flying headfirst into the ground. The prevailing winds carried east Oklahoma's red soil, so that in the winter of 1934 the snow that fell in New England was bright pink.

"FutureWorld," said Mitchell. "It's a matter of death and death."

"FutureWorld," said Jane. "Every silver lining has a cloud."

They worked during lunch in the conference room of Future-World's new office. A long window overlooked the corner of Central Park and its brown softball fields. Directly below was the Columbus Fountain, which had run dry and was now the home of nesting pigeons, and their shit. Mitchell caught Jane staring into the distance.

"What is it?" he said.

"When you were a kid did you ever look at a cloud and try to figure out whether it was an animal or an object?"

"Kansas City has the highest number of clouds per capita of any medium-sized American city. That's not a joke."

"So what's that one?"

Mitchell squinted, searching the sky. He reached for his glasses.

"I didn't know you wore glasses," said Jane. "They make you look . . . professorial. I think I like you better without them."

"Me too." Mitchell snapped the glasses back into their case and squinted again. On an otherwise clear day, a single cloud had appeared over the Central Park reservoir. It had an oblong shape, with tendrils flying off concentrically, like curls on an infant scalp.

"I'm going to say a galaxy. The Milky Way."

"The Milky Way is kinda cloudy, I suppose."

"There's that thick bar in the middle, see. And then the swirls coming out of it? Those are the arcs of the stars."

"I'd say a white laundry bag. The soiled clothing at the bottom—see how it's heavier and darker there? The swirly lines are gym socks, flying out of the bag."

"Flying out? Why?"

"Maybe because the person is running. Running the bag down the block to the Laundromat."

"Why is she running?"

"She's running because . . . it's raining?"

The cloud stung the earth with a bolt of lightning.

Jane hiccuped.

"Did you just hiccup?"

"I hiccup when I'm surprised. Or scared."

A noise like God cracking His knuckles. Silence—and then cheers from the people on the sidewalk.

"Jumping baby Jesus."

"A bomb," said Mitchell.

"No," said Jane. "It's much bigger than that."

They approached the window, pressing their foreheads against the pane. Mitchell was careful not to hit his nose on the glass. There was another boom. They both lurched back.

"Thunder."

"No way."

"Unreal. Thunder. Unreal."

A crack of lightning tore across the sky. More cheering.

"Wait a minute," said Jane. "Is this going to be bad for business?"

"What are you talking about?"

"I was just hoping we could milk this drought for a few more weeks."

Mitchell stared at her, uncomprehending. He was reminded that they saw the world in very different ways.

"Is this actually happening?" Charnoble had rushed into the room. His fists were clenched, like a child having a tantrum. "We have at least a dozen special drought consultations scheduled this week. No, this is no good—"

Beneath the cloud the sky was streaky and fish gray. On Columbus Avenue the crowds were gazing upward, their hands over their foreheads to block the sunlight. There was another crack in the sky, a gunshot to start a footrace, and they started running toward the park—a few people at first, then in bunches—whooping and laughing and pulling on their hair in disbelief.

Tewilliger appeared beside Charnoble. Seeing the crowds in the park, she shook her head with disapproval.

Jane grabbed Mitchell's hand. Mitchell looked at their hands touching.

"C'mon," said Jane.

"Where?"

She tugged on his hand.

"Might want to bring an umbrella," said Charnoble, but they were already past him, racing down the hall.

⊞ ⊞ ⊞

A gray curtain of rain drew across the Great Lawn. Mitchell could hear it before it was upon them, a vociferous lashing of dried leaves and baked soil. Angry fist-size droplets detonated on the ground in front of them, and the sagging, wounded belly of the cloud passed over their heads. It was like walking under a waterfall or into a car wash. The rain pelted like hurled stones. The force was staggering. The people around him, raising their hands over their heads, laughed at its comical, bullying strength. They were like children being tossed around by a half-playful and half-malicious older brother.

The two futurists ran to the Great Lawn. A crowd had assembled in an impromptu dance circle. It was one of those blue-moon New York exuberant moments when strangers made eye contact, slapped hands, even embraced flesh to flesh. A utilities worker held his construction helmet in his outstretched hand; when it filled with water, he dumped it over his head, roaring with glee as the water cascaded down his shirt. Then he held the helmet out again. A woman in a beige business suit was carrying her heels in one hand, her bare feet clomping in the mud, her white blouse quickly becoming transparent. Children extended their arms like prophets, their heads back and mouths open. They caught the rainwater until their cheeks were full and then spouted it out like cherubic fountain statues. Jane grabbed Mitchell and pulled him into the circle. Without thinking he spun her around and dipped her, the rain splashing into her bright open face, and she burst into happy laughter. She had a distinctive laugh—a laughter arpeggio, accelerating from low quickly to high before descending again as she ran out of breath. She clenched her eyes shut and tilted back her head. The rain bounced off her exposed neck and gathered her hair into wild tendrils.

Yet Mitchell couldn't help but notice how, as the water pelted the dirt, it did not seep into the ground. It collected in pools, as it would on a tarp. He was suddenly desperate to do research. He knew that most droughts ended not in a single rainstorm, but over weeks and even months—just as droughts didn't begin overnight, but over months as rains came with less frequency. Normally a drought ended only once a certain minimum amount of rainfall had been recorded over the course of a season. But what happened when a major rainstorm followed a major drought?

He had stopped dancing. His pant legs were glutinous with leaf pulp.

"What is it?" Jane yelled over the water's loud patter.

"We should probably go."

"C'mon, Mitchell! *Live.* Live just a little bit."

Jane started dancing with someone else, a cleanly shaved young man whose tie was winsomely dripping with mud. The crowds of people kept pushing past, running like mad to the Great Lawn.

Mitchell turned and walked against the crowd, back to the office. He felt very damp, and very alone.

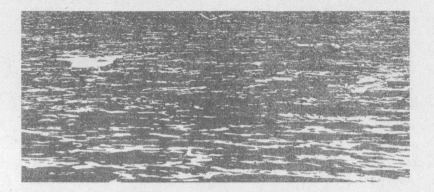

# 3.

What to make of the mayhem on the streets, the adults frolicking like children under a park sprinkler? Was this what everybody had been waiting for? A sign of divine intervention? On television it seemed so: the weathermen were in ecstasies. After so many empty predictions of advancing storms, their jobs—if not their entire scientific discipline—had been on the line. Now they appeared live on every station, enjoying the bliss of exoneration. They gesticulated manically in front of their painted maps, fist-bumping their amused anchormen. Their speech was infected with grand metaphors and meteorologically themed clichés.

"There have come soft rains!"

"Gray skies *aren't* gonna clear up. Put on a happy face!"

"Good day, *no* sunshine. Put on a happy face!"

The tristate area Doppler radar maps were obscured by a heavy neon green swirl. It was a large, messy storm system. There were low winds and heavy rainfall, a combination that indicated the storm would linger in the metropolitan area. It was moving in a

northeasterly course; from what Mitchell could determine, Camp
Ticonderoga stood directly in its path. And it seemed as if there
were more storms to come. In the Atlantic Ocean, just north of
San Juan, Tropical Storm Tammy was rapidly coalescing, and now
seemed poised to pursue its weaker predecessor up the coast. Over
on Channel 4, Big Henry D.'s eyes were spinning, mini-cyclones.
In his high-pitched ecstasy he swayed back and forth, his legs
pressed tightly together, like Tweedledum. He appeared not to
have urinated since the storm first glided onto his Doppler.

Mitchell called Augusta General.

"Patient Bruner, huh? You the guy who phoned this morning?"

"That's me."

"I'm sorry. There's been no change."

"A big storm is coming your way," said Mitchell. "Thought you
might want to know."

"Weatherman's been predicting that for months," said the receptionist. "He's lying."

Mitchell paused, wanting to ask her something else, to find out
more information about the body of the foolish girl in the hospital
bed. How closely were they monitoring her? Had they contacted
her mother? Had they considered sending her to a hospital in, say,
New York City, so that she could be examined by world-class specialists using state-of-the-art machines with names that the hum-
ble country doctors of Maine would not even be able to pronounce?
But the receptionist had hung up.

A marine climatologist from the National Weather Service appeared on the office flatscreen. This man, pale faced and slightly
cross-eyed, clearly lacked his colleagues' exuberance. If anything, he
appeared uneasy—an attitude that the anchorwoman seemed to find
insulting. He spoke in a quiet, restrained voice and was distracted.
He kept looking off camera to a live satellite feed of the tropical
storm developing in the Atlantic Ocean just west of Bermuda.

"Dr. Walsh," said the anchorwoman, "why aren't you more

pleased about this storm? Isn't this what we've been begging for all summer? What we've been *praying* for?"

The camera cut to images of children playing on the beach at Sandy Hook, New Jersey. They were running around in the pouring rain with their arms held aloft like wings.

"Well, Vivian, it's not that simple. Given the duration of the drought, the intensity of this storm is troubling. As is the prospect of Tammy making landfall as soon as tomorrow evening, by which point it will likely achieve hurricane strength. The erosion of the beaches in the metropolitan East Coast region has accelerated dramatically in the last several months. The coastal wetlands have been decimated, not to mention—" He paused, glancing offscreen. "Is that—is that a live image? Those children should get off that beach. No one should be allowed on the beach!"

The camera abruptly cut away from him and back to the image of the children playing.

"Dr. Walsh, with all due respect to your expertise, do you actually mean to suggest that rain is a bad thing?"

"Rain in and of itself is not a bad thing. But all the analytics indicate that this storm is going to bring excessive rain. The drought has inhibited the land's ability to accommodate sudden large amounts of precipitation. The soil simply cannot absorb it. Especially at this stage in the tidal cycle, when we're two days short of a full moon—"

"Dr. Walsh? Thank you for your time. We're going to have to cut away—"

"Please, Vivian? You need to inform the public that they must retreat from the coasts—"

"We're going live now to Central Park, where an improbable display of jubilation has broken out on the Great Lawn. You just gotta see this—it's the kind of thing that makes me proud to be a New Yorker. Actually—Harry? You want to take over? I might just run down there myself—"

Mitchell flipped off the television and raced back to the conference room, where his drought files were arrayed across the table: historical weather tables, local news articles, reports from the USDA, the USGS, NOAA, books with titles such as *The Worst Hard Time*, *The Drought*, and *The End of Nature*. This Walsh was right, at least about the soil. During the drought the region's topsoil had dried out and turned to dust. Just the previous week, farmers in New Jersey had seen large, glowing towers of cloud passing over their farms— what one man interviewed on the nightly newscast had described as a "black blizzard." The dust sprayed houses and seeped through the thinnest cracks in the walls, around the windows and under doors. "The grit gets into every crevice, even into a man's soul, if I may say so," said a Newark contractor. One of the tabloids profiled a woman in Morris County who woke up to find that overnight, a fine layer of dust had invaded her house, settling on every surface, including her china, the rugs, and her sheets. When she rose from bed, the only clean part of her pillow was the outline of her head.

In New York there was a run on window washers. The waiting list was three weeks, and that was only if you could afford the jacked-up rates—Charnoble had paid one guy four hundred dollars an hour. When you were on the street, you saw them every time you looked up; they dangled from their nets like tree caterpillars. Mitchell could have used one himself: brown plumes of sediment had appeared like mold on his own apartment window, blotting out the meager view he had. On the street level the problem was compounded by the automobiles' trapped exhaust, which was too heavy to rise, especially in the absence of breeze. The pillars of buildings were ribbed with soot; you couldn't lean against a street corner without ruining your shirt. For months the earth had been drying out and flaking away. The land had been starved to death, abused, murdered.

He realized that, having dedicated his research to extreme drought scenarios, he'd suffered a failure of the imagination. He hadn't considered what might happen in the case of a deluge.

There were precedents, he quickly discovered. Most recently

the 2011 Queensland floods, which drowned nearly a quarter of Australia, had followed a decade of drought. He tried to run down what he knew about extreme rainfall in New York City. He recalled, for instance, that lower Manhattan began to flood when the sea level rose five feet above average levels. On December 11, 1992, a nor'easter caused a surge of eight and a half feet. The storm closed the PATH and subway systems. An L train reversed course under the East River when the Fourteenth Street tunnel began to fill with water. Three hundred passengers had to evacuate a G train and walk a thousand feet out of a flooded Greenpoint tunnel. The FDR Drive was submerged. The major bridges all closed down.

In late October 2012, Hurricane Sandy, though only a Category 1, brought a near fourteen-foot tide to Battery Park, flooded sections of lower Manhattan, and left 850,000 people without electricity. Staten Island and south Queens suffered the greatest damage; the Rockaway Beach boardwalk was stripped to its piers. The New York Stock Exchange closed for two consecutive days for the first time since 1888, schools shut down for a week, and it was more than two weeks before subway service was fully restored. The lessons of Sandy were soon forgotten, however, even though conditions continued to deteriorate in the years following the storm.

Mitchell pulled the numbers. It didn't take long to isolate the bad news. With depleted salt marshes, narrower beaches, eroded soil, and a higher water table—the East River and the Hudson had each risen eight inches in the past twenty years—the city had never been more susceptible to flooding. They were close to a full moon, which meant high tides: water two feet higher than the mean. A storm surge would raise the water level of the New York Bight, which would overflow into the rivers. The question was how large a surge there would be. Under extreme drought conditions, could a regular storm cause flooding?

Mitchell was verifying erosion figures with the city's Department of Environmental Protection office when Jane returned. She had pulled her hair back in a ponytail to keep the water from dripping down her face. She carried a single shoe, the other one having been lost somewhere in the park. Her makeup had washed away, and her eyes were dewy and soft.

"You missed a lot of fun." Her bra, pale blue and webbed, was visible beneath her wet cream blouse. "Have you seriously been working all this time?"

"A little. I think we should review our flood scenarios."

"A flood?" She gave him a sideways look. "Are you kidding?"

"Droughts often lead to floods. I'm trying to figure the odds." Charnoble appeared at the doorway.

"They're calling," he said, grinding his forefinger into his palm. "They're *call*ing. They want meetings. And meetings mean more money. Money, money, money—" An obscene grin, like a water stain, crept across his face.

# 4.

The newspapers led with photographs of ecstatic New Yorkers. Under the headline SINGING AND DANCING IN THE RAIN, the cover of one tabloid ran a picture of the casts of Broadway musicals dancing outside in Times Square, arm in arm in avenue-wide chorus lines. The markets had advanced nearly six percentage points, led by a massive surge in the agribusiness sector. Traders were photographed on the steps of the New York Stock Exchange, spinning in the rain, pinwheeling their arms, their ties plastered to their shoulders.

He'd slept terribly. Wasn't rain supposed to lull you to sleep? Insomniacs paid for the privilege: there were machines, little speakers, that projected incessant pitter-patter all night. But what he heard outside his window was violent, erratic, a wild drunkard careening through the streets with sledgehammers in his hands. The rain continued all night. It wasn't cleansing, at least no more than a blitzkrieg could be considered cleansing. It was obliterative. It wiped the sludge right off his window. He was only surprised that it didn't wipe the windows right off his building.

It had slowed to a drizzle by the time he headed for the subway the next morning, but the city had been noticeably altered. The sewer grates were clogged with crushed plastic bags, creating muddy ponds that gathered around each street corner. The sidewalk smelled of fresh soil. The exultant mood had already given way, overnight, to one of fatigued irascibility. It was typical New York City, this whiplash effect, one day's exuberance followed the next day by a hangover and the shakes. The sudden rains had overwhelmed many of the city's basic operations. Underground, Mitchell took his place behind a mob of exasperated commuters standing five-deep back from the tracks. A voice over the loudspeaker reported in a mechanical, stroboscopic bellow that several downtown stations had been closed due to flooding. A man next to him was so furious that he burst into tears.

He blamed himself for not anticipating this sooner. Then he blamed Elsa. Her mystic optimism had brainwashed him into seeing his work as just, well, work. But it wasn't just work. It was life and death. He had been completely disengaged, zombified. On the previous afternoon he had returned to the library and examined the city's basic water blueprint. What he found haunted him.

In the days when Times Square was a red maple swamp and St. Mark's Place a hickory forest populated by hawks and ravens, more than forty brooks and streams covered the island of Manhattan. During high tide, the Lenape Indians could canoe from the East River straight through to the Hudson River across what is now Canal Street. His old office at Fitzsimmons Sherman stood over a little body of water called Sunfish Pond, which was beloved by early settlers for its profusion of sunfish, flounder, and eels. For all he knew, the pond was still there beneath the Empire State Building, percolating below the subbasement, the sunfish and flounder gone, but perhaps not the eels.

All of these waterways were buried when the city was built in the eighteenth and nineteenth centuries, but the water didn't disappear—it still pumped through the undersoil. Even during a drought Manhattan's natural water table gushed thirteen million gallons of groundwater into the subway tunnels daily—water that once had been absorbed by roots, marshes, and streams. Every day, eight hundred electric-powered municipal pumps diverted the excess water into the sewer system. Whenever a sizable storm hit, the pumps were overtaxed and the subway tunnels flooded. After just twenty minutes of rain, Brooklyn's sewage pipes began to overflow and human excrement spilled into the Upper New York Bay, Gowanus Canal, and Newton Creek. This was the price of having the entire island overlaid by concrete and a subway system buried deep in the earth—below the sewer pipes. The underground city was a water balloon filled to bursting. It just needed one sharp poke.

When he called the office, Tewilliger picked up before the first ring finished chiming. Charnoble had trained her well.

"Future."

"It's Mitchell. I'm going to be a little late this morning—"

"No, you're not."

"Excuse me?"

"Hold."

The hold music came on the line. It was a pop song from around the turn of the century, set against plaintive piano chords:

*As logic stands,*
*you couldn't meet a man*
*who's from the future.*
*But logic broke,*
*as he appeared he spoke*
*about the future.*
*We're not going to make it . . .*

The song had been Jane's idea. She screamed with laughter every time she was put on hold. It was starting to get under Mitchell's skin.

"Zukor!" Charnoble came on the line. He had never addressed Mitchell as Zukor before. He was out of breath.

"Alec. What's happening?"

"We need you here now. The phone is ringing off the hook, in a manner of speaking. This may be our first live disaster."

The excitement in his voice was extreme, bordering on grotesque. Charnoble explained that Tammy had been upgraded to a Category 2 hurricane, gusts as high as 105 miles per hour.

"You should see the Doppler," said Charnoble, and Mitchell could picture the spittle on his lips. "Overnight the beast spun into a tight spiral."

"Where is it going to make landfall? Is it coming here?"

"Too early to tell. Weather Channel says Chesapeake Bay. CNN is reporting the Delaware coast. But Big Henry D. thinks farther east, near Ocean City."

"Ocean City would be very bad," said Mitchell. "But Atlantic City—Atlantic City would be catastrophic."

"Let's pray for Atlantic City!"

Mitchell didn't bother to explain that a storm passing through Atlantic City would likely head straight to Manhattan. He worried that this information would only multiply Charnoble's giddiness. Instead he asked Charnoble to pull out his hurricane files so that Jane could review them before her meetings. The first file was a collection of material about the 1821 storm, one of the only hurricanes to have passed directly over Manhattan. During that storm the tide rose thirteen feet in a single hour, causing the East River to meet the Hudson in what is now SoHo.

Charnoble had already booked both of them through the day. Mitchell volunteered to go straight to his first appointment. He was up-to-date on the literature now, he didn't need his notes. The client was Jason Tanizaki, a vice-president of Lady Madeline, the perfume giant. Lady Madeline was concerned about what damage a hurricane might cause to their scent-production factory in Middlesex County, less than a mile from the ocean.

It seemed easier to work than to think of everything that might happen. Work, his old savior, would clear his brain, or at least distract him. It had been the same thing his whole life: when the hot panics came, he turned to math for relief. During high school he had seen an episode of *Mega Disasters* about the massive volcano, larger than the state of Rhode Island, that lay beneath Yellowstone National Park. The Yellowstone volcano had erupted three times. Each time it had covered the western half of North America with a foot of volcanic ash. Winds carried sulfur aerosols and ash particles around the entire planet, causing temperatures to plummet. Nearly all life on earth went extinct. The volcano erupted roughly every six or seven hundred thousand years; the last eruption had occurred 640,000 years ago. It seemed that we were due. With a shaky hand Mitchell had turned off the television. The host of *Mega Disasters*—a bearded man best known for hosting a dating show—had said that the volcano had erupted 2.1 million years ago, 1.3 million years ago, and .64 million years ago. Mitchell wrote the figures on a pad and took out a calculator. If you added the intervals between eruptions and divided by three, that meant the Yellowstone volcano's average dormancy period was 730,000 years. After plotting a probability graph, he determined that the chance another massive eruption would occur in the next one hundred years was 0.00055 percent, or 1 in 181,000. An exceedingly low number, one that did not justify the ominous tone used by Mr. Megadisasters. Those zeroes on the LCD face of his TI-89 calculator had made all the difference. They were like little white pills that faded out his anxiety. They put him to sleep.

But the information he had found at the library, reading about Manhattan's full bladder, had not yielded anything that suggested he was overreacting. And with the schedule of meetings today, there would be no time to call the top people at the local universities: the hydrologists, fluviologists, geomorphologists—anyone, really, who could tell him what the future would cost him.

The Lady Madeline Tower was only five blocks away, so he abandoned the crowded subway station and set off on a sprint, his eyes turned upward, not caring where his feet landed. The gray clouds had sapped the coloration of the skyscrapers; every glass, stone, and steel surface had the same dull slate hue. It was as if Manhattan were assuming the qualities of his skycity—it lacked only the brilliant cobalt-blue sky of his dreams. When he reached the office building he was panting. A dismayed security guard stared pointedly at his shoes. They were leaking black dye onto the expensive carpet. He might as well have been walking on ink pads.

"I'm here to see Jason Tanizaki," said Mitchell. "I'm from FutureWorld."

The guard kept his eye on Mitchell while he dialed the intercom.

"Mr. Tanizaki has a visitor." The guard paused and stared balefully into Mitchell's eyes. "He says he is the man from the future."

# 5.

Seven people were seated around the oval marble conference table. Six of them stood when Mitchell entered the room.

"The man of the hour," said Jason Tanizaki, extending his soft fingers.

Mitchell had liked Tanizaki as soon as they met, a month earlier. He was a thin, tall man with elongated features, and he dressed like a Ferragamo model; today he wore uncreased chocolate loafers, a trim navy suit, and a thickly knotted aqua-blue tie. His elegance extended even to his posture. During their consultations he sat with his ankles crossed, hands pressed together, and head cocked, as if in pleasant anticipation of whatever Mitchell had to say. Watching Tanizaki, Mitchell marveled at the natural effortlessness with which the powerful administered their affairs. No matter how hard Mitchell worked at it, his every action seemed to him freighted with the weight of Kansas City, his father, the Zukorminiums, thick Hungarian gravy on fatty sides of veal, saggy pelican-mouth briefcases with chipped bronze clasps.

Mitchell walked right up to the edge of the table so that no one could see his leaking shoes.

"Please," he said, "sit." He noticed there was nowhere for him to sit, so he remained standing.

"You will be pleased to know," said Tanizaki, "that Lady Madeline has purchased a headset for every one of our employees."

In their previous session they had discussed the problem of widespread cell phone use among Lady Madeline's staff, particularly their traveling salesmen.

"Glad to hear that," said Mitchell. "You've spared yourself innumerable negligence lawsuits and a surge in oncology-related health-care expenses."

Tanizaki introduced his colleagues, who nodded as they were named. Finally he came to the slumped batrachian form at the head of the table. It was Lady Madeline D'Espy herself, the company's founder, whose legendary beauty hadn't faded so much as expired; she was decades past the sell-by date. Her face, blotted with heavy rouges and pinks, rested low in the hollow of her neck, but the eyes had retained a sharp brown lucidity. They peered out beneath eyebrows that had been sketched slightly too high up on her forehead, giving the impression of being raised, perpetually, in skepticism.

Mitchell began his doomsday hurricane analysis by explaining that Lady Madeline needed to move quickly. The Middlesex factory had to be shut down immediately. All chemical substances and laboratory equipment should be moved belowground, preferably to a sealed storm cellar. The New York office must close tomorrow, the day the hurricane was expected to make landfall. Employees who lived in the city should leave for higher ground inland. Anyone with no choice but to remain in New York should consult the city's online flood map to see whether his apartment lay in an official evacuation zone. If so, he should locate the nearest hurricane shelter. No apartment higher than the tenth floor or lower than the fourth floor was safe. All employees had to prepare a Go Bag, containing bottled water, nonperishable food items, a flashlight, batteries, latex gloves, medical history information, iodine tablets—

D'Espy raised a stiff, maculated hand from the table. Though subtle, this gesture seemed to have activated some buzzer beneath each person's seat cushion—all her employees abruptly turned to face her. She released a long, profound sigh that seemed to emanate from the pit of her soul. Finally, assured that she had their attention, she blinked her eyes deliberately several times and the edges of her mouth began to rise. It slowly dawned on Mitchell that this was meant to be interpreted as a smile. D'Espy spoke in a hoarse monotone.

"I don't buy it."

Surprised, Mitchell waited for a signal.

"Oh, and Jason," she said, turning to Tanizaki, "I don't buy the business about cell phones causing cancer either."

Tanizaki's expression—open mouth, wide eyes—was one that Mitchell would never have imagined possible on such a professional, elegant face. It was a look of pure, abject fear.

"I've known two Tammys in my life," said D'Espy. "One was a Puerto Rican maid who did the dishes for me back in the nineties. Tampíco Tammy. Mentally deficient, she was. You had to remind her, every single time, to wash both sides of a plate, or else you'd find it grimy with last night's rice or some other horror. The other Tammy, Tammy Martin, used to run with my sister in high school. Big fat slutty girl, that one. Both Tammys, I should add, were extremely docile. Wouldn't hurt a bug."

Her employees, other than Tanizaki, chuckled ostentatiously.

"Ms. D'Espy," said Mitchell, "with all due respect. The National Weather Service is now reporting that Tammy is a Category Two hurricane. It may strengthen to a Category Three, or even Four. We've already had some flooding today. You see, the drought has made the land incapable of absorbing such massive rainfall."

"I've been in this city, in this business, for forty-five years. I've never seen anything like what you're predicting. On the Gulf Coast, maybe. Not here."

"In 1938 a Category Three hurricane hit seventy miles away, on Long Island. But still the East River flooded three avenues inland."

"Even I wasn't born then."

"On December eleventh, 1992, a storm shut down Manhattan. That was only a nor'easter."

"I remember that day, and I remember the storm in 2012. Very windy. We all came to work anyway, and there were no serious problems at the factory. Do you have any idea how much it would cost us to close the factory?" As she glared at him Mitchell began to wonder whether her eyes, like her eyebrows, had been painted on. "Closing the factory," she continued, "is a lot more expensive than purchasing these moronic earpieces for everybody's little phones."

Mitchell felt unpleasantly warm all of a sudden.

"Ms. D'Espy," said Tanizaki. He paused, blinking, as if in an effort to catch his breath. "I believe that Mr. Zukor is suggesting that we might be encountering a once-in-a-lifetime storm. A natural disaster that might threaten our lives."

For whatever reason—D'Espy's skepticism or the look of alarm on Tanizaki's immaculate face—the hurricane began to feel more real. It was like stepping out of a movie theater and into the street when the light is too sharp. The air went out of Mitchell's throat. He stared at the green vase in the middle of the conference table, and there, in the rippling glass, was the shifting surface of the horseshoe-shaped lake that lay beside Camp Ticonderoga. The water was swirling now, faster and faster, spinning like a black hole, and it was exerting a gravitational pull on the table, on the people in their cleanly pressed business suits, sucking them into its vortex, where they would drown.

"Mitchell?"

He looked up. They were waiting for his response. D'Espy rocked in her chair like a judge.

"Ms. D'Espy," he said. "I apologize. You are correct."

Tanizaki stiffened in his chair.

"It is true that a Category Four hurricane—even a Category Three hurricane—would have a catastrophic effect on the city. Windows, walls, and exterior cladding would fall to the sidewalk, killing anyone unlucky enough to be standing below. Pedestrians seeking shelter underground would drown. Every rail-tunnel system, including most subway stations, would flood. At high tide, the rivers could surge as high as thirty-two feet above normal water levels. Much of Manhattan could be submerged. Days, if not weeks would pass before the authorities would be able to restore any semblance of order. A factory like yours in Middlesex, just a mile from the coast, would suffer tremendous damage. The windows would shatter and the building would flood. The chemicals stored in the laboratories would be released, causing explosions and releasing poisonous gas into the atmosphere. Overnight your business would lose most of its value."

Mitchell glanced around the room, avoiding eye contact with Tanizaki. He had their attention. There was the white-knuckled concentration he had grown accustomed to in his months at FutureWorld, the dry mouths and anxious, tapping fingers. For him these subtle signals were like the roar of applause. He took a deep breath, then continued.

"But what are the odds, really, of this happening? I mean, it's one thing for a Category Four hurricane to hit the East Coast. But in order to create the kind of worst-case scenario I've outlined, the hurricane would have to follow an extremely specific course. It would have to make landfall east of Atlantic City and then continue on a north-northwest path into the New York Bight, with the eye of the storm passing within fifteen miles of Staten Island. And the odds of that, despite the latest trajectory analyses, remain fairly low."

"How low?" asked D'Espy. She leaned forward; her expression had softened.

"I haven't done all the math yet. But I'd estimate odds of less than one in eight. There's a high probability of some damage regardless, of course, but nothing worse than the 1992 storm." He smiled uneasily.

"Oh," said D'Espy. "Is that so?"

"Yes," continued Mitchell. "I think we'll all be OK. Soon everything will be back to normal." He tilted backward slightly, and for balance he grabbed the edge of the table, his fingers smudging the glass.

"Mitchell," said Tanizaki. "Are you all right?"

If he could only get the most recent numbers out of the National Hurricane Center, he'd be able to determine the odds precisely. Was it really one in eight? Might it be higher? The truth was that he had invented the figure. Twelve point five percent seemed a safe, low number. It was a hunch—no more, no less. The calculations were vague because the data was vague. He needed better numbers. When could he get better numbers?

"Bring the boy some water," said Ms. D'Espy. The others around the table muttered and ruffled their papers.

The first thing he'd do, once he got the new figures from the National Hurricane Center, was calculate the odds of the storm maintaining its Category 2 status. He'd have to cross tab those odds against the storm's range of potential trajectories. A graph would help. The x-axis would represent the distance from the center of the New York Bight at which the storm would pass; the y-axis would represent the strength of the hurricane, measured by the Saffir-Simpson scale. At $x = 0$ and $y = $ Category 5, the storm would be at its most powerful, and it would make a direct hit on New York harbor—

"I don't think he's telling us the truth," said D'Espy. "Mitchell? Do you hear me talking to you?"

At the right end of the x-axis, mark one thousand miles. Set the y-axis between Category 1 and 5. Plot each data point with a hash mark. Connect the points. What would the line look like? What kind of shape would form? Would it be a Poisson distribution? A parabola? A sine curve? Or would it be pure chaos, the marks like drops of water in a rainstorm? Any hash mark that landed near the point of origin would represent variations on the worst-case scenario—high probability of major impact, high Saffir-Simpson rating. High casualties. High chaos. Out rushes Cerberus, barking with all his heads—

Rough material abraded the back of Mitchell's neck. He was annoyed to discover that it was carpet pile. Someone pressed a cold, damp paper towel to his forehead. A large drop of water leaked down the side of his face and trickled into his ear. Water seemed always to be trickling down his face—first in the high-rise on Spruce Street, then in the rainstorm, and now. What the hell did it mean?

"Mitchell? Are you OK?"

He looked into a reassuring, smoothly contoured face, a face like a well-made bed.

"Jason?"

"You gave us quite a scare." The others had gathered behind Tanizaki in a circle around Mitchell's body. "Give him air," said Tanizaki.

Once the others backed away Tanizaki removed the compress. "You especially scared Ms. D'Espy," he said in a confidential, prideful tone. His voice softened to a whisper. "I think you scared yourself."

◫ ◫ ◫

The rest of the day proceeded much the same way, minus the fainting spell. The rain intensified slightly. It collected in pools that eddied by the sewer gutters, conveying trash from every alley and garbage can into the avenues. The breaking reports about the hurricane grew increasingly dire—now it was veering straight at New York, now the gusts were as high as 130 miles per hour, a robust Category 3—and Mitchell had to work harder in order to convince himself that the worst could be avoided. This put him in an unusual position with clients. They had not seen him like this before. Never had his prophecies been so optimistic, so full of hope. Those who knew him, like Tanizaki, seemed disturbed by this transformation. It was obvious that something was wrong with him. Mitchell's phony optimism fooled nobody. His speech became erratic; even his math began to suffer. When Nybuster pointed out that one of his calculations was off by a factor of ten, Mitchell turned pale.

At the office Charnoble greeted him with a handshake and a broad paternal smile.

"Whatever you told Lady Madeline, it worked. They're scared shitless, in a manner of speaking."

"It's not really a manner of speaking, Alec."

"I'll be the judge of that," said Alec, winking. "In any case, they want a follow-up meeting tomorrow morning."

"Tomorrow morning might be too late."

"They've already started shutting down their Middlesex factory. I received a personal call from Madeline D'Espy herself. She wanted to express her gratitude for FutureWorld's foresight and wisdom. Madeline D'Espy herself!"

The phone rang continuously. Tewilliger yelled out the names of the callers to Charnoble. As soon as he was gone Jane entered Mitchell's office.

"What in the world have you been telling your clients?"

"I'm telling them not to worry," said Mitchell. "That the odds of Tammy hitting the region at the point of greatest impact are extremely low."

"But they didn't believe you?"

"Not at all."

"God, you're good." Jane shook her head. "I never would have thought of that. Brilliant."

"I'm lost out there."

Jane seemed not to hear him.

"With an imminent natural disaster," she said, "the only thing scarier than confirming their worst fears is to be crazily optimistic. It's as if the threat is too atrocious even to discuss. You mind if I use that?"

Mitchell slumped over in his chair.

"Charnoble was right," she said. "You are a natural-born terrorist."

"Jane, be honest—aren't you a little bit scared?"

"Of what?"

"This thing might really hit, and hit hard. What if it's Galveston in 1900? No one foresaw that hurricane either."

She smiled, her eyes comically wide. "C'mon—we'll be fine. An itty-bitty Category Four ain't gonna hurt us! At least not for a day or two. This is New York City. *Winnetka*, it'd be another story. Or Kansas City. Don't you worry: we'll stick together. Jane will take care of you."

"I might hold you to that."

Jane chuckled. She began to leave the room, but when she reached the door, she turned back.

"Refresh my memory. What happened to Galveston in 1900?"

"You don't know?"

"What, was Galveston badly damaged?"

"Damaged?" Mitchell laughed—or choked. He couldn't tell which. "Galveston disappeared. The city completely disappeared."

# 6.

Mitchell had spent most of the night in the skycity. Or a version of it. In his dream, when he looked outside his window, instead of cobalt-blue sky and sparkling skyscrapers extending infinitely, he saw trees—giant, soaring oaks perforating a green-black night. Below was a green lake on which there floated a canoe, rocking in the slow waves. On the bottom of the boat lay a girl in a plain brown dress, sprawled on her back in an irregular position. Her arms were bent at strange angles. Her eyes were open. The eyes stared at him from an impossible depth.

When he'd awoken at five in the morning, a pale glow had just started to creep across the parquet floor of his living room in the shape of a lady's fan. It looked like a beautiful day. Could the storm have veered off course? Once, in kindergarten, his school was closed because of a twister-spawning thunderstorm that was buzz-sawing its way across Johnson County, headed straight for Kansas City. Old Tibor boarded up the windows with plywood and secured them with duct tape.

"We're not on the ground, Toto!" yelled Tibor.

"Oh stop it," said Rikki.

"*The Wizard of Oz*," said Tibor, "starring a certain Miss Judy Garland."

Mitchell hadn't been able to sleep the night before, he was too afraid; he remembered stumbling to the bathroom in the middle of the night and sitting in the empty bathtub with his pajamas on, as if in a bomb shelter. But when the dreaded morning arrived, they awoke to the music of two woodpeckers cautiously tapping the plywood on their windows. The family gathered in the dimmed living room, and Tibor tentatively peeled off strip after strip of duct tape. Then, in a single dramatic gesture, he snapped back a sheet of plywood. A rectangular shaft of clear blue light shot through. It landed like a spotlight on the face of Mitchell's mother. She laughed, startled, and they all joined in, snapping off the plywood, as if a normal sunny day were the craziest thing they'd ever seen.

Rikki, in fact, had called Mitchell several times since Tammy had strengthened to a Category 3. He hadn't picked up, and he didn't have the heart to call her back. No matter how calm he pretended to be, the moment she heard his voice, she would sense his terror. There was no need to worry her any more than she was already. In her last message she asked whether he had thought about where he could go in case the hurricane was as bad as some were predicting. Of course he had thought about where he could go. He had no place to go.

But am I still dreaming? Out the window the sky over the East River was a weird curdled pink—the color of fresh scars, inflamed gums. It sparkled like fish scales.

The phone rang. Was Rikki already up? Had she never gone to sleep? It was just after 5:00 a.m. in New York, which meant 4:00 in Overland Park. He picked up.

"Zukor! Glad I got through. You up?"

"It's early, Alec."

"I know, it's just—I couldn't go to sleep. Too excited."

"Can we talk at the office?"

"Listen, at two a.m., after the latest numbers came in from the NHC, the mayor issued an executive order. Mitchell, he's ordered an evacuation. All zones."

The sun itself was a bloody disk. There were clouds—a linty blanket of them—white on top, fading to lavender below.

"Mitchell? You there?"

"They waited too long," Mitchell said. "They should have made the announcement yesterday. By the end of the workday."

"I know. Because of that, I don't see our clients taking the warning seriously."

"You're saying you want me to go to consultations. You want me to work today? During an evacuation?"

"We don't have a choice. Besides, the evacuation is a political thing. It's stopped raining, for godsakes! I've even been hearing that the storm might miss us completely. And if our clients request meetings and we stand them up, well—how will that make us look? No, no, that won't do."

"Nobody's canceling?"

"Listen, we won't be foolish about it: we'll monitor the weather minute by minute and act accordingly. Besides, you yourself spent all of yesterday telling people that we'd be safe." Charnoble was speaking very quickly now. "We may never get another chance like this. This is the day by which FutureWorld will be judged from here forward. If we fail, our business is in jeopardy. If we succeed, we'll be the leaders of the most important new sector in the financial industry. Mitchell, this is it! This is what we've been working for. I need this from you. *We* need this from you—all of us. Tewilliger, Jane, and me. We are in this nest together."

Across the street from his apartment, at the entrance to the Queens Midtown Tunnel, traffic accumulated. New Yorkers weren't leaving so much as fleeing. There were no cars heading in the other direction except for the occasional police van. Pedestrians were running into the tunnel wearing backpacks, carrying suitcases, tripping in their galoshes.

"When I said that about the hurricane yesterday," said Mitchell, "about how it wasn't going to come? No one believed me."

"I believed you."

"They didn't believe me because I didn't believe it myself."

The cars were loaded to their roofs with baggage, sleeping bags, moving boxes, and whatever else could fit: a basketball, a television, a stack of women's dresses on hangers, a bubbling fish tank. Children's faces pressed against the windows. Sleeping children; flushed faces. The adults were determined but feverish. They yelled at each other, pounded on the windshield, punched the roof of the car. They glanced frequently in the rearview. One man took a final look at the Chrysler Building before the tunnel swallowed him up. Or perhaps he was staring at the sky. The sky had gone cuckoo. On the horizon the streaks of cloud were curved like the grains of an oak board—brick-dust red speckled with curling yellows and oranges. God doing van Gogh. Mitchell had seen these colors only one other time, during a winter vacation he had taken with his mother on Vancouver Island. He must've been eight or nine. At a highway rest stop they happened upon a stream where salmon were spawning. The huge fish lay spent on the rocks, their roe already discharged, the water rushing over their bloated bodies. Their skin was the same unusually strong pink hue, almost bloody. The fish weren't quite dead yet—they still flicked their tails and blinked idiotically—but sections of their flesh had already begun to decompose and flake away. The skeletons started to show; a fin detached; an eyeball hung loose from its socket. He asked his mother why the salmon, having already given birth, didn't just drift back to the ocean. Why, even as they died, did they still face upstream, fighting against the current?

Three reasons, she said. First, they know, on a primitive level, that they won't survive long enough to make it back to the ocean. Second, they want to keep the way clear for their offspring. And finally, like human beings, their instinct is to die looking up.

Charnoble cleared his throat.

"I appreciate this, Mitchell." He paused. "Oh, and Mitchell? Enjoy yourself. This may be the most glorious day of our lives."

"Wait—Alec. Have you looked at the sky? This sky—"

But Charnoble was gone.

# 7.

When he went to the bathroom to splash water on his face, the tap sputtered. In the refrigerator he found a jug of purified water. He bent over the sink and poured the cold water over his head. There was something absurd about drenching himself while a monsoon was speeding in his direction, but the cold slap of wetness on his neck and cheeks achieved the desired result. His thoughts clicked into place. His first resolution: no way was he going to work. He'd escape. If the trains weren't running, he'd follow the traffic through the Midtown Tunnel, weaving between the stopped cars, escaping to Queens, then on to—no. Long Island, surrounded by water, would be even more dangerous. Better to head west to New Jersey, then Pennsylvania. The phone rang.

"You talk to Alec?" It was Jane. She sounded exhausted and bored.

"Yes, but . . ."

"You're not thinking of bailing, are you?"

"You saw the scenarios. If we stay here too long, we'll be trapped. Stuck. Cut off—"

"Hold on a minute. It's not even raining."

"The mayor ordered an evacuation," he said.

"Wait. Are you freaking out?"

"No. Yeah. Maybe a little."

She paused, and when she spoke again her voice had dropped an octave. The note of playfulness had vanished.

"Don't abandon me," she said.

The sound of her voice did something physical to him. It entered him, diving into his abdomen and extending prickly brambles into the soft parts of his stomach. He thought of his family, begging him to leave. And of Elsa, lying in a hospital bed in Augusta. Was her brain working? Did she know what had happened to her?

*Psycho! Where Do You Go When You Sleep?*

"I'd never abandon you," he said. Despite the water dripping off his face, he suddenly felt flush. "You know that, right?"

She paused for a second, as if she were trying to figure out whether he was joking.

"FutureWorld," she said at last. "Hope springs infernal."

"FutureWorld," said Mitchell. "You made your bed. Now die in it."

"We'll check in with each other, OK?" said Jane. "In a couple of hours?"

Mitchell nodded.

"Are you there?"

"Sorry." He took a breath. "Yes. I'm here."

◫ ◫ ◫

The storm broke at six-thirty. As soon as he stepped out of his cab on Broad Street, large, pregnant drops sopped his hair and soaked his neck. They detonated in giant asterisks on the sidewalk, the backsplash drenching his pant cuffs. The sewers were stopped up and beginning to flood; estuaries bulged around each street corner. At the building where he was scheduled to meet with his first client, Affiliated Data Systems, the revolving door was jammed with a crowbar. He sprinted north to Anchor Liberty's office on Beekman Street. An anxious janitor stood outside the shuttered lobby ordering workers to go home. As the janitor shook his head, a file of water dripped from the brim of his hat onto his chest.

"I have an appointment," said Mitchell. "Harold Harding."

"Nobody there," said the janitor. "I'm telling you, I don't get paid enough for this. I don't know how to swim. Look at this shit."

He pointed upward. Mitchell understood the man's apprehension. The sky had begun to darken. It looked enraged, a livid sky, full of eggplant colors, purple yielding to cast-iron black. There was something thrillingly exotic about the angry blackness of it, tense with intermittent electricity. The clouds were scowling. Mitchell walked away, but the janitor didn't seem to notice. He was still staring upward, transfixed.

On Cortlandt the wind started playing tricks, swirling one minute, swooping upward the next. Sometimes it pushed down from above like a giant sole crushing a bug—Mitchell the bug. The streets were a honking chaos: cars, overloaded with possessions, continued to drive toward the bridges while giant white NYPD buses, packed with people who had no other way of escaping, formed a procession up Broadway. In the windshield of each bus was a placard with the name of the evacuation center where it was headed; Mitchell saw Wassaic, Weehawken, Fort Lee, Randall's Island. The subway was running on an enhanced schedule, express trains running north to the Bronx at brisk intervals, but dozens of skeptics were still emerging from the stations on Fulton Street. They stepped outside into the swirling winds, opened their umbrellas, threw down their umbrellas when they bent, and walked with brisk determination to their offices, purposefully oblivious to what was going on around them. The New York business day would brook no storm. It occurred to Mitchell that he was just like these people. On a day when an actual disaster might very well unfold, here he was, working! He supposed he could run away now, hop one of those white buses—but Charnoble, viper that he was, had attacked Mitchell's weak point: his sense of logic. There was only one more client on his itinerary that morning, just four blocks away, an annuities executive named Howard Schmitz; all Mitchell had to do was check in and deliver his final warnings. Charnoble was right: If Mitchell couldn't do his job when an actual disaster was approaching, how could he, or FutureWorld, have any credibility during calmer times? Then again, if he were honest with himself, he wasn't staying in New York because of integrity. He was staying for Jane.

When he reached the H. R. Hayes building he found the front door open, though no one was at the security desk. Mitchell hurdled the turnstile and took the elevator to Howard Schmitz's office. It was empty, and Mitchell was punching the elevator button when he noticed a pair of black flats on the carpet, connected to stockinged feet behind the front desk. The feet were twisting from some type of exertion.

"Hello?" he said.

The feet froze. Slowly a mop of brown hair rose above the desk.

"Who are you? How did you get in here?"

"I'm Mitchell Zukor? From FutureWorld? Mr. Schmitz is expecting me."

"No, he is not." The woman stood up. She was still wearing her wet raincoat. "The only thing he or anyone else is expecting is that hurricane. Tammy. What a name—who would've thought a storm with a fat girl's name would do so much damage."

Mitchell stared at her, perplexed.

"Haven't you been watching the news?" she said. "You've been outside, I can see that."

"Mr. Schmitz isn't in?"

"Not him, not no one else neither. I left my car keys here somewhere and my car is parked downstairs. I don't know how the hell I'm going to get out of town without my car. That's my excuse for being here. What's yours?"

"Well—I—I'm going around warning people to leave."

"They're already warned! And they're terrified. One thing I learned these last years is that the heavens don't follow historical precedent. People are afraid. Bad things are happening. This is a new world we've made."

Mitchell slowly backed away. This woman was unstable. Maybe all the water had gotten into her brain.

"I'd take the stairwell if I were you," said the secretary. "They're going to cut the electricity any second. The pipes are already out."

On the street again, he saw he had missed a call from Jane. He buzzed her back.

"Have you *met* with anybody?" Her voice was less casual than before, almost pinched. If he hadn't seen her name on his phone, he wouldn't have believed it was Jane.

"I think everyone's gone," said Mitchell.

"Alec didn't pick up when I called his phone. When I called the office, Tewilliger said he hadn't been in all day."

"Huh."

"So I told her to go home."

"What'd Tewilliger say?"

"She hung up on me."

Many of the workers he'd seen filing into the office towers were now running across the avenue, trying to reach the City Hall subway station before it closed. Hats and umbrellas flew through the air, colliding into the sides of buildings and falling back to the street. He'd be safer once he got back home, but he dreaded the three miles that lay between him and the apartment. Three miles of humanity shoving and racing. The same as any other day, really, only damper, even more desperate.

"Mitchell," said Jane. "It's hard for me to say this."

"What? What is it?"

"I guess I was faking it before."

"Wait a minute—" He really didn't like the tone in her voice. Where was the unflappable Jane, the demure Jane, the sarcastic, fearless—

"I'm scared," she said. "I'm really scared."

"No way. Don't give me that."

"Everyone I know has already left the city. We're the only ones left."

"What did we talk about before?" His mind raced. He realized how much he had been relying on her. If she was cool, he could be cool. He nearly shouted. "We could have left! We could be on the George Washington Bridge by now, or at least the Henry Hudson. There are probably ferries—"

"Stop. Mitchell?"

"What?"

"Right now I don't want to be alone."

# 8.

She gasped audibly when the power went. There was a sound like a record player flipped off mid-song. The lights shuddered. Somewhere in the distance a man screamed.

They had been watching television at the time, long enough to see the local news switch over to the national broadcast. The streets were finally empty, the ground white with the force of the rain exploding in steady bursts. The George Washington Bridge, thronged with cars and stragglers walking with their heads bent under the punishing rain, rocked gently from side to side, a cradle over the churning abyss of the Hudson River. The wind hammered like a crowbar at the Victorian houses on Rockaway Beach. Slate shingles boomeranged through the air in Bay Ridge. The East River breached the barricade of the FDR Drive, the impact of the waves creating vertical geysers of arctic-white spray that fixed in the air like holographic mist. In one particularly unsettling tableau, a cameraman had filmed the iridescent purple corpses of pigeons floating in the Central Park reservoir; in other parts of the park the rain had fallen with such ferocity that it filled the birds' overhead nostrils and drowned them where they stood. There were reports of looting but also of supermarkets providing their stocks of fresh food to whoever passed by—the electricity was out, so the frozen meat was thawing, the ice cream melting. There were press conferences in Washington, Albany, Hartford, Brooklyn, City Hall. The politicians wore expensive rain slickers, but as if in solidarity with their constituents their hair had been carefully drenched and lay on their heads like wilted cabbage.

"He's terrified," said Jane when the mayor spoke from his podium. "You can see it in his eyes. He looks like a little boy who lost his mother in the supermarket."

Though the window was shut, a sour mist sprayed into the room with each strong gust. Jane was the first person Mitchell had let into his apartment, and he couldn't quite get comfortable. He kept looking around for things to tidy up, but after nudging the Psycho Canoe against the wall, he didn't really know where to begin. The disorder was suddenly impossible and unbearable.

"I have to make a phone call," he said, handing her the remote.

Jane pursed her lips as if she were going to say something, but one look at Mitchell and she turned back to the screen. He went into his bedroom, closed the door behind him, and made the call.

As usual, the nurse at Augusta General explained that nothing had changed. Yes, they were doing everything they could. Yes, they had a backup generator in case a storm put the electricity out. Yes, she had his number and would alert him if Elsa's condition changed. He hung up and returned to Jane.

Outside the wind was calling to them. *Oooh*, it said. *Oh oh oh ooooooh. Oh. Oh. Oh!*

Jane was watching a live press conference held by a Colorado Springs preacher. The man spoke like a high-ranking general: curt, supercilious gestures and a magnanimous tone, with significant, heightened pauses. He wore delicate spectacles that magnified his gentle blue eyes. The Colorado sky was bright and wide.

"Never has the wickedness of mortal man been greater than now," he said. "When the earth was filled with blood violence and all flesh had been corrupted, God did not tell Noah that the destruction of man would come by gun, bomb, or missile launcher. No, death would not come by any tool of man. God said, 'I will destroy them with the *earth*.' And today you can see that our modern Babylon is being overwhelmed by the earth in a great alluvion. Every man, beast, fowl, and thing that creepeth across the earth must repent."

"What a preposterous man," said Jane, hugging herself. She changed the channel back to the local news. It was broadcasting an image of the Hudson, which was now melted caramel, muddied with sediment dredged from the riverbed. Splinters of wood whipped through the air. Newscasters were no longer reporting from the street—it was too dangerous—so the pictures were taken by cameras that had been left behind, beaming their images to satellites. There were no people visible anywhere, in fact. Tammy had already accomplished what financial collapses and terrorism and heat waves had failed to do: it had emptied New York's streets of its people.

"I guess I was wrong about FutureWorld," said Jane. "You have to give Charnoble credit."

"For what? Exploiting fear to make money?"

"Well, yeah. You do have to give him credit for that. I mean, just last week I bought a dress that costs more than my monthly rent, even though I have no place to wear it. I can see you've been indulging too." She tilted her head toward the Psycho Canoe.

"Impulse buy," he said.

"Yeah, exactly—we're making enough money now to buy almost whatever we want, when we want it. But there's another side to this thing. I mean, as crazy as it sounded at the time, the advice

I gave my clients about hurricane evacuation is going to be useful. The numbers we ran were valid, after all. The time series was accurate and the stochastic process bore out. Our warnings might save lives."

*Unnnh*, said the wind. *Ummmm. Unnnh.*

"I don't think Charnoble cares about anyone's life but his own."

"You're right. But the business will help people despite that. Look at what's going on." She pointed to the television, where water was shown galloping up the steps of a subway station entrance on Eighth Avenue. "You can't just pretend anymore that the unusual will never happen. It will."

"I know it, believe me."

"Every business needs a bank, a law firm, an insurance company, an advertising firm. I think they're going to realize soon that they also need a future consultant. Not just to protect them from lawsuits, but to protect them from, well, *this*."

The power cut out with a tapering electronic sigh, as if it were relieved to exit the scene before the real destruction began. Mitchell tried his cell phone, but the signal was gone. After the surprise wore off, he realized he was grateful for the darkness, the silence. For a long time he and Jane sat listening to the squealing wind and the thunder that was like the roar of an ensnared beast.

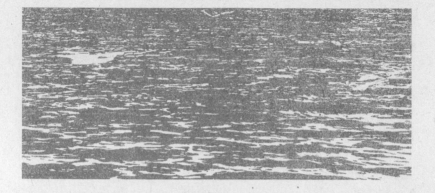

# 9.

Everything got worse.

If he weren't on the third floor he would have sworn there was a man outside the window, a huge man pounding with his fists against the glass, demanding to be let in. They had to barricade it. Mitchell went over to the corner where the pile of wooden staves from the canoe crate still lay in a messy pile. As soon as Jane realized what Mitchell was doing, she pitched in, carrying the staves to the window and snapping the longer pieces over her knee. They laid the wood over the window in horizontal bands, using duct tape to hold them in place, following the example Tibor had set on that long-ago day in Overland Park. It was the only window in the apartment, but they weren't losing much of a view. The city had been blanketed by an uncanny iron darkness. The only time they could see anything was when the lightning struck, filling the sky with baroque blue designs. What they saw in those brief flashes hurt Mitchell's stomach.

Third Avenue was now a canal, the water so high it had begun to spill over the curb. The ramp that led from the avenue to the Queens Midtown Tunnel was a cascading stream, the water leaping over itself as it rushed down the incline. The wind levitated the crushed skeletons of umbrellas, garbage cans, chunks of scaffolding. Bricks blurred through the air, hurtling like poorly thrown footballs until they pulverized against the sides of buildings. Or shot through windows.

"These things do happen," he said. "They really do."

"I don't think anyone's doubting you anymore," said Jane, but she seemed very far away. There were blinking bursts of light at the edge of Mitchell's vision and everything else was getting hazy. Was this the tragedy he'd been preparing himself for all these years, a world-cleansing flood of biblical proportions, straight out of the preacher's sermon? *Every man, beast, fowl, and thing that creepeth across the earth must repent.* I've spent a lifetime worrying about this moment, doing the calculations, taking the measurements, trying to render catastrophe in calculable, precise dimensions, and still I'm not prepared? But real catastrophe was like that. It was a form of genius. It astounded expectations, was unlike anything that came before.

*Whee!* shouted the wind. *Whee! Wheeee!*

He squeezed his eyes and opened them. In order to ignore the frantic Morse code of his heartbeat, and the sweat edging his hairline, he forced himself to concentrate on the task at hand. His mother's old advice: Do something!

He forced himself to focus on barricading the window. They worked together, Jane holding the slats in place while Mitchell taped them to the window frame. They worked slowly, deliberately, making sure not to leave any gaps, and slowly Mitchell began to breathe. Slat over window, tape, repeat. Slat, tape, repeat. They made progress. Jane glanced at him out of the side of her eye; it seemed she wanted to ask him something but didn't quite know how to do so.

"Let's hear it," said Mitchell finally.

"Don't take this the wrong way or anything. But why *is* there a canoe in your living room?"

"It's actually a work of art. From the New Psychedelia School."

She nodded, as if giving this serious consideration.

"It was made by a young Nova Scotian woman named Sylvan who collects objects from her natural environment and paints them in unexpected ways, using organic laminates and gold leaf and nontoxic enamel in an effort to capture the eternal unity of—"

"That's enough," she said. "What's going on, exactly? Are you worried that the window is going to blow in?"

"We're safe here," he said. "At least for now. I have provisions. I have a Go Bag."

The wind sobbed. *Whaaah! Whaaah! Aaaah!* The wind screamed murder.

"You're in control of the situation, is what you're telling me," she said, doing her best impression of Charnoble's wispy voice. She twisted her finger in her palm. "You're a man of action."

"A man of action?" His voice came out bitter and clipped. He tore a strip of duct tape with a loud rip. "A man of *action?*"

She put down the wood.

"What was that phone call about?" she said.

"It's a long, boring story."

"It looks like we're not going anywhere for a long time. It'll get dull if we just have to sit here in silence, listening to the rain and wind."

"Here's a question: Do you ever have the desire to do something irrational? Then you stop and think about it for a second and realize it's a stupid idea. But you actually go ahead and do it anyway?"

"Sure. I mean, I didn't get any offers out of Wharton. I guess you didn't know that. Bad timing with Seattle and all. But I came to New York anyway, no money, sleeping in a foldout chair in a

Bushwick hallway. I was the only bartender at the All-Ways Lounge with an advanced degree."

"Yeah, but a Wharton degree—it was just a matter of time. I'm talking about real risk. Something that could ruin you."

"Why are you asking?"

"Because I don't know what that feels like. I don't know if I'm capable of it."

She looked at him with a strange little smile. "There is one other thing. But I don't want to scare you."

"I'm not easily scared."

"That's a good one," she said, and without hesitation she pulled down the collar of her V-neck sweater, revealing the latticed trim of a white bra. A word was tattooed in a neat blue cursive, arcing in a rainbow over her left breast.

"I can't read it," he said in a whisper. He cleared his throat and tried again. "It's too dark."

She laughed. "Look closer, buddy."

He moved in, close enough to see the goose bumps on her pale skin and read the word: SLUT.

"My ex-boyfriend's idea," she said, snapping her shirt back. "I thought I was going to marry him. Typical Winnetka. We were eighteen. It didn't bother me because I figured it'd be our private dirty joke. I don't know why, but it turned him on. I guess I was a romantic back then."

He nodded gravely, testing with the back of his fingers the tension of the duct tape over the window.

"Are you going to have it removed?" he said finally.

"When my mother saw it she burst into tears, then fell down on the carpet and began to pray. I can't blame her, really. But I guess that's why I want to keep it."

"To piss off your mom?"

"No. Because it's a reminder of a time in my life when I didn't care about the future, or silly things like pride or self-respect."

"Mm. I think I respect you more."

She punched him on the shoulder. "Yeah, well, now you owe me."

So he told her about the Zukorminiums. He told her about his mother's long despair in Overland Park and the Hungarian Revolution that was waged every night in his father's dreams, his fainting spells at Eight Spruce Street and Lady Madeline, the dazzling skycity of his nightmares, and, at last, Elsa Bruner, the human worst-case scenario. While Mitchell continued to barricade the window, adding vertical pieces for reinforcement—an activity that allowed him to avoid making eye contact—Jane listened. She watched him closely and asked questions. Why, for instance, had Elsa corresponded with him in the first place? In retrospect, he said, it seemed it was because he was the only person she knew who might see through her wild delusions. It was the first time his instincts for disaster avoidance had really been tested, but he had failed her, and the ridiculous girl was now lying comatose on a Maine hospital cot.

By the time his story ended they had finished the window. At Jane's request, they left a small area of the glass uncovered—a rectangular slot six by three inches—so that they could see what was going on outside. Jane was quiet for a moment, making herself busy by checking whether all the slats were properly aligned and the tape was secure.

In the darkness it was impossible to read Jane's expression. She turned toward him.

"That girl wasn't a test. What were you supposed to do, kidnap her?"

"I could have tried."

"She was having an argument with herself." Jane shook her head. "No, you haven't been tested. When you're really tested, you'll know it."

"How?"

There was a tremendous crackling noise. He was afraid to look outside. It sounded like a meteor shower on Third Avenue. The wall thumped. Jane laughed in surprise.

"That's how."

⊡ ⊡ ⊡

He couldn't fall asleep—the constant banging was even louder than the pulsing noise in his head—and after twenty minutes he got out of bed and quietly stepped over to the window. He knelt and looked through the slot. After some time an intricate mosaic of lightning filled the sky and he could see that the water had risen. The curb was gone; the few cars still parked on the street were almost completely submerged.

"What do you see?"

Mitchell jerked around. Elsa Bruner was standing behind him. She must have emerged from the canoe. Then he saw the swoop of brown hair and the half-shut eyes, and Elsa's face became Jane's face.

"There are waves," he said. "Coming up Third Avenue."

Jane knelt next to him, hip to hip. They looked together through the section of glass. Obscure objects bobbed in the water like fallen logs, before being dragged beneath the surface.

The lightning sizzled again. Embedded in the foaming arc of a wave was, unmistakably, a black baby grand piano. There was a rending, creaking sound as some crucial structural brace peeled off a building and cartwheeled over the rooftops.

Neither of them dared to move. Their heads touching, their bodies pressed together, they waited. Beneath the eruptions outside the window, Mitchell could hear Jane's slow intake of breath. Her shoulders rose and fell, rose and fell.

A jagged streak of lightning flashed very close by, and in that instant he could see a red blur flying through the air straight at them. They fell backward, shielding their faces as the brick crashed into the window. There was a small explosion of glass, then a burst of mist, and the rain started to spray into the apartment.

"Jane?"

She lay next to him, her arms covering her face. She started to tremble, and then she hiccuped.

Mitchell touched her shoulder. "Are you hurt?"

Jane flung back her arms, and all at once her peculiar melodious scale-climbing laughter filled the room. She started to brush the broken glass off her sweater, but that only made her laugh harder, and Mitchell laughed too—more out of shock than anything else. Still laughing, Jane flopped her leg over Mitchell's waist and sat on top of him. She flung off her sweater, casting shards of glass across the parquet floor. She unbuckled her jeans; she found his hand and put it on her breast. When she lowered her face to meet Mitchell's, her laughter stopped.

Then the only noise was the storm throwing itself against the wall.

# Sternman

## I.

He was standing on a cliff after a storm. Waves fell gently against the shore, a vaporish drizzle fell on the rocks, the air was shivery and moist. The seagulls were starting to return, searching, with forlorn chirps, for their lost friends. Then a mechanized stentorian voice, amplified by a loudspeaker, interrupted.

"If you are safe and secure and have enough food and water for the next twenty-four hours, please remain where you are. If you are hurt or in danger, *please call out.* This is the United States Coast Guard. Is anyone in danger? Is anyone in danger?"

Mitchell made his way gingerly across the living room to the window, circling a huge puddle flecked with needles of broken glass. Though the hole in the window he peered out at a new world.

It wasn't quite dawn. The sun touched lightly upon the balustrade of the tenement buildings across the street. Most of the windows were shattered or blown out entirely; one had been plugged with a waterlogged queen-size mattress. A white spotlight advanced north along the river that was once, very long ago, Third Avenue. The waters of the flood were upon the earth.

He suddenly felt as if everything that happened before that moment had been a dream, but this world into which he'd awoken—this was real.

He looked at Jane—she was asleep on the floor, partially covered by his shirt. Her head was pressed into the hollow of her shoulder; her mouth was slack; her hand was outstretched, grasping for something just out of reach. Most people look peaceful when they sleep. Jane looked as if she'd been knocked over the head.

The Coast Guard patrol boat drifted into view. Its searchlight fanned across the width of the avenue, picking up a car, a half-submerged couch, the piano, and bloated, humped shapes the color of oyster meat. These last Mitchell feared were bodies. An officer leaned over the side of the boat, a grappling hook in hand.

"Is anyone in danger?" asked the man through the loudspeaker.

The grappling hook snagged something heavy in the water. With a grunt the man hauled his catch onto the boat. When the spotlight passed over the deck, Mitchell saw a pair of jeans, a clump of black hair, a puckered blue arm.

He started frantically to remove the tape and the slats over the broken window. They couldn't come off fast enough. Once the opening was large enough he put his mouth to it and yelled.

"Up here! Up here! Hey! Help!"

But the boat had passed.

Jane was moving behind him. Before he could say anything, she was running into his bedroom, carrying her clothes, covering her body as best as she could. The door clicked shut behind her. Mitchell threw a towel over the puddle and found his Go Bag in the closet. He turned the transistor radio to the NOAA All Hazards station. Static kept interrupting the broadcast, but he could make out "massive flooding . . . known dead . . . preliminary . . . hundreds of thousands still unaccounted for, though many are hoped . . . no electricity for at least a week . . . damages that are already approaching . . . fog, calm, overcast . . ."

Beyond his little apartment, beyond the shard of city visible from his window, something vast and nameless had happened—and was, to some extent, still happening. Yet as scary as the news was, the measured tone of the reporter's voice gave the tragedy an eerie semblance of normality. Switching on the radio, Mitchell had expected to hear inchoate wailing, the brass of crashing machinery, the rush of cascading water. But even a catastrophe of this proportion, it turned out, could be described in simple English—word after word, sentence after sentence. A barbaric nausea passed over him. The storm was being discussed in the same way that one might recount the highlights of a ball game, a summit meeting between prime ministers, a recipe for butternut squash. Chaos was seeping under the cracks of doors and through the seams in the carpentry, wrathful Kali was dancing at the door, the Valkyries were hurtling through the air with flashing spears, chanting their death hymns—yet somehow a story could still be told. Even on the precipice of hell, here was introduction, thesis, cliff-hanger, conflict, resolution. Somewhere in the world, possibly as close as Newark, there existed a radio studio in which a woman sat at a desk wearing a business suit; makeup, perhaps. Set before her, a printed script and a pen, a computer screen logging minute-by-minute updates. Staff members tested the microphones, wrote copy, balanced the sound frequencies, received reports from journalists flying over the wreckage in helicopters. Just another Thursday morning: microphone check one two three four.

"There's something wrong with your pipes."

Jane emerged from Mitchell's bedroom in her jeans and T-shirt, her hair pulled back, her face still puffy from sleep. "I'm going home. I want to make sure my computer didn't get totally drenched." She began to move toward the door.

"What?"

She walked past him.

"I don't think you understand," he said. "The city is flooded. Look outside."

She squinted at him. Mitchell, suddenly aware that he was wearing nothing but his boxer shorts, slipped quickly into his room and pulled over his head a ratty old T-shirt he'd made in high school. When he emerged again, Jane was at the window. As if doing him a favor, she bent to look through the window.

"Oh." She hiccuped loudly. "My goodness."

Mitchell started picking through his Go Bag.

"Ten snack bars, a gallon of bottled water, three cans of red beans, two boxes of animal crackers. There's a can of tuna in my cupboard, and three bottles of lemon-lime Gatorade. Maybe a beer or two. Mustard, ketchup." He walked into the kitchenette and opened the refrigerator door. "And a small plastic container of coleslaw from a deli sandwich I ordered last week. That's probably turned, though." He opened the lid and sniffed. "Yeah. It turned."

Jane was still at the window, shaking her head.

"And we'll need some of this," said Mitchell, opening the freezer. He began removing the rubber-banded stacks of bills from their ziplock bags. Each stack contained two hundred bills. A stack of twenties therefore was four thousand dollars. A stack of hundreds was twenty thousand. He took two of each. Then a third stack of twenties for good measure. "Cold, hard cash," he said from the kitchen. Jane didn't seem to hear him. "Frozen assets."

Jane's voice, when she finally spoke, was altered; she sounded like a scared little girl.

"How long are we going to be trapped here?"

"They're saying it might be a few days. But who knows?"

"You. You know. You're the genius futurist, aren't you?"

"No one can say how long it'll take for the flooding to subside. Then they'll have to restore electricity and test the water supply—that could take a while. A week? Months? I have enough food for five days, which is what the DHS advises. But I only planned for one."

"What are you saying?" Her eyes were wide. She did not faintly resemble the impish, chattering woman he had met at the Future-World offices only a couple of weeks earlier. A fog passed over her, as behind a smudged window on an old elevator door when it clangs shut, leaving visible only a sad, vague blur where there was once a human face.

"I'm not saying you should leave," he said. "That's not my point. But buildings that have had structural damage can crumble any second. It's as dangerous now as it was during the storm, if not more so. The roof above us might collapse. The floor could cave in."

He scanned the room. Had he missed anything? The apartment was actually in pretty good shape, considering: couch, puddle, canoe, broken glass, pile of wood, cushions and blanket, chair, desk, television, bookshelf . . . canoe.

"No way," said Jane, following his eyes. "You heard what the Coast Guard said: stay indoors."

Mitchell closed his eyes, found the depth, plunged the air down. A peculiar calmness radiated through him. When he opened his eyes his small, safe, ugly apartment had been transformed into a prison. The Psycho Canoe, its paddles stowed safely beneath the seats—the idea of a water escape, an exhilarating flight to safety—that was freedom. For the first time in his life he could laugh at risk. What was risk, anyway? Risk was a canceled check, a fever dream that flees from daylight, a stubbed toe.

"If we wait here to run out of food, we might not have the strength to escape. We just missed a rescue boat. Who knows when the next one will come?"

He picked up the two Day-Glo-orange PFDs and held one out for her.

"Have you gone out of your mind?"

Mitchell nudged the PFD into her shoulder.

"No chance," said Jane. "Let's think about this rationally for a minute. First of all, that thing is an artwork. An attempt to capture the eternal unity of something or another."

Mitchell stood smiling back at her like a maniac.

"You're not acting like yourself."

"Yeah, I know." He gave a low laugh. "I know."

# 2.

He heard a sound that was like continuous thunder and it became louder, roaring in his ears, a powerful, overwhelming noise, and he realized it was the silence, the colossal silence of the emptied city, that was making the sound.

The water was on fire. Low blue flames danced on the surface like floating bowls in a Thai river festival. He didn't want to think about what was burning: sewer discharge, most likely, chemicals leached by ruptured pipes. But he was grateful for the fires. Without them it would be impossible to see the way. The morning fog had limited visibility to a fifteen-foot radius, the circumference marked by a heavy wall of white-blue mist, the color of skim milk. Out of this murkiness the larger shapes emerged first: the curved seat of a wicker chair; a strip of rubber insulation curled like an octopus's tentacle; an inflated red yoga ball, like a candy apple; and the smooth black hull of a plasma television, bubbles coalescing and darting on its screen as it rocked in the current. Then the pigeon corpses. They were bobbing everywhere, lobster buoys in a Maine cove. And stationary objects—the studded plastic corner of a refrigerator door, a radiator's white corrugated grill—protruded from the water like unnatural icebergs. On either side of the avenue, the steel beams of traffic lights were rotted trees bending into the river, their roots the bundles of severed copper cables. Where the floodwater reached its highest point it traced, along the sides of buildings, an uneven line of filth that continued the length of the avenue as far as they could see.

"Gentle Jesus," said Jane. "Gentle Jesus, meek and mild."

The reek of sewage was overwhelming at first, then faint, and then—most unsettling of all—they stopped noticing it. The surface of the water was coated with a foamy scum that had collected into it cigarettes, gum wrappers, straws, plastic cups, bottle caps, and whatever other debris resisted sinking. Mitchell tried not to let the toxic water touch his skin, but it couldn't be avoided the way Jane paddled. She had obviously never been in a canoe before, and every clumsy stroke produced a coppery spray that whipped into Mitchell's face. It was no use telling her to go more gently. When he did, her exaggeratedly careful strokes were so feeble that she might as well not have paddled at all.

Slowly they drifted uptown. Jane was in the bow, responsible for calling out directions. Mitchell was the sternman. He executed hard rudders and wide sweeps to pivot around obstacles. A foreign

sensation pulsed through him. He thought it might've been tri-
umph, but he didn't have much experience with that, and he didn't
trust it.

"Right! Right!" shouted Jane. "Wait."

"What is it?"

"Left. Hard left!"

The birds had returned, at least some of them. Seagulls, king-
fishers, even a few pigeons. In the absence of traffic and human
voices, their calls filled the air. The melodies weren't particularly
joyous—it was mostly a furor of confused squawking, their imbecilic brains having lost all sense of orientation. Still they were a
reminder of a life that existed beyond the fog and the alien gray
river. Or rather, if life did exist somewhere beyond the fog, the
birds would be the first to discover it. Noah's big idea: release a
dove. If it didn't come back, that meant it had found a place where
the floodwaters had abated.

"Do you have any idea where we're going?" asked Jane after
they had paddled about two blocks north. It was difficult to tell
where the street ended and the sidewalk began. The best indica-
tions were the silver caps of fire hydrants, which peeked out of the
water like soldier's helmets.

"We're going to Bennett Park," said Mitchell.

"Never heard of it. Is that the one near the United Nations?"

"No, it's way uptown—on Fort Washington Avenue and One
eighty-third. It's the highest land in Manhattan. More important,
it's next to one of the narrowest sections of the Hudson. It's also
near the northern end of the island, so even if the current pulls us
south as we cross the river, we should be able to make it to New
Jersey before we're carried off into the bight."

They were quickly entering midtown, the beige apartment
towers and redbrick tenements giving way to black towers of glass
and steel. He was reminded of the drawings made by the early
explorers of the Grand Canyon, the Colorado gushing between

black vertical walls, the lone canoe in the foreground, its paddlers two insignificant specks.

"I'm not sure I follow," said Jane. "I know you're not saying that you want to canoe to New Jersey, because only a crazy person would say something so obviously crazy."

He saw how it would be to surge through the wave breaks, the river licking up against their prow, Bergen County vastly looming ahead.

"So I'm stuck in a boat with a lunatic," she said. "A raving, deranged—"

"Not at all. It doesn't get more pragmatic than this."

"You're not doing this to be romantic, are you?"

"I'm doing it to survive. Our worst-case scenario is also the most likely one. We stay indoors, we starve. Or worse—we're attacked by looters searching for food. It's safer on the water."

"I guess . . . Maybe we'll come across a police boat. I thought I heard a helicopter, but I don't think they can see down here until the fog clears."

The canoe had veered, without Mitchell's notice, toward the east side of the street, and now they were over the sidewalk, floating beneath the arcade of a fifty-floor office building. The canoe skidded over a round planter in which a ficus tree had somehow survived the storm. Its sodden leaves dragged in the water. The glass windows and doors that separated street from lobby had blown out, and Mitchell had the impression of entering an aquarium tank. There was a disturbance on the surface, and he noticed a pair of fish, each roughly three feet long, with large, puckering mouths and upper bodies streaked with olive and brown lines. They swam in lazy figure eights in front of the half-submerged security desk.

"Striped bass," said Jane. "Why not."

With a hard pull Mitchell pivoted the canoe around a black column and they were back into the middle of the avenue.

"I'm thinking we stay east," said Mitchell, "then we can cut across once we're farther north."

"Why not go west? That way we can at least make it to dry land. The flooding must be worst closer to the East River. Doesn't the elevation drop as you move east?"

"Yeah, the gradient is pretty sharp. The middle of the island is probably dry. But if we abandon the canoe, we might end up stranded, and surrounded by water. Out here at least we can move around."

But Jane, on the verge of tears, insisted, and Mitchell conceded that there was probably a better chance of being rescued on the dry part of the island. At the corner of Fortieth Street they turned west. The water level dropped the farther inland they went. By the time they reached Lexington it was shallow enough that they could see the pavement beneath their oars.

"Almost there!" said Jane. Her brow was smudged from the black water. "I knew it."

He felt good. Strong even. But then he started to hear the noises.

⊡ ⊡ ⊡

First there came a large splash directly ahead of them. This, in itself, was not particularly odd; they'd been hearing objects falling into the water ever since the moment they'd left Mitchell's apartment building: burning debris, chunks of plaster. For that reason they'd kept to the middle of the street. But this first splash was followed directly by a second, and then a third, so it began to seem as if someone were tossing objects into the water on purpose. A window exploded, as if struck, and finally, unmistakably, they heard the sound of hollering men. It was difficult to make out words, but the voices were anxious and violent. After they glided past Park Avenue Mitchell told Jane to stop paddling and they drifted, listening. Once they were within about twenty yards of Madison, the canoe ran onto dry macadam, coming to rest behind a van parked in the middle of the street. There was a crash ahead and they began to make out through the mist the dark forms of men swinging metal bars into the windows of a deli on the corner. When the windows shattered, the men kicked the glass into the street. Then they attacked the store, overturning shelves and counters, grabbing as many liters of soda, beer cans, bags of potato chips, and boxes of candy they could carry. Already they had become animals. Snarling, brutish, hateful. Was it that easy, the transition into savagery? Was it also inside him?

In the middle of the avenue two men wrestled on the ground. Beside their entangled bodies stood a shopping cart loaded with bundles of logs and bags of charcoal. The cart tipped over when a gang of young boys ran by; they were chasing a bald man with a liver spot on his forehead. He wore a torn blazer. The boys laughed and shouted obscenities; the man was sweating profusely despite the cool, foggy air, and screaming for help. In his arms he cradled a gallon-size tank of water like it was a fat baby.

"We should never have left your house," said Jane, her voice a frantic whisper.

Mitchell hooked one leg out of the canoe, pushing backward until the water was deep enough to float it.

"It's OK," he said, as much to himself as to her. He began back-paddling frantically. "We're OK. We'll go east."

"How do you know that will be safe? The water will be higher."

"You can trust me," he said.

The crazy thing was that he actually believed it.

# 3.

Grand Central was darker than he expected—larger too. As they glided in, the two-tiered concourse opening around them, it was like passing from the mouth of a river into a lake—or a sea, since it was impossible to perceive its boundaries. The great arched windows on the terminal's west wall had lost hundreds of panes during the storm, and the light that filtered through was viscous and gray. The expansive vaulted ceiling was as dark as the night sky, and the pinprick constellations were impossible to make out with their LED lights extinguished. The water was flat and still, some three feet deep. Only the marble counters glowed dimly, picked out by the faint shaft of light that fell diagonally from the lunette windows on the north wall.

"Thanks," said Jane. "I needed this." It was difficult to hear her. The cavernous room had a muting effect. It swallowed up her voice.

She removed her PFD and rested it over the thwart behind her. She lifted her legs onto the gunwales, and leaned back until her head came to rest on the orange pillow.

"Ten minutes," said Mitchell. "Then we have to make another push."

The clock over the information kiosk emerged from the darkness, a giant yellow cat's-eye. It read 5:22: the time power had cut out.

"I can make out one of them," said Jane, staring upward. "Andromeda."

"I don't even see any stars."

Jane, without sitting up, lifted one of her arms and pointed overhead. Mitchell tried to follow her finger, but all he saw was blackness.

"The Chained Woman," she said. "That's what Andromeda means."

Mitchell didn't have his glasses—after Jane had expressed her distaste for them he put them in the drawer of his office desk and they were still there—but even when he squinted he couldn't see the stars. He decided that Jane couldn't either.

Slowly she lowered her arm and closed her eyes.

He would let her sleep. She needed it. He also needed it, but he wouldn't be able to turn himself off while the adrenaline was so high in him. Too much was happening, too much, much too much: the future was on him, and he was trying to make sense of it all, but there was too much. He paddled past the kiosk, listening. No voices, no footsteps, no life. Only the sound of the water, parted by the canoe, lapping gently against the limestone walls. The stairwell to the lower level, on the eastern end of the concourse, was completely submerged, as were the tunnels off the main floor that led to the Metro-North tracks. And somewhere ahead, at the western end of the concourse, was the twinned staircase that led to Vanderbilt Avenue and high ground. And there were Mitchell and Jane in the Psycho Canoe, floating slowly across the giant floor of the concourse.

It was like being in the middle of a lake all right, or a grand swimming pool, peaceful and quiet, and Mitchell understood how Jane, exhausted and addled, could fall asleep. But he was only becoming more agitated. It wasn't the thought of all the people who might have been trapped in stalled trains when the tracks flooded that did it, or the scattered pieces of luggage that bobbed in the water here and there, each no doubt containing a person's most valued possessions, packed frantically at the last moment. It was the silence. The silence didn't make any sense. Grand Central Terminal was the perfect place to wait out the storm: large, impregnable, stone, with restaurants stocked with food. It was one of the first places rescue teams would target. If nobody was here, there was probably a reason.

Then he saw the reason. The Psycho had drifted past the kiosk, and the western staircase had begun to emerge from the blackness. The tunnel between the twin marble staircases was like a large, greedy mouth drinking the water. But clogging that mouth, and against the bottom of the stairs, were bodies. Not just one or two, as he thought he might have glimpsed on Third Avenue, but at least fifteen, maybe twenty, and the number kept getting larger the closer he got. He began to make out bare arms and legs and gray, puffy faces. It was as if they had been stacked there on purpose. And then came the smell—a sour, mildewed ghastliness. Mitchell backpaddled, hard, and the boat rocked. Jane shifted but did not open her eyes.

And the horror pounced on him, the roaches scrambling in his stomach, the panic sharp, cutting off his breath—he could see it all now, the waves rushing in from the East River, the water rising more quickly than anyone could imagine, surging through the Lexington Avenue entrances and down the long halls into the concourse. There must have been dozens, maybe hundreds of people in the terminal then, standing or sitting on the floor of the concourse, seeking shelter from the storm and waiting until the trains started running again. When the water began seeping into the

station those people would have known better than to head down
the ramps to the underground train tracks. Most likely they raced
up the stairs, some of them abandoning their luggage, and ran out
toward Vanderbuilt Avenue.

A second group of people would have been on the lower level,
sitting in the open train cars, maybe lying across the seats, naively
hoping to be on the first train out, once service was continued.
As the water started rising in the tunnel, some of the people on
the trains—the New Yorkers, the daily commuters—would have
known to run out to the concourse and up the stairs, and they too
would have escaped to higher ground.

But a third group, whether out of ignorance or pure panic,
would have stayed put. That, after all, was the natural human response to disaster. Psychologists called it the incredulity response,
or normalcy bias: most people, having never experienced a real
catastrophe firsthand, don't actually believe their eyes. This is why
some pleasure cruisers don't leave their cabins even as their ship is
sinking, why some office workers continue sending e-mails even
after they've learned that, on a lower floor, their building is on fire,
why a stunningly high percentage of people who die in skydiving
accidents are found to have never pulled the backup parachute
line. The people waiting in the trains needn't have waited very
long. In the tunnels the pipes would have soon burst, and with the
pumps overwhelmed, the water would have risen quickly from
the ground. The whole thing might have been inundated within
ninety seconds. Those people would still be there this minute,
entombed in the submerged trains.

Yet there was also a final category of people: those who waited
in the trains until it was *almost* too late, and then, rather than
limply succumbing to their watery fate, came to their senses and
ran out of the tunnel just in time. These people would've had to
work hard, racing up the ramps against the cascading water—it
would have been like running up a waterfall—only to reach the

concourse. But by then the terminal would have been like the ocean, for in the first stage of flooding the water was undoubtedly deep and turbulent, gushing in from several directions, seeping up from the tunnels and in waves from Lexington Avenue. The flood-waters would have lifted the desperate people off their feet and swept them toward the western end of the concourse, as if the flood wanted to nudge them toward safety but didn't know its own strength, until finally it crashed their bodies against the marble staircase. And so they would rest there, in a grotesque human dam, until the water subsided and the rescue crews arrived.

Mitchell didn't wake Jane until they were back on Lexington Avenue.

"Why are you breathing like that?" she said.

"Like what?" he said, and they were under the real sky again, blinking in the sunlight.

# 4.

On Forty-fifth Street and Lexington a man was wailing. The noise seemed to be coming from an old tenement building that was barely standing; it leaned into the street at a cockeyed angle. They gave it a wide berth. On Forty-fifth and Third a woman was barking gibberish: "*Ungh. Ronned. Shmoft.*" And on a fire escape off Forty-fifth and Second a man was preaching to the sky, a waterlogged copy of the Bible bloating in his hands like a sea sponge. "Alas, that great city! God hath remembered her *iniquities*. In one hour so great riches is come to nought!"

They saw things they instantly tried to forget. The swollen corpse of a tabby cat, its head unnaturally inclined; doggy-paddling rats; a child's coloring book, the bleeding ink turning the water different colors; a red sports bra. On Forty-sixth and Second, a brownstone had capsized, effectively damming the street with brick sections of wall and squat sandstone plinths. The rooms were completely bare inside; even the wallpaper in some places had been torn off by the wind. And once in a while they saw bodies. These tended to gather at street corners and beneath the parked cars. They were all half submerged, limbs sprawled and distended. Many were naked, their clothes having been torn off by the force of the flood.

"I can't," said Jane. "Oh, help us. Please help us."

"Don't look. I'll do the looking. I'll steer. Just paddle."

It was not always possible to avoid looking. They passed very close to an old woman, a young man, another woman. But they rarely saw the faces. By some compassionate force of nature the drowned bodies floated facedown.

If they didn't name what they saw, the things maintained an unreality. But just say the words "drowned cat" and, like a witch uttering abracadabra, the bloated belly, matted brown fur, twisted mouth, grasping paw, eyes watery with terror—the drowned cat appeared in their canoe, a third passenger, never to disappear. So they limited their conversation to canoeing directions, calling out debris and other obstacles. Almost immediately Jane had settled upon a simple code. Whenever they encountered a hunk of machinery, personal item, or a formerly living thing, she simply called out "flotsam" or "big flotsam"—or, in the case of the capsized brownstone, "really big flotsam"—and left it at that. Jane had become almost cartoonishly playful, as if determined to transform their journey into some kind of awful game. At first Mitchell was bothered by such blatant self-delusion. But as time elapsed and the fog held steady, he started to appreciate the tactic. It reflected one of the qualities that had made Jane so good at her job: she was a genius at beating back denial, at making improbable scenarios seem likely to occur. One of her favorite rhetorical tricks in consultation meetings had been to point out that an event that happens once every thousand days occurs on average, according to the math of probability, every two years. As it turned out, Jane was equally persuasive in making the case *for* denial. If Mitchell stared at the back of her head and avoided looking at the water, he could almost convince himself that he was back on Little Elkhart Lake, where the only obstacles he had to avoid were boulders and floating branches.

He wondered whether Elsa was dead.

About ten blocks ahead First Avenue passed through a short tunnel under the Queensboro Bridge. Since there was not much room between the surface of the water and the tunnel ceiling and Mitchell did not particularly relish the idea of canoeing through a dark cave, especially when the water level might suddenly rise at any moment, he hooked east, to Sutton Place. They'd have to veer even closer to the East River, but that seemed safer than heading west, back to Babylon.

A woman cradling an infant sat in a second-floor window in the middle of the block. The baby shrieked painfully, as if being assaulted. The mother spotted Mitchell and Jane and asked whether they had water or food to spare.

"I'm sorry," said Mitchell.

"God bless you anyway. Be careful out there."

They pushed their paddles hard into the water and glided away, as from another obstacle.

"That was hard," said Jane. Her face was polluted by black, greasy smudges—residue of the oil and sewage in the water. It was all over their hands, and she kept touching her face to pull back her hair. "But it was the right thing to do. Once we see a rescue worker, we can tell them about her."

He couldn't stop thinking about the scene they had witnessed on Madison. The men running through the street, smashing glass, bags of chips falling from their arms. In his futurist calculations he had always counted on bad things happening. But he hadn't considered the brutality of it, the primitive, selfish desperation that took hold when one's life was threatened. He pulled his oar out of the water. Then he started to paddle in reverse.

"What are you doing?" said Jane. The fear in her was strong, animal, instinctual. But she maintained her composure while Mitchell handed the woman a carton of animal crackers and lemon-lime Gatorade. When they set off again, her relentless spirit of denial cracked.

"I'm sorry. *That* was the right thing to do. I'm sick. What's wrong with me? I'm sick." She put the oar on her knees.

"Don't be sorry," said Mitchell. "Just look out for flotsam."

But she had frozen.

"Jane?"

They were drifting toward a floating skerry of flame. It had the circumference of a hula hoop. When Jane finally turned, black, greasy tears were sliding down her face.

"I can't do this," she said, shaking her head. "It's too horrible."

"Hey. Listen—"

"Why is this happening to us? A whole city . . ."

"Try not to think about it."

"All the destruction. The *death*. Everything is dead. This city is dead. It's a graveyard."

"If we think like that," he said, catching her eye, "we're going to run into something and the boat is going to flip. And then we'll really be in the shit."

"Right." She seemed uncertain. She seemed to be trying to convince herself of something. "Right."

The floating hula hoop of fire was drifting very close now. But if Jane felt the heat behind her back, she didn't show it.

"It's not just New York," she said. "It's like *I'm* being destroyed too. I know this sounds silly, but really, I never fantasized about being successful in Boston for crissakes, or Washington. What can you even *buy* in Boston?"

"The city will come back. This is temporary. Everything is temporary."

"Whenever you say something hopeful, it sounds like a curse. Nobody believes you. Lady Madeline didn't, Nybuster didn't, and I don't either."

"Just look out for flotsam, OK? *Flotsam*."

"Yeah." She tried to wipe away her tears, but she managed only to spread the grease in a horizontal streak across the bridge of her nose. "Flotsam."

He pulled hard to avoid the oil fire, and the boat disappeared into a cloud of acrid smoke.

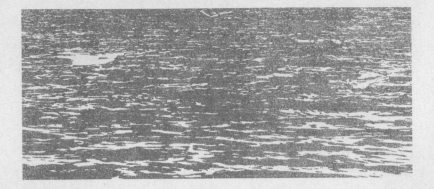

# 5.

*"Oh take me back to Elkhart Lake, where the cotton candy grows."*
*"POOF! POOF!"*
*"Where the little marshmallows hang from the trees—"*
*"SAY WHAT?"*
*"And the lollipops grow on the ground!"*
*"NO! NO!"*
*"YES! The LOLLI-pops grow on the GROUND GROUND*
*GROUND."*

The camp songs were Jane's idea. It seemed incongruous, if not shameful, to be singing about lollipops while mattresses and house pets and who knows what else floated by, but it worked. With Tammy's full horrors hidden from sight and their progress north unchecked, their immediate fear of disaster subsided and was replaced by a lightness that flirted with mania. Jane sang her choruses louder and louder in a desperate effort to dispel the sepulchral silence of Sutton Place.

*"POOF! POOF!"*

The day was becoming brighter too. The fog had diminished. The sleepy residential neighborhood had acquired a kind of diseased Venetian charm. The ornate battlements and bay windows of its town houses were reflected in jaundiced tints on the oil-streaked water. At the intersections, which had been most heavily exposed to the storm gusts coming off the East River, the trees that lined the avenue had been de-leaved, de-branched, even de-barked. All that remained were pitiful yellow stumps. On the west side of the street almost every window was gone; on the east side, leeward, they were mostly intact.

By Fifty-fourth Street they were seeing signs of life. In one window a fire burned wildly on a shag rug; next door a young boy ran in circles with a model airplane in his hand, making vrooming noises. Standing at the railing of a third-story balcony was an impossibly well-dressed young man. Pin-striped gray suit, royal-blue silk tie, a pink oxford with starched white lapels. His right hand dangled a cigar; the fingertips of his left encircled the rim of a snifter filled to overflowing with an emerald liquid. A golf club leaned against the wall beside a plastic bucket of white balls. His pose reflected an attitude of lethargy and casual refinement almost psychopathic in this context. But what would be sane in this context? Singing camp songs?

Just one thing about this man could not be reconciled. In place of shoes, he wore on his bare feet Kleenex boxes.

The slap of oars in the water shook the man from his reverie. He spun toward them.

"No," he said. "Nuh-uh." He stomped the length of the balcony, the Kleenex boxes trampling on broken glass. "What is this? Motherfucking *FutureWorld?* In a *boat?*"

Then Mitchell recognized him. They were too close now, Mitchell couldn't pretend not to see him. He pulled up alongside the building and the canoe came to a rest beneath the Kleenex-box-clad feet of young Ned Nybuster.

"A full-service operation," he was saying, giggling to himself. "FutureWorld to the rescue! But a motorboat might have been a better choice. I mean, if you're going to consider all the angles, all the *scenarios*, you're going to want a big, powerful engine"—his voice kept getting faster and quieter—"and maybe like a wedge to put on the front, and fishing rods and spears, or whatchucallem, harpoons like, rope of course, lots and lots of rope—"

"Not a good idea," said Jane under her voice.

"He's a client."

"Client of what? If you think we're still on the clock, you're even dumber than I thought. As of yesterday, the clock is broken. The clock drowned."

"Come to rescue me?" Nybuster peered down at them, a dark glint in his eye. "Guys?"

"We're just passing through," said Mitchell. He tried to lighten his tone. "On our way north."

"Funny thing. My father and his wife left for Long Island as soon as they heard about the storm. Course they didn't bother to inform me of their plans. All they did was leave a note."

Nybuster removed a balled-up paper from his pocket and spent a tedious minute unfolding it, flattening it, smoothing the creases. He cleared his throat and held the page at arm's length.

*"Junior,*
*Off to Montauk with Lori and kids.*
*Call when I can.*
*Feel free to avail yourself of the liquor in the library cabinet.*
*Dad"*

Nybuster started to snigger. "Please . . . avail yourself. *Avail* yourself!" He exploded into a bout of cruel, obscene laughter.

"Let's get out of here," whispered Jane. "He's wrecked and probably violent."

"Oh, I felt free, Zukor. Never felt freer, in fact. Took on the wine cellar first—the old French bottles. Now I'm working through the liquor, starting with the Benedictine. But please—be my guest. Would you like to avail yourself?"

"Thanks, Ned, but we have to be going. We'll send help as soon as we find someone."

"Hey, let me ask you something. Did you know how many different kinds of herbs and spices there are in a bottle of Benedictine?"

"I'm sorry, I don't even know what Benedictine—"

"Twenty-*seven*! But the identities of these herbs and spices are a secret. The only people who know the secret are the French monks who make the stuff." Nybuster stared, transfixed, into his snifter of green liquid, holding it up to the sun. It cast green flickers across his face. "It's a conspiracy."

"Well," said Mitchell. "Off we go."

"You know something about conspiracies, don't you?"

"No. Not really."

"I think one of those spices must be salt, because I'm thirsty. Do you have any water? In the fridge there's only green olives and Gruyère. I'll trade you a case of Benedictine or even cognac for a bottle of water. There's something here called Kelt Petra—is that OK? Or does the lady like champagne? I have regular and pink."

Jane glared at Mitchell.

"It's funny that in all our little catastrophe sessions, I never heard about a flood." Nybuster's eyes narrowed to coin slots, sharp and metallic. "*Never a flood*. Robot invasions, sure. An earthquake and a fleet of terrorists arriving from the sea armed with vials of bird flu. And the drought, Jesus—I have a lifetime supply of bottled water at the office, if it still exists. But if you're such a good prophet, why didn't you mention a flood?"

"I did."

"*No!*" he shouted, with surprising force. "Never a flood. I see it now, what you were after all along. You weren't trying to protect me. You were trying to disguise the disaster that you knew was coming."

"That's ridiculous."

"Mitchell," said Jane. "Mitchell, stop. He's baiting you."

It didn't matter. He would have his revenge. Nybuster was powerless over him now.

"It was during the natural disaster sequence," Mitchell said. "I talked about a hurricane-flood scenario. The worst case was a Category Four or Five headed straight into the New York Bight. Tammy's trajectory was dead-on, but it was only a high Category Three. It could have even been worse, especially given the rising sea levels—"

Nybuster waved him off, his drink splashing into the canoe. "Yeah, yeah, but why didn't you *emphasize?*"

"What do you mean? I did emphasize it." His face was hot.

"Whatever. Listen—you got any water?"

He was reminded of their very first meeting, Nybuster's lips closing around one grape and then the next, popping them off the vine, the juice splashing all over the white glass of the conference table. And those tiny water bottles, which he downed in a single gulp, then tossed to the floor.

"Mr. Nybuster," said Jane. "We really have to go."

"Why didn't you *emphasize*, Zukor?" Nybuster's voice started rising, herky-jerky, up the scale. "You thought you could keep this from me? I guess you figured you'd be the only one to know. And look at you now. You had a boat all ready. You knew this was coming—"

"And you said, if a flood came, you'd just get in your family helicopter and fly to your country house. Actually, the word you used was 'hop.' You'd *hop* over to Montauk."

"My father and his wife and their kids took the fucking helicopter!" It seemed that the glass would shatter in his fist. Then the cloud passed. Nybuster cracked his neck from side to side like a prizefighter right before the bell. "By the way, have you heard anything about Long Island? Is it flooding?"

"I haven't heard," said Mitchell. But he had seen the flood charts. During the 1992 nor'easter the ocean breached Westhampton Beach, creating a new inlet a quarter of a mile wide; sixty houses were destroyed, including one that was carried several hundred yards into the bay. Barring some unusual quirk of the storm winds, it was likely that Tammy had overridden Long Island at all its narrow points, turning the island into an archipelago. Montauk, at the far eastern end, was at the highest risk. Sandy Sherman's beachside house in Sagaponack might have washed away too, and for some reason this thought saddened Mitchell. He'd been given his start in that house, after all, speaking up at a meeting when he'd been too young and too stupid to know any better.

"Before you go," said Nybuster, "let me show you one thing." He tilted the remainder of his Benedictine over the edge of the balcony and dropped the glass into the water after it. Mitchell noticed streaks of black mud on Nybuster's suit jacket and on his bare ankles. Nybuster grabbed the golf club and pointed it at Mitchell. "You a golfing man?"

Nybuster cued the golf ball on the balcony and launched it. It screamed through the air, a rising line drive, flying through an empty window frame on the fifth floor of the building across the street. It ricocheted loudly off the walls and bounced out of a different window, plopping into the water below.

"Birdie!" Nybuster cried madly.

Jane grabbed the gunwales so hard it looked like her knuckles would pop. "Mitchell! This is preposterous. *Please*."

But he didn't want to go. Everything had become strange and he didn't want to miss what happened next. He was a spaceman encountering an alien landscape for the first time. Several hundred yards up Sutton Place a large segment of plaster wall drifted across the wide Fifty-seventh Street intersection. On this crumbling raft squatted three Siberian huskies. They hissed at their reflections in the water.

"You've always despised me," said Nybuster. "I could tell. Bright midwestern Jew, star of your rinky-dink suburban high school, come east to be a big man. But you never learned how the game is played. Numbers alone would take you through, that's what you hoped. But you're *weak*." He spat the word. "The ways of the world, of power—you don't understand them. You thought you could scare me with your ridiculous ghost stories. But you're the one who lives in constant fear, not me. I'll be fine even if this entire fucking city falls into the sea." His voice suddenly softened into a blandishment. But for Mitchell the spell was broken. He picked up the oar. "So why don't you just come up here, give me some of that water? I won't hurt you. Bring the girl. We'll have some fun, the three of us. Come just a little bit closer. I can pull you the rest of the way."

"Go!" said Mitchell, but Jane was already at it, spraying away. They plunged hard, plowing into the canal, a wake beginning to ripple behind them. Nybuster disappeared into the house, only to reemerge a few seconds later with his arm full of brown bottles. He threw a half-filled whiskey bottle first; it landed several feet from the boat, splashing them with water that was like cold grease. A wine bottle came next, hurtling directly at Jane's head, and Mitchell blocked it with the blade of his oar. Then a series of thumps, and golf balls were launched into the sky. He could hear them slicing through the air, but the angle was off and the balls crashed against the buildings across the street. When they were more than a block away, Nybuster finally put down his golf club. He stood with middle fingers extended as the canoe faded out of view.

Jane started laughing then—her unruly arpeggioed laughter, a laughter that climbed through the broken windows, kicked off its shoes, and danced in the abandoned rooms. She turned around to look at Mitchell. It was probably an effect of the grease, but her face was shining.

"*Poof!*" she said. "*Poof!*"

Nybuster was right. Living in fear was no kind of life. Not long ago—that very morning!—Mitchell had been weak. Soft fibered. Defeated every morning, defeated every night.

No more.

# 6.

"I haven't had these since I was ten," said Jane, her lovely, delicate teeth decapitating a tiger.

Mitchell's mouth was full of crackers so he could not immediately reply.

"Noah took two of every animal," he said at last. He reached into the box for another cracker. "So did I."

They had wedged themselves between the wide crowns of two oak trees near the northeastern corner of Central Park. Manhattan was narrower up here, the water deeper; Mitchell suspected that the Hudson River had flooded as well and the two rivers had converged in the middle, as in the era of the Lenape Indians. Branches poked from the water, their shredded leaves floating in the tide.

"FutureWorld," said Jane. "When it rains, it floods catastrophically."

"FutureWorld," said Mitchell. "Don't go with the flow."

"FutureWorld: when the going gets tough, the tough jump into a tie-dyed canoe like a couple of half-wits."

They were sitting at the height of nesting birds. Baffled sparrows pecked at the water and then hurried back to the treetops, cautious and uncertain. The trees along Fifth Avenue had served as a kind of filter—their branches were cluttered with garbage—but in the interior of the park the water was calm and unusually clear. You could follow the brown trunks down for several feet below the surface. This underwater forest had seemed a good place for a noontime snack, hidden away from the rest of the floating city. They'd removed their PFDs, and Mitchell took out his last box of animal crackers. As soon as he cracked the box, he realized he was starving.

"Another thing I've been meaning to ask you," said Jane. She took a rhinocerous and nibbled on its tusk.

Mitchell braced himself.

"Who's that?" She pointed to his T-shirt.

"Oh." He looked down. "It's an old shirt. I mean, high school old. His name is Leonardo Fibonacci. You know, the Fibonacci sequence?"

Jane laughed, shaking her head. "Ah. Good old Leonardo Fibonacci. I didn't know people silk-screened shirts with his face on it."

"*People* don't. But I did."

"This flood is making me bughouse crazy."

Jane's forehead was smudged black from the floodwater and her hair tangled in muddied clumps. But still her face retained its brightness. Even now, bedraggled and exhausted, the light was still on. Only twice, briefly—first when it seemed they were trapped in the apartment and later when they had passed the woman stranded with her infant—had the light gone out. He couldn't help his mind's eye from drifting back to the previous night. Her hair falling on his face like a caress, the action of her hips, her warm hands.

She was looking at him as if she'd read his mind.

"What happened last night," she said.

"Yes."

"It was an extreme situation."

"I know. This is an extreme situation too." He gestured at the tree canopies that boxed them in like a garden maze.

"Right," she said. "Exactly."

Mitchell fed a zebra into his mouth.

"I'm trying to say that I like you," she said. "A lot. And not just because today, well, I don't know any other way to say it: you probably saved my life. It's just that—"

"We're not out of the woods yet."

She laughed. "I do like you."

"Don't worry about it."

He actually felt relieved. Earlier that afternoon he'd prepared a little speech, explaining that he had no expectations. He was planning to say something like *It was a crazy night, but that's all it was, one night. Neither of us is exactly in a position to look for anything more . . . involving.*

Jane relaxed. "I'm glad we agree. You won't take it personally. Just as I won't take it personally. We can be friends and forget it ever happened."

Mitchell nodded and tried to smile. "Bowwoman and Sternman. Paddling to salvation."

Jane tossed her cracker box over the side of the canoe.

"I know—don't litter."

"You get a pass."

The box drifted into a small current that trailed between two leafy islands several dozen yards distant. Then, with a plop, it sank into the water—pulled under by something swimming there. But it seemed to have been rejected, for a few seconds later it bobbed back to the surface.

Jane shook her head. "The loss of life, the damage. It's incalculable."

"Don't think about it."

"That seems to be your approach—not thinking."

"I haven't figured out anything better."

"Maybe you should try."

"Maybe I will. Later."

"That's the thing—the scale is too great. It's impossible. We can only see what's immediately in front of us. It's difficult to imagine the next avenue, let alone the entire city. All the people."

"Most people were smart enough to evacuate," said Mitchell.

"Let's be wildly optimistic. Say ninety-nine percent evacuated. There are one million five hundred and eighty-five thousand people on the island of Manhattan. What's one percent of that? Fifteen thousand?"

"Fifteen thousand eight hundred and fifty."

"So fifteen thousand eight hundred and fifty people didn't get out."

Mitchell didn't know what to say. Bubbles rose to the surface several feet from the canoe, gurgling loudly.

"Not to mention the museums, the libraries, the theaters."

"The big ones will be safe. They were built on rock, Manhattan schist. The museum founders thought about floods. So did the rich, who built their mansions on Fifth Avenue—as far away as possible from both rivers. High ground. The central library stands on the side of a hill, eighty feet above sea level."

"Grand Central was flooded."

"It's all rock: limestone, marble, granite. It'll be fine." He was not going to mention the bodies. Maybe not ever, to anyone.

"What about the United Nations? That's right on the river."

"The UN is in trouble. It was built on land twelve feet *below* sea level."

"So the Secretariat Building is a fish tank now."

"It's a sunken ship in the East River."

"Maybe the very unreality of it all is what's making me come back again and again to the same terrible thought. I just can't shake it."

"That you're just happy to be alive?"

"Yes," said Jane. "That is nice, of course. But that's not it."

"You can say it."

She paused, trying to find the right words. "I suppose it's something like this: if the storm was so horrific, then why is everything now so beautiful?"

As if on cue, a large black bird swooped over their heads, so low that the water rippled beneath its rush. The crow shrieked as it flew past and landed on a branch several yards away from them. It perched there unsteadily, maneuvering for balance, its talons scratching the bark, its vast wings beating several times in quick succession. Finally it settled. Slowly, with a regal, almost contemptuous motion, it rotated its head to examine the two figures sitting in the garishly stippled canoe. Mitchell and Jane watched in awe. No doubt perturbed by the sight of such large creatures so high in the sky, the crow sprang from the branch with a loud clap of its wings. They watched it soar in the direction of New Jersey.

"Was that beautiful?" said Mitchell. "Or horrible?"

They put on their PFDs, snatched up their oars, and resumed paddling. The fog had lifted and the air was clear, if not particularly fresh. The flooding wasn't as severe once they got north of the park, since the elevation was higher. Harlem was empty and still. There were times when, the water depth having dropped enough that the hull began to scratch the pavement, they had to get out of the canoe and walk alongside it for a block or two, but they never ran aground. Their voyage had settled into a routine; there were no imminent threats to their safety and yet the spookiness never entirely dissipated. The cloudless sky seemed a kind of madness after the storm. But it wasn't until they got to 135th Street that he realized what was unsettling him.

Déjà vu. Of course he'd never seen before anything like a flooded city. But now the blueness of sky, the bright cobalt blueness . . . He stared at the place where the buildings touched the still floodwater. It was difficult to tell exactly at what point the buildings stopped and their reflections began. The buildings might have continued forever in either direction.

It was his skycity. In his dreams what he had thought to be an infinite city, floating in space, was in fact a flooded New York. The sun was unusually bright because it bounced off the glassy surface of the water. If he fell from his tower, as in his dreams he often feared, he wouldn't plunge forever, like Alice in the rabbit hole. He'd splash into the water. Maybe the reason the sky was so blue was because the rains had ended. All the filth of the world—its parasites and disease and wormlike anxieties—had been wiped away, just like the bacterial sludge on his living room window. His skycity had been rinsed by the flood. And what a glorious place it was.

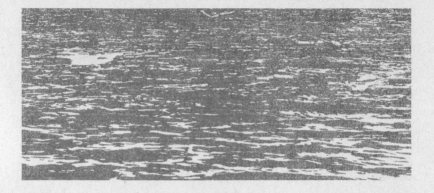

# 7.

He was in no kind of physical shape, but as the day had progressed, he felt stronger. He looked forward to the challenge of crossing the Hudson—a true test of his sternman prowess. He began estimating the velocity of the Hudson's current, the angle at which he should direct the Pyscho Canoe, the distance between the shores.

But he never had the opportunity. As they turned onto Fort Washington Avenue, Jane gave a celebratory whoop, startling him from his calculations. Amid aid tents and portable toilets, a crowd of flood refugees stood around the edge of Bennett Park. They regarded Mitchell's canoe perplexedly but quickly lost interest. After all they'd seen in the past twenty-four hours, what was a tie-dyed canoe?

An aid worker ran to meet them, taking pulses and checking temperatures before they could even step out of the boat. As soon as they were on solid ground Jane pushed past the worker and jumped into Mitchell's surprised arms.

She kissed him greasily on the cheek, then withdrew so she could look him in the eye. "That was courageous. You're the best sternman a bowwoman could ever hope for."

Mitchell hugged her back. From spending all day in the canoe, he was uneasy on his feet. He clung to her like an invalid. He shut his eyes tight, and when he opened them, everything was blurry. For a moment he felt as if the canoe had capsized and they were now sinking underwater.

There was nothing to do with the Psycho but abandon it. He dragged it under a tree and turned it upside down, leaving the paddles and orange PFDs beneath it so that someone else in need could use it. Then he walked away. He wasn't sad to leave the Psycho behind. In fact he hoped never to see it again for the rest of his life.

A makeshift terminal had been established beneath the George Washington Bridge. Shell-shocked refugees were ferried across the river to New Jersey, where a shuttle ran them to Fort Lee High School. From there government-commandeered buses left every few hours, headed across the country in all directions: Los Angeles, San Francisco, Miami, Houston, and Portland, Maine. The country's second cities were preparing to receive the humbled New Yorkers.

In the mobbed gymnasium of Fort Lee High School Mitchell and Jane registered at an information desk and filled out Red Cross questionnaires. Mitchell wrote down the locations of Ned Nybuster, the wailing man, and the woman with the infant. They were given water bottles and cheese sandwiches and told to find a place on the floor. After seeing next to no one all day in the abandoned city, it was overwhelming to smell, hear, and see so many people packed into a single room. Laughter, bawling, manic ranting, furtive mumbles, and the now-familiar scent of dried sewage water, obscene body odor, urine, old sweat—too much too soon.

"You going to Kansas City?" said Jane.

He honestly hadn't thought about it. "We'd be on the same bus, right? Are you going back to Chicago?"

"Winnetka, you mean?" She shook her head. "Here's the thing you have to understand about my parents. I'm the first person from my high school ever to attend Princeton. Then I was accepted at Wharton and finally hired for a high-paying job at a financial firm. I earn enough that I start saving to buy my own Manhattan apartment. But every time we talk, my parents ask me when I'm going to do something with my life. Why can't I be like my sisters—all of them married, all of them pregnant. Perpetually. Perpetually pregnant, like feral dogs in heat. Two of them are younger than me. You know what else they ask me, my parents? They ask me when I'm going to make them proud."

"So which bus are you going to take?"

"None of them, if I can help it. I'll wait until the water subsides. It can't be more than a week or two, right? New York is where I always wanted to be. I don't think that will change. The city is invincible."

"You still believe that?"

"You'll see. It'll come back. You said so yourself. It always has. I don't want to go so far away that I can't return."

It occurred to Mitchell that Jane might be right in the short term—New York would come back, certainly Manhattan and perhaps certain swaths of Brooklyn. But what about the long term? For the long term was now upon them. According to the scientists, these would become the presiding conditions. Over the next years and decades, things would not be as before. Things would be, for starters, a lot wetter. The floods would keep coming, more and more frequently. Soon the coastal cities would lose the will to rebuild the old seawalls and levees. No one would have to pay to hear about worst-case scenarios—they'd be living them, night and day. The future would vanish as a preoccupation; the present would consume man's full energies. The nation's money and power would gradually transfer to the largest inland cities. Chicago, Dallas, Atlanta—even Kansas City—ascendant. Miami, San Francisco, New Orleans, Houston: drowning. Or would the major cities retreat inland? Boston to Worcester? Los Angeles to Orange County? Invincible New York would persist, but it would be rebuilt as a canal city. Amsterdam on the Hudson. Amsterdam *in* the Hudson. Boats instead of cars. Canoes instead of bicycles. In a floating world, Sternman would be king.

Cell service was still out, so they took turns waiting in line to use a public phone. After nearly two hours Mitchell was finally able to call his parents. His mother gasped when she heard his voice. She was too overcome to speak so she handed the phone to Tibor.

"Mitchell! Very good. Very, very good to hear your voice. We've been calling your phone every second the last two days."

"I'm OK, Dad."

"We were worried. But then I thought to myself, you know what the Lion King says."

"'I laugh in the face of danger.'"

"That's my son!"

Mitchell could hear his mother sobbing hysterically in the background.

"Your room is all ready for you," said Tibor. "And the Zukorminiums—well, the business could always use a smart young executive with big-city know-how. I have an office space for such an executive. Should one day he happen to appear on my doorstep."

His mother grabbed the phone. "Honey, you do whatever you want to do. You're welcome to stay with us as long as you want, of course. But you make your own decisions."

"Rikki," said Tibor, warning her.

"Your son is grown. It's not for us to say what he should do.

Mitchell, just because of this disaster you don't need to change who you are."

But the storm had already changed who he was. He hung up and, despite the groans of irritation from the people behind him, dialed his voice mail and punched in his passwords. He deleted the twelve messages from his parents and skipped five messages from Charnoble—he didn't have the patience just now—before arriving at a recording from a man whose voice he didn't recognize. The man sounded confused, and he kept trailing off; Mitchell could make out only the words "Billy," "attack," and "sealed," and he would have assumed it was a wrong number if he hadn't heard, at the very end, another word: "Bruner." He pressed the phone hard into his ear and replayed the message:

"Hey. I'm calling for a Mitchell Zukor? This is Billy. Elsa's boy-friend. Well she's still sleeping, but they let us move her back to the infirmary at Ticonderoga. When we were moving her be-longings from her old room, I found a note. It said that if any-thing happened to her—like an attack, actually she specified another attack—that I should give you this other letter she wrote. It's in a sealed envelope. So: I wondered where I should send it? My phone number is 207-685-4441. Again, this is about Elsa. Elsa Bruner.

"Also, man? If you need a place to stay. You know, with the flood? We've got plenty of space now, unfortunately. So. This is Billy—"

He found Jane. She was defending a few square feet of floor against a woman who kept trying to insert her child into the space where Mitchell had been sitting. The woman was using her elbows and her knees.

Mitchell didn't bother to sit down.

"You can't stay here."

Jane narrowed her eyes.

"You should come with me," said Mitchell. "We'll tough it out together."

"In Kansas City? I don't think so. That's a bit too close for comfort. I can already see my folks driving down from Winnetka to pick me up. No way. I can't go back to the Midwest."

"We're not going to the Midwest," said Mitchell. "We're going north."

# Part Three

*There's no such thing as courage. There's only fear. A fear of getting hurt and a fear of dying. That's why the human race has lasted so long.*
                                        —DAVID GOODIS

## Future Days

——

# I.

"It's just ridiculous." Jane was getting worked up, her grimy hair dangling across her cheek. "You don't owe her anything."

"Just want to visit her."

"Why?"

"To see what she built. I want to see what she was so proud of. This farm, this life that made her feel safe. Despite everything."

He wasn't being entirely honest, and Jane seemed to know it. Of course, he wanted a chance to talk to her, but even if she were still in her blind limbo, a million miles from Earth, maybe it would be enough just to see her. Maybe it would be enough just to take her hand in his own.

Jane was giving him one of her death stares.

"Besides," he said, in a brusque tone that he did not himself recognize, "there's a letter."

"What kind of letter?"

"I don't know. It's waiting for me."

"That's really wonderful. But I don't see why I need to come along for the tearful reunion."

"I want to go, but not alone. I don't know another way to say it."

"Mm."

"Look," he said, "what happens if they close this center down tomorrow? Would you rather go back to Winnetka?"

"That's your most logical argument yet," she said. "But it's not going to happen."

They were jolted by a loud electronic trill. It was the first time in two days that they'd heard the sound of a machine. The woman beside them leaped to her feet. Like a soldier checking himself after an explosion to make sure all his body parts were intact, she patted herself down and located the ringing phone in her jacket pocket.

The signal had been restored. It was the first service to come back, before running water and hospitals and even dry ground—the cellular towers and their omnipenetrative electromagnetic fields. Mitchell could feel the electric current zipping through his temporal lobes.

"I have seven messages from Charnoble," said Jane after listening to her voice mail. "They're all for you."

A generator was activated, and a television screen that had been rolled into a corner of the gymnasium zapped on. The national news aired hallucinatory images of flooded New York. A traffic light bent like a cheap spoon. A frenzied school of orange carp fed on the torn garbage bags outside a half-submerged Chinese restaurant on First Avenue. A Gramercy Park brownstone had caught on fire; because the adjacent buildings had crumbled, the brownstone appeared to be standing alone in the water, a fiery monolith. And finally the watery outlines of bodies floating like lily pads on Second Avenue. Mitchell looked away.

He turned on his portable and listened to the messages he had skipped earlier at the public phone. The first three were from Charnoble. A frightening urgency distorted his voice. Charnoble had checked the FEMA website and seen that Mitchell had registered at the Fort Lee relief center.

"Mitchell!" said Charnoble. "I am *so* pleased you've survived."

He explained that FutureWorld was the only consulting firm to have predicted the flood. Word had gotten out—Jason Tanizaki at Lady Madeline had talked to a reporter from *Forbes*, and now it was everywhere. "I've been getting calls all day. Everyone wants to talk to you. Mr. Brumley and even old Mr. Sansome have called me personally. So have cable news, networks, websites. They want to talk to the man they're calling the Prophet."

There were several more like this, interspersed with increasingly frantic messages from his parents and several from college friends he hadn't seen since graduation. One, who reminded Mitchell that they had sat next to each other in Sputnik for Nudniks on the day of the Seattle earthquake, was now a journalist; he had been assigned to write a feature about Mitchell for *The Wall Street Journal*. There was a final message from Charnoble. "This is big," he said. "This is mega. FutureWorld is going mega." Mitchell thought of megaton nuclear bombs. When he was standing on Beekman Street—the wind crushing umbrellas and hurling them into buildings, the rain like falling ice picks, the security guard's tired, terrified eyes—Charnoble must have been scurrying to a secure location. The coward was probably in the company car, escaping, at the very moment he'd called Mitchell.

"What does that monster want?" said Jane.

She had just spoken with her mother and stepfather. The conversation seemed to have exhausted her. At the beginning of the call she had tried to sound calm, reassuring, but after a few minutes she hung up in exasperation. Just the sound of Winnetka was enough to make her skin pucker.

"They're reporting that FutureWorld is the only firm to have predicted the flood," said Mitchell.

"That's right. We were. You were."

"Charnoble wants me to do interviews. Though I don't see why I should help him at this point."

"But the flood scenario—you came up with it yourself. Charnoble doesn't deserve the credit."

"They'll lose interest soon. They've got more important things to cover than some consulting firm's predictions about things that have already happened."

Jane wasn't listening anymore.

"What," said Mitchell. "What is it now?"

She was staring at the television, her mouth open. Mitchell turned.

A patrol boat was ferrying patients from New York Hospital up the East River to the Bronx. Semiconscious bodies doubled over the railing; others lay sprawled on the deck. They had wild eyes and gaping mouths, like astonished fish heaving on the bottom of a fishing boat.

"Exactly. They don't have time for FutureWorld when this kind of thing—"

"No," said Jane, impatient. "Read the crawl!"

Squinting, he focused on the text scrolling beneath the images: *". . . Zukor, a consultant at the firm, the only financial analyst to have foreseen the tragedy . . ."*

"Jesus King," said Jane. "No wonder Charnoble wants you to call."

Mitchell's phone started to ring. It was an unlisted number. When he picked up, the caller introduced himself as a producer from the *Morning Show.*

"Morning, like top of the *morning*?" said Mitchell. "Or mourning, like *mourning* an unspeakable tragedy."

Jane gestured at him frantically. "Tell them you'll call back."

Mitchell hung up.

"Let's think about this," she said. *"Strategize."*

"There's nothing to think about. I'm not going to shill for FutureWorld."

"No," said Jane. "You should talk to them."

Mitchell's phone buzzed again, a different number. They stared at it. Mitchell pressed REJECT INCOMING CALL.

"Look, Charnoble sent you out in the hurricane too," said Mitchell. "Just so you could make him a few extra consulting dollars. We might have died back there. We *should* have died. By all odds."

"That's just it. You do the interviews, but only on one condition: they don't credit FutureWorld."

"What would it say under my name—freelance consultant? What's the point?"

"It doesn't say freelance consultant. It says 'Founder and Director, Future Days.'"

"Future Days?"

"Your new consulting firm."

"*Hold* on."

"You were the soul of FutureWorld. Charnoble was just an administrator, a scheduler. Brumley was the money behind the whole operation—and it was their idea anyway. But you've been devising worst-case scenarios since you were a kid. *You're* the talent."

"No way. I appreciate the thought. But I'm not interested."

"Every scenario we presented to our clients, you created. You did the research. Most important, you were the one who scared the bejesus out of all those Nybusters we met with."

"Thanks. You were pretty scary yourself."

"Glad you think so. Because now that you're the director of Future Days, I was hoping you might consider hiring a number two."

"Have you been plotting this?"

"*Plotting* sounds devious. But yeah, I've been planning some future scenarios myself the last couple of days. Mitchell, the money is going to be flooding in."

He raised his eyebrows.

"In a manner of speaking," said Jane. "Look, you deserve this. Now's the time to move. It's a new market. We could make serious, *consequential* money. For you, frankly, the flood is a best-case scenario."

"Listen to yourself. You sound like Alec."

"Alec had his points. He was a good salesman, at least. He knew how to turn fear into capital."

"Mm."

"We might as well make the best of a bad situation, right?"

There was a heightened mania in her eyes. Passionate Jane had seized on another passion. She was like a puppy with a new toy clenched between her teeth. Mitchell remembered how she looked in Central Park, dancing when the storm broke, the rain bouncing off her exposed neck, her hair in wild tendrils, giddy and free.

"I can't think about this now," he said. "It's too soon."

"If we wait much longer, other people, other firms, will jump in. You know Brumley will."

Mitchell thought of his father, gaping in awe of the high business machinery of New York City. The moral of the Hungarian Revolution: Greed is Good.

His phone rang. Jane tried to read the number that popped up on his display.

"Television calling?"

It was Anchor Liberty, a FutureWorld client. Mitchell plugged in his earphones and connected.

"Zukor, thank God." It was Harold Harding, the investment firm's boss. "You're alive."

"Mr. Harding? I showed up yesterday morning for our appointment, but the building was closed. The security guard didn't let me in."

Jane tapped Mitchell on the shoulder, indicating that she wanted to listen to the conversation. She nudged close to him, and he handed her one of his earbuds.

"Yesterday morning?" said Harding. "You mean the morning Tammy hit? You're goddamned right it was closed."

"Oh. Sure."

"We assumed you left once the storm started bearing down. Why, we were following the directions you gave us yourself."

"I suppose Alec wanted us to be sure—"

"Charnoble! He made you stay? I never trusted the guy. You, I've always respected. Always thought you had a real ability. You know that."

"Yes sir."

Jane, next to him, was smiling.

"But he forbade you from leaving the city," said Harding, incredulous. "He made you go against your own recommendations? Frankly I'm stunned."

"I'm stunned myself. I'm still in a state of stun."

"We evacuated all our employees in time—not just the Manhattan office but also Fairfield. Followed your scenario to the letter. Everyone with an Anchor Liberty Go Bag. They avoided the traffic too, sticking to your escape routes."

"They took Tenth Avenue, then?"

"Tenth to Amsterdam to the 181st Street bridge."

"So it worked. I'm glad to hear it."

"A bonus will be arriving with the first mail. Count on that. And now I see you're some kind of national celebrity. Well, this has been a nightmare, a hell of a nightmare. But we're grateful to have had your wisdom guiding us through."

"See what I mean?" said Jane, after Mitchell disconnected. "They depend on you now."

"It's not a bad idea."

"There's a logic to it, right?" she asked. "A *logic*, no?"

"Yes," he said, humoring her. "I see the logic. But how? We have nothing. We might not even have access to our apartments or the office for weeks."

"That's my job. All we need is our clients' information, and I have that on my phone. They know you're more valuable than Charnoble. We'll call Anchor Liberty and Lady Madeline and a few other firms right away—those contracts will stake us while we develop our business plan. Especially since you'll be able to bill more than FutureWorld. A lot more."

"Future Days, huh?"

"It has a certain ring. If I don't say so myself."

"We'll need a financial team, office space, a marketing strategy."

"There are profits to be made," said Jane, "in being prophets."

"Yep. Got it. But first I'm going to Maine."

Jane cocked her head, as if he had suddenly started speaking Farsi.

"All right, how's this," said Mitchell. "Come with me, and we'll sort out the details of Future Days on the way."

The phone rang, another unlisted number.

"Let me take it."

Mitchell handed Jane his phone.

"I'm his representative," she said. "Only on one condition," she said. "Future Days," she said. "Founder and director."

Jane hung up.

"This," she said, "is going to be mega."

# 2.

In the ziplock bag the bills had thawed and were lightly perspiring. But he hadn't needed them yet. All bus and train transit had been government commandeered. The refugees received frequent handouts: sandwiches, bananas, Jell-O cartons, phone chargers, water bottles. There were no longer any shortcuts out of the city. They had to follow the masses; they had to ride the motorcoach. Traveling so slowly was exhausting. They might have made it more quickly on foot. The highways had been transformed into parking lots, shrouded in clouds of exhaust. But it wasn't just the roads that were crowded; the cars were packed too, crammed full of possessions that had been accumulated over lifetimes. Save two of everything, so that they can replicate in the new world: two flatscreens, two laptops, two gaming consoles.

In the torn-up fields beside the interstate, sinuous white vapor rose like smoke in the wake of an explosion. Tammy had spent the greatest portion of her rage on New York and had weakened once she reached Connecticut, but not considerably. The earth had still been scoured, as by a vast cloud of steel wool. And the road itself was an obstacle course: car crush-ups, roadkill, fallen trees. It took half a day just to reach the Rhode Island state line. Every few hours Mitchell tried to call Billy, but there was not even a ring signal, just an empty, scratchy noise, the sound of a record that keeps spinning after the side is over. The Ticonderoga phone, or the wires, seemed to be dead. Anything that was frail before the storm was now dead.

When television or radio producers called, Jane answered his phone. She introduced herself as Mitchell Zukor's publicist. She coached Mitchell to speak with humility and formality, and she limited interviews to five minutes. When newspaper and magazine journalists called, Jane introduced herself as Mitchell Zukor's spokeswoman. She did those interviews herself.

"This is just the very beginning," said Jane. "Keep them wanting more."

At one point in almost every conversation he was asked, "What's going to happen next? To New York, to America, to the world?"

"That information," said Mitchell, "we reserve for our clients."

Nobody on the bus paid them any attention.

After midnight the driver pulled over at a turnpike motel in Warwick, where power and electricity had been restored. Mitchell and Jane were given a room with a queen-size bed, dingy yellow carpeting, fluorescent lighting, and a dense cigarette aroma with a urine finish. The bus would leave again in less than six hours. When Mitchell entered the bathroom he was surprised by his reflection. The face in the mirror looked unhappy. In fact the face was giving a very strong suggestion of tears.

Mitchell dumped his sewage-stained clothes into the bathtub: slacks, Leonardo Fibonacci T-shirt, socks, even the boots. He emptied the contents of his Go Bag onto the sink counter—opening the ziplock bag to let the bills air—and then tossed his backpack into the tub as well. He twisted the hot faucet as far as it could go. When the water hit the clothes it released a metallic smell that thickened into something raunchy, animalistic. Mitchell squeezed the microbottle of courtesy shampoo into the tub. He tore open the microbar of courtesy soap and scrubbed at his shirt, trying not to let the blackening water splash on his naked body. But it couldn't be helped. The stray drops left blue stains on his flesh. Mitchell let the tub drain, then refilled it. This time he emptied the microbottle of courtesy conditioner; it bubbled into an ashy foam. After thirty minutes the clothes, while not clean by any measure, had at least regained their original hues. He hung them on the towel rack and, with the last butter pat of soap, took a shower. When he came out of the bathroom Jane was asleep under the covers, in her clothes.

At rest stops, fast-food chains donated value meals. The bus passengers, blandly dipping their french fries into ketchup splats, didn't speak very much. For Jane, revived by three cups of coffee, the long silences were maddening, a source of stress. She filled the vacuum with talk about her mother in Winnetka, a fastidious woman who forbade Jane from playing in the sandbox.

"Fear of germs," she said. "When I came home from school I had to scrub my hands twice with soap and hot water. My little washerwoman hands, raw and red."

"You didn't get sick, though, did you?"

"That wasn't the end of it—after the soap and hot water she sprayed me with disinfectant. Of course it didn't really matter if my hands were dirty because everything was covered in vinyl. Slips over the furniture. But I did get sick. Often."

"Because you cheated. You told her you'd washed your hands when you hadn't."

"No—because I *didn't* cheat. That was the problem. I never built up a proper immune system. When I was given the chicken pox vaccine, I actually contracted full-blown chicken pox. The infectious disease specialist at Skokie Hospital said mine was the first case in Chicagoland in a decade."

The shoulders on I-95 were plugged with cars. Many people had run out of gas; others had given up and, in some cases, pitched tents in the median, waiting for the traffic to subside. The exhaust was so dense on the road that it seeped into the bus's air circulation system. It thickened into a large pillow, and the pillow pressed into Mitchell's face, stopping his breath. He felt like he was being asphyxiated and he was only surprised that nobody else seemed affected by the recirculating exhaust—nobody was passing out or keeling over in the aisles. Nobody on the bus, in fact, was doing much of anything. The traffic, or traumatic shock, or just pure exhaustion had left the refugees in a narcotized stupor. They leaned against each other to sleep, or stared out the windows with expressions of horror and wonderment, preparing, perhaps, for the next crisis.

At the New Hampshire border, Jane began calling Future-World clients to introduce them to Future Days. The clients had heard Mitchell's voice on television and radio, had seen the *Wall Street Journal* piece. Charnoble's messages and e-mails, frantic coming on enraged, went unreturned.

But Jane's constant phone chatter, her interviews and her repeated pitch to the FutureWorld clients she was busily poaching, finally became too much. Mitchell took the phone from her hand and turned it off.

"Why'd you do that?" She looked wounded.

"Let's take a break."

Jane sighed. "I suppose I was getting a little carried away. It's just . . . incredible. How things can turn."

"What do you mean?"

"A year ago today I was at Lippincott Library doing research for my thesis."

"A day ago you were an analyst. Now you're a mogul."

"It's been a long day."

She needed to talk, needed chatter. It was almost a compulsion with her. The phone calls to clients were as much a manifestation of nervous energy as shrewd business planning. He couldn't fault her. Set adrift, in a bus headed into unknown territory, it helped to grasp onto something familiar. Besides, he was responsible, after all, for the mess they were in.

That was the one thing unspoken between them. He should have told her to leave the city as soon as the storm came. But he had said no such thing. He did the opposite, in fact: when she asked him to wait for her, he had agreed. Very well, but—let's be honest now—he wasn't just being timid, or thoughtless, or kind. He was succumbing to a different voice, a whispering voice inside his own head. It was a reasonable, patient voice. It said, if he had to be trapped in this hurricane, wouldn't it be nice to be trapped with Jane Eppler?

"And a year from now?" he said.

"Future Days signs its one hundredth client? Two hundredth?"

The bus passed over Memorial Bridge. A sign showing a church steeple in front of brown mountains announced LEAVING NEW HAMPSHIRE: LIVE FREE OR DIE. They passed beneath a sad, crooked pine tree, its crown bent like the head of a man whose neck has been snapped. Another sign said WELCOME TO MAINE: VACATIONLAND.

The traffic slowed to a stop. A hundred yards distant, the interstate passed over what had been, at normal water levels, a marina. The flood had receded, but the boats were stuck on the shore, in trees. A motorboat sat jackknifed across the shoulder, blocking two lanes.

And then he couldn't think any longer—not a *single second longer*—about Jane or her business plan for Future Days or the horrors they had left behind. For up ahead, on the horizon, loomed

Elsa Bruner. And if she were hurtling ever farther into outer space—past constellations and galaxies, pulled by some dark energy, flying faster and faster to the outer reaches of the universe—then she was also becoming larger, vaster, boundless even, drawing into herself all his fears but reflecting nothing.

▣ ▣ ▣

Portland, though structurally sound, was still damp; the streets shone like black ice. The government booked them into the Eastland Park, a towering 1930s-era redbrick hotel with a grand lobby lit by dim electric candlesticks. The bellhops wore pillbox caps and blazers with brass buttons. Nobody appeared to be staying there besides the bussed-in flood refugees, whose numbers had depleted with every stop after Lowell, Massachusetts. Even Portlanders had fled the storm, headed farther north, into the woods—to Aroostook County, Quebec, Prince Edward Island.

The double room granted to Jane and Mitchell was trying badly to be something it was not. There was a divan upholstered in apricot plush, a crimson-and-yellow-checkered marble table, an oval mirror squatting on curved cane legs. The sense of disorientation was extreme. It wasn't only that they were in an unfamiliar place; it was another era, an alternate universe. There was a television, but it didn't work. They had to lie in separate beds, as in a black-and-white movie. Perhaps it was better this way. No missed signals, no ambiguity. Safe.

After the lights went out, just as Mitchell was falling asleep, Jane rose. She stepped over to his bed and lifted his blanket.

"Hi," she said.

"Hi," he said.

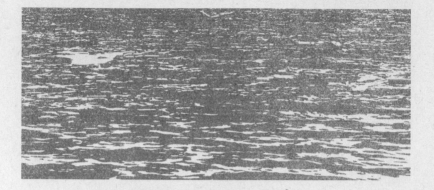

# 3.

This time, to his surprise, he actually got a ringtone. Then the machine answered. Billy's voice had a distant, befuddled quality, as if he had been awakened in the middle of a dream.

> "I'm afraid . . . I'm sorry. This is Billy, from Camp Ticonderoga. I'm afraid that we are not able to offer positions—bunks, or, I mean, shelter and food or . . . water to any more refugees from Tammy. I'm sorry. It's just that we're out of space. We ask you please. We have heard that other camps have been set up in Augusta and Bangor and the north country. But we're overwhelmed. I—I'm sorry."

An automated voice interrupted to tell Mitchell he could not leave a message because the mailbox was full.

The bus departed Portland at eight in the morning, destination Montreal. It was suddenly full summer again, indigo sky, the windows hot to the touch and fogging from the refrigerated air. Mitchell and Jane were the only passengers to debark at Augusta

State Airport, which doubled as the Augusta bus station. There were no airplanes in sight. The terminal was closed. The only vehicle on the runway was a brown station wagon. Its side was crosshatched with scrape marks.

The door to the station wagon opened and a freckled, large-limbed woman clumped out. She wore a baseball hat that struggled to stay perched above her cloud—a feathery, cumulonimbus cloud—of bottle-brown hair. Her face was abnormally tall and creased, a billowing sail of a face. Across her T-shirt was written, in shaky letters, GENUIS.

"You need a ride?"

"Are you a livery driver?" asked Jane.

"I'm Judy. From two ten Winthrop Street." She pointed at a row of houses several hundred yards away. "But I'm afraid that will have to do."

"Can you take us to Starling?"

"Let me guess: Camp Ticonderoga."

"You know it?"

She chuckled, shaking her head. "I've been running people the last two days. Desperate people."

Mitchell pretended not to notice Jane's death stare.

"I can take you as far as Kents Hill," said Judy. "That's under two miles from the camp. Then you'll be on your own. I'm not going any deeper."

What else could they do? They got into the station wagon. It had a warm smell, burnt wood and burnt cigarettes. The interior paneling was simulated wood grain. Judy removed a copy of that morning's *Kennebec Journal* from the passenger seat to make room for Mitchell. He caught the headline: TAMMY WAVE CRASHES ON CENTRAL MAINE. There was a photograph of flood refugees lined up in a tent city that had been erected in downtown Augusta by the local chapter of the Elks Lodge.

"Going rate's fifty bucks," said Judy. "Can you pull it?"

"Yes," said Mitchell, glancing at his Go Bag. After paying for snacks at the vending machine in the Eastland Park lobby, his cash supply was down to $51,996.50. "I can pull it."

Judy sped off the runway and turned onto Winthrop. They passed graveyards.

"Why won't you go any farther than Kents Hill?" asked Jane.

Judy caught Jane's eyes in the rearview mirror. "You never know what happens when you throw a bunch of city people into the woods. They can lose their bearing." Judy was withholding information—there was a dark suggestion on her face as she turned back to the road. Mitchell was relieved that Jane, in the backseat, didn't catch it. Otherwise she would have asked Judy to elaborate. And that would have only created more problems. They had already escaped from Hell. It was difficult to imagine that whatever awaited them in Starling could compare with the floating children's books, cats, corpses. Besides, if Elsa was in some sort of danger, he owed it—to himself, if not to her—to help. And what secrets would be revealed in her letter to him?

"I have nothing against the hippies," Judy continued. "Heck, I'll admit it, I even went in eighty-eight to see the Grateful Dead play at Oxford Plains Speedway. But there's a hundred miles between talking about the land and living on it."

Augusta gave way to apple orchards and blueberry fields, which yielded to forest. After twenty minutes they reached a fork in the road. Judy stopped the car.

"You have second thoughts," she said, "call me."

She tore off the front page of the *Kennebec Journal* and scrawled her phone number.

"I'll take that." Jane reached over the seat to snatch the paper from Judy's fingers. She folded it carefully into her wallet. When she looked up, Mitchell was staring at her.

"I just don't want it to get lost," said Jane. She hiccuped.

Judy drove right at the fork. Mitchell and Jane went left onto a dirt road, where they were greeted by a porcupine.

◻ ◻ ◻

Jane gasped when she saw it, the clumsy black beast with little swords protruding from its swaying haunch.

"After all we've been through," said Mitchell, "this scares you?"

She started laughing. Then, in the space of another hiccup, she was crying.

"Jane?"

She looked down, her hand over her eyes, and the sob passed. After a brisk shake of her head she looked up. Her smile was bright, if insincere. She wiped her eyes.

"Sorry." She cleared her throat. "That happens sometimes."

Who was this woman? Had they met?

"Anyway. I'm not *scared* of him." She indicated the porcupine, who watched from behind a bush. "But why isn't he scared of us? Aren't animals supposed to run away when they see people? It's like he owns the place."

"By rights he does. You can tell from the way he's marked the turf."

His hand on her shoulder, Mitchell guided Jane around a sturdy stack of porcupine feces.

"That's why I moved to New York," she said.

"To avoid porcupines."

"I like my nature domesticated, housebroken, manicured, neutered, fearful. I take that back. I don't like nature at all. I like buildings and cement and electrical wires. *Love* them. I'd kill for a nice flat stretch of pavement right now. A stoplight. Those little green gates they put around every single tree on the sidewalk." Jane sniffled one more time and wiped away the last of her tears.

So this was Maine. The air actually did smell like taxicab pine fresheners. Only it was fuller, deeper, rich with wet dirt.

"Listen, Mitchell." She gave him a sharp look. "I wasn't very sensitive back in Fort Lee. I'm sorry. I know this matters."

"I was going to drag you along with me one way or another. I just didn't realize I'd have to go so far as create a new business."

"No, that's not enough. Your sense of loyalty to this girl is impressive. Crazy, definitely. But I respect it. And I'm not just saying that as your new deputy at Future Days. Or because you saved my behind in the storm. I'm saying it as a friend."

"That isn't necessary."

"I mean it."

The road became muddier, sucking at their sneakers. The forest on both sides became thicker. It was choked with gigantic floppy ferns the size of elephant ears, black spruce, and tall firs, their needles shivering with insects.

"I'm not sure what exactly you're after here," said Jane, and Mitchell could sense in her voice a coy sexual insinuation that made him uneasy. Because hadn't he considered it himself—that there was a scenario, not necessarily a best-case scenario but not a worst-case scenario either, in which Mitchell might just stay there with Elsa, at Ticonderoga? That Elsa would come out of her trance and cure him of Fear once and for all, and that she might find comfort in his presence too, and then she might, perhaps, offer herself to him? Right there in the middle of the softball field, surrounded by heirloom tomatoes and zucchini and whatever the hell else they planted there, and she'd want it quickly, *quickly*, before Brugada could strike again—

"I'm not sure what you're after," Jane was saying, "but if it all goes bad, I want you to know that you've still got me. I may not know how to hunt a moose or grow carrots, but I know how to listen. And I know what you're worth."

"What am I worth? The profits of Future Days?"

He was sorry as soon as he said it.

"I deserve that. Sure I do. But I mean what I said."

There was nothing casual about her. Fiercely opportunistic one moment, fiercely devoted the next. She did everything with an intensity that charmed and unnerved him equally. From her spastic canoe stroke to her chatty telephone manner with business clients, she was always committing her full energy, exhausting herself—total engagement all the time. And then his thoughts returned to Elsa, or rather all the Elsas—Elsa the Cripple, Elsa the Hippie, Elsa the Black Star, and Elsa, Nymph of the Fields—and he tried to figure out whether any of them existed in the place that she called the Actual World.

After half a mile the road bent again, now to the right. They turned the corner, and Mitchell understood why Judy wouldn't drive them any farther.

# 4.

Were the circumstances different, were this the same world as the one into which he'd awoken on the day before Tammy hit, he might have assumed that the people were assembling for a county fair. Fried Dough, Tilt-A-Whirl, Milk Bottle Toss. Only their eyes were all wrong: fluttery, blinking, bloodshot. The mood was not carefree, not at all. This was high panic.

Families dragged luggage on wheels, college kids lumbered under hiking backpacks, and children sullenly kicked their sneakers on the ground as they walked. No one acknowledged anyone else. Several cars with New York license plates began to pass at speeds too high for a twisting dirt road. He wondered if any were the same cars he'd seen from his window before the storm, sitting in the traffic on the ramp to the Queens Midtown Tunnel.

"Is there some kind of refugee center around here?" asked Jane.

"That's what I'm afraid of."

By the time they reached the lake they could hear the mumbling noise of a crowd. Mitchell was out of breath. Not because of anxiety, he realized, but because he and Jane were rushing to keep pace with the others.

They found themselves in a traffic jam of dozens of abandoned vehicles. Past the cars were tents, set up in haphazard rows, facing the rock wall that marked the boundary of the Ticonderoga property. Personal belongings were scattered everywhere, as if at an auction. Two boys urinated beneath the broad wooden sign that welcomed visitors to Ticonderoga. The camp's slogan had been rewritten in a graffiti scrawl.

CAMP TICONDEROGA

~~A PLACE FOR KIDDIES!~~

WHERE THE NEW LIFE BEGINS

There were more than a hundred people, perhaps twice that, sitting and standing and lying in sleeping bags. And lighting fires—campfires, bonfires, pyromaniac fires. But still there was too much smoke. Ash was falling like snow. Then he noticed a darker plume rising above the trees of the property itself.

"What the hell is going on?" said Mitchell.

"Hell," said Jane. "Hell is going on."

Mitchell felt a sharp prodding behind his knee. A skinny woman sat beside them in a lawn chair, a tattered issue of *Glamour* on her lap. She looked exhausted, lines cutting sharp diagonals from her nostrils. Her gray eyes were soft and watery in the smoke. Thick, straight black hair hung from her skull like overcooked spaghetti.

"Who's that?" said the woman, pointing at Mitchell's stomach. "On your shirt. Leonardo Fibo, Fibo—?"

"Fibonacci," said Jane. "Hall of Fame field-goal kicker. Green Bay Packers. What, you never heard of him?"

The woman frowned. "Sounds like a dago."

"Can I ask," said Mitchell, "what exactly you are doing here?"

"Reading. Got a better idea?"

"I mean here." He gestured at the road, the people camping out, the smoke, the chaos. "What is this?"

"Ticonderoga." Seeing Mitchell's confusion, she sat up straight and flipped her magazine over on her lap. "What, you just stumbled on this?"

"In a matter of speaking," said Jane.

"It *was* a real good thing," said the woman. "For the first couple days at least. If you could make yourself useful on the farm, you could stay. Indefinitely. They didn't pay nothing, but they served food and the cabins have cots. Vegetables in the fields, water from a natural well. The water was clean and fresh. *Cold*. Bottom-of-the-ocean cold."

Jane regarded this woman suspiciously, uncertain of her sanity.

"Ma'am," she said, in a patient, anthropological tone, "if you don't mind my asking—if things are so good in there, why are you out here?"

"It's not safe *now*," said the woman. "And law enforcement won't come for days. They're overwhelmed in the capital. It's sad. This place was a little treasure, but they've ruined it now. Like they always do."

"Who ruined it?"

"People. Human beings. Well, to be specific, men. It's the men that did it. They're doing it still."

And Mitchell then noticed something about the crowd milling around them on the road: it was composed almost entirely of women and children. There were only a few elderly men, sprawled in the shade like wounded soldiers.

"What exactly is happening in there?" said Mitchell. "In the camp?"

"You want to know?" said the woman. She gave him a vicious sneer. "Take a look for yourself."

Mitchell approached the front gate cautiously, Jane following. The gate—a black metal bar on a hinge—was unlocked. They entered the property. Fifteen feet ahead loomed a stand of pine trees. Behind it a slope led down to the camp. The dirt was soft under his sneakers; after the toxic filth they'd waded through in the ruined city, it might as well have been milk chocolate. The smoke grew thicker. Blackened pine needles cracked beneath their feet like little bones. When they came to the pines they could see the camp below. Jane grabbed his arm.

"Sweet Jesus," said Jane. "Shine on."

A series of buildings and fields lay arranged in a long strip along the plateau at the bottom of the slope. To the right were the softball and soccer fields. They were now bare dirt. The vegetables had been uprooted and messily devoured, as if by wild beasts; all that was left were scraps of torn vine and the occasional tomato lying on the ground, rotten and burst, oozing white bugs. To the left of the fields lay the tennis court, cleaved in half by a fallen electric pole. Directly below them was the large three-story wooden building that Mitchell knew to be the old infirmary. This is where Elsa and the others had slept. But no one would sleep there again. It was burning down. The wood walls shifted and bent, engulfed by wild curtains of flame. The roof had already collapsed in several places. The fire was deeply entrenched; it had moved in, taken up quarters. You could see it through the blown-out windows, lapping thirstily at the lintels from within. A file of elm trees stood beside the building; their leaves had vaporized. All that remained of their branches were attenuated fingers of charcoal. Mitchell could feel it even from where they stood, the crackling heat. Glowing embers floated over them like falling fireworks. He wondered if any of the embers were made of the letter Elsa had left for him on the bureau inside the infirmary.

"The new life," said Jane. "This must be the new life."

Farther left, across the plain, stood the mess hall and a smaller administrative cabin, its windows shattered. Another churned field, then a curving path that reached into the woods. Along the path you could see the bright green roofs of the wooden bunks where the campers had once slept. Additional bunks were visible in the distance, extending toward the shore. The lake seen through the trees was like jewelry hanging in the branches.

The full horror of the scene took a few seconds to reach him. His eyes, as upon entering a cave, had to adjust to the darkness. But now he could see them—the men. Most of them were shirtless. They roamed the bunk areas like foxes, uncertain, fidgety, huddling low to the ground, moving in packs. When the air cleared momentarily between puffs of smoke, Mitchell noticed other men, deeper in the woods, their faces covered with mud and leaves, branches tucked into their pants in a crude camouflage. They were hunting.

But where, in this madness, was Elsa Bruner? Where was her design? His escape from the city, sternman—it felt meaningless in the face of this pandemonium.

"Retreat!" yelled Jane in his ear. "*Re*-treat!"

And then they were both running as fast as they could. But they went in opposite directions: Jane back to the gate, Mitchell down the hill. The dry, rocky soil, covered by the blackened pine needles and charred acorns, raced beneath him. As he sprinted toward the burning infirmary, the warmth became heat, then the heat became a blaze, and he was a comet entering the atmosphere. His face was burning off.

"Mitchell! Oh God! Mitchell!"

When he heard the pain in Jane's voice, the howling agony, he started to veer—it'd be so easy just to peel off to one side and avoid the house, run out into the field, away from danger and back to Jane. Yes, he realized, that would be the most logical option. And he remembered what Billy said in the message: *They let us move her back to the infirmary at Ticonderoga.*

So he kept running, accelerating as he flew down the slope. He was breathing deeply, and now the smoke, sharp and hot, was getting deep into his lungs, and it felt like he was ingesting the pine needles. He coughed bitterly, spitting black saliva. The air blurred. His eyes burned into the blurriness and he tried to make out details but there was only the nauseating blurriness. When he was within twenty feet of the building his foot caught and twisted, hard, spinning him, until the turf came up impatiently to smash his chin. The pain shook his mind into clarity, at least long enough to acknowledge the madness of what he was doing, and he felt the perverse satisfaction of total recklessness. It felt nothing like the canoe exodus from the city. That was dangerous, but it was calculated danger, better than the prospect of being marooned in his apartment without food and water. You couldn't make the same argument for running into a burning building.

He was lying beneath one of the elm trees. He had tripped on a root, which now, like a crooked elbow, pressed into his ribs. The air at the ground was relatively clean. He inhaled deeply, and his exhalations were little puffs of smoke. It was just like breathing steam in the winter. From this position he was at an angle to the infirmary and could see slightly around it, to a section of the building that seemed to have been spared by the flames. It was a back entrance. There was a step that led to a green screen door. The door rattled slightly in its frame, breathing in and out. He didn't want to get up, the air on the ground was so sweet and clean, but he begged himself to get up because he knew that Elsa was behind that door.

The tree above him was crackling and the smaller branches glowed golden. Mitchell felt dizzy and forgot what he was doing here, lying on the ground. It would be quite pleasant, he decided, to sleep at the foot of this tree. But as his eyes closed something pulled him, and he knew that it was Elsa, the Black Star, drawing him toward her, and then he was stumbling back to his feet and running the last twenty feet to the infirmary.

He tried to hold the clean air in his lungs but when he ran around the side of the building he found that the air was clearer; a breeze was blowing from the lake, pushing the smoke up the hill. He prepared himself for what would come next. First he would have to remove whatever tubes were plugged into her. He'd make sure she was wearing her gown. Then he'd roll her out of the bed and over his shoulder. It wouldn't be difficult to lift her; she was very small and no doubt had lost weight during her hospitalization. He would carry her away, not up the hill, at least not at first, but to the softball field. Then he could return, grab whatever medication or tubes or serums he could find in her room, and stuff them into his pockets; and finally, assuming none of the men from the bushes tried to interfere—just let them try!—he would carry Elsa up the slope to safety.

Some distant part of his brain told him to stand out of the way when he opened the door, that the surge of oxygen might ignite a spark, but the other part of his brain, the part that was now dominant, made him pull the door back hard and rush in without hesitation. And then he was inside the infirmary.

He was in a dark yellow room. There was no fire or smoke. But the walls were melting. Brown spots bloomed on the dark yellow wallpaper, and the paper was curling off in wide strips, exposing a glutinous, whitish plaster. It looked as if he were surrounded by bananas that were peeling themselves. He realized that this was not a bedroom at all, but a small doctor's office. There was a shelf that held cardboard boxes of gauze and latex gloves and pill bottles. The glass pill bottles had burst, and there was brown and green glass sprinkled on the floor. There was a small examination table with dark yellow padding and a metal scale and a steel sink. There was a steel counter on which there were arrayed steel tongs, a plastic bowl filled with dark yellow lozenges, a reflex hammer, a blood pressure cuff, and the remains of a shattered jar of tongue depressors. The depressors had spilled onto the floor, which was a pattern of checkerboard squares done in brown and silver. An old thermometer lay at the edge of the counter, and Mitchell bent to read it. It must have been broken, because it read 208°F. Mitchell wiped a great sleeve of sweat from his face. There was no other person in the room.

At the far end, there was a brown door. Mitchell's thinking began again to slow down and this time he decided to feel the door before opening it. It was not any hotter than the air, so he opened the door and looked into a second room.

This was not a bedroom, not exactly, more like an alcove, though there was a single bed in it. The bedsheets had been pulled back, revealing the mattress. There was an IV stand beside it, and on a table near the doorway there were about a dozen empty orange prescription bottles. Mitchell looked at one of the labels. It said, in a sloppy cursive: "Isoproterenol—dissolve 10mg in 1 gallon purified water/BRUNER, ELSA."

He scanned Elsa's room for an envelope with his name on it,

but he saw nothing. There was another doorway leading out of the not-exactly-bedroom, but flames were licking around the jambs. When he angled over to look into the hallway, all he saw was a curtain of bright blue fire. He realized that he was coughing again, only worse than before, and the pine needles in his lungs had become small scalpels that were excavating his chest from the inside. He backed away, out of Elsa's room and into the office, where two small arms grabbed him around the waist.

She dragged him outside, and he didn't resist. They stumbled into the softball field, coughing, and collapsed into the dry dust.

"Your face," said Jane, coughing. "Oh dear God."

She gave him a bottle of water and he drank, pausing every few gulps to cough and spit and breathe. Jane bent over his face and gently wiped away the inky soot.

"I don't understand you," she was saying. He didn't tell her how much it hurt when she touched his face. Her fingers trembled as they brushed his skin.

"Is it bad?" he asked, when he could speak.

"It's not good," she said, pouring water on his scraped chin. "But it could've been worse. You could be dead."

"She wasn't there."

Jane pulled back, squinting down at him quizzically. She nodded. "Now I know what it is that's getting me."

"What?"

"You don't have eyebrows anymore."

◫ ◫ ◫

At the gate they found the woman with the squid-ink spaghetti hair.

"See? They're fighting for control. It's a zoo. A *war*. I just know my husband won't come back. He's off in the woods. Thinks he's back in his regiment." She looked at Mitchell more closely. "You should put some Neosporin on that. What did you do, run into the fire?"

"The people who ran the farm," said Mitchell. "What happened to them?"

"The kids? They're *gone*."

"Gone? Gone how?"

"I don't know. No one does."

"You haven't heard anything."

"Oh, I have heard things. I have heard Canada. I have heard the Midwest. And I have heard that they never made it out of the infirmary."

"You tried," said Jane, handing Mitchell the folded page from the *Kennebec Journal*. "But now it's time to call Judy."

They sleepwalked through the billowing smoke, past a young girl defecating in the middle of the road and a woman curled on the shoulder bawling for her husband and a boy of twelve or so crawling through the brush, his arm bandaged and bloody—they walked away from Ticonderoga and Elsa Bruner's exploded dream.

Judy's station wagon was waiting just past the fork in the road. She had never left.

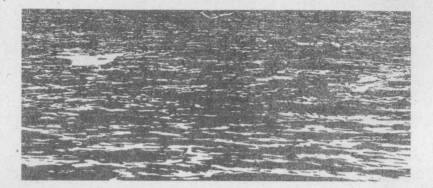

# 5.

**"As in the *prophet* Mitchell Zukor?"**

"Excuse me? No. Um. I don't think so."

"The financial consultant Mitchell Zukor, the guy who predicted . . ." The FEMA representative, struggling to put it into words, overwhelmed by the magnitude of it all, finally just gestured around her to the white trailers and the snaking food lines and, in the distance, the smoke billowing from the Manhattan skyline. The skyline looked like photographs of Beijing, the smoke blurring the contours of the buildings into a swampy gray soup.

"Yes," said Jane. "*This* guy. Mitchell Zukor. Z-u-k-o-r. He is also the founder and director of Future Days, a new futurist consulting firm."

"*My*. What are you doing here? Of all people—"

"We'd like a trailer," said Jane. "Our own trailer. If possible."

"I'll see what I can do." But then the FEMA employee turned back to Mitchell and a tremor passed through her body. Her bureaucratic seemliness cracked and split open. "Mr. Zukor, if you don't mind. What is going to happen to us next?" She was becoming mucousy. "God help us, what will happen next?"

⊡ ⊡ ⊡

It had been a lively drive back from Vacationland—a shorter one too. The trip to Augusta had taken three days; they made the return in six hours. But first Judy had stopped at her house on Winthrop Street, where she found a bandage for Mitchell's chin, a tube of first-aid cream, and a jar of aloe vera.

"You look like a Martian," said Judy as Jane gingerly applied a dressing of the green goo to Mitchell's pink face. "Does it hurt?"

Mitchell shrugged, as if to suggest that he couldn't feel the burn. But he felt it, oh Lord did he feel it, the skin tender and already beginning to blister. When Jane accidentally applied pressure to his cheek the pain caused his eyes to water.

Jane ordered Mitchell into the backseat and explained to him that she would be making the decisions from now on. She asked Judy to take them to the nearest police station so they could report what they'd seen at Ticonderoga.

"The cops?" said Judy in mock disbelief. "The cops are overwhelmed. They've never seen anything like this before. Most of these folks work on call, part-time, and they never had to govern a crowd or do much more than write folks speeding tickets. They're stuck in the cities. At the state refugee centers in Augusta, even in Lewiston, there are breadlines for miles. A man in South Portland was stabbed to death because he cut the line. And Canada is squeezing the border."

"Fine, but *something* has to be done."

"It'll improve once all the power comes back. People will resettle elsewhere. But for now there is nothing to do. Only panic."

Jane, having taken control of Mitchell's Go Bag and the cash inside of it, offered Judy an extra hundred dollars to drive them to the Portland bus terminal. There Jane found a Greyhound driver named Herman Loaiza who had been contracted by FEMA. He was about to return to New York, on two hours of sleep, to collect a new batch of refugees.

"You want to go back *there*?" said Herman, looking suspiciously at Mitchell, whose face still glistened with the green aloe. "What, you forgot something?"

"We have nothing keeping us here," said Jane.

"New York is admitting nobody. Not even buses."

"Then where are you going?"

"Randall's Island. FEMA Trailer City. That's where the folks are waiting to evacuate. Nope, sorry."

Jane opened Mitchell's Go Bag and showed Herman the cash-stuffed ziplock.

The northbound lanes were still jammed but the southbound road was empty. Herman kept it at eighty miles an hour. Mitchell lay across a pair of seats and tried to figure out why he had wanted to run inside the burning infirmary. Perhaps he had just wanted to see it for himself, the incineration of Elsa's Ticonderoga dream. There was a grim satisfaction in that, as there was in the sight of the men stalking the woods. Elsa's fantasy had been overrun by the actual world and its desperate hordes, and the tragedy—which was really almost a comedy—was how plainly predictable this outcome should have been. Even without the flood, a design so excruciatingly naive couldn't have survived very long. What confused Mitchell was how he had failed to see it coming himself. If anyone should have been able to predict the chaos that Ticonderoga had become, it was Mitchell. This was his profession, after all. He didn't have to do historical research on utopian communes or cooperative societies in order to know that most of them ended in disillusionment, pettiness, and, yes, violence. If he could insure behemoth corporations, shield them from risk, why hadn't he tried harder to save the life of a single sick girl?

"How is it?" Jane asked Herman. "In New York?"

"You *know* it's real bad," said Herman, "because you can't *see* anything. I mean, there's news videos, things like that? I seen waves—I'm saying whitecaps—on Broadway. Right in front of Lincoln Center. Taxis—a dozen? Floating in a pack down First Avenue. Like a school of whales. Yellowback whales."

"Have you heard any numbers?" asked Jane.

Herman shook his head. "The problem is that you can't tell which of those pictures is fake."

"Fake? How?"

"You seen the Swimming Boy?"

They had. It aired on the television in the Fort Lee gymnasium, and they had caught it again at a service station near Lowell where the bus driver had taken a fifteen-minute smoke break. The clip was an instant smash; it had already been viewed online half a billion times. The video was shot from several stories up, presumably from a window across the street. The subject of the film was a blond-haired boy, no older than twelve, who finds himself standing alone on the roof of a car in the middle of a residential block. It might be the Lower East Side, Carroll Gardens, perhaps Bay Ridge. The car sits like a boulder in a fast-moving channel, the water galloping wildly on either side. At the beginning of the clip the boy waves across the street at someone, trying to communicate. The camera pans down to reveal a second, older boy—his brother, by the looks of it—halfway down the block, standing on a high stoop that is not yet submerged. He gestures for his younger brother to join him, to swim across the street.

The little towheaded boy takes a deep breath, his shoulders rising and falling. He leaps—headfirst, arms outstretched—into the churning water. He wheels his arms and kicks wildly, but he is no match for the current. He flies past his brother, who is now screaming in despair, and careens to the next block. There, just before it seems he will collide with a parked van, he bobs beneath the water—apparently for good.

Then, out of nowhere, a police patrol airboat sweeps into the intersection. The officer, leaning over the guardrail, reaches into the water and pulls the boy out by his wrist. The boy spits and heaves, but he is alive. Newscasters asked viewers to identify the savior and the courageous swimming boy.

"Did they find him?"

"Sure did," said Herman. "It's fake. It's actors."

"Impossible."

"That's the story today. Producer in Hollywood has politician friends. He had footage that never made it into some old disaster picture. Does a little touch-up to make it look like New York. Then the government sends it to the news programs."

"But why would they do that?" said Jane. "That's sick."

"They need to tell a story. Distract from what's actually going on. Hell, even if people find out the truth, that's no worse—one more day of distraction. Point is, they don't want us to know how bad it is."

It occurred to Mitchell that Herman was right. Tammy was worse than anyone could imagine. Like all major catastrophes, it surpassed the limits of imagination. And what was human imagination, after all, but the reconfiguration of past events? Tammy—like Seattle—was an innovative disaster. Its horrors were unprecedented. It created images that man had never seen before, but once seen, could never be unseen.

Yet Jane, as they drove at eighty miles per hour back to the flooded city, seemed emboldened. Exhilarated even.

"Do you think this is just the beginning?" she asked Mitchell.

"Beginning of what?"

"That there will be more hurricanes and more floods?"

"That's the trend. Natural disasters have been trending upward for the last three decades."

"But what do *you* think?"

"It will get worse, but by how much I have no idea. Our expectations are constantly being surpassed. The scales need to be recalibrated."

"Then we're in the right line of business. Wouldn't you say? The more uncertainty, the higher the stakes—Future Days will only get bigger and bigger. Futurism is the way—"

"Don't."

"*Of the future!* Sorry. It wanted to come out."

They laughed, a bit too hard. It wasn't funny. They just wanted to laugh. And as they laughed, Mitchell realized how badly they had been craving human things—laughter, certainly, also intimacy, cleanliness. But they'd wanted animal things too: food, water, sex. The animal things they had wanted even more desperately.

"I don't know why I'm laughing," said Jane. "If I didn't, I guess I'd cry."

He didn't know whether it was the sight of Jane about to break down that did it, or the thousands of people gridlocking on the northbound side of the interstate, the fossils of their destroyed lives strapped to the roofs of their cars, or the highway signs twisted like paper clips, or the roadkill, which was everywhere, not just deer and skunks but birds and a black bear lying flat on its back, its teeth gleaming an unnatural white, and cats and dogs by the dozen with name tags around their broken necks. But it was only now that it occurred to him that Elsa, most certainly without medical care, had entered some new hell. For all he knew, she was dying this very second. Maybe she was already dead.

As the bus passed Hartford (PLEASE ENJOY THE "INSURANCE CAPITAL OF THE WORLD"!), the vast absurdity of the whole enterprise became a cattle prod and he was the dumb bovine, and the cattle prod was pushing one simple message into his animal brain. The message was: disorder always won in the end. The idea that man could order the world to his own design was the most pitiful fairy tale ever told. An empty house, left alone for just a single year, begins to return to the earth. It starts with a storm, a ceiling leak. Pollen and rainwater seep in, and before long, a tree has taken root in the living room, its branches pushing out the windows, the birds and squirrels invading. This was true of man too. Even the most brilliant mathematician, late in life, was infantilized by old age. He lost his memory, motor skills, potty skills. It was a universal rule. Not even the universe itself was spared. It too was going senile. Space was cooling, and one by one all the stars would go out in the sky. Disaster: from Latin *dis-* "ill-" and *astro* "starred," a calamity caused by an unfavorable configuration of the stars.

Everything was disintegrating, yet here was man, the poor schlemiel, running around with his glue and his tape. Back in the city the federal government was now probably dredging Manhattan, repairing the bridges, planning task forces and emergency construction jobs. There was something insane about it. Pathetic too. The next flood would come, then another one. You could only delay the inevitable. Every arrow pointed down. All the king's horses and all the king's men wouldn't be able to unbreak the egg. What was the point?

Jane, of course, was right—this was where the futurist came in. Essentially a futurist was asked to prevent the future from happening. He was paid to devise solutions that might halt change. The solutions were obvious: build higher seawalls, reinforce the concrete, use stronger alloys. Vaccinate and immunize; pack a Go Bag and a PFD. Preservation was the human instinct, or at least the American instinct. Those in power wanted to be told that everything will stay just as before—as long as you purchase a little insurance. And this was the service that Future Days would provide. In the short term, it would be a lucrative business. And the short term was all that mattered. He was beginning to think there would be no long term.

"We should get an office in SoHo," Jane was saying. "Or Tribeca. Somewhere downtowny. The public relations team will be crucial. We need to hire professionals."

Returning to Manhattan was impossible to imagine, but then everything was impossible to imagine. His imagination, once whorled and baroque with theories of superfiasco, had become a casualty of Tammy. Now when he thought about the future, all he found was blankness. *There would be no long term.* Jane's scenario, in which he founded a new futurist firm, would certainly make him money—lots of it, enough to force his parents into retirement in Mission Hills. But the worst-case scenarios would return. That would be part of the bargain. They would be waiting for him in the middle of the night.

And for the first time since the flood, cockroach eggs began to hatch in the pit of his stomach.

◫ ◫ ◫

The future had arrived. It assumed the shape of a long white rectangular box with two windows looking out over the narrowest part of the East River. A coffin with a view.

"I guess this counts as prime real estate," said Jane, taking in the sight.

Their trailer, number 2199, looked no different from the thousands of other trailers arrayed in long rows across the baseball and soccer fields of Randall's Island. The bedroom was just large enough for a double bed. In the bathroom the toilet nudged the shower stall. The main room contained a kitchenette with propane stove and mini fridge, a sofa upholstered in peach polyester, a matchbook-size dining table with two chairs. Two navy mesh FEMA baseball hats sat on the table, compliments of the federal government. The furniture was bolted to the floor. There was, significantly, no television. FEMA didn't want the refugees to understand how bad it was in the city, how long they'd be stuck on Randall's Island.

"Beachfront property," said Jane. She went straight for the bed and flopped onto it.

The air in the trailer was tropical. Mold smeared the window-sills. The bedroom window gave a view of the northern tip of Astoria. A power plant stood there, its white smokestacks standing like the columns of an ancient ruin.

"Sleeping now," she announced, her eyes already closed.

In the kitchen Mitchell set down his Go Bag and opened the fridge. The shelves were lined with aluminum cans. Across each can, in large black letters: FILTERED DRINKING WATER. Mitchell cracked one open and drank. The water had a mildly astringent aftertaste. Was that chlorine? Fluoride? Arsenic?

This was unsustainable. But was it worse than Overland Park? That was the calculation. If he returned, he'd immediately be pressed into service by Tibor. Mitchell, after all, was slumlord-in-waiting.

"New York is a wonderful place," Tibor had said the last time they walked among the Zukorminiums. "Don't get me wrong." It was the week between graduation and Fitzsimmons, and Mitchell had reluctantly agreed one morning to accompany his father to his office. It was a decision he soon regretted.

They were truly hideous structures, the Zukorminiums, even worse than he'd remembered—redbrick, cruciform, seven stories tall, with laundry racks and satellite dishes hanging as ornaments from the windows. The buildings had been built to maximize profit per square foot; Tibor hadn't taken human dignity into account. On the way to the administrative offices you had to follow a winding gravel path lined by shrubs flecked with plastic bags, dodging bottles of hobo wine, syringes, and soiled diapers. The condition of the Zukorminiums was shameful, but the shame didn't reflect on the inhabitants. It reflected on Tibor. And Mitchell claimed it too; he felt the shame. It posed uncomfortable questions. For instance: Deep down, how different was his father from, say, Sandy Sherman? Both men were obsessed by financial gain; they were, in this way, sociopathic, seeking profit at the expense of human dignity. The protesters who picketed the Zukorminiums weren't wrong when they argued that Tibor cared more about their checks than their human rights. "We have insects, terrible mold, rodents, insecto-infestations," one woman told a local news reporter. "I'm up all night long making sure things don't crawl on my kids."

But none of this seemed to daunt Tibor. If anything, his pride had caused him to grow bolder. And now he was preparing Mitchell to take his place.

"Isn't it dangerous for you to stay here?" Mitchell had asked. "Don't you fear for your safety?"

Tibor laughed, stepping over a pile of what appeared to be human feces. "New York is also dangerous. You never know when something terrible will happen. I lived through Budapest in 1956. The revolution can burst out at any moment. That's one of the great things about this place. There is no chance of revolution in Kansas City."

A bag of garbage fell from the sky and detonated on the path behind them. They froze and looked up. An old woman was leaning out of her window, shaking her fist.

"Go back to commie Russia, Zukor!"

They hurried into Tibor's office and shut the door, but even then Tibor seemed unbowed.

"*Monty Python and the Holy Grail*, starring a certain Mr. John Cleese," said Tibor.

Mitchell waited for the rest of it.

"'One day, lad, all this will be yours.'"

No, he had thought. It most certainly would not. What was the Hungarian word? *Nem*. He would *nem* return to Kansas City, *nem* take over the Zukorminiums. *Nem soha*.

The FEMA trailer rattled. Someone was smacking the front door.

There were ten people standing outside. They wore ingratiating smiles. Mitchell's first thought was that they were a delegation from the Zukorminiums, delivering complaints about asbestos and lead pipes.

Their leader, or at least the person who had knocked, was a pretty young Hispanic woman in librarian glasses. She held a newborn child against her shoulder.

"Are you the gentleman they call the Prophet?"

Mitchell stared at her in confusion.

She laughed apologetically. "I'm sorry to intrude. My name is Marcy Rosado. It's just that, you see, we have some questions. And, well—" She gestured with her head to the baby. "We need the answers."

"I'm sorry, I—"

"Mr. Zukor?" She wasn't laughing anymore. "We need answers."

# 6.

Who were all these people? Waiting on line outside the food tent, taking fluids intravenously in the medical trailers, lingering by the administrative desk in the hope of hearing news, any news, the children racing wildly around the island in unsupervised games of tag, the babies screaming. It was clear what they weren't: Manhattanites. Many were first-generation immigrants. They didn't have friends with guesthouses in other parts of the country; they couldn't afford hotels or airfare. In many cases their entire family had lived on the same block. They were also stubborn: they didn't want to start over. They planned to move back to their old neighborhoods and rebuild. A fog of high irritation had fallen over the camp. Hysteria, too—it buzzed in the air like a cloud of wasps. Occasionally the buzzing blistered into violence. Mitchell had already witnessed three fistfights. At breakfast a woman pulled another woman's hair out over a bowl of cereal.

But the refugees seemed to be going out of their way to be friendly to Mitchell and Jane. If anything, they were too friendly.

By the end of the meal Mitchell had met the Lipinskis of Rego Park, the Diazes and Motas of Gravesend, the Wolaczes of Greenpoint, and a passel of McIntyres, nearly twenty in all, great-grandpa Miles through baby Lola. The McIntyres were from Broad Channel, a narrow island in Jamaica Bay between Howard Beach and the Rockaways that, during the storm, had been entirely submerged. Since the side streets in Broad Channel alternated with canals, many residents owned boats. The McIntyres had stayed afloat in their own family fleet, sheltered in the inundated but relatively protected bay. Mitchell didn't meet anyone from the narrow Rockaway peninsula, the city's first line of defense against the Atlantic Ocean. The Rockaways were missing.

"What's your story?" asked Joseph McIntyre, a man with a flat nose and large brown eyes who looked as if he hadn't slept for a week. He sidled up with his lunch tray. "How'd you end up here?"

"We took a canoe through the flooded city," said Jane. "We went to Maine, but the situation there was even worse. So we came back."

"You don't say."

Jane nodded, smiling uneasily. "I do," she said, but Joseph McIntyre just gaped back at her. Finally Jane asked for his story. The man smiled in gratitude.

This became a pattern. Strangers asked questions, but they didn't seem particularly interested in answers. Even when Jane recited the gruesome details—the floating bodies, the brush with Nybuster and his caroming golf balls—they gave her only blank stares and patient smiles.

"Is that so?" said Ruben Mota. "That sounds scary."

"Really?" said Olga Lipinski.

"My," said Harold Wolacz. "You had it rough."

Their friendliness, Mitchell began to realize, was the first part of a ritual. In certain African societies, when you meet a person in the street, you can't merely ask how he's doing; you must also inquire about his health, family, and occupation before exchanging various blessings and hymns. The encounters at the camp worked in a similar way. The refugees would listen, patiently, to another person's story, but only so long as they could share their stories next. They were desperate to unburden themselves of their personal horrors. The Lipinskis had waited for two days on their roof, dehydrating, until they were airlifted by a rescue basket into a Coast Guard helicopter. The Motas, a Dominican couple in their fifties, were trapped in their dining room; they stood on a coffee table for eighteen hours watching as the water slowly rose to their chins. A patrol boatman, hearing their screams, took an ax to their door and rescued them. Finally there was Maya Dupre, a robust college sophomore who told her story with wild gesticulations. She had swum out the window of her second-floor apartment in Homecrest. The night after the storm she slept on the elevated F train platform above McDonald Avenue, lying out in the open air. "For the first time in my life," she said, "I could see the stars." She was proud of that line. She repeated it and repeated it.

"I could make her see some more stars," said Jane between bites of a government-issued ham sandwich. Then her mouth puckered, and she removed a curled strip of plastic wrap from her mouth.

And there were those who, like Mitchell, didn't want to talk. These were the diminished people, unnaturally drawn and tortured, who haunted the Red Cross table. Aid workers gamely took down names and any information that might be used to identify a body. Some of the bereaved carried photographs of the missing; some wore the photographs on chains around their necks. They walked around the camp like zombies, from trailer to trailer, hoping in their desperation to discover a familiar face. Others gathered around the muted flatscreen television that had been hung from the side of the Red Cross trailer. The television was tuned to a local news network that periodically flashed images of the missing and scrolled the names of those who had registered at FEMA checkpoints. But nearly every time Mitchell walked by this television, his own picture appeared on the screen. It was the photograph Charnoble had taken on his first day of work at FutureWorld; he looked baffled and alarmed, and the flash had turned him several shades paler. It was like seeing a ghost—a ghost of a former self, a painfully naive young man who had no idea what kind of nightmare was about to swallow him. He told himself to stop going near the Red Cross trailer, but every hour or so he found himself back there, where he would linger until his face appeared under increasingly large font with increasingly hysteric captions:

HE CAME FROM THE FUTURE

WHY DIDN'T WE LISTEN?

THE MAN WHO KNEW TOO MUCH

While Mitchell wandered the camp, Jane gave interviews. Once, when Mitchell's photo appeared on the television, a tagline at the bottom of the screen appeared: "On the line: Jane Eppler, spokeswoman, Future Days." He looked around and spotted Jane standing at the shore forty yards away, speaking into her headset, making exuberant motions with her hands.

Nearly five days had passed since Tammy made landfall, and everyone who could leave Randall's Island had already left. The refugees who remained were determined to stay put. They were ready to return to their homes. It was a reasonable position. There was only one problem: the water hadn't gone down. Behind the administration desk, set up on what had been public tennis courts, a large whiteboard listed neighborhoods next to their flood-depth figures. Every hour the numbers were updated by a woman in one of the ubiquitous navy FEMA baseball caps. She read the latest depths from a clipboard. With her other hand she gripped a marker, using the side of her fist to dab away the old figures and scribbling the new ones in red ink. There was a mood of frantic expectation around the clipboard. Other than the Red Cross television, this was the refugees' main portal to the rest of the world. All they knew of the devastation was what they had seen first-hand, and rumors. Some reported that the city was completely empty; there was no electricity, no drinking water, and the flood-water was tainted with toxic waste. Others claimed that hundreds of thousands of New Yorkers were already returning to their neighborhoods, that outside of lower Manhattan and the coastal areas, there was little damage other than fallen trees. So they scrutinized the only hard data they had: the water level figures on the whiteboard. They puzzled over them, as if the numbers alone could reveal the myriad unknown stories of the storm-wrecked city.

The water in the neighborhoods along the East River—Vinegar Hill, Brooklyn Heights, Sunset Park, and, to a lesser extent, Red Hook—had dropped from feet to inches. But those neighbor-hoods that fronted the sea, in lower Brooklyn and Queens—from Sea Gate (12.5 feet) to East New York (5 feet) and even parts of East Flatbush (10 inches)—had barely changed. By evening the numbers decreased, but in the morning they returned to their previous levels. Every time a higher figure appeared there were groans of outrage from the crowd. The FEMA woman, shrug-ging, blamed imprecise measurements, but Mitchell knew better. The fluctuations weren't due to faulty equipment; the culprit was the tide. Washing in and washing out. And every time the wa-ter receded, it swept out traces of civilization—walls, furniture, bodies.

Nor were the refugees pleased to see that while their neighbor-hoods in the outer boroughs were turning to swamp, the water in lower Manhattan was dropping rapidly. Manhattan, however, had help. The island had been surrounded by Mosquitoes—supertankers with suction pumps built to clean up oil spills. The Mosquitoes vacuumed millions of barrels of water every hour and pumped the effluent into the bight. Another day of the Mosquitoes slurping up Manhattan's water and, according to the whiteboard, the borough would be dry.

"How about that?" said Jane. "We could be having dinner at the Palm tomorrow night. I could use a steak. Rare. Salted and charred. Side of half-and-half. Side of creamed spinach."

"Jane."

"Side of thick-cut *bacon*."

"Dry doesn't mean safe. They'll have to send thousands of assessors, engineers, garbage crews. Imagine the amount of trash. Millions of tons, mountains, skyscrapers of trash."

Jane's mouth went slack.

"What," said Mitchell. "What is it?"

"It's like you don't even *want* to go back."

"That's not true," he said. But it was true. He could admit that much to himself.

"I don't get it. Would you rather stay *here*?"

"No! Of course not."

Jane turned abruptly, advancing toward the woman with the clipboard. Her name tag read LANORE.

"Lanore? Excuse me, but when do the buses start leaving for Manhattan?"

"I'm sorry," said Lanore. "I don't have that information."

"But you work for FEMA, don't you? You must know something. We need to get back."

"I know. We all want to go home."

"Jane," said Mitchell, touching her shoulder. "It's OK."

"No, it's not." Jane shook him off with a violent twitch. Her eyes were blazing. He'd never seen her like this. "She has a *job* to do."

"Yeah!" said a man standing behind Mitchell. "We want answers!"

"Hey lady, what about Gowanus?"

"Lady, why is the water getting *higher* in Dyker Heights?"

"She making up shit."

Lanore looked around anxiously, as if for backup. But no other staff was near. Just a crowd of angry, scared people.

"I don't know anything," said Lanore to Jane. "I just don't."

"Do you even work for FEMA?"

Lanore shook her head, her lips trembling.

"I'm a receptionist for the Brooklyn Transit Police," she said, unable to stifle a sob. "District Thirty-nine. I don't know nothing. My family—I haven't heard from them since this whole mess started. I don't know where they are."

"I'm sorry," said Jane. "That's horrible."

"She's crying. Look at that."

"At least she got a fancy trailer."

"At least she *got* family."

Lanore, her cheeks damp, focused on Mitchell. The sight of him seemed to embolden her.

"But you—you're the so-called Prophet. And you're telling me that *you* don't know what's happening?"

The crowd turned to Mitchell. The crowd turned—and Jane turned too.

Mitchell put up his hands.

"I'm just a financial consultant," he said.

"He doesn't know anything," said Jane a bit too firmly, but it was too late. No one would listen to her. At the trailer the previous evening, when he had made his apologies, Marcy Rosado and her friends had appeared unconvinced, but they had left him alone. It helped that they had recognized his name from the news. At lunch, two of the McIntyre kids had even asked him to autograph their napkins. But now the mood was different. Nobody here wanted his ink. They wanted his blood.

A circle closed around him. The shouting faces moved in, their breath hot on his neck, on his brow.

"Jane!" said Mitchell. "Jane!"

Jane was yelling somewhere, but very quietly. The other voices were louder and angrier.

"What are you keeping from us?" said an old man in a cloth cap and grimy overcoat, very close to Mitchell's ear.

"I've heard about you," said a woman with a crumpled, washed-out face, on the other side of him. She smelled of detergent. He thought she might have been one of the McIntyres.

"Tell us what you know." This was a skinny white man with five-day stubble and a ghastly Oklahoma-shaped scab across his nose. He shook with rage, spittle forming on his lip. His fists clenched. "Tell us, kid!"

The man reached out and nudged Mitchell's shoulder. "Tell us!"

Mitchell raised his arms in front of his face. He was trapped within a tiny chamber of noise and saliva.

And then a very strong and very large hand came down on his head.

# 7.

They met after midnight at the northern tip of the island, beneath the railroad overpass.

It was too dark to see faces. That was the point. If the expedition failed, they didn't want to get arrested. Already there were rumors that the jails were swelling, that a person who stole bottled water would be tossed into the same cell as the murderers. In case they needed a further reminder, the yellow blinking lights of Rikers Island were visible across the river, the searchlights cutting scythes in the black water.

It was too dark to see faces, but Mitchell could tell that there were eight people in all, only three of whom he could identify: himself, Jane, and Hank Cho. It wasn't difficult to pick out Hank. He was six three, about 230 pounds, with a powerful torso and a broad, flat head like a tombstone. His arms, too, were brawny, but short, as if the bulk he had added to his arm muscles caused them to contract. The general resemblance was to one of those carnivorous bipedal dinosaurs. Mitchell had felt the power in Hank Cho's fingers that afternoon, when Hank placed his palm over Mitchell's head.

"Leave the boy," Hank had said. "He don't know shit."

The fingers exerted a remarkable pressure on Mitchell's skull.

"And they call him prophet," yelled one of the McIntyre men.

Hank gave McIntyre a defiant glare. McIntyre shrugged, and turned his back. The crowd dissipated, the refugees wandering to their trailers. Once the danger had passed, Hank lifted his hand.

"Thank you," said Mitchell. "They wanted to kill me."

"I have a proposition for you," said Hank. He gestured at Jane. "And your friend."

And so they ended up at the midnight meeting beneath the railroad overpass.

The plan was simple. They were going to get off FEMA island. Where they ended up would be their own business, but for safety they would escape in a single group. They'd leave in the middle of the night. The plan was simple, but the execution posed problems.

"They patrol the roads," said one man. "You trying to swim?"

"They patrol the three highway bridges. But not the Hell Gate. That's only for freight trains. It spans the Bronx Kill."

"What?"

"The water between here and Queens." Hank pointed in the direction of the RFK Bridge. "*That*. The Hell Gate is the little bridge, without the lights. In front of the big one."

The RFK was lit brightly now, electricity having been restored, but the old railroad bridge stood in complete darkness. In the moonlight all you could see were the triangle cutouts of the steel trusses and the squat towers on either shore. Mitchell had never seen the bridge before, but he remembered it from disaster assessments of New York. The Army Corps of Engineers concluded that the Hell Gate would be the last bridge standing in New York after a nuclear explosion. Left to nature, it would outlast every other bridge in the city by a millennium.

"Hell Gate over Bronx Kill?" someone said. "I don't like the sound of that."

"Looks dangerous."

"We have to walk on train tracks?"

"This is ludicrous." That was Jane.

Inwardly Mitchell cursed Alec Charnoble. In some way, he was convinced, this was all Charnoble's fault.

"The Hell Gate will take us into Astoria," said Hank. "It's a freight track, but there are no trains running now. We stay on the track past the bridge. It goes over Woodside, then bends south to Middle Village, Ridgewood, all the way to Broadway Junction."

"How do you know all that?"

"I work for the MTA."

"Yeah, right. Doing what?"

"Track maintenance foreman."

"I don't live but ten blocks from Broadway Junction," said someone.

"I'm two stops east."

"From Broadway Junction," said Hank, "you can go wherever you like. I'm planning on heading south."

"You from down there?"

"Nope. Flushing. But I've been hearing that Flatlands and below got clean swept away."

"Why you going, then?"

"I'm looking to start again."

No one had anything to say about that.

"What are the Flatlands?" This was Mitchell.

"It's just about the end of the earth," someone said. "Or as close as you can get without leaving New York City."

"It's east of Flatbush Avenue, west of Ralph," said Hank. "Near Mill Basin and the Belt Parkway, protected by the Rockaways from the sea. No subways go there. It was working class—mostly West Indians and Orthodox Jews. Now it's a giant patch of dirt.

You can bet the government won't be rehabilitating it anytime soon."

"It's cold," Jane whispered in Mitchell's ear. "Can we go?"

"One second," said Mitchell. "Let's hear him out."

"When's this supposed to happen?" someone said.

"Tomorrow night," said Hank. "We meet at the far end of the tennis courts. I'll bring flashlights. But we don't turn them on until we're over Hell Gate."

The only sound was the river slapping playfully against the rocks.

"Any other questions?"

"Yeah," said one woman. "Why are you in charge?"

"You got a better idea, pop it."

They waited.

"I'll see you tomorrow midnight. Don't let the word out. We don't know who's watching."

Mitchell and Jane separated from the others and walked quickly back to their trailer.

"Who could be watching us?" said Jane after they were out of earshot. "He's not just paranoid. He's delusional."

"Paranoia has its advantages. Did you see his arms?"

"Yeah. That dude is a piece of meat."

The smell engulfed them as soon as they entered the trailer, a sour, moldering, damp animal rot—the smell of despair.

"It's intolerable," said Mitchell.

"I know. I'd open the windows, but then we lose the AC. Lose-lose." She cracked open a can of water and took a swig. "We have to get out of here. But we have to be smart about it."

"Mm."

"You're thinking about going," she said. "You're actually thinking about leaving tomorrow. With Korean G.I. Joe."

"The man is Chinese."

"What about me?"

"We go together."

"And Future Days?"

"The FEMA people say it'll be at least a week until the city opens. That's optimistic. We have time." He watched for her reaction. She didn't react. "We can't stay here."

"Look, I don't feel safe here either. But it's better than the Flatlands."

There was more to it, of course. It wasn't only fear for their safety that made the Flatlands seem like a promising alternative. Unless he had some time to concentrate, in solitude, and consider everything that had happened, he wouldn't be able to figure out the next thing, the big thing to which FutureWorld, Tammy, and even Ticonderoga were inexorably leading him. And there had to be something else, didn't there? For if not, what had all this been for?

"You saw the way they went after me yesterday," said Mitchell. "They wanted to kill me. If it weren't for Hank Cho, what do you think would have happened?"

"I realize. But casting out into the unknown? It's just so not like you."

"I'm not like me anymore."

There had to be a big, perfect thing right ahead, some pursuit more vast and profound than fear prediction. Now that his old way of life was gone, nothing remained. He was as bare as the floodgrounds. So there had to be something larger up ahead, because if not, then the only thing was destruction and chaos—

"So you would just leave me here," said Jane. She looked frantically around the trailer: the stained cabinets, the wilted, understuffed polyester couch, the linoleum floor that curled up at the edges like a piece of burning paper.

"Of course not. I'm just saying the guy's plan is worth some thought."

Jane went into the bedroom. Out flew a pillow, then the extra blanket.

"You can think about the plan all you want," she said, "over there." She pointed to the couch.

The door closed, then locked.

He switched off the overhead fluorescent panel and spread the moth-bitten blanket over his body. That was Jane for you. Determined, devoted, never casual. She demanded full devotion in return. And she deserved it. But could he give it to her?

He had a picture of Jane carefully wiping the soot off his face outside the infirmary at Ticonderoga, cradling his head in her trembling hands. He blocked it out. He turned on the couch and tried to hit the cushions into softness, but nothing worked, and then an uncomfortable sensation covered him like a heavy woolen blanket and he couldn't escape from under it. For the first time he could remember, he was making a plainly irrational decision. Jane's logic was sound. Futurism, as she'd put it on Herman Loaiza's bus, was the way of the future. After Tammy, the risk market would be at peak demand. It was important to establish Future Days immediately. Futurism was now a job for specialists, but it wouldn't be much longer. A few more years of these new meteorological patterns, a few more disasters, and every person on the street would be able to speak intelligently about drought, methane pollution, UV poisoning. The intricacies of planetary collapse would be general knowledge. Kid stuff. So Jane had every reason to act with urgency. And Mitchell had every reason to join her.

What was the alternative? Elsa's Ticonderoga dream of a self-sustaining farm, toxin-free food, the creation of so much natural energy that the surfeit could electrify the rest of the county? Sure, all that was noble, that was fine. Elsa had been a kind of futurist herself, her behavior driven by her fear about what was happening to the planet—and to herself. But Mitchell had been in finance too long to lose sight of the truth about Ticonderoga. What, after all, was its source of income? Billy's father's money. That wasn't a business model. It was a charity, financed by good intentions. This put Ticonderoga squarely on the wrong side of history. It was a local, virtuous, and limited enterprise. The Nybusters of the universe would never invest in a Ticonderoga. They wanted to be insulated from transformational change. That's why Future Days was the present, if not also the future. The question was whether it was *Mitchell's* future.

He realized that he was pacing around the room. He reached into the refrigerator for a water. As he popped the can, he heard a knocking behind him. So—Jane had reconsidered.

"Jane?" he said. "Should I come in?"

"That wasn't me," Jane called out from inside the bedroom.

There was more knocking. The trailer rattled. He went to the front door. Marcy Rosado was back, with her child. This time she had brought twenty-five people.

"Mr. Prophet," said Marcy. She was rocking the baby on her shoulder to the erratic rhythm of her own agitation. Her teeth were bared. "Is *now* a good time?"

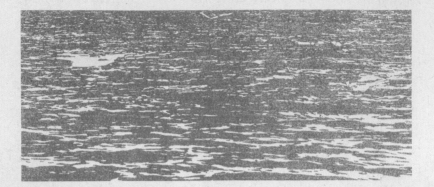

# 8.

What would Tibor do? A ludicrous question under normal circumstances, but here was one situation in which the experiences of father and son overlapped. A city destroyed, and nowhere to go. What would he do? Tibor would flee, as he had Budapest in the winter of 1956, hiding under a tarp in the bed of an apple truck until it reached Nickelsdorf, on the other side of the Austrian border. Rikki? She'd be halfway to Kansas City by now. She could take better care of herself than any government agency, thank you very much. And Elsa? Saint Elsa of the Fields? That was easiest of all. She'd be gone already—lost in the urban wilderness. It seemed to be Elsa's preferred state, lost in the wilderness. The wilderness of idealism, the wilderness of Maine, the wilderness of unconsciousness. Wherever she might be, she was lost.

But Jane Eppler was the only person who counted now. And her feelings on the subject were a tad more nuanced.

"You've gone fucking in-*sane*."

She was foaming at the mouth. She had stepped out of the

bathroom while brushing her teeth and the toothpaste foam was spilling down her chin. She caught it with her free hand and dodged back into the bathroom cubicle. Mitchell sat up on the couch and checked the clock. It was seven in the morning. It occurred to him that he had never heard Jane curse before.

She rinsed and spat, forcefully. She appeared again in the little stretch of space between the bathroom and the living room, what might be called a hallway if it were longer than three feet.

"After everything we've been through."

"Why do you keep saying that? I wasn't going to abandon you."

"Hold on." She went back into the bathroom. The water ran. She spat again.

When she emerged, she scrutinized his face, squinting, as if to detect some hidden pattern there. Whatever she saw couldn't have worked to his advantage. His skin still tender and pinkish from his little adventure in the Ticonderoga crematorium. A yellow scab on his chin that was just beginning to peel. His flat hair whorled in cowlicks like an electrocution victim; his eyes red, scummy with sleep; and his semi-beard, a growth of five days— what Rikki called his "Mexicano look," which had something to do with the fact that only his mustache grew in fully, the hair on his cheeks growing out sparsely and in different directions, like spines on a saguaro. He knew this much about his appearance without consulting a mirror. He also realized that his mouth was hanging open, like a taxidermied bear.

"Fine," she said at last. "I believe you."

"Really?"

"I have no choice, do I? What else can I do? Even if I wanted to go home, all the buses have left. I don't know what is happening in the city; there's no way to tell what horrors are raging there. And I'm not going to stay by myself in this camp. It wouldn't be safe. So I'm completely vulnerable. Another way of saying that is,

I'm screwed." Her voice lowered. "Besides. We have to trust each other if we're going to try to make Future Days work."

"Right. Good point." And that was the moment of cowardice. *Wrong,* he should have said. *I'm not going to work at Future Days.* But that would have started a conversation he was not prepared to have. A conversation that would end with her leaving him. So he just sat there with a bland smile, like the selfish weasel he was.

"So," said Jane. "Breakfast?"

They followed the crowds to the food tent.

"It's really not so bad here," said Jane. "See?"

He saw. It really was so bad. Five men stood in a line outside a trailer just twenty yards down. None of them talked with each other. Mitchell knew what they were waiting for. The previous night Marcy Rosado had, through tears, cataloged the depredations she had seen on FEMA Island: propane tanks were being filched right and left; small children found syringes in the field and used them in unsupervised games of doctor; and women who had lost everything in the storm were turning tricks. He hadn't mentioned this to Jane, and he didn't now, but one look at those men standing outside the trailer, hands in pockets, the red ribbon dangling from the door handle, and he knew that the trailer was open for business.

Those men were patient, but no one else seemed to be. Breakfast wasn't served until eight o'clock, but even now the line was growing—Mitchell could see it from their trailer on the other side of the camp. The other refugees streamed by them, quick-walking or jogging toward the food. It was unsettling, this mania at every meal, the people rapacious in their hunger. It was like they were racing against one another. It was like they were running for their lives.

They waited ninety minutes before being handed their microwaved breakfast burrito. It was cold. Biting into the tortilla, the flaky eggs coming loose all over the paper wrapping, the congealed salsa oozing like berry preserves, Mitchell thought of the frozen burritos he had stocked in his freezer before it had been crowded out by his money, and he had a strange pang of nostalgia for his old apartment. What condition was it in now? If an empty house, left alone for a single year, begins to harbor animals, what happens to a New York City apartment, its window blown in, its electricity out, in the week after a hurricane? Do rats make nests in the bathtub? Does the couch bloom moss? He didn't want to think about the refrigerator. Undoubtedly by now the leftovers from Chosan Galbi had colonized the shelves, employing crude biological warfare, entrenching for a long occupation.

"This is gruggy," said Jane, washing down a bite with a gulp from her allotted pint of orange juice. "But I'm going to eat every morsel." She appeared to gag slightly as she pushed the burrito into her mouth.

They sat on a bench crushed between the Motas and the Watkins family of East New York. The Watkinses had been behind Jane and Mitchell in line. Between increasingly violent imprecations to their misbehaving children—there seemed to be about eleven of them in all—they had recited a tedious story about taking a public bus for eight hours through Queens with a band of manacled convicts.

"We're too rich for this," Mitchell whispered. He was trying to eat quickly and avoid eye contact with the other refugees, wearing his FEMA baseball hat low on his head. He worried about a repeat of yesterday's encounter. Perhaps Marcy Rosado would see him and arouse her mob. Only this time the mob would include the entire camp.

"Exactly," said Jane. "We should be eating baked Alaska or something. Though I'd settle for a hamburger."

She did look starving. Like a refugee.

"I can't stop thinking of that building you ran into at Ticonderoga," she said.

"The infirmary. Where Elsa lived."

"How the walls were collapsing in on themselves. That's how it's been since Tammy, isn't it? The walls collapsing in on themselves?"

Mitchell put down his burrito. He leaned in so that the Motas and Watkinses couldn't overhear.

"You think I'm good at predicting disasters?"

"Not really," said Jane. "I'm just betting my career on it."

"Well, this?" He gestured around the meal tent, at the impatient refugees still standing in line, at the Watkinses screaming at their children, who were stealing one another's burritos. "This is a disaster waiting to happen."

"I know," said Jane, and she put down her burrito. "I can't eat this anymore. Let's just go back to the trailer. *Now.*"

They hadn't gone more than twenty yards when a bomb detonated. A plume of smoke burst into the air three rows down. They approached cautiously, following the crowd across the field. A trailer's propane tank had burst. Gas fumes blurred the air. The couple who lived there were lying on the grass, blackened by the smoke.

"They're dead," said Jane.

But the couple began to cough and wheeze, and slowly they crawled away from the wreckage. The crowd stood by and watched until the flames had burned themselves out. And then they began to line up for lunch.

# 9.

The corner of the chain-link fence was occluded by the blocky form of Hank Cho. "Blocky" wasn't quite the right term: he really resembled a single block, as of granite or wood. A human two-by-four. Even from twenty-five yards away, in the darkness, there was no mistaking his girth. Jane squeezed Mitchell's arm.

"Where are all the others?"

"Maybe they're coming."

"Maybe this is a *trap*."

It was an argument that would have persuaded the old Mitchell. If he had worried that Alec Charnoble, at their first meeting, might slaughter him in the middle of the night on the seventy-fifth floor of the Empire State Building, where surveillance cameras and motion sensors and keystroke recorders detected their every move, then shouldn't he be alarmed at the prospect of meeting an inordinately built Korean—or Chinese—man in the middle of the night on an island that had minimal security and was descending briskly into *chaos*? Soon the men would be stalking one another as at Ticonderoga and at the flooded deli on Madison Avenue. What would stop Hank Cho from dismembering them right there and then? He could boast to the rest of the refugees that he had killed the false prophet. Yet even as Mitchell's brain went through the familiar convolutions of worst-case scenarioism, he felt oddly removed from himself. His brain's logical infrastructure still functioned, but the fear, the hot animal fear, was absent. He yanked Jane the final fifteen yards toward Hank Cho.

"Hey guys," said Hank. He sounded sleepy. "Glad you came."

"Where is everybody?" said Jane.

"Guess they're scared." Hank looked at his watch. "I think it's just us three."

They stood in silence for several moments. Jane hiccuped.

"Yeah," said Hank. "Let's probably go." He started walking in the direction of the bridge.

Jane took Mitchell's hand, and squeezed it.

"I'm putting all my trust in you," she said.

"And I'm putting all my trust in Hank Cho."

Jane stopped in her tracks. "You've completely lost it."

Laughing, they followed the giant into the darkness.

◻ ◻ ◻

Queens was invisible. From the span of the Hell Gate they could see, ahead and to the left, the white glare of the klieg lights over LaGuardia Airport. The Mosquitoes were doing their work, sucking the polluted water from the runways and spraying the slurry into the bay in geysers that sparkled like formations of dark quartz. The rest of the borough was dark. It was a cloudy night, the moon as invisible as the Rockaways, so it was impossible to assess the damage in the neighborhoods beneath the train tracks. Still, Mitchell thought he could glimpse forms moving in the blackness—anxious, darting movements, like scurrying rats. Only much larger. He told himself it was a figment of his imagination.

"Just follow the light," said Hank, like a deathbed priest. Once they'd crossed the bridge, he aimed a yellow industrial flashlight in front of him. A second, dimmer model was tucked into his belt, mostly illuminating his buttocks but also spilling down to trace the narrow gravel strip between the northbound and southbound tracks. The gravel bounced and flickered as he walked, the light wobbling with each of his lumbering steps—for such a strong man he was rather clumsy of gait. They walked single file, Jane in the middle. And they didn't talk. What was there to say? Any efforts at trivialities sounded absurd, even blasphemous against the night's silence. There were no birdcalls, no crepitation of insects, not even frogs—only the crunch of the gravel and the light *phthapping* of the flashlight against Hank Cho's bottom. After about half an hour, or an hour, or two—it was impossible to tell anymore—Hank halted their procession. He passed out cans of water and they drank greedily. When they were finished they tossed the empty cans over the railing and listened closely, as if the clink of the cans might describe the terrain of the streets below. But all they heard were three large plops. They kept walking, more quickly now.

What were they doing? What were they thinking? Mitchell tried not to think at all by concentrating on the path. He had to be careful to walk in a straight line so as not to veer off the tracks.

But of course he had already veered off the tracks. That's exactly what he had done! He had run himself off the rails: the rails of his career and perhaps of his sanity. He had never adhered to them well—they'd always been slick, his sanity rails. And now the train was careening into the darkness, the engineer slumped unconscious over the wheel, his shoulder pressing on the accelerator. But this newest excursion was not entirely inconsistent with his past behavior. He had been running away from things for as long as he could remember: from Overland Park, the Zukorminiums,

Fitzsimmons Sherman, FutureWorld, New York, Ticonderoga, Randall's Island. The more he ran from things, the less he knew where he was. Where would it end?

"Are you still there?" Jane asked without turning.

"Yeah," he said. But he wasn't so sure.

"I'm still here," said another voice in the darkness. It was a female voice, but it wasn't Jane. And it spoke without sound.

"I don't think you are," said Mitchell, soundlessly. "I don't think you're anywhere."

"Then why can you hear me?" said Elsa.

Mitchell didn't have an answer to that one.

"It's like this for me," she continued. "Walking down a long track through darkness, unable to see or hear anything."

"Are you in pain?"

"I am not going to answer that."

"We're more similar than we're different, aren't we?"

"We do have something in common," said Elsa.

"Obsession."

"There aren't so many like us, you know. We are crippled by extreme beliefs."

"*Extreme* seems a bit extreme. I would say strongly held."

"We don't listen when others try to tell us something."

"We don't listen unless it suits us," said Mitchell. "You didn't listen to me."

"You still aren't listening to me."

"I'm trying. I am."

"Obsession gives us purpose. I don't think your friend understands that."

Mitchell looked at Jane ahead of him, walking lazily over the gravel.

"Without obsession," said Mitchell, "I have nothing. All I have is wandering through a shapeless black void."

"What are you going to do when you get to the Flatlands?"

"I don't know. I'm afraid. What am I going to eat? Drink? Will there be anything resembling a bathroom? Will there be more violence? And say I do make it a few days, what happens next? Can you tell me?"

"I cannot."

"But do you know? Do you know what's waiting for me in the Flatlands?"

"Oh yes," said Elsa, and there was something dark and tinkling in her voice. "I know what is waiting for you."

Elsa was laughing and the track curved slightly to the right and the dancing light from Hank Cho's flashlight bounced over the tracks, disrupting the darkness. And Elsa was gone.

How good his fears had been to him! While they lingered, he had that thing so exalted by schoolteachers and guidance counselors: an All-Consuming Passion. He had a profession too. He missed them, his fears, just as he missed his skycity and even, in a perverse way, the cockroaches. Now there was only the void. With every step he took on the elevated tracks, the barrier weakened—the barrier that separated what was inside him and what was outside of him. The broken world beyond the tracks was seeping inside him. Or was it the other way around?

He reached for Jane's hand. She squeezed it. But since he was walking behind her this soon became awkward and she pulled her hand away.

◫ ◫ ◫

"How long do you think it's been?" said Jane. She was on the edge of tears.

"Two and a half hours?"

"I'd say six." She sighed. "Please, God, let this end soon."

They were taking a bathroom break. During the last stretch the track had run for several minutes through an underground tunnel—a short but horrifying tunnel, which was like walking through an ink blot—and when they emerged they were at ground level, the tracks hemmed between two lines of trees. It looked like they had entered a forest. Had they left the city? Were they in Long Island? Were they back in Central Park? Jane had squatted ten yards behind him, several paces from the tracks. Mitchell was pissing on the southbound track. He wasn't going to piss in the woods. He didn't want to know what was in the woods.

"Six hours, the sun would be out."

"Who knows. The same rules don't seem to apply."

"It's been four hours and twenty-five minutes," said Hank. It was the first thing he'd said other than announcing the bathroom breaks. "And that over there? Way up ahead? That's Flatlands Avenue."

"Where?" said Mitchell.

"*There,*" said the giant, pointing at a vague, slightly paler patch of darkness in the distance, past where the trees ended.

"So this is the Flatlands," said Jane.

"It's Canarsie," said Hank. "But close enough."

They walked several minutes longer, until the tracks began to angle to the right. Hank continued straight, stepping over the tracks. They were now on a dirt road littered with trash.

"Keep walking," said Hank. "Try not to get your feet stuck."

Mitchell obeyed. The ground was still muddy. Occasionally his shoe landed on something squishy, a bloated rat carcass perhaps or something larger, but he didn't dare look down. They kept to the median, where the ground was slightly higher and there was less debris. Finally they came to a stretch of smooth cement. Before them appeared an area of low brush. At the horizon the sky was beginning to lighten.

"Flatlands," said Hank.

"What do we do here?"

"I'm going to rest," said Hank, lowering himself to the concrete. "I'm tired."

"We're just going to sleep on the ground?"

"That's right."

"And then?"

"Then we make sure that we're alone."

# IO.

It wasn't so bad if you wrapped a towel around your face like a keffiyeh. There was an art to it. You had to cover as much of your face as possible, but the fabric couldn't entirely cover your eyes. If you yanked the towel down too much, the stink got in—and then it invaded you, gumming up your pores and pricking your eyes. But if you tucked the edge of the towel just below your eyes and pressed the fabric close to your cheeks, you could endure five minutes, which was enough time to fill most of a shopping cart.

Jane hadn't mastered the technique. Almost instantly she had sprinted, gagging, for the exit. And she did not return. When Mitchell rumbled his shopping cart out of the warehouse, she was gone.

There was only the loading dock and the stacks of cans in their carts and the empty expanse. Hank Cho had been right about the Flatlands. The lands had been flattened. There was little evidence that buildings had stood here just one week earlier, and just as little evidence of the flood: only a puddle here and there, as after a light rain. Few structures remained three-dimensional—a tepee of cracked plywood, brick foundation slabs, two concrete walls leaning on each other for support like a pair of old drunks. Most everything else had been pounded into the ground or wiped into the ocean, rinsed like a soiled plate after dinner. The only surviving buildings appeared to be the oldest ones.

Before Mitchell and Jane had even awoken that morning, Hank had discovered a stone church standing on what he believed had been East 100th Street (he found the street sign several yards from the building, spiked halfway into the ground, though he'd also found signs for East 101st Street and East 99th Street farther down the block). There was no bathroom—no plumbing or electrical wire—but the interior was surprisingly clear. The floor was dry. Other than a smattering of bloated loofahs that, in the antediluvian era, had been prayer books, the only evidence of a flood was the peculiar arrangement of the wooden pews. They crowded in the entrance, stacked nearly to the ceiling. It was as if the pews had tried to climb over one another in a desperate attempt to save themselves from drowning. The pews had remained in this configuration when the floodwaters drained from the church, but the structure was flimsy; Hank gave a shove and like a scaffold it tumbled to the ground with a riotous clatter.

One of the stained glass windows was intact. It depicted two serpents, two deer, and two eagles. The background was royal blue, and the animals stared with large eyes toward the heavens.

Mitchell and Jane found roomier quarters on what had been Flatlands Avenue. The Canarsie Bank Trust Company was an old financial fortress, the kind built in the early twentieth century, modeled after an Italian Renaissance palazzo, with touches of brazen American showmanship. It was eerie to come across this beacon of high business authority in the middle of the desolate, flood-ravaged badlands—like encountering a monolith on the moon. The facade was white limestone brick, and the double-high top story was set behind a series of columns. The attitude of the three-story building was best expressed by the granite eagle that perched over the high entry arch; it seemed excessively prideful, the eagle, the way it surveyed the wreckage of the neighborhood. The newer, cheaply constructed buildings that had crowded around it in recent years were now less than rubble. The Canarsie Bank Trust had outlasted them all.

Jane's phone rang.

"Who is it?" said Mitchell.

"Tewilliger," Jane whispered. She gestured for him to continue inside the building.

The front door had shattered, but it still hung on by the hinges; it looked as if someone had burst through the center of it with a battering ram. Mitchell reached inside and turned the bolt lock. Then he pushed the door. It fell flat over.

The interior was grander than the exterior. A dark floor of red travertine, stately brown teller counters, globe-shaped pendent lamps. Since the front entrance was raised, the flooding hadn't been catastrophic; the waterline reached only to chest level. As in the church, the loose furniture had huddled together in fear. The clerical desks and chairs were piled in one corner like a beaver dam.

Mitchell stepped across the atrium and creaked through an ancient turnstile. The air was thick with dust; it rose in puffs from the blood-colored floor with every step. A flight of stone stairs took him to the second level. Here was a lounge, lined with bookshelves and metal cabinets, the drawers all open, files spilling out. It looked as if it had been ransacked by burglars unable to find what they were looking for.

He forgot everything and decided he was exploring an abandoned world at the edge of the universe. There was no sleep or sadness here and beside him was a beautiful girl with long blue hair and soft violet eyes who would live with him happily ever after in a castle by the sea. They would speak to each other without sound and daydream their lives away.

"Mitchell?" Jane's voice was frantic and it made everything rush back to him, especially the fear.

"Up here."

When she appeared in the stairwell she was holding the collar of her shirt over her mouth.

"Phone died," she said. "But we were about finished anyway." She coughed. "This place is not to code."

"Yeah, but it's beautiful."

"Compared to its neighbors."

"Everything OK with Tewilliger?"

"She sat out the flood in the office. The tower was leaning in the winds, but she survived. She's with a nephew in Virginia. And quite pissed."

They climbed to the third floor. The dust puffed around them. In the inner chambers they found couches that had been shielded from the rain. Jane sat on one; the leather gave generously.

"I could sleep on this," she said. "But last night I slept on asphalt."

In the outer offices—those facing the street—the storm had sucked out the windowpanes and the rooms were caked with bird droppings that rose in bent, conical stalagmites. The water stains on the white plaster wall looked like cat's eyes, concentric circles in alternating shades of brown.

"Another thing about Tewilliger," said Jane. She bobbed on the leather cushion.

"Yeah?"

"She's suing Charnoble."

"Why?"

"Intentional infliction of emotional distress. For making her work on the day Tammy hit."

"Wow. Good for her."

"She has a case. She can prove that Charnoble understood exactly the danger of the hurricane. It's all in your memos, after all. A suit could bring down the whole company. Just look at Seattle."

"Wouldn't she just qualify for some type of worker's comp?"

"That's the best part. Apparently Charnoble neglected to sign FutureWorld's own insurance forms. He's not insured."

"I guess I shouldn't be surprised."

"He wasn't a true believer."

"He was a salesman. He believed in that."

"Just wait till we start our own firm," she said. "He'll never know what hit him."

"Judging by his phone messages, I think he's starting to get a pretty good idea."

"Future Days," said Jane. "Where there's life, there's no hope."

"Future Days," said Mitchell. "No prophet is accepted in his own country."

"No. That's not a proper one. Was that scripture?"

"Future Days," said Mitchell. "Foresight is always twenty-twenty."

"We're going to have to work on those."

Mitchell walked to the windows.

"Don't fall, please," called Jane from the couch.

"The structure at least seems solid, though."

"I have no idea. It's stone. Isn't it the stone house that the big bad wolf can't blow down?"

"Well it's not the straw house, or the one made of sticks."

But from this height you could see that it was exactly straw and sticks that had saved the Canarsie Bank Trust. Across from the building, on the other side of Flatlands Avenue, lay a long marsh, a dense scrabble of destroyed trees and dried brush. It was two blocks wide and extended some six avenues long, until it touched the sea. The entire acreage was clogged with trash and plaster and splintered shingles, which meant that the marsh had done its job: it had buffered the winds and the rising water.

And so the Canarsie Bank Trust was a real castle; it even had a moat.

◻ ◻ ◻

They began in the outer rooms. The wood floor was still damp. Beneath the windows a pattern of mold—black and green polka dots—had begun to climb the wall. There was a sharp, rotten odor, and they soon found the source: a toad, its flat green head crowned with glass shards and fragments of sash. Using a hard manila folder as a shovel, Mitchell scooped the carcass off the floor and flopped it out the window.

"If this were cleaned up," said Jane as they began to pick the branches and muddy tufts of grass off the floor, "it wouldn't make a bad temporary office for Future Days."

The sunlight, hitting the broken glass, cast prismatic shapes across the floor—rhombuses, triangles, diamonds. The breeze, washing through the room in a continuous flow from the sea, flushed out the scent of the dead frog. Through the windows you could see clear to the ocean. Even the Belt Parkway, which crossed the far end of the marsh, was still visible in the sunlight, though its platform was still a foot underwater. A furry animal with a bouncier gait than a dog was jogging along Flatlands Avenue. Was that a fox? Mitchell had never seen a fox. "It wouldn't make a bad office," said Jane, "if it weren't in the middle of a postapocalyptic wasteland."

She chucked a clump of moss out the window.

It was a warm day, and they were sweating, but the work was satisfying. It was brainless, mechanical labor and you could chart your progress by comparing the amount of dirt inside the offices with the amount on the street below. Jane was smiling at him.

"What?" said Mitchell.

"You look . . . different."

"Like strong? From the canoeing?"

"No. Like confident," she said, but there was something bittersweet in her smile. "Like happy."

"Aren't you happy? Isn't it a relief to be off that island?"

"Manhattan? Or Randall's?"

"Well, both. But especially Randall's."

"Yes." But she wasn't looking at him anymore. Her fingers palpated the surface of a long maple desk that was dappled with white water spots. She began rubbing away at one of these spots. This was not particularly useful—the water spots were the least of their problems. Nor was she making much progress, though she seemed to be putting significant effort into it. It would be more helpful to get started on, say, the birdshit stalagmites. But Mitchell sensed it was best not to interfere. He was doing more of that, he found. Sensing. Less logic, more intuition. He wasn't confident that it was working.

Once they were down to their last two cans of water they went to find Hank Cho at his church. It was about fifteen blocks away, but blocks no longer made sense as a unit of measurement—the distance was shorter because now you could walk diagonally through the grid. Hank was waiting for them on the stairs outside. There was a peculiar, stretched expression across his face. Mitchell realized it was the first time he had ever seen Hank grin.

"I found it," said Hank. He was rocking from one foot to the other like a kid who had to pee.

"Found what?" said Jane.

"Jackpot!"

☒ ☒ ☒

Jackpot Eastern Market Supply was an enormous cement warehouse near the corner of Flatlands and Pennsylvania, about a mile east of the Canarsie Bank Trust. It had been run by a Chinese import agency that specialized, apparently, in everything. Square sections of ceiling had collapsed in the storm, and the warehouse had partially flooded. The merchandise on the shelves closest to the ground was mush, leaching a chromatic array of industrial dyes that pooled on the cement floor. But the pillars of sunlight lancing through the ceiling at least allowed them to see. As Hank led them down an aisle they passed parcels of fish food, copper pots, propane stoves, knife sets, beach towels. Mitchell stepped over a torn bag of fertilizer that had been colonized by a scraggly beard of orange moss.

"Is there an organizing principle here?" said Mitchell.

"It's in alphabetical order," said Hank. He handed beach towels to Jane and Mitchell. "In Chinese."

They smelled it before they could see it. And before they could smell it, they could feel it—on their faces, in their eyes. Their eyes filled.

"Put them on," said Hank. He demonstrated the technique with his own towel.

They emerged into an open section of floor, where thousands of cans and sealed bags of food and plastic water jugs were stacked on pallets in magnificent towers that rose to the ceiling. It was a city of food. That was the good news. The bad news: the back wall was lined with freezers. They had been thawing for nearly a week. Sludge, the color of kidneys, oozed gently from the vents. White worms pullulated within the freezers. You could see them churning, pushing against the glass panels.

Hank, pressing the towel firmly across his face, pointed to a set of shopping carts and then to the towers of cans. "Get going," he said, his voice muffled by the terry cloth. "Before we run out of time." They looked at the bank of freezers. One of the doors was beginning to bulge.

◘ ◘ ◘

Outside Mitchell heard a violent heaving. He found Jane around the corner, several yards down the side of the warehouse, her forehead against the wall. A plastic water jug was on the ground next to her, half empty.

"Just leave me," she said.

"Here. Take this."

She glanced quickly at him, but when she saw the towel she recoiled, as if he'd offered her a scorpion. Shuddering, she covered her mouth.

"It's the smell," she gasped. "It's an atrocity."

"Where?"

"It's on the towel. It's on *you*."

He had already become used to it. After the reek of sewage in flooded Manhattan and the mold in their trailer on Randall's Island, what was a little rotting meat?

"I'm leaving," she said.

"Wait a minute."

"No." She turned to face him. Her hair hung in loose clumps; her eyes were strained. "I'm going back."

"Just stay outside—I'll handle the rest of the shopping."

"And then what?"

"And then," he said. "Well—"

"You want to stay here. In *this*." She waved at the littered expanse, the dirt fields.

"You saw the bank building. It's nice."

She laughed—a short, caustic burst of air—and shook her head. "You've already decided."

"I don't know yet."

"I do. And I know how you feel about Future Days."

The smell hit him all at once then, and he felt he was about to be sick.

"You've made up your mind," said Jane. "You probably made up your mind as far back as Maine. Fort Lee, even."

In his mind he was floating with her again in Central Park, she was laughing and chewing animal crackers, the crow was shrieking, the sky was brightly scrubbed blue, and Mitchell and Jane were enclosed by the branches of the oak trees, laughing and floating together.

"I've been trying to imagine what it'd be like," he said. "Starting a new company."

"And?"

"It's not for me. The business of fear. All day stuck in a cell, creating worst-case scenarios. Doomsday every single day."

"So you lied to me," said Jane.

"That's not it."

"You've changed. I don't understand it."

"Look, the FEMA camp is going to hell. FEMA camps always do, you know. Let's try this. For a little while, at least."

"I went to the roof this morning."

"The roof?"

"At the bank building. While you were in the front room, I slipped upstairs. From the roof you can see the tip of Manhattan."

A silence stretched between them, stretched taut, and then it snapped.

"What did you see?" Mitchell said.

"The Mosquitoes are gone."

"Really."

She cocked her head, as if listening to something he was saying. But he had stopped speaking. So she was listening to some other voice, one he couldn't hear. When this internal voice finished delivering its message, her eyes snapped back to his.

"I want to be there when the city comes back," she said. "I want to be part of that. Hank was right. This neighborhood will take months to come back. Years, even. They might forget about it altogether."

Mitchell nodded.

"That's why you want to stay, isn't it?"

"I haven't thought it through," he said. "For the first time in my life I'm not thinking anything through."

"Yeah? Well, I've thought it through."

She was right. He *had* changed. But she hadn't. She was the same: passionate, committed, loyal Jane Eppler. Her loyalty had shifted, however. It was not with him anymore. Her loyalty was with Future Days, with New York.

"You can use my name," he said. "If it helps you. My scenarios, too. Take them all."

"I might do that."

"I'd like you to."

With a sudden, almost deranged intensity, Jane lunged toward him with arms outspread. The embrace didn't last long. Just as abruptly she pulled away from him, as in disgust. She picked up the water jug. Without looking back, she set off in the direction of the train tracks.

Mitchell let her go.

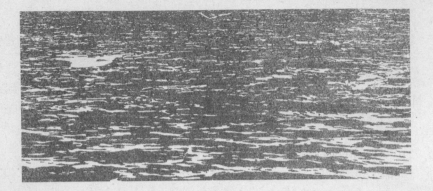

## II.

Order, logic, reason. Order, order, order, *order.* If you said "order" enough times in a row, you were guaranteed to drive yourself mad.

Think of it as a geometry problem. The first step was demarcation: draw the x- and y-axes, name the variables. Most important of all, define the boundaries. Otherwise you were just beckoning chaos.

The rectangular plot adjacent to the bank building on Flatlands Avenue was about half the size of a basketball court. The surface soil was orange. That was the only indication that a structure had stood there a week earlier, for the building itself had vanished. Mitchell scouted the surrounding land for any materials he could find. He loaded bent ribbons of wood and shattered masonry and sections of granite tile into a wheelbarrow that had been generously donated by Jackpot Eastern Market Supply. He dumped the debris along the border of his estate, where it began to accrete into a ramshackle perimeter wall. It would take days before the wall became functional—it was no more than a couple of feet at its highest point. But it seemed crucial to create a border to the property. A barrier would be necessary once the garden began to grow, if only to keep out the rats. They were everywhere, the rats. Without buildings or walls to shelter them, they had been forced out into the open. They raced, bewildered and terrorized, across the scarred landscape in search of any scrap that might shelter them. Many of them darted into the marsh, though few emerged from it. That's because other, larger animals were moving in, no doubt attracted by the increasing availability of rodents. He'd now seen two foxes, an opossum, and a raccoon. On his second night he had been kept up by what he assumed must have been an owl, though it did not hoot. It gave a wounded cry: *Ow! Ow-ow-ow-ow-ow*—like a child rubbing his boo-boo. Or being stabbed. *OW OW OW!* Yes, it would be important to build the wall high. At least to the height of a tall human being. It was impossible to know what was lurking in this wilderness—or who.

The ground floor was still a mess, but at least now it was an orderly and relatively hygienic one. Mitchell had stockpiled supplies from Jackpot—not just food but clothing (ersatz Benetton T-shirts and cotton-polyester blend slacks and triple packs of boxer briefs), an ax with a two-foot haft, rubber gloves, sanitizing wipes, bleach, barrels, shovels, padlocks. He kept the more valuable tools, along with his cash, in the old vault, which the previous tenants had cleaned out before the storm.

One afternoon, his third, or fourth—he was already beginning to lose track of the days—he ran into Hank outside of Jackpot.

"Your friend," said Hank. "She gone?"

"I'm afraid so."

"She didn't want to be here."

"How do you know?"

"You could tell. The way she walked, even. Like she was being punished." He looked at Mitchell closely. "You going to stay?"

"For now," said Mitchell.

"Then you're going to want these." Hank pointed at three bags of compost in his shopping cart. "Third aisle. With the garden supplies."

Mitchell looked at him in confusion.

"You dig a hole in the ground. As deep as you can. Then you dump in a full bag of compost."

"OK. Then what?"

"Then you take a shit, man."

"Oh. Right."

He would deal with the latrine later—for now the marsh would have to serve. Besides, there were more immediate problems. With Jane gone and Hank ensconced in his cathedral, he was deeply, emphatically alone. It wasn't only that he was without other people—that he could deal with. He had been without other people for so much of his life. But now he was without belief. He had forsaken the cult of fear, had abandoned the order of the futurists. For what was obsession anyway but a kind of intense faith? Yes, a new faith was required, something rigorous, ascetic, all-encompassing. Because if he couldn't find one, then all he had was order order order order order order order order order order order order order order order order order order.

He couldn't help but think of Ticonderoga. It was the only comparable scenario he knew. In Starling they had repurposed the land to create a self-sufficient habitat. Sure, it had ended badly, but only because of the twin blows of Brugada and Tammy. Maybe something could be learned from Elsa's blueprint. Upon reaching Maine, what was the first thing she had done? He thought back to her first letter. *In April,* she had written, *we tilled the baseball field.*

He wasn't a true believer, but what else was available to him? He had to have time to think, and during that time he'd need to eat, give himself shelter, work. Most of all to work.

He began by pounding the ground with a hoe, breaking up the

dirt. The undersoil was still damp, so the surface crust punctured easily and the chalky layer beneath gave little resistance. But that didn't matter—the pain began almost immediately. His knees grumbled, his back sobbed, his shoulder shrieked.

He wondered what Jane was doing.

He lugged a water jug outside and began again. It was October now, and the temperature was starting to drop into the sixties, maybe even the high fifties, but soon the sweat was so heavy that he took off his T-shirt and then his pants. Orange dirt descended in rivulets down his chest. Blisters appeared in the crooks of his fingers. By the time he'd finished smashing up the entire field the sun was nearly touching the horizon. He dropped the hoe and stumbled into the marsh.

You had to go slow, hesitatingly, careful not to get hooked by a loose nail or a stubborn branch. Sections of warped plywood and broken trees were tangled with the brush. It was like walking through dirty, matted hair. He stepped carefully around a toppled tree trunk that had landed upside down in the earth. Its crown was lodged in the ground, and its root system spread in the air like branches. He heard a song in his head:

*Oh take me back to Elkhart Lake, where the cotton candy grows.*
*Where the little marshmallows hang from the trees.*
*And the lollipops grow on the ground!*

After a hundred yards he found a muddy finger of land that pointed into a calm pool. Here the earth was smoother, covered only by a light blush of moss. This was where the ocean began. Beyond this pool the creek snaked around a bend before expanding into a wide channel that fed Jamaica Bay. He removed his sneakers and waded in, the mud slimy beneath his feet, until the water rose to his armpits. The creek was rust colored, silty, and very cold. Without thinking, without caring, he dunked his head.

The water flooded his ears, tickled his face, cradled his brain. The coldness was shocking, but when he resurfaced, everything had sharpened. The whiteness of the sky, the marsh's clicking insect choruses, the breeze against his face like a fresh shave.

On the way back to the bank building he congratulated himself for not worrying about the toxins that might have tainted his little bath—mercury, PCBs, dioxins, sewage. But perhaps they'd had an effect. A prickly wooziness settled over him, and as soon as he reached the upstairs couch he was dizzy. When he lay down the cushion under his head became a brick and knocked him into unconsciousness.

◻ ◻ ◻

He was tamping down the soil one afternoon, speculating about the alimentary properties of the marsh breeze—would it nourish the spinach or desiccate it?—when he began to hear the voices.

He had started by planting spinach because it was the only vegetable he recognized among the small pouches of vegetable seeds he'd found at Jackpot. His haul had included snow peas, kohlrabi, bitter gourd, soybean, burdock, and ten-pound bags containing soil the color of crushed brownies.

How the mighty had fallen. Mitchell Zukor, the internationally renowned prophet, with $1,996.50 sitting in a backpack twenty yards away—he had given the balance, $50,000, to Jane for use as start-up capital—was now on his hands and knees, scrounging in the orange dirt, choking on it, getting it into his eyes and underwear.

But whatever had started to happen to him in the cold waters of the marsh continued to happen. The long stretches of quiet labor narcotized him. Time was again becoming strange. It moved in erratic ways: in large bounds, when he worked in the fields. During other activities, as when he bathed in the marsh, it halted altogether. Light determined everything: his sleep schedule, his mealtimes, his bodily functions. The mineral smell of freshly turned earth also contributed, as did the sharp, wet breeze of the swamp, like the whip of a wet towel, that passed freely through the exploded windows of the third floor where he slept. The general sensation was of mindlessness. He didn't know what he was going to do next, though that didn't bother him. All that mattered was that he was now doing something.

But then he heard the voices. And they were calling his name.

So this is how it would happen. Hadn't he, to a certain extent, been waiting for it? First the inexplicable impulse to follow Hank Cho on his kamikaze mission, then the rolling about nearly naked in the dirt, and finally the voices calling out to him, singing hymns, telling him to drown himself in the ocean.

"Mitchell Zukor?"

The voices weren't quite inside his head, but they weren't far away either. They were coming from the direction of the marsh.

"Mr. Zukor?"

He turned, expecting to see nothing, or worse—a seven-foot-tall cockroach, for instance, wearing a monocle—but instead there were two people, a man and a woman, roughly his own age. They stood directly beside each other on an archipelago of sidewalk that was all that remained of Flatlands Avenue. Each wore a bulky backpack; the girl had a blue bandanna wrapped around her head. They looked like hikers who had taken a wrong turn off the Appalachian Trail. A disastrously wrong turn.

"Jane told us we'd find you here," said the boy. "Jane Eppler."

"Who are you?"

"Ronald. This here's Cassie."

"Hey," said Cassie. She took one step forward, stepping to the edge of the garden plot.

Mitchell leaped up. "Listen," he said, glancing nervously at Cassie's feet, "I just spent two full days tilling this land."

Ronald reached for Cassie's hand and pulled her back. "Oh," said Cassie. "Of course. It looks good."

These social niceties, their tentative, smiling approach—there was something vestigial about it all. It was pathetically antediluvian. He had no time for it. State your purpose, then be on your way. And leave me alone.

"Jane asked us to check on you," said Ronald. "Make sure you're OK." He was looking at Mitchell very closely.

"It's only been, what, five days? What could've happened to me in that time?"

The two of them glanced at each other.

"It's been almost two weeks. At least since Jane came back to the island."

"Hm. I don't know about that."

"We just wanted to make sure everything was . . . OK."

"I'm fine," said Mitchell. "You can go back to Randall's Island and tell Jane I'm *fine*."

"We're not going back," said Ronald.

"And she's not on Randall's Island anymore," said Cassie. Her mouth opened wide when she spoke, disclosing a winking pearl within. A tongue stud: another quaint, even nostalgic touch, a relic from the early part of the century, like fax machines or vitamin supplements. "Jane is in Manhattan. They opened it up. On Wednesday."

"Wednesday," said Mitchell. He chewed on it like a recalcitrant wad of taffy. "*Wed*-nes-day."

"Three days ago."

Three days. Knowing Jane, she'd probably already rented an office, hired a staff, designed a website, issued press releases, negotiated contracts with all of FutureWorld's old clients. Joined Tewilliger's suit against Alec Charnoble. Ate a steak at the Palm, side of creamed spinach, side of half-and-half.

"You said you were staying here?"

"We want to do what you're doing," said Ronald.

"You walked away from 'Mitchell Zukor,'" said Cassie. "You walked away from everything, all the old systems. We want that too. A lot of people want that."

"No," said Mitchell. This wouldn't do. "I can't help you."

"We're not asking to stay with you," said Ronald. "We found a structure about a mile down. A school. And Jane told us about Jackpot."

What was Jane after? Was she sincerely worried about what might happen to him, left to his own devices, all alone in this storm-ravaged wasteland? Or was this a subtle poke, an effort to get him to return to Manhattan and help launch Future Days?

"There's really no reason for Jane to worry," said Mitchell. "I'm self-sufficient."

The couple exchanged another look. "You know," said Cassie, "this area is part of the Dead Zone. Canarsie, Flatlands, across to Sheepshead Bay and Gravesend—the whole swath along the water—it's been classified as Zone Five."

"What's a Zone Five?"

"The unflooded areas are Zone One. Lower Manhattan is Zone Two. Downtown Brooklyn is Zone Three. They've had to prioritize the rebuilding effort."

"So this is last."

"Dead last. They're saying they might let it go back to nature. Wetlands restoration. To serve as a natural buffer against future storms."

It was a farsighted policy. Perhaps they'd learned the lessons of recent meteorology. The refugees on Randall's Island who had lived in Zone 5 wouldn't be pleased, of course. But it wasn't anything to get concerned about now. If Seattle were any model, those legal battles wouldn't be resolved for years. Mitchell's thinking was now decidedly short-term.

"So, if you need us," said Cassie, "for anything? We'll be at the school."

Mitchell nodded warily.

"Or we'll see you around, I guess."

*"Cassie,"* said Ronald under his breath.

"What?"

He took her by the arm. "Let's go. He's working."

"There are others, you know," said Cassie, shirking off Ronald. "There are others coming. Others like us. We want to start something here."

Mitchell turned his back on them and bent to the dirt. But he watched the couple out of the corner of his eye as they walked away. They watched him too, glancing back every few paces. When they finally disappeared behind a ruin—not a structure, exactly, but a mound of wooden planks and bent telephone poles, like a mammoth funeral pyre, festooned with tangled copper cables—Mitchell dropped the bag of spinach seeds. The garden would have to be postponed. He needed more debris. He had to build up his wall faster. If word had gotten out, if more people were coming, he needed to insure his privacy. He would also have to make another trip to Jackpot before others started competing for supplies. And before the maggots and rats colonized the entire warehouse.

He was under no illusions. Out here in the neighborhood formerly known as Flatlands—or was it Canarsie?—he wouldn't unearth Eden, or even some agrarian ideal. Most likely his work here wouldn't amount to very much at all. He knew nothing, after all, about farming, fertilization, engineering, construction. Problems would arise that he could not anticipate, and he'd be comically unprepared to fix them. The weather would only become increasingly erratic. The fields might go fallow or flood. Winter would be excruciating. And a single serious injury or illness would force him to give up. There was also the danger that he might lose his nerve.

Yet he doubted this. The only thing stronger than his desire to stay in the Flatlands was his aversion to the idea of returning to his old life.

A time would come, perhaps even in the next month, when he would need to sneak back to the city for supplies: a generator, a water filtration system, perhaps even wind turbines or photovoltaic panels, the kind Elsa had installed at Ticonderoga. And books: on energy harvesting, basic engineering, agriculture. Best-case scenario, he would create a few hundred square yards of farmland next to the bank building and another plot, half that size, behind the building. He had enough bottled water to last a couple of months, and after that he supposed he could collect rainwater and boil it. He'd be away from the world, yet in it more intimately than he had ever known. *Doing:* finally. At night he would go to bed with the smell of the orange dirt in his nostrils, the sour taste of it in the back of his throat.

The cynic in him laughed derisively. The logician in him, however, responded curtly, and not without condescension: it wasn't a question of idealism; it was survival. In the Canarsie Bank Trust Company building he would create his own self-contained universe. This was a future. It might not be the best possible future or even a particularly comfortable future, but it was a future that he could see.

He trundled the wheelbarrow across the dirt, and the heaviness didn't bother him because he could feel within him the first flickers of obsession, the electricity sparking in his brain like a live wire. This obsession, after all, would not be very different from those he'd already mastered. It would be based in mathematics and logic, even scenario planning and risk analysis, only now the application would be practical instead of theoretical. The work would demand much more from him than his fanciful scenario planning at FutureWorld. The stakes would be higher, too: miscalculations could lead to injury or hunger. Precision was essential.

There was no escaping math, after all. It was everywhere, especially in nature. You could go so far as to say that math *was* nature. Pi described the arc of a rainbow, the way ripples spread in a body of water, the dimensions of the moon and sun. Fractals could be observed in halved sections of red cabbage, the topography of deserts, the branching of lightning bolts. And take the old man glaring out from his shirt, Leonardo Fibonacci, who discovered that a basic number sequence predicted the arrangement of scales on a pinecone, the distribution of petals on flowers, the spiral of a snail shell, the furcation of veins in the human body, even the structure of DNA. When all the people were gone, the numbers would persist. Always the numbers, an infinite chain running to the edge of the universe.

Once the property was running, he might even invite his parents to visit. Rikki would be glad that he had escaped Kansas City and its nightmares forever, and Tibor would be proud to see the landownership gene resurface in his son. Slumlord begetting fieldlord. From the haystacks of a farm outside of Győr to giant rotating turbine blades above his castle in the Flatlands.

And yet—and yet—despite all this, he would be alone.

Yes, there was Hank, there were Cassie and Ronald, who seemed like neo-hippies from Ticonderoga, and perhaps there would be others, settlers from Randall's Island and elsewhere. But he would keep his distance, and the wall around him would grow tall with trash and plaster. The purest intellectual pursuits were always solitary, weren't they? You had to be uncompromising and self-disciplined. No great mathematical problem was ever solved by a team of mathematicians (there was the Appel-Haken solution to the four-color theorem, but really their supercomputer deserved the credit); no brilliant machine was ever conceived in tandem (the Wright brothers were good engineers, but they honed technology developed by others); and no literary masterpiece was ever written by a group of collaborators (the Bible notwithstanding). Elsa had understood this. There were others working with her on the farm, working *for* her, but it was her plan, and she was uncompromising in its execution. And what Mitchell was after—an impregnable, self-contained, self-sustaining fortress—would require the same level of dedication. No place would be reserved for anyone else.

The wheelbarrow hit against a single red brick wedged into the earth. He kicked at it, hard, and it budged enough so that he could pull it out of the soil, like a rotten tooth from a gum.

His plan had other satisfactions. There would be no one for him to grow attached to, no one he would have to rely on but himself. He would avoid nostalgia; forget the past, forget FutureWorld, forget the whole tangled cycle of anxiety and fear and paranoia that got him here. Instead, his teeming energies—or, to be honest, his *fanaticism*—his fanaticism would be spent in the fields, building-shaping-making-growing-spreading. Then, at night, to bed alone. Alone with his numbers and their cold, metallic comforts.

He would live, in other words, the life that Elsa Bruner had wanted. It was her ideal scenario: self-reliant, sovereign, irreproachable. Having created his own world, he'd be protected from the world. And he began to make out, like a distant cloud formation, the vast shape of her loneliness.

It occurred to him then, as he pushed the wheelbarrow toward the funeral pyre of telephone poles and wiring, the wheels twisting restively on their axles, jarring on every divot and pebble. It occurred to him that he now understood another fact about Elsa Bruner, his paragon of solitary idealism, of single-minded devotion to higher purpose. He understood now that Elsa Bruner was dead.

▣ ▣ ▣

It was three days after the encounter with Cassie and Ronald—or was it four?—when he discovered the tree.

He had gotten into the habit of eating dinner at what must have been five o'clock. He couldn't help it; by that time he was too starving to hold off any longer. But it gave him an hour of sunlight to kill before he could sleep. That was too long without working. These were the hours when, at Fitzsimmons Sherman and Future-World, he'd been at his most productive. Unhassled by the constant shocks of the business day—news reports, meetings, e-mails—he could concentrate on his scenarios. But now what was there to do? He had finished planting the seeds, after all, and he'd cleared the second and third floors of debris. Fortunately the wall could use more work. Though "wall" wasn't the most accurate term for the uneven, steadily accumulating pile of rubble that rose in clumpy hillocks around the perimeter of the property. Every object that remained, every stray plank, roof tile, and cement block within about a hundred yards that he could stack in his wheelbarrow, he had added to his barricade. He hadn't yet foraged in the marsh— the ground was too uneven for the wheelbarrow—but he had seen plenty of dead wood there. The smaller sections he could haul away by himself, as long as they weren't too splintery. And for the most part they weren't, the turbulence of the floodwaters having smoothed the wood, sanding down its burrs and jagged edges.

In the vault he found what he was looking for: the ax. It was heavier than he'd expected, tugging aggressively at his shoulder as he lifted it. It was a powerful weapon. Walking around the property, swinging the ax, he felt for the first time as if he owned the land. The Canarsie Bank Trust, as well as the adjacent plot, whatever it had been, was his domain. His shoulder began to smart. He paused to rub it.

He walked gingerly to avoid cutting himself. Navigating the matted swamp grass and the chaotic brambles, he entered the marsh. Here there were only the crushed branches of smaller trees, nothing substantial. But farther down, just past where his little bathing pool debouched into a wider creek, the trunk of a fallen oak lay on the shore. It was not native to that strip of land, but the storm had deposited it there and divested it of its crown. It was perfect. He wouldn't be able to drag it home, you'd need a tractor for that, but he could chop it into thick stumps and use those to reinforce his wall's foundation.

As he approached he saw that the tree had split open near its midpoint. Where the trunk had cracked there was a wide crevasse, chocolate near the outer levels and reddening farther down. He raised his ax, aiming the blade. But he couldn't follow through. Something was moving in the tree. He bent over to examine it more closely, and then he was on the ground beside it, and then his head was nearly inside the tree.

The first thing he noticed were the mushrooms, orange with caps the size of buttons, projecting from the walls of the crevasse. Their fleshy undersides were lined with gills that ruffled like lace. These gills secreted a toothpasty substance that branched into a plexus of lines that descended deep into the trunk's core. But that was just the beginning. When Mitchell moved closer, he saw eruptions of brightly petaled clover; exotic spindly-legged spiders with bodies the same exact hue as the tree itself; a flesh-colored worm as long as his arm; a fiery procession of red mites snaking between piles of school-bus-yellow spores and thick, translucent bubbles of slime; a downy pink fungus like a speck of cotton candy; a bark beetle sheathed in an iridescent shell; and canals of thick syrup in which tiny flies had gotten stuck, flapping their broken wings and twitching in panic. What had appeared to be no more than a dead log was everywhere crawling, munching, slurping, rotting, liquefying, cannibalizing—a grotesque insectopolis. As his shadow moved across the log, the bark beetle, sensing a larger presence, folded completely into itself—head into shell, encased and protected, a gray oval disk without edges or openings. Protected against its predators. Protected even against the air.

He tried not to think about Elsa, where her body now lay,

in what state of decomposition. But then the awful flesh-colored worm, propelled by its wet, clenching suckers, glided sinuously along the surface of the log, and Mitchell felt that he was going to throw up.

He rose, unsteady on his feet, and grabbed the handle of the ax. This time he would bring it down with all his force, explode the decayed wood, spattering worm pulp and tree rot and larva across the grass. But now the ax was much too heavy. The poll dug into the small of his back and he couldn't begin to hoist it over his head.

Did he really want to obliterate this festering micro-universe? Or might it be nicer simply to join it? To stretch out under the sky until night came and all the creeping things mistook him for a second log to explore and infest. If he were to lie there, simply lie there on the wet ground until he lost consciousness, how long would it take for anyone to notice? Who would discover his absence? Who would care? If Hank or the new settlers didn't find him in the bank building, they'd assume he had given up and run back to New York. Days would pass, maybe weeks, before someone found him. By then his corpse would have already merged, like the rotting oak, into the marshy soil.

Gingerly he let himself down beside the log. His ears were full of the sound of the creek washing against the shore just several feet away, and above him spread the sky, more vast than any he'd ever seen in New York. That was another result of the flood and its destruction: it had not only wiped clean the ground, it had also expanded the sky. It used to steal through the narrow slivers between skyscrapers, a petty thief; now it had been restored its dominion. It was radiant with its pride.

There was only one stubborn cloud, a cumulonimbus, directly overhead. It was an odd cloud: it didn't seem to be drifting at all. It just sat, motionless, looking down at him. Mitchell lay there for what seemed like ten, even fifteen minutes, but the cloud refused to move. How was this possible? It didn't expand or contract, just stayed fixed in the highest part of the sky. And it really was watching him, wasn't it? Just staring at him, waiting for him to move.

"You first," said Mitchell without sound.

"Nope," said the cloud.

"I got nowhere to be."

"That's two of us."

"Fine," said Mitchell. "Suit yourself."

Even as the swamp flies, or whatever they were, started flapping around his eyes, as the bark beetles scaled his bare arms and the grass scratched at his neck, he would stay there. This was his land now. If he wanted to lie on it all night long, or even for weeks, until he wasted away and his flesh sloughed free from his bones—well, if he wanted to lie there for eternity, nobody could stop him, certainly not an intangible mass of vapor in the upper atmosphere.

But then something very peculiar happened. Almost imperceptibly, the cloud, cowed by his will, began to drift away.

# Flatlanders

**Mitchell Zukor was missing.**

The condition of the atrium was the first indication that something was wrong. The atrium was immaculate. Last month it had still resembled a forgotten storage unit, with disorderly clusters of tools, chairs, and bank-teller desks, long sacks of fertilizer and compost, and pallets from Jackpot loaded with vegetable cans and packages of instant ramen. The red travertine floor tiles had been all but obscured by dirt and plastic wrappers and what appeared to be animal droppings. Mitchell's appearance then had alarmed her; he had not looked good. He hadn't shaved since, well, probably not since Randall's Island. Gone was the Mexicano; this was the Elderly Wino. She could barely recognize him. The most disturbing thing was the beard. It was full and wild, getting into the corners of his mouth, and it was coming in white. Now he really looked the part of a mad old oracle, she told them back at the office. Like Tiresias himself, frail and muttering and blind.

It was a slight exaggeration. Mitchell wasn't frail. Far from it, in fact, he was broader in his shoulders and neck—his body, in a state of shock, frantically adding muscle to cope with the intense physical exertions it had been forced to endure for the first time in

its existence. And Mitchell wasn't blind either, except in one respect: he had no idea what he looked like, not having glimpsed a
reflective surface for six months other than the rippled, silty waters of the Fresh Creek Basin. When she mentioned the whiteness
of his beard, he had no idea what she was talking about, and when
she clarified it for him, he just shrugged. He didn't seem to care.
His clothes were filthy too. He cleaned them every few weeks in
the marsh, he reported, as if this achievement were worthy of a
trophy. Gold star for marsh boy.

So in addition to the other supplies he had requested and several that he had not, she had brought him a gift: a mirror. She'd
had it wrapped in brown paper, tied with a red bow. She carried it
to the door, leaving the rest of the things—the floor wax, the new
pack of filtration cartridges, the fresh vegetables—in the truck. He
didn't answer the intercom at the front gate, which was typical, so
she punched the security code, passed through the arbor, and un-
bolted the front door with her key. But now, upon entering the old
bank building, she was so disturbed by what she saw that she lost
her grip on the mirror. She clamped down as it fell, pinning it
against the side of her knee just before it hit the floor.

"Mitchell?" she called out. "It's me."

The supplies were still there—they had barely been dented—
but he had stacked them neatly in the bays along either side of the
atrium, behind the U-shaped bank that in a distant age had separated the bank customers from the tellers. The floor had been
mopped clean, the travertine tiles glowing dimly in the twin shafts
of sunlight that passed through the two first-floor windows. Emptied of the clutter, the room somehow seemed taller, and she was
astonished to see that the original lighting fixtures—twin domes
hanging at the end of white stalks like the eyes of a hermit crab—
had been polished to their original splendor. There were no light-
bulbs in them, of course, but still the glass globes absorbed the light
that bounced off the floor, projecting solar systems on the walls.

She first checked the vault—if Mitchell was inside, he might not have heard her enter. The door gave with a startled gasp, revealing its treasures: the portable generator, the canisters of gasoline, another half dozen pallets of canned vegetables, about a hundred gallons of water, and the black suitcase that she figured must by now contain nearly half a million dollars in rubber-banded stacks of hundreds. Everything seemed in order. There was no sign of a break-in. But there was also no sign of Mitchell.

On the second floor he had shelved the books she had brought him, and the couches had been arranged around the center of the room. A stack of books lay on the low coffee table in front of the couch. The thick volume resting on top was titled *Textbook of Domicilic Engineering: Systems and Processes*.

"Mitchell?"

Her voice came out strangled. Every time she visited she was reminded how ridiculous it was to leave him here like this, in isolation. But what else could she do? He'd refused every alternative. Even her offer of a cabin on the Maine coast, off the grid, outfitted with the latest in bioenergy technology, with a full garden already planted—even that he had refused with a scornful head shake.

"That's not the point," he'd said cryptically. He'd developed a disquieting habit of combing his fingers through his beard, where they inevitably found little pieces of fuzz or food that he held up to his eyes for examination before tossing aside. "I have to do it by myself, for myself." He refused to say anything else on the subject.

On the third floor his sleeping bag was unrolled. His clothes were piled tidily on the conference table. The desk he kept by the windows was the only messy thing in the place: scattered papers, pencils, a calculator, and open books on electric engineering and building design, their pages heavily annotated. It could not look more different from his FutureWorld office. This room felt lived-in, thought-in, alive with knowledge. At FutureWorld the offices had felt choked by knowledge—choked to death.

On the tall windows he had done a near-professional job: the putty was almost invisible at the edges of the new panes, the glass unsmudged. The weather monitor sat on the sill, its silicon dish exposed to the sunlight. She walked over and looked out. Mitchell wasn't visible in the garden below, though the large, flat leaves of the canna plants, flapping in the breeze like pterodactyl wings, obscured part of it. Nor was he in the outhouse; she could see that the door was ajar. And she doubted he was in the marsh; he never left the property by daylight, as far as she knew. In any case there wasn't anyone now visible in the marsh, except for the Motas and their young daughter. A fat white opossum was sauntering lazily down Flatlands Avenue. She hiccuped.

"Mitchell!"

She ran down the stairs, her hiking boots *thwaping* on the burnished stone steps. She had bought them upon returning to Manhattan—a six-hundred-dollar pair of black Mountainsiders with injection-molded supports, antibacterial linings, open-cell foam sock liners, and thick, chunky treads. It was a silly purchase: she wore them only during visits to the Flatlands, and even then they were hardly necessary. Still, the boots had become part of the monthly ritual. Going to the wilderness? Throw the heels into a bag, slip on the hiking boots. Then call the armored limousine. That was the other indispensable part of the ritual: the armored limousine, which was really closer to a cargo truck, with its giant trunk compartment, off-road wheels, and Large Keith, the 280-pound retired defensive end who served as her driver.

Outside, as she passed from the entryway to the front gate, something flashed in the garden behind the canna plants. Squinting, she ran to it, past the tomato trellises and some kind of purple lettuce, her boots kicking soil onto her calves. Was he playing games with her, hiding in the garden?

But no one was there. The glimmer was a shard of glass wedged into the boundary wall at shoulder height. It was attached to a cracked window frame, one of the thousands of pieces of debris that formed the wall to Mitchell's fortress, nearly every component with rough surfaces and jagged edges. You couldn't climb a wall like that—you couldn't even touch it. That seemed to be the point.

Sweet jumping Jesus, get me out of here.

"Everything all right, Ms. Eppler?" said Large Keith. He was standing in the gate, his arms crossed in front of his sequoia chest, keeping an eye on the neighbors. His titanic dome gleamed in the sunlight, slippery with perspiration. "You need me to go in?"

Behind him she could see that the couple from down the block—David and his wife with the overbite, what the heck was the poor girl's name?—were sauntering over. She stepped outside the gate.

"Andrea and I have been worried about him," said David, waving. "He still only comes out at night. We watch him from our house. You know, just to make certain he doesn't get into any trouble."

"He's fine," she said. "Same as always."

"Could you tell him the offer still stands?" said Andrea. "Our shack isn't finished yet, but we'd really love to have him over sometime. I mean, once he's ready."

"I'll tell him."

"The Tildas are having a party tomorrow," said David. "Everyone's going to be there. We'd like very much to see him."

She nodded. "I'll stop by when we're done here. I have the PV modules." She could see the relief on their faces.

Once they'd returned to their hut and were safely out of earshot, she informed Large Keith that Mitchell was missing.

"This kind of thing?" Keith shook his head. "It's not sustainable. No man can live like this."

"I don't know what to do."

"Want me to unload the supplies?"

"Maybe we should wait," she said. "I mean, maybe the best—"

They were interrupted by a skitter of falling gravel, then three loud *plunks* as something bounced off the top of the perimeter wall, then off the roof of the limousine, and landed in the dirt. Jane looked up. There was nothing to see except a thin plume of dust where the object had skimmed the top of the wall. They ran around to the other side of the limousine. On the ground lay a fat metal bolt.

"Mother Mary."

"The roof," said Large Keith. "I'm coming this time. That could've killed one of us."

"Keith? Stay here."

He gave her a long, cold, squinty stare, the kind of look he must have used to traumatize the offensive tackle at the line of scrimmage.

"Please. You know how he feels about visitors."

She ran back through the arbor, fumbled the keys, dropped them in the dirt, picked them up, turned them in the lock. She sprinted across the atrium, through the creaking turnstile, up the stairs—*thwap-thwap, thwap-thwap, thwap-thwap*—to the third floor. Then—of *course,* why hadn't she thought of it before?—she walked to the back of the building, where she ascended the final half flight of steep metal stairs. She pushed with all her weight on the security bar. The heavy steel door burst open, and she was in the open air. And there on the blacktop, facing her, was a filthy bearded man with curly hair that danced mazurkas off his head in every direction. He was shirtless, his chest a dull brown, his arms nicked and blemished like someone who has run through brambles. Of course he probably *had* run through brambles. He probably did every time he went for a night marsh soak. He was wearing only dirty green slacks and a pair of black boots. She recognized the boots, of course. They were Mountainsiders. She'd given them to him.

Every month she had scrutinized him for signs of impending

madness. There were signs, starting with the beard (which looked more feral than ever, a chaotic blizzard), but until now they hadn't added up to anything verifiable—or certifiable. Mitchell didn't rant about pantheism or spirit liberation, he didn't wear energy bracelets or anti-EMF diadems, and he hadn't sworn off soap or toothpaste (though deodorant, based on anecdotal evidence, appeared to have fallen out of favor). But the jury was still deliberating. She was the jury.

"Jane?" said Mitchell.

"I was worried."

"Why?"

He was holding a hammer. She noticed now the white PVC tubes, the power drill, the open toolbox with its contents disgorged around it like a split belly, the boxes of nails and screws—and bolts.

"What are you doing?"

"Trying to improve the rain catchment system," he said. "What's wrong with you?"

"Nothing. I was just . . . annoyed. I couldn't find you."

Mitchell put down the hammer and put his hand on her collarbone. He smelled awful. Like a wild animal.

"Jane. How many times do I have to tell you."

"I know."

"I'm fine."

"Great. But you need to take a shower. I know you're not in modern society anymore, but this is crazy hobo territory."

"Actually that's what I'm doing up here." He smiled faintly, from a faraway place, and lowered his arm. "The gutters catch the rainwater, it drains through the PVC into barrels on the ground. I'll warm the water with the solar heater. And then I can take a hot shower."

"Well," said Jane. "That's neat."

"Isn't it?"

"I have the stuff you wanted."

"Thanks. I'll help Keith unload."

"I also got you a present. You can open it after you take your first shower."

"Hm. I think I know what it is. Hey, did Tibor and Rikki write?"

"There's a package in the car. Also the guy from *The Wall Street Journal* keeps calling. Did you ever read his article?"

"I don't read articles."

"Well now he has a book deal. A kind of biography. It begins with his memories of you in college. The day of Seattle and all that."

"Convenient."

"He's a nice guy. Smart. But he does want you to sit for an interview, or several. He says if you don't, he'll be forced to imagine things from your perspective so that he can put the reader inside your head."

"Is that supposed to be a threat?"

Jane shrugged. "Look, I don't care. What should I tell him?"

"He can talk to you or my parents, or even Charnoble. But I don't want to hear about it again."

"I have one other message for you."

"Who?"

She smiled uneasily.

"Did you give them the spiel? Off the grid, no interviews, no donations—"

"No."

"What? Why not?"

"The message is from Elsa Bruner."

"Elsa Bruner."

"She called Future Days."

Mitchell recoiled. His mouth underwent a violent contortion. It was like he had seen a ghost.

"She's *alive*?"

Jane told him about Elsa's recovery, her decision to undergo open-heart surgery to implant an automatic cardiac defibrillator—a device that carried a number of risks, but seemed necessary given the alternative. There were three months of physical therapy, during which she had begun to study for the LSAT.

"Absurd. She didn't even finish college. You're lying. This isn't nice."

"But she's been accepted. Stanford."

The look on Mitchell's face was a mixture of befuddlement and high skepticism. At least that's what she guessed. The beard blocked everything. It was like the perimeter wall. It not only kept you out, it kept you from getting too close.

"I can't believe it."

"I don't think she would lie about it."

"I can't believe she's alive."

"She's going to study environmental law."

"It doesn't sound like the Elsa Bruner I knew."

"She's not the Elsa Bruner you knew."

"I don't want to see her."

"You have about three months to think about it. She has a summer job downtown at some environmental law firm. Not far from Future Days, in fact."

"That's ridiculous."

"She'd like to visit you."

"Enough."

"Fine. But she wanted you to have this." Jane pulled a crinkled envelope from her back pocket. Mitchell's name was written on the front in Elsa's neat, girlish script. The envelope smelled like smoke.

"The letter," said Mitchell, and his eyes got very wide behind his whiskers.

He tore it open with such force that the envelope fell out of his hand and the breeze carried it skidding toward the edge of the roof. He stepped on the envelope finally, hard, and opened it more carefully. It contained a postcard. It was one of those cheap promotional postcards they gave away for free at restaurant cash registers. This one was from a crappy Korean dive in midtown, Chosan Galbi. Mitchell was looking at the note with disgust. He showed it to Jane. It read "By the time you get this, I'll be a futurist." It was in Mitchell's handwriting, with his signature. Only Elsa had crossed out Mitchell's name and signed her own.

"What the hell is that supposed to mean?" said Mitchell.

Since he seemed to be addressing himself and not Jane, she thought it best not to answer.

Downstairs, Large Keith had already carried the supplies and the crate of vegetables into the atrium. Mitchell handed Jane the envelope containing his monthly update to his parents and his supplies list for the following month. Jane gave him the Zukors' care package and the mirror.

"Business good?"

"Business," said Jane, trying not to laugh, "is *quite* good."

"And the recovery?"

"It's going great, actually. Even some of the subway lines are coming back."

"I imagine only the old IRT lines, right? And none of the outer boroughs."

"Yeah. Just the old IRT lines."

"And the water supply—do you still have boil water advisories?"

"Mm."

"And I bet the insurance claims aren't being processed quickly, so you have uninhabited, structurally unsound buildings all over. And the side streets, especially outside of Manhattan, are probably still riddled with cracks and craters and holes."

"OK, yeah, there's work to be done. Glad you haven't lost your powers of divination."

"I had an idea for you. New slogan."

"Let's hear it."

"Future Days: because the future is not quite what it used to be."

"You still have it," said Jane, and she smiled as if she meant it.

The sun shifted, and Mitchell seemed to squint.

"It was nice to see you," he said. His voice got quieter. "Always is."

She tried to read his expression, but it was impossible behind the tangles of hair. All she could make out with any clarity were his eyes. They were as sharp as ever, like the points of swords.

"Mitchell."

"Yeah."

She paused. "Aren't you lonely?"

Mitchell kicked the gravel. "I'm alone. I've been alone for six months. But that's not the same thing as lonely."

"There are a lot of people outside who want to meet you."

"Mm. Are there more?"

"Sorry?"

"More settlers. I mean other than Hank and those two kids—Ronald and Cassie? And that other family from Randall's. The Motas."

She had suspected it before; there had been signs, though it seemed too preposterous. But now she was certain: he had no idea. None. He hadn't left the property for months, at least not during the day, and at night he only sneaked across the street to the marsh, which was hidden from most of the neighborhood. "Can't you see them?" she said. "From the windows?"

"The windows look out to the marsh. Then the sea."

"From the roof, then?"

"I just started on the roof this morning." He lowered his eyes, breaking eye contact. "I guess I haven't looked down just yet."

"Well," she said, "maybe you should."

They said their goodbyes, and she left the property. She didn't have time to linger. There was a full staff meeting at the office in three hours, and she had to make the rest of the deliveries. There were David and Andrea with the overbite, Hank Cho, and Ronnie and Cassie. Then there were the Motas, the Wachtels, the Herreras, the Chopras, the Reburns, the Castillos, the Mendozas, the Tildas, Dr. Valentine and his children, Sara Watson with the squint eye, Andy Nguyan, Brian Petersen, Amy Macias, Stuart and Lacey, Sissie and her daughter, Larry Rocha, Dennis and Rodney Archer, the LaGarde brothers, and the camp of runaways, whose names she never remembered except for their leader, the one with the eye tattoos, who went by Lizard, or Zard. Even if she kept chitchat to a minimum and made her rounds as quickly as possible, she would no doubt be delayed by the newest settlers. She had seen them even on the drive over—they were still arriving, more every day. They walked in from Brooklyn and Queens, lugging camping backpacks like mules, ducking under the unmanned police barricades that separated the rest of the city from the Dead Zone. And they were building: hackneyed, unprofessional, ramshackle homes with mismatched walls and askew floors straight out of Dr. Seuss. But the disorderliness seemed welcomed, if not intentional.

The whole place was a mess—a sprawling, chaotic, giddy mess—but for a brief moment, as Large Keith opened the door to the armored limousine and the refrigerated air wafted into her face, it occurred to her that there *was* something intoxicating about this new way of life in the Flatlands. Their little experiment in self-sufficiency might even end up succeeding. Ticonderoga failed, sure, but hadn't mankind done it before—started from scratch? And this time it would be easier. They were cheating, after all, with Future Days providing the essentials, and a bit more besides. New nonprofits were chipping in—the Easties, We're All Mitchell Zukor, New Americans for a New America. For a passing moment, as Jane took one final look at the high entryway of the grand old bank building surmounted by its silly granite eagle, she felt that she would like to live in the Flatlands herself one day. She felt that she wanted to live in the Flatlands rather desperately.

Large Keith slammed the door. The cold darkness of the limousine enclosed her, the seat gave gently beneath her, and her thoughts turned to that afternoon's meeting. It was an important meeting. They were going to make final hiring decisions for the new class of Cassandras, review the new ad campaign, announce the second quarter earning reports, and set profit goals for the third quarter. A fortune was at stake. She buzzed Keith.

"Ms. Eppler?"

"Let's move this along," she said.

"Ms. Eppler? Everything all right back there?"

No, she thought. Everything is not right, not at all.

I am *scared*.

But she choked back the words.

"I'm fine," she said at last. "I just need to get back to New York. We don't have a lot of time."